A Note on the Text

This authoritative text of *The Reef* is reprinted from the Library of America edition of *Novels* by Edith Wharton, and is based on the first American edition of *The Reef,* published in New York by D. Appleton and Company in 1912.

Also Available from Collier Books

THE HOUSE OF MIRTH
MADAME DE TREYMES AND THREE NOVELLAS
SUMMER
THE AGE OF INNOCENCE
ROMAN FEVER AND OTHER STORIES

The Reef

by

EDITH WHARTON

With an Introduction by Louis Auchincloss

Collier Books
Macmillan Publishing Company
New York

Macmillan Publishing Company
866 Third Avenue, New York, N.Y. 10022
Collier Macmillan Canada, Inc.

Library of Congress Cataloging-in-Publication Data

Wharton, Edith, 1862–1937.
The reef.

Reprint. Originally published: New York :
Scribner, 1965.
I. Title.
PS3545.H16R4 1987 813′.52 86-30780
ISBN 0-02-055410-9

First Collier Books Edition 1987

10 9 8 7 6 5 4 3 2 1

The text for this edition is reprinted from *Novels* by Edith Wharton, published by the Library of America, 1986, by permission.

Printed in the United States of America

Introduction

by Louis Auchincloss

BEFORE opening *The Reef* the reader must be prepared for a moral climate in which extra-marital physical love is considered damning to a woman and only mildly reprehensible to a man. If Anna Leath is going to strike the reader as a prude for opposing her step-son's engagement to a woman who has been another man's mistress, and as a fool for attempting, for the same reason, to break off her own pending marriage to that other man, then *The Reef* is not for him. Why is it that we can put ourselves so easily, in reading historical fiction, into the shoes of barbaric emperors and slaveholders, and yet stumble our toes on yesterday's prejudices? Probably because yesterday's morality seems absurd and hypocritical, while that of the day before yesterday has some of the dignity of antique things.

Yet the effort *can* be made, and more easily than one might think. Darrow, after all, has his affair with Sophy Viner after he has proposed to Anna and while she is still considering her answer. Even the most conscientiously modern woman might raise an eyebrow at this. Furthermore, Sophy is manifestly an inappropriate wife for young Owen, who is much too immature, anyway, to get married. Pushing on, our persistent reader will find himself rewarded by seeing Edith Wharton successfully engaged in doing something that she was supposed by many critics to be always doing, but that in fact she never did but once: in writing a Jamesian novel.

Great as was her admiration of Henry James, she wanted to stand on her own feet and deplored the reviews of her early books that bracketed her name with his. But by the time she came to write *The Reef*, she had so firmly estalished her independent literary personality with *The House of Mirth* (1905), *The Fruit of the Tree* (1907) and *Ethan Frome* (1911), three utterly unJamesian novels, that she must have felt that she could afford at last to indulge a Jamesian mood. This is why *The Reef* stands apart from the rest of her work. It is not as rich in content as *The House of Mirth* or as strong as *Ethan Frome,* but it has the quiet dignity and mellow charm of the old château in which its highly civilized characters come tensely to grips with their fate.

James called the book "Racinian," which is the right word. Although the characters go to and from Paris, and although some months are encompassed in the action, the spirit of the classic unities is observed. It is against the background of Givré that Darrow and Anna work out the problem posed by her discovery that her child's governess has been his mistress. As in *The Golden Bowl,* where the ramifications of the Prince's adultery with his step-mother-in-law are seen alternately through the minds of the Prince and the Princess, so are the complications brought on by Sophy's fall from grace seen through the consciousness of Anna and Darrow. One wonders if Mrs. Wharton's protestation that she did not like James' final style and could not finish his last novels was not exaggerated. Surely, *The Reef* owes some of the tightness of its organization to *The Golden Bowl.*

James was enchanted by it. He wrote her from Rye:

> "It all shows, partly, what strength of subject is, and how it carries and inspires, inasmuch as I think your subject in its essence is very fine and takes no end of beautiful things to do. . . . The beauty of it is that it is, for all it is worth, a Drama, and almost, as it seems to me, of the psychological Racinian unity, intensity and gracility."

His only question was "why the whole thing, unrelated and unreferred save in the most superficial way to its milieu and background; and to any determining and qualifying *entourage,* takes place *comme cela,* and in a specified, localised way, in France—these non-French people 'electing,' as it were, to have their story out there." This question he went on to answer for himself by suggesting than an "exquisite instinct" back of her Racinian inspiration absolutely prescribed "a vague and elegant French colonnade or gallery, with a French river dimly gleaming through, as the harmonious *fond.*"

I would agree with James that the role of Givré is justified simply by Mrs. Wharton's ability beautifully to delineate it. It is the best of all the wonderful houses of her fiction, shimmering in color yet clear of line, like an early impressionist canvas, or like a painting by Walter Gay, who made a small niche for himself in twentieth century art by doing charming studies of his own château. As the story unfolds we see Givré in different lightings. We see its high roof, its brick, and yellow stone first in the light of a mild October afternoon, the breadth of its grassy court "filled with the shadow and sound of limes." We see its garden at noon when the sunlight sheets with gold "the bronze flanks of the polygonal yews." We see it in the deep blue purity of a mistless night when the moon blanches "to unnatural whiteness the statues against their walls of shade." But it is never any part of the lives of the characters. Anna will not live in it. Owen does not want it. Madame de Chantelle will have to leave it to Effie who is too young to object.

The lack of any real connection between Givré and its inhabitants dramatizes what was happening in Mrs. Wharton's own life. Because she had chosen to live in France she was increasingly losing touch with her native land and source material. James warned her about this but she ignored the warning, probably thinking that he was his own best rebuttal. In *The Reef* the problem had not yet become acute for her as an artist, but it was there: the characters might be acting out a contemporary play against the settings of an old classic.

Givré is too removed to cast a frown on Sophy Viner, but not so her one-time lover. We are told exactly why Darrow cannot suffer her to be either Effie's nurse or Owen's wife: she is unclean. Mrs. Wharton regards her hero's instinct in this matter as basic to a man. "He tried to get away from the feeling, to isolate and exteriorize it sufficiently to see what motives it was made of; but it remained a mere blind motion of his blood, the instinctive recoil from the thing that no amount of argument can make 'straight.' " This is the kind of thinking in the book that is hardest for us to accept today. Still, remembering that Dumas Fils, a generation earlier, would have thought murder of the girl justifiable, we can try to accept it in a man of Darrow's upbringing. But how can we accept his hypocrisy in telling Sophy that he is thinking only of *her* happiness in doubting if Owen is a good enough match for her? Sophy knows how to deal with this.

"You'd rather I didn't marry any friend of yours," she tells him flatly, and he has the grace not directly to deny it.

This would still be all right if Mrs. Wharton saw Darrow as we do. But she doesn't. She clucks a bit at his affair with Sophy, but very mildly, and she evidently sympathizes with his embarrassment at finding the girl in the employ of his future wife. She seems to be telling us that Darrow's blundering clumsiness in his talks with Sophy is what must be expected of men. The real reckoning in such matters is always between the women.

We now know that the period of the writing of *The Reef* was the most trying of Mrs. Wharton's life. Her husband's nervous instability was approaching insanity, and at the same time, as shown by her secret diary, she had fallen in love with Walter Berry, a distinguished lawyer, an exquisite aesthete but a confirmed bachelor. In 1913, a year after *The Reef* was published, she obtained a divorce, but although she and Berry remained the closest friends, they never married. Many of her circle believed that the reluctance was on his part.

In any case, *The Reef* offers the psychological puzzle that Mrs. Wharton, in depicting Anna's husband, Fraser Leath, whose rare kiss drops on her face "like a cold smooth pebble," gives us a figure who corresponds more closely to what we know of the man with whom she was actually in love than it does with her hero. Leath is one of the best of her long gallery of dilettantes:

> In the first year of her marriage the sober symmetry of Givré had suggested only her husband's neatly-balanced mind. It was a mind, she soon learned, contentedly absorbed in formulating the conventions of the unconventional. West Fifty-fifth Street was no more conscientiously concerned than Givré with the momentous question of "what people did"; it was only the type of deed investigated that was different. Mr. Leath collected his social instances with the same seriousness and patience as his snuff-boxes. He exacted a rigid conformity to his rules of non-conformity and his scepticism had the absolute accent of a dogma. He even cherished certain exceptions to his rules as the book-collector prizes a "defective" first edition.

Does it not call to mind Percy Lubbock's description of Walter Berry as a dogmatic and snobbish egoist, the "evil genius" of Edith Wharton's life? "None of her friends," he put it bluntly, "thought she was the better for the surrender of her fine free spirit to the control of a man, I am ready to believe, of strong intelligence and ability—but also, I certainly know, of a dry and narrow and supercilious temper."

Anna Leath is a widow as the story opens, and it is Darrow who awakens her, as Walter Berry did her creator, on the threshold of middle age. She must not lose him, but the final solution of her problem makes a weak ending for an otherwise excellent novel. James was apt to find solutions for his characters in renunciation: Stretcher gives up Maria Gostrey; Maggie Verver gives up her father; Merton Densher gives up Kate Croy. But Mrs. Wharton knew Anna Leath too well to allow her to give up Darrow. Anna simply would not have done it. She is too much a woman of flesh and blood, so much so that there are moments when we wonder what she is doing in Givré, what she is doing in France, what she is doing in a late Jamesian novel. Her problem has to be resolved at the cost of Sophy Viner. The latter reveals in the final chapter—or, rather, allows to be revealed for her by a bloated disreputable sister who receives the disdainful Anna in bed—that she has gone off to India in the company of a Mrs. Murrett who, like the sister, is no better than she should be.

Poor Sophy! Does she deserve it? Mrs. Wharton has strung little hints through the book to warn us not to get too upset about Sophy's fate. In Sophy's very first talk with Darrow on the boat train she refers to one Jimmy Brance, with whom she has exchanged some indelicate confidences, and who, we discover on the last page of the novel, is her sister's lover. But it is no good. We refuse to be convinced that the Sophy who is such a good sport about the advantage that Darrow has taken of her and who gives up a great match because she has the delicacy and decency, being in love with him, not to wed another, has found her proper niche with Mrs. Murrett.

Sophy is never really alive at Givré; she is sacrificed there to the exigencies of the plot. But she successfully dominates the long Paris prologue, a novelette in itself, beginning with her meeting Darrow at the pier in Dover and ending with the rainy days that turn an artless adventure into a drab affair. Here her particular combination of fineness and coarseness, of brightness and banality, of shrewdness and bad taste, is both convincing and touching. The change of scene from the dreary hotel room with the rain beating on the window (Sophy is always associated with bad weather) to the glory of Givré on a mild October afternoon seems to lower the curtain on vice and raise it on virtue. The contrast may be a bit harsh for Sophy, but it is pictorially effective, and it is for such effects that the novel is most remarkable. When I think of it, I think of the serene face of an old house seated in its park among poplar-bordered meadows. *The Château* might have been a more appropriate title than *The Reef*.

Book One

I.

"UNEXPECTED obstacle. Please don't come till thirtieth. Anna."

All the way from Charing Cross to Dover the train had hammered the words of the telegram into George Darrow's ears, ringing every change of irony on its commonplace syllables: rattling them out like a discharge of musketry, letting them, one by one, drip slowly and coldly into his brain, or shaking, tossing, transposing them like the dice in some game of the gods of malice; and now, as he emerged from his compartment at the pier, and stood facing the wind-swept platform and the angry sea beyond, they leapt out at him as if from the crest of the waves, stung and blinded him with a fresh fury of derision.

"Unexpected obstacle. Please don't come till thirtieth. Anna."

She had put him off at the very last moment, and for the second time: put him off with all her sweet reasonableness, and for one of her usual "good" reasons—he was certain that this reason, like the other, (the visit of her husband's uncle's widow) would be "good"! But it was that very certainty which chilled him. The fact of her dealing so reasonably with their case shed an ironic light on the idea that there had been any exceptional warmth in the greeting she had given him after their twelve years apart.

They had found each other again, in London, some three months previously, at a dinner at the American Embassy, and when she had caught sight of him her smile had been like a red rose pinned on her widow's mourning. He still felt the throb of surprise with which, among the stereotyped faces of the season's diners, he had come upon her unexpected face, with the dark hair banded above grave eyes; eyes in which he had recognized every little curve and shadow as he would have recognized, after half a life-time, the details of a room he had played in as a child. And as, in the plumed starred crowd, she had stood out for him, slender, secluded and different, so he had felt, the instant their glances met, that he as sharply detached himself for her. All that and more her smile had said; had said not merely "I remember," but "I remember just what you remember"; almost, indeed, as though her memory had aided his, her glance flung back on their recaptured moment its morning brightness. Certainly, when their distracted Ambassadress—with the cry: "Oh, you know Mrs. Leath? That's perfect, for General Farnham has failed me"—had waved them together for the march to the dining-room, Darrow had felt a slight pressure of the arm on his, a pressure faintly but unmistakably emphasizing the exclamation: "Isn't it wonderful?—In London—in the season—in a mob?"

Little enough, on the part of most women; but it was a sign of Mrs. Leath's quality that every movement, every syllable, told with her. Even in the old days, as an intent grave-eyed girl, she had seldom misplaced her light strokes; and Darrow, on meeting her again, had immediately felt how much finer and surer an instrument of expression she had become.

Their evening together had been a long confirmation of this feeling. She had talked to him, shyly yet frankly, of what had happened to her during the years when they had so strangely failed to meet. She had told him of her marriage to Fraser Leath, and of her subsequent life in France, where her husband's mother, left a widow in his youth, had been remarried to the Marquis de Chantelle, and where, partly in consequence of this second union, the son had permanently settled himself. She had spoken also, with an intense eagerness of affection, of her little girl Effie, who was now nine years old, and, in a strain hardly less tender, of Owen Leath, the charming clever young step-son whom her husband's death had left to her care . . .

A porter, stumbling against Darrow's bags, roused him to the fact that he still obstructed the platform, inert and encumbering as his luggage.

"Crossing, sir?"

Was he crossing? He really didn't know; but for lack of any more compelling impulse he followed the porter to the luggage van, singled out his property, and turned to march behind it down the gang-way. As the fierce wind shouldered him, building up a crystal wall against his efforts, he felt anew the derision of his case.

"Nasty weather to cross, sir," the porter threw back at him as they beat their way down the narrow walk to the pier. Nasty weather, indeed; but luckily, as it had turned out, there was no earthly reason why Darrow should cross.

While he pushed on in the wake of his luggage his thoughts slipped back into the old groove. He had once or twice run across the man whom Anna Summers had preferred to him, and since he had met her again he had been exercising his imagination on the picture of what her married life must have been. Her husband had struck him as a characteristic specimen of the kind of American as to whom one is not quite clear whether he lives in Europe in order to cultivate an art, or cultivates an art as a pretext for living in Europe. Mr. Leath's art was water-colour painting, but he practised it furtively, almost clandestinely, with the disdain of a man of the world for anything bordering on the professional, while he devoted himself more openly, and with religious seriousness, to the collection of enamelled snuff-boxes. He was blond and well-dressed, with the physical distinction that comes from having a straight figure, a thin nose, and the habit of looking slightly disgusted—as who should not, in a world where authentic snuff-boxes were growing daily harder to find, and the market was flooded with flagrant forgeries?

Darrow had often wondered what possibilities of communion there could have been between Mr. Leath and his wife. Now he concluded that there had probably been none. Mrs. Leath's words gave no hint of her husband's having failed to justify her choice; but her very reticence betrayed her. She spoke of him with a kind of impersonal seriousness, as if he had been a character in a novel or a figure in history; and what she said sounded as though it had been learned by heart and slightly dulled by repetition. This fact immensely increased Darrow's impression that his meeting with her had annihilated the intervening years. She, who was always so elusive and inaccessible, had grown suddenly communicative and kind: had opened the doors of her past, and tacitly left him to draw his own conclusions. As a result, he had taken leave of her with the sense that he was a being singled out and privileged, to whom she had entrusted something precious to keep. It was her happiness in their meeting that she had given him, had frankly left him to do with as he willed; and the frankness of the gesture doubled the beauty of the gift.

Their next meeting had prolonged and deepened the impression. They had found each other again, a few days later, in an old country house full of books and pictures, in the soft landscape of southern England. The presence of a large party, with all its aimless and agitated displacements, had served only to isolate the pair and give them (at least to the young man's fancy) a deeper feeling of communion, and their days there had been like some musical prelude, where the instruments, breathing low, seem to hold back the waves of sound that press against them.

Mrs. Leath, on this occasion, was no less kind than before; but she contrived to make him understand that what was so inevitably coming was not to come too soon. It was not that she showed any hesitation as to the issue, but rather that she seemed to wish not to miss any stage in the gradual reflowering of their intimacy.

Darrow, for his part, was content to wait if she wished it. He remembered that once, in America, when she was a girl, and he had gone to stay with her family in the country, she had been out when he arrived, and her mother had told him to look for her in the garden. She was not in the garden, but beyond it he had seen her approaching down a long shady path. Without hastening her step she had smiled and signed to him to wait; and charmed by the lights and shadows that played upon her as she moved, and by the pleasure of watching her slow advance toward him, he had obeyed her and stood still. And so she seemed now to be walking to him down the years, the light and shade of old memories and new hopes playing variously on her, and each step giving him the vision of a different grace. She did not waver or turn aside; he knew she would come straight to where he stood; but something in her eyes said "Wait", and again he obeyed and waited.

On the fourth day an unexpected event threw out his calculations. Summoned to town by the arrival in England of her husband's mother, she left without giving Darrow the chance he had counted on, and he cursed himself for a dilatory blunderer. Still, his disappointment was tempered by the certainty of being with her again before she left for France; and they did in fact see each other in London. There, however, the atmosphere had changed with the conditions. He could not say that she avoided him, or even that she was a shade less glad to see him; but she was beset by family duties and, as he thought, a little too readily resigned to them.

The Marquise de Chantelle, as Darrow soon perceived, had the same mild formidableness as the late Mr. Leath: a sort of insistent self-effacement before which every one about her gave way. It was perhaps the shadow of this lady's presence—pervasive even during her actual brief eclipses—that subdued and silenced Mrs. Leath. The latter was, moreover, preoccupied about her step-son, who, soon after receiving his degree at Harvard, had been rescued from a stormy love-affair, and finally, after some months of troubled drifting, had yielded to his step-mother's counsel and gone up to Oxford for a year of supplementary study. Thither Mrs. Leath went once or twice to visit him, and her remaining days were packed with family obligations: getting, as she phrased it, "frocks and governesses" for her little girl, who had been left in France, and having to devote the remaining hours to long shopping expeditions with her mother-in-law. Nevertheless, during her brief escapes from duty, Darrow had had time to feel her safe in the custody of his devotion, set apart for some inevitable hour; and the last evening, at the theatre, between the overshadowing Marquise and the unsuspicious Owen, they had had an almost decisive exchange of words.

Now, in the rattle of the wind about his ears, Darrow continued to hear the mocking echo of her message: "Unexpected obstacle." In such an existence as Mrs. Leath's, at once so ordered and so exposed, he knew how small a complication might assume the magnitude of an "obstacle;" yet, even allowing as impartially as his state of mind permitted for the fact that, with her mother-in-law always, and her stepson intermittently, under her roof, her lot involved a hundred small accommodations generally foreign to the freedom of widowhood—even so, he could not but think that the very ingenuity bred of such conditions might have helped her to find a way out of them. No, her "reason", whatever it was, could, in this case, be nothing but a pretext; unless he leaned to the less flattering alternative that any reason seemed good enough for postponing him! Certainly, if her welcome had meant what he imagined, she could not, for the second time within a few weeks, have submitted so tamely to the disarrangement of their plans; a disarrangement which—his official duties considered—might, for all she knew, result in his not being able to go to her for months.

"Please don't come till thirtieth." The thirtieth—and it was now the fifteenth! She flung back the fortnight on his hands as if he had been an idler indifferent to dates, instead of an active young diplomatist who, to respond to her call, had had to hew his way through a very jungle of engagements! "Please don't come till thirtieth." That was all. Not the shadow of an excuse or a regret; not even the perfunctory "have written" with which it is usual to soften such blows. She didn't want him, and had taken the shortest way to tell him so. Even in his first moment of exasperation it struck him as characteristic that she should not have padded her postponement with a fib. Certainly her moral angles were not draped!

"If I asked her to marry me, she'd have refused in the same language. But thank heaven I haven't!" he reflected.

These considerations, which had been with him every yard of the way from London, reached a climax of irony as he was drawn into the crowd on the pier. It did not soften his feelings to remember that, but for her lack of forethought, he might, at this harsh end of the stormy May day, have been sitting before his club fire in London instead of shivering in the damp human herd on the pier. Admitting the sex's traditional right to change, she might at least have advised him of hers by telegraphing directly to his rooms. But in spite of their exchange of letters she had apparently failed to note his address, and a breathless emissary had rushed from the Embassy to pitch her telegram into his compartment as the train was moving from the station.

Yes, he had given her chance enough to learn where he lived; and this minor proof of her indifference became, as he jammed his way through the crowd, the main point of his grievance against her and of his derision of himself. Half way down the pier the prod of an umbrella increased his exasperation by rousing him to the fact that it was raining. Instantly the narrow ledge became a battle-ground of thrusting, slanting, parrying domes. The wind rose with the rain, and the harried wretches exposed to this double assault wreaked on their neighbours the vengeance they could not take on the elements.

Darrow, whose healthy enjoyment of life made him in general a good traveller, tolerant of agglutinated humanity, felt himself obscurely outraged by these promiscuous contacts. It was as though all the people about him had taken his measure and known his plight; as though they were contemptuously bumping and shoving him like the inconsiderable thing he had become. "She doesn't want you, doesn't want you, doesn't want you," their umbrellas and their elbows seemed to say.

He had rashly vowed, when the telegram was flung into his window: "At any rate I won't turn back"—as though it might cause the sender a malicious joy to have him retrace his steps rather than keep on to Paris! Now he perceived the absurdity of the vow, and thanked his stars that he need not plunge, to no purpose, into the fury of waves outside the harbour.

With this thought in his mind he turned back to look for his porter; but the contiguity of dripping umbrellas made signalling impossible and, perceiving that he had lost sight of the man, he scrambled up again to the platform. As he reached it, a descending umbrella caught him in the collarbone; and the next moment, bent sideways by the wind, it turned inside out and soared up, kite-wise, at the end of a helpless female arm.

Darrow caught the umbrella, lowered its inverted ribs, and looked up at the face it exposed to him.

"Wait a minute," he said; "you can't stay here."

As he spoke, a surge of the crowd drove the owner of the umbrella abruptly down on him. Darrow steadied her with extended arms, and regaining her footing she cried out: "Oh, dear, oh, dear! It's in ribbons!"

Her lifted face, fresh and flushed in the driving rain, woke in him a memory of having seen it at a distant time and in a vaguely unsympathetic setting; but it was no moment to follow up such clues, and the face was obviously one to make its way on its own merits.

Its possessor had dropped her bag and bundles to clutch at the tattered umbrella. "I bought it only yesterday at the Stores; and—yes—it's utterly done for!" she lamented.

Darrow smiled at the intensity of her distress. It was food for the moralist that, side by side with such catastrophes as his, human nature was still agitating itself over its microscopic woes!

"Here's mine if you want it!" he shouted back at her through the shouting of the gale.

The offer caused the young lady to look at him more intently. "Why, it's Mr. Darrow!" she exclaimed; and then, all radiant recognition: "Oh, thank you! We'll share it, if you will."

She knew him, then; and he knew her; but how and where had they met? He put aside the problem for subsequent solution, and drawing her into a more sheltered corner, bade her wait till he could find his porter.

When, a few minutes later, he came back with his recovered property, and the news that the boat would not leave till the tide had turned, she showed no concern.

"Not for two hours? How lucky—then I can find my trunk!"

Ordinarily Darrow would have felt little disposed to involve himself in the adventure of a young female who had lost her trunk; but at the moment he was glad of any pretext for activity. Even should he decide to take the next up train from Dover he still had a yawning hour to fill; and the obvious remedy was to devote it to the loveliness in distress under his umbrella.

"You've lost a trunk? Let me see if I can find it."

It pleased him that she did not return the conventional "Oh, *would* you?" Instead, she corrected him with a laugh—"Not *a* trunk, but *my* trunk; I've no other—" and then added briskly: "You'd better first see to getting your own things on the boat."

This made him answer, as if to give substance to his plans by discussing them: "I don't actually know that I'm going over."

"Not going over?"

"Well . . . perhaps not by this boat." Again he felt a stealing indecision. "I may probably have to go back to London. I'm—I'm waiting . . . expecting a letter . . ." ("She'll think me a defaulter," he reflected.) "But meanwhile there's plenty of time to find your trunk."

He picked up his companion's bundles, and offered her an arm which enabled her to press her slight person more closely under his umbrella; and as, thus linked, they beat their way back to the platform, pulled together and apart like marionettes on the wires of the wind, he continued to wonder where he could have seen her. He had immediately classed her as a compatriot; her small nose, her clear tints, a kind of sketchy delicacy in her face, as though she had been brightly but lightly washed in with water-colour, all confirmed the evidence of her high sweet voice and of her quick incessant gestures. She was clearly an American, but with the loose native quality strained through a closer woof of manners: the composite product of an enquiring and adaptable race. All this, however, did not help him to fit a name to her, for just such instances were perpetually pouring through the London Embassy, and the etched and angular American was becoming rarer than the fluid type.

More puzzling than the fact of his being unable to identify her was the persistent sense connecting her with something uncomfortable and distasteful. So pleasant a vision as that gleaming up at him between wet brown hair and wet brown boa should have evoked only associations as pleasing; but each effort to fit her image into his past resulted in the same memories of boredom and a vague discomfort . . .

II.

DON'T you remember me now—at Mrs. Murrett's?"

She threw the question at Darrow across a table of the quiet coffee-room to which, after a vainly prolonged quest for her trunk, he had suggested taking her for a cup of tea.

In this musty retreat she had removed her dripping hat, hung it on the fender to dry, and stretched herself on tiptoe in front of the round eagle-crowned mirror, above the mantel vases of dyed immortelles, while she ran her fingers combwise through her hair. The gesture had acted on Darrow's numb feelings as the glow of the fire acted on his circulation; and when he had asked: "Aren't your feet wet, too?" and, after frank inspection of a stout-shod sole, she had answered cheerfully: "No—luckily I had on my new boots," he began to feel that human intercourse would still be tolerable if it were always as free from formality.

The removal of his companion's hat, besides provoking this reflection, gave him his first full sight of her face; and this was so favourable that the name she now pronounced fell on him with a quite disproportionate shock of dismay.

"Oh, Mrs. Murrett's—was it *there*?"

He remembered her now, of course: remembered her as one of the shadowy sidling presences in the background of that awful house in Chelsea, one of the dumb appendages of the shrieking unescapable Mrs. Murrett, into whose talons he had fallen in the course of his headlong pursuit of Lady Ulrica Crispin. Oh, the taste of stale follies! How insipid it was, yet how it clung!

"I used to pass you on the stairs," she reminded him.

Yes: he had seen her slip by—he recalled it now—as he dashed up to the drawing-room in quest of Lady Ulrica. The thought made him steal a longer look. How could such a face have been merged in the Murrett mob? Its fugitive slanting lines, that lent themselves to all manner of tender tilts and foreshortenings, had the freakish grace of some young head of the Italian comedy. The hair stood up from her forehead in a boyish elf-lock, and its colour matched her auburn eyes flecked with black, and the little brown spot on her cheek, between the ear that was meant to have a rose behind it and the chin that should have rested on a ruff. When she smiled, the left corner of her mouth went up a little higher than the right; and her smile began in her eyes and ran down to her lips in two lines of light. He had dashed past that to reach Lady Ulrica Crispin!

"But of course you wouldn't remember me," she was saying. "My name is Viner—Sophy Viner."

Not remember her? But of course he *did*! He was genuinely sure of it now. "You're Mrs. Murrett's niece," he declared.

She shook her head. "No; not even that. Only her reader."

"Her reader? Do you mean to say she ever reads?"

Miss Viner enjoyed his wonder. "Dear, no! But I wrote notes, and made up the visiting-book, and walked the dogs, and saw bores for her."

Darrow groaned. "That must have been rather bad!"

"Yes; but nothing like as bad as being her niece."

"That I can well believe. I'm glad to hear," he added, "that you put it all in the past tense."

She seemed to droop a little at the allusion; then she lifted her chin with a jerk of defiance. "Yes. All is at an end between us. We've just parted in tears—but not in silence!"

"Just parted? Do you mean to say you've been there all this time?"

"Ever since you used to come there to see Lady Ulrica? Does it seem to you so awfully long ago?"

The unexpectedness of the thrust—as well as its doubtful taste—chilled his growing enjoyment of her chatter. He had really been getting to like her—had recovered, under the candid approval of her eye, his usual sense of being a personable young man, with all the privileges pertaining to the state, instead of the anonymous rag of humanity he had felt himself in the crowd on the pier. It annoyed him, at that particular moment, to be reminded that naturalness is not always consonant with taste.

She seemed to guess his thought. "You don't like my saying that you came for Lady Ulrica?" she asked, leaning over the table to pour herself a second cup of tea.

He liked her quickness, at any rate. "It's better," he laughed, "than your thinking I came for Mrs. Murrett!"

"Oh, we never thought anybody came for Mrs. Murrett! It was always for something else: the music, or the cook—when there was a good one—or the other people; generally *one* of the other people."

"I see."

She was amusing, and that, in his present mood, was more to his purpose than the exact shade of her taste. It was odd, too, to discover suddenly that the blurred tapestry of Mrs. Murrett's background had all the while been alive and full of eyes. Now, with a pair of them looking into his, he was conscious of a queer reversal of perspective.

"Who were the 'we'? Were you a cloud of witnesses?"

"There were a good many of us." She smiled. "Let me see—who was there in your time? Mrs. Bolt—and Mademoiselle—and Professor Didymus and the Polish Countess. Don't you remember the Polish Countess?

She crystal-gazed, and played accompaniments, and Mrs. Murrett chucked her because Mrs. Didymus accused her of hypnotizing the Professor. But of course you don't remember. We were all invisible to you; but we could see. And we all used to wonder about you——"

Again Darrow felt a redness in the temples. "What about me?"

"Well—whether it was *you* or she who . . ."

He winced, but hid his disapproval. It made the time pass to listen to her.

"And what, if one may ask, was your conclusion?"

"Well, Mrs. Bolt and Mademoiselle and the Countess naturally thought it was *she*; but Professor Didymus and Jimmy Brance—especially Jimmy——"

"Just a moment: who on earth is Jimmy Brance?"

She exclaimed in wonder: "You *were* absorbed—not to remember Jimmy Brance! He must have been right about you, after all." She let her amused scrutiny dwell on him. "But how *could* you? She was false from head to foot!"

"False——?" In spite of time and satiety, the male instinct of ownership rose up and repudiated the charge.

Miss Viner caught his look and laughed. "Oh, I only meant externally! You see, she often used to come to my room after tennis, or to touch up in the evenings, when they were going on; and I assure you she took apart like a puzzle. In fact I used to say to Jimmy—just to make him wild—: 'I'll bet you anything you like there's nothing wrong, because I know she'd never dare un—' " She broke the word in two, and her quick blush made her face like a shallow-petalled rose shading to the deeper pink of the centre.

The situation was saved, for Darrow, by an abrupt

rush of memories, and he gave way to a mirth which she as frankly echoed. "Of course," she gasped through her laughter, "I only said it to tease Jimmy——"

Her amusement obscurely annoyed him. "Oh, you're all alike!" he exclaimed, moved by an unaccountable sense of disappointment.

She caught him up in a flash—she didn't miss things! "You say that because you think I'm spiteful and envious? Yes—I *was* envious of Lady Ulrica . . . Oh, not on account of you or Jimmy Brance! Simply because she had almost all the things I've always wanted: clothes and fun and motors, and admiration and yachting and Paris—why, Paris alone would be enough!— And how do you suppose a girl can see that sort of thing about her day after day, and never wonder why some women, who don't seem to have any more right to it, have it all tumbled into their laps, while others are writing dinner invitations, and straightening out accounts, and copying visiting lists, and finishing golf-stockings, and matching ribbons, and seeing that the dogs get their sulphur? One looks in one's glass, after all!"

She launched the closing words at him on a cry that lifted them above the petulance of vanity; but his sense of her words was lost in the surprise of her face. Under the flying clouds of her excitement it was no longer a shallow flowercup but a darkening gleaming mirror that might give back strange depths of feeling. The girl had stuff in her—he saw it; and she seemed to catch the perception in his eyes.

"That's the kind of education I got at Mrs. Murrett's—and I never had any other," she said with a shrug.

"Good Lord—were you there so long?"

"Five years. I stuck it out longer than any of the

others." She spoke as though it were something to be proud of.

"Well, thank God you're out of it now!"

Again a just perceptible shadow crossed her face. "Yes— I'm out of it now fast enough."

"And what—if I may ask—are you doing next?"

She brooded a moment behind drooped lids; then, with a touch of hauteur: "I'm going to Paris: to study for the stage."

"The stage?" Darrow stared at her, dismayed. All his confused contradictory impressions assumed a new aspect at this announcement; and to hide his surprise he added lightly: "Ah—then you *will* have Paris, after all!"

"Hardly Lady Ulrica's Paris. It's not likely to be roses, roses all the way."

"It's not, indeed." Real compassion prompted him to continue: "Have you any—any influence you can count on?"

She gave a somewhat flippant little laugh. "None but my own. I've never had any other to count on."

He passed over the obvious reply. "But have you any idea how the profession is over-crowded? I know I'm trite——"

"I've a very clear idea. But I couldn't go on as I was."

"Of course not. But since, as you say, you'd stuck it out longer than any of the others, couldn't you at least have held on till you were sure of some kind of an opening?"

She made no reply for a moment; then she turned a listless glance to the rain-beaten window. "Oughtn't we be starting?" she asked, with a lofty assumption of indifference that might have been Lady Ulrica's.

Darrow, surprised by the change, but accepting her rebuff as a phase of what he guessed to be a confused and tormented mood, rose from his seat and lifted her jacket from the chairback on which she had hung it to dry. As he held it toward her she looked up at him quickly.

"The truth is, we quarrelled," she broke out, "and I left last night without my dinner—and without my salary."

"Ah—" he groaned, with a sharp perception of all the sordid dangers that might attend such a break with Mrs. Murrett.

"And without a character!" she added, as she slipped her arms into the jacket. "And without a trunk, as it appears—but didn't you say that, before going, there'd be time for another look at the station?"

There was time for another look at the station; but the look again resulted in disappointment, since her trunk was nowhere to be found in the huge heap disgorged by the newly-arrived London express. The fact caused Miss Viner a moment's perturbation; but she promptly adjusted herself to the necessity of proceeding on her journey, and her decision confirmed Darrow's vague resolve to go to Paris instead of retracing his way to London.

Miss Viner seemed cheered at the prospect of his company, and sustained by his offer to telegraph to Charing Cross for the missing trunk; and he left her to wait in the fly while he hastened back to the telegraph office. The enquiry despatched, he was turning away from the desk when another thought struck him and he went back and indited a message to his servant in London: "If any letters with French postmark received since departure forward immediately to Terminus Hotel Gare du Nord Paris."

Then he rejoined Miss Viner, and they drove off through the rain to the pier.

III.

ALMOST as soon as the train left Calais her head had dropped back into the corner, and she had fallen asleep.

Sitting opposite, in the compartment from which he had contrived to have other travellers excluded, Darrow looked at her curiously. He had never seen a face that changed so quickly. A moment since it had danced like a field of daisies in a summer breeze; now, under the pallid oscillating light of the lamp overhead, it wore the hard stamp of experience, as of a soft thing chilled into shape before its curves had rounded: and it moved him to see that care already stole upon her when she slept.

The story she had imparted to him in the wheezing shaking cabin, and at the Calais buffet—where he had insisted on offering her the dinner she had missed at Mrs. Murrett's—had given a distincter outline to her figure. From the moment of entering the New York boarding-school to which a preoccupied guardian had hastily consigned her after the death of her parents, she had found herself alone in a busy and indifferent world. Her youthful history might, in fact, have been summed up in the statement that everybody had been too busy to look after her. Her guardian, a drudge in a big banking house, was absorbed by "the office"; the guardian's wife, by her health and her religion; and an elder sister, Laura, married, unmarried, remarried, and pursuing, through all these alternating phases, some vaguely "artistic" ideal on which the guardian and his wife looked askance, had (as Darrow conjectured) taken their disapproval as a pretext for not troubling herself about poor Sophy, to whom—perhaps for this reason—she had remained the incarnation of remote romantic possibilities.

In the course of time a sudden "stroke" of the guardian's had thrown his personal affairs into a state of confusion from which—after his widely lamented death—it became evident that it would not be possible to extricate his ward's inheritance. No one deplored this more sincerely than his widow, who saw in it one more proof of her husband's life having been sacrificed to the innumerable duties imposed on him, and who could hardly—but for the counsels of religion—have brought herself to pardon the young girl for her indirect share in hastening his end. Sophy did not resent this point of view. She was really much sorrier for her guardian's death than for the loss of her insignificant fortune. The latter had represented only the means of holding her in bondage, and its disappearance was the occasion of her immediate plunge into the wide bright sea of life surrounding the island of her captivity. She had first landed—thanks to the intervention of the ladies who had directed her education—in a Fifth Avenue school-room where, for a few months, she acted as a buffer between three autocratic infants and their bodyguard of nurses and teachers. The too-pressing attentions of their father's valet had caused her to fly this sheltered spot, against the express advice of her educational superiors, who implied that, in their own case, refinement and self-respect had always sufficed to keep the most ungovernable passions at bay. The experience of the guardian's widow having been precisely similar, and the deplorable precedent of Laura's career being present to all their minds, none of these ladies felt any obligation to intervene farther in Sophy's affairs; and she was accordingly left to her own resources.

A schoolmate from the Rocky Mountains, who was taking her father and mother to Europe, had suggested Sophy's accompanying them, and "going round" with her while her progenitors, in the care of the courier, nursed their ailments at a fashionable bath. Darrow gathered that the "going round" with Mamie Hoke was a varied and diverting process; but this relatively brilliant phase of Sophy's career was cut short by the elopement of the inconsiderate Mamie with a "matinée idol" who had followed her from New York, and by the precipitate return of her parents to negotiate for the repurchase of their child.

It was then—after an interval of repose with compassionate but impecunious American friends in Paris—that Miss Viner had been drawn into the turbid current of Mrs. Murrett's career. The impecunious compatriots had found Mrs. Murrett for her, and it was partly on their account (because they were such dears, and so unconscious, poor confiding things, of what they were letting her in for) that Sophy had stuck it out so long in the dreadful house in Chelsea. The Farlows, she explained to Darrow, were the best friends she had ever had (and the only ones who had ever "been decent" about Laura, whom they had seen once, and intensely admired); but even after twenty years of Paris they were the most incorrigibly inexperienced angels, and quite persuaded that Mrs. Murrett was a woman of great intellectual eminence, and the house at Chelsea "the last of the *salons*"— Darrow knew what she meant? And she hadn't liked to undeceive them, knowing that to do so would be virtually to throw herself back on their hands, and feeling, moreover, after her previous experiences, the urgent need of gaining, at any cost, a name for stability; besides which—she threw it off with a slight laugh—no other chance, in all these years, had happened to come to her.

She had brushed in this outline of her career with light rapid strokes, and in a tone of fatalism oddly untinged by bitterness. Darrow perceived that she classified people according to their greater or less "luck" in life, but she appeared to harbour no resentment against the undefined power which dispensed the gift in such unequal measure. Things came one's way or they didn't; and meanwhile one could only look on, and make the most of small compensations, such as watching "the show" at Mrs. Murrett's, and talking over the Lady Ulricas and other footlight figures. And at any moment, of course, a turn of the kaleidoscope might suddenly toss a bright spangle into the grey pattern of one's days.

This light-hearted philosophy was not without charm to a young man accustomed to more traditional views. George Darrow had had a fairly varied experience of feminine types, but the women he had frequented had either been pronouncedly "ladies" or they had not.

Grateful to both for ministering to the more complex masculine nature, and disposed to assume that they had been evolved, if not designed, to that end, he had instinctively kept the two groups apart in his mind, avoiding that intermediate society which attempts to conciliate both theories of life. "Bohemianism" seemed to him a cheaper convention than the other two, and he liked, above all, people who went as far as they could in their own line—liked his "ladies" and their rivals to be equally unashamed of showing for exactly what they were. He had not indeed—the fact of Lady Ulrica was there to remind him—been without his experience of a third type; but that experience had left him with a contemptuous distaste for the woman who uses the privileges of one class to shelter the customs of another.

As to young girls, he had never thought much about them since his early love for the girl who had become Mrs. Leath. That episode seemed, as he looked back on it, to bear no more relation to reality than a pale decorative design to the confused richness of a summer landscape. He no longer understood the violent impulses and dreamy pauses of his own young heart, or the inscrutable abandonments and reluctances of hers. He had known a moment of anguish at losing her—the mad plunge of youthful instincts against the barrier of fate; but the first wave of stronger sensation had swept away all but the outline of their story, and the memory of Anna Summers had made the image of the young girl sacred, but the class uninteresting.

Such generalisations belonged, however, to an earlier stage of his experience. The more he saw of life the more incalculable he found it; and he had learned to yield to his impressions without feeling the youthful need of relating them to others. It was the girl in the opposite seat who had roused in him the dormant habit of comparison. She was distinguished from the daughters of wealth by her avowed acquaintance with the real business of living, a familiarity as different as possible from their theoretical proficiency; yet it seemed to Darrow that her experience had made her free without hardness and self-assured without assertiveness.

The rush into Amiens, and the flash of the station lights into their compartment, broke Miss Viner's sleep, and without changing her position she lifted her lids and looked at Darrow. There was neither surprise nor bewilderment in the look. She seemed instantly conscious, not so much of where she was, as of the fact that she was with him; and that fact seemed enough to reassure her. She did not even turn her head to look out; her eyes continued to rest on him with a vague smile which appeared to light her face from within, while her lips kept their sleepy droop.

Shouts and the hurried tread of travellers came to them through the confusing cross-lights of the platform. A head appeared at the window, and Darrow threw himself forward to defend their solitude; but the intruder was only a train hand going his round of inspection. He passed on, and the lights and cries of the station dropped away, merged in a wider haze and a hollower resonance, as the train gathered itself up with a long shake and rolled out again into the darkness.

Miss Viner's head sank back against the cushion, pushing out a dusky wave of hair above her forehead.

The swaying of the train loosened a lock over her ear, and she shook it back with a movement like a boy's, while her gaze still rested on her companion.

"You're not too tired?"

She shook her head with a smile.

"We shall be in before midnight. We're very nearly on time." He verified the statement by holding up his watch to the lamp.

She nodded dreamily. "It's all right. I telegraphed Mrs. Farlow that they mustn't think of coming to the station; but they'll have told the *concierge* to look out for me."

"You'll let me drive you there?"

She nodded again, and her eyes closed. It was very pleasant to Darrow that she made no effort to talk or to dissemble her sleepiness. He sat watching her till the upper lashes met and mingled with the lower, and their blent shadow lay on her cheek; then he stood up and drew the curtain over the lamp, drowning the compartment in a bluish twilight.

As he sank back into his seat he thought how differently Anna Summers—or even Anna Leath—would have behaved. She would not have talked too much; she would not have been either restless or embarrassed; but her adaptability, her appropriateness, would not have been nature but "tact." The oddness of the situation would have made sleep impossible, or, if weariness had overcome her for a moment, she would have waked with a start, wondering where she was, and how she had come there, and if her hair were tidy; and nothing short of hairpins and a glass would have restored her self-possession . . .

The reflection set him wondering whether the "sheltered" girl's bringing-up might not unfit her for all subsequent contact with life. How much nearer to it had Mrs. Leath been brought by marriage and motherhood, and the passage of fourteen years? What were all her reticences and evasions but the result of the deadening process of forming a "lady"? The freshness he had marvelled at was like the unnatural whiteness of flowers forced in the dark.

As he looked back at their few days together he saw that their intercourse had been marked, on her part, by the same hesitations and reserves which had chilled their earlier intimacy. Once more they had had their hour together and she had wasted it. As in her girlhood, her eyes had made promises which her lips were afraid to keep. She was still afraid of life, of its ruthlessness, its danger and mystery. She was still the petted little girl who cannot be left alone in the dark . . . His memory flew back to their youthful story, and long-forgotten details took shape before him. How frail and faint the picture was! They seemed, he and she, like the ghostly lovers of the Grecian Urn, forever pursuing without ever clasping each other. To this day he did not quite know what had parted them: the break had been as fortuitous as the fluttering apart of two seed-vessels on a wave of summer air . . .

The very slightness, vagueness, of the memory gave it an added poignancy. He felt the mystic pang of the parent for a child which has just breathed and died. Why had it happened thus, when the least shifting of influences might have made it all so different? If she had been given to him then he would have put warmth in her veins and light in her eyes: would have made her a woman through and through. Musing thus, he had the sense of waste that is the bitterest harvest of experience. A love like his might have given her the divine gift of self-renewal; and now he saw her fated to wane into old age repeating the same gestures, echoing the words she had always heard, and perhaps never guessing that, just outside her glazed and curtained consciousness, life rolled away, a vast blackness starred with lights, like the night landscape beyond the windows of the train.

The engine lowered its speed for the passage through a sleeping station. In the light of the platform lamp Darrow looked across at his companion. Her head had dropped toward one shoulder, and her lips were just far enough apart for the reflection of the upper one to deepen the colour of the other. The jolting of the train had again shaken loose the lock above her ear. It danced on her cheek like the flit of a brown wing over flowers, and Darrow felt an intense desire to lean forward and put it back behind her ear.

IV.

As their motor-cab, on the way from the Gare du Nord, turned into the central glitter of the Boulevard, Darrow had bent over to point out an incandescent threshold.

"There!"

Above the doorway, an arch of flame flashed out the name of a great actress, whose closing performances in a play of unusual originality had been the theme of long articles in the Paris papers which Darrow had tossed into their compartment at Calais.

"That's what you must see before you're twenty-four hours older!"

The girl followed his gesture eagerly. She was all awake and alive now, as if the heady rumours of the streets, with their long effervescences of light, had passed into her veins like wine.

"Cerdine? Is that where she acts?" She put her head out of the window, straining back for a glimpse of the sacred threshold. As they flew past it she sank into her seat with a satisfied sigh.

"It's delicious enough just to *know* she's there! I've never seen her, you know. When I was here with Mamie Hoke we never went anywhere but to the music halls, because she couldn't understand any French; and when I came back afterward to the Farlows' I was dead broke, and couldn't afford the play, and neither could they; so the only chance we had was when friends of theirs invited us—and once it was to see a tragedy by a Roumanian lady, and the other time it was for 'L'Ami Fritz' at the Français."

Darrow laughed. "You must do better than that now. 'Le Vertige' is a fine thing, and Cerdine gets some wonderful effects out of it. You must come with me tomorrow evening to see it—with your friends, of course. —That is," he added, "if there's any sort of chance of getting seats."

The flash of a street lamp lit up her radiant face. "Oh, will you really take us? What fun to think that it's tomorrow already!"

It was wonderfully pleasant to be able to give such

pleasure. Darrow was not rich, but it was almost impossible for him to picture the state of persons with tastes and perceptions like his own, to whom an evening at the theatre was an unattainable indulgence. There floated through his mind an answer of Mrs. Leath's to his enquiry whether she had seen the play in question. "No. I meant to, of course, but one is so overwhelmed with things in Paris. And then I'm rather sick of Cerdine—one is always being dragged to see her."

That, among the people he frequented, was the usual attitude toward such opportunities. There were too many, they were a nuisance, one had to defend one's self! He even remembered wondering, at the moment, whether to a really fine taste the exceptional thing could ever become indifferent through habit; whether the appetite for beauty was so soon dulled that it could be kept alive only by privation. Here, at any rate, was a fine chance to experiment with such a hunger: he almost wished he might stay on in Paris long enough to take the measure of Miss Viner's receptivity.

She was still dwelling on his promise. "It's too beautiful of you! Oh, don't you *think* you'll be able to get seats?" And then, after a pause of brimming appreciation: "I wonder if you'll think me horrid?—but it may be my only chance; and if you can't get places for us all, wouldn't you perhaps just take *me*? After all, the Farlows may have seen it!"

He had not, of course, thought her horrid, but only the more engaging, for being so natural, and so unashamed of showing the frank greed of her famished youth. "Oh, *you* shall go somehow!" he had gaily promised her; and she had dropped back with a sigh of pleasure as their cab passed into the dimly-lit streets of the Farlows' quarter beyond the Seine . . .

* * *

This little passage came back to him the next morning, as he opened his hotel window on the early roar of the Northern Terminus.

The girl was there, in the room next to him. That had been the first point in his waking consciousness. The second was a sense of relief at the obligation imposed on him by this unexpected turn of events. To wake to the necessity of action, to postpone perforce the fruitless contemplation of his private grievance, was cause enough for gratitude, even if the small adventure in which he found himself involved had not, on its own merits, roused an instinctive curiosity to see it through.

When he and his companion, the night before, had reached the Farlows' door in the rue de la Chaise, it was only to find, after repeated assaults on its panels, that the Farlows were no longer there. They had moved away the week before, not only from their apartment but from Paris; and Miss Viner's breach with Mrs. Murrett had been too sudden to permit her letter and telegram to overtake them. Both communications, no doubt, still reposed in a pigeon-hole of the *loge*; but its custodian, when drawn from his lair, sulkily declined to let Miss Viner verify the fact, and only flung out, in return for Darrow's bribe, the statement that the Americans had gone to Joigny.

To pursue them there at that hour was manifestly impossible, and Miss Viner, disturbed but not disconcerted by this new obstacle, had quite simply acceded to Darrow's suggestion that she should return for what remained of the night to the hotel where he had sent his luggage.

The drive back through the dark hush before dawn,

with the nocturnal blaze of the Boulevard fading around them like the false lights of a magician's palace, had so played on her impressionability that she seemed to give no farther thought to her own predicament. Darrow noticed that she did not feel the beauty and mystery of the spectacle as much as its pressure of human significance, all its hidden implications of emotion and adventure. As they passed the shadowy colonnade of the Français, remote and temple-like in the paling lights, he felt a clutch on his arm, and heard the cry: "There are things *there* that I want so desperately to see!" and all the way back to the hotel she continued to question him, with shrewd precision and an artless thirst for detail, about the theatrical life of Paris. He was struck afresh, as he listened, by the way in which her naturalness eased the situation of constraint, leaving to it only a pleasant savour of good fellowship. It was the kind of episode that one might, in advance, have characterized as "awkward", yet that was proving, in the event, as much outside such definitions as a sunrise stroll with a dryad in a dew-drenched forest; and Darrow reflected that mankind would never have needed to invent tact if it had not first invented social complications.

It had been understood, with his good-night to Miss Viner, that the next morning he was to look up the Joigny trains, and see her safely to the station; but, while he breakfasted and waited for a time-table, he recalled again her cry of joy at the prospect of seeing Cerdine. It was certainly a pity, since that most elusive and incalculable of artists was leaving the next week for South America, to miss what might be a last sight of her in her greatest part; and Darrow, having dressed and made the requisite excerpts from the time-table, decided to carry the result of his deliberations to his neighbour's door.

It instantly opened at his knock, and she came forth looking as if she had been plunged into some sparkling element which had curled up all her drooping tendrils and wrapped her in a shimmer of fresh leaves.

"Well, what do you think of me?" she cried; and with a hand at her waist she spun about as if to show off some miracle of Parisian dress-making.

"I think the missing trunk has come—and that it was worth waiting for!"

"You *do* like my dress?"

"I adore it! I always adore new dresses—why, you don't mean to say it's *not* a new one?"

She laughed out her triumph.

"No, no, no! My trunk hasn't come, and this is only my old rag of yesterday—but I never knew the trick to fail!" And, as he stared: "You see," she joyously explained, "I've always had to dress in all kinds of dreary left-overs, and sometimes, when everybody else was smart and new, it used to make me awfully miserable. So one day, when Mrs. Murrett dragged me down unexpectedly to fill a place at dinner, I suddenly thought I'd try spinning around like that, and say to every one: '*Well, what do you think of me?*' And, do you know, they were all taken in, including Mrs. Murrett, who didn't recognize my old turned and dyed rags, and told me afterward it was awfully bad form to dress as if I were somebody that people would expect to know! And ever since, whenever I've particularly wanted to look nice, I've just asked people what they thought of my new frock; and they're always, always taken in!"

She dramatized her explanation so vividly that Darrow felt as if his point were gained.

"Ah, but this confirms your vocation—of course," he cried, "you must see Cerdine!" and, seeing her face fall at this reminder of the change in her prospects, he hastened to set forth his plan. As he did so, he saw how easy it was to explain things to her. She would either accept his suggestion, or she would not: but at least she would waste no time in protestations and objections, or any vain sacrifice to the idols of conformity. The conviction that one could, on any given point, almost predicate this of her, gave him the sense of having advanced far enough in her intimacy to urge his arguments against a hasty pursuit of her friends.

Yes, it would certainly be foolish—she at once agreed—in the case of such dear indefinite angels as the Farlows, to dash off after them without more positive proof that they were established at Joigny, and so established that they could take her in. She owned it was but too probable that they had gone there to "cut down", and might be doing so in quarters too contracted to receive her; and it would be unfair, on that chance, to impose herself on them unannounced. The simplest way of getting farther light on the question would be to go back to the rue de la Chaise, where, at that more conversable hour, the *concierge* might be less chary of detail; and she could decide on her next step in the light of such facts as he imparted.

Point by point, she fell in with the suggestion, recognizing, in the light of their unexplained flight, that the Farlows might indeed be in a situation on which one could not too rashly intrude. Her concern for her friends seemed to have effaced all thought of herself, and this little indication of character gave Darrow a quite disproportionate pleasure. She agreed that it would be well to go at once to the rue de la Chaise, but met his proposal that they should drive by the declaration that it was a "waste" not to walk in Paris; so they set off on foot through the cheerful tumult of the streets.

The walk was long enough for him to learn many things about her. The storm of the previous night had cleared the air, and Paris shone in morning beauty under a sky that was all broad wet washes of white and blue; but Darrow again noticed that her visual sensitiveness was less keen than her feeling for what he was sure the good Farlows—whom he already seemed to know—would have called "the human interest." She seemed hardly conscious of sensations of form and colour, or of any imaginative suggestion, and the spectacle before them—always, in its scenic splendour, so moving to her companion—broke up, under her scrutiny, into a thousand minor points: the things in the shops, the types of character and manner of occupation shown in the passing faces, the street signs, the names of the hotels they passed, the motley brightness of the flower-carts, the identity of the churches and public buildings that caught her eye. But what she liked best, he divined, was the mere fact of being free to walk abroad in the bright air, her tongue rattling on as it pleased, while her feet kept time to the mighty orchestration of the city's sounds. Her delight in the fresh air, in the freedom, light and sparkle of the morning, gave him a sudden insight into her stifled past; nor was it indifferent to him to perceive how much his presence evidently added to her enjoyment. If only as a sympathetic ear, he guessed what he must be worth to her. The girl had been dying for some one to talk to, some one before whom she could unfold and shake out to the light her poor little shut-away emotions. Years of repression were revealed in her sudden burst of confidence; and the pity she inspired made Darrow long to fill her few free hours to the brim.

She had the gift of rapid definition, and his questions as to the life she had led with the Farlows, during the interregnum between the Hoke and Murrett eras, called up before him a queer little corner of Parisian existence. The Farlows themselves—he a painter, she a "magazine writer"—rose before him in all their incorruptible simplicity: an elderly New England couple, with vague yearnings for enfranchisement, who lived in Paris as if it were a Massachusetts suburb, and dwelt hopefully on the "higher side" of the Gallic nature. With equal vividness she set before him the component figures of the circle from which Mrs. Farlow drew the "Inner Glimpses of French Life" appearing over her name in a leading New England journal: the Roumanian lady who had sent them tickets for her tragedy, an elderly French gentleman who, on the strength of a week's stay at Folkestone, translated English fiction for the provincial press, a lady from Wichita, Kansas, who advocated free love and the abolition of the corset, a clergyman's widow from Torquay who had written an "English Ladies' Guide to Foreign Galleries" and a Russian sculptor who lived on nuts and was "almost certainly" an anarchist. It was this nucleus, and its outer ring of musical, architectural and other American students, which posed successively to Mrs. Farlow's versatile fancy as a centre of "University Life", a "Salon of the Faubourg St. Germain", a group of Parisian "Intellectuals" or a "Cross-section of Montmartre"; but even her faculty for extracting from it the most varied literary effects had not sufficed to create a permanent demand for the "Inner Glimpses", and there were days when—Mr. Farlow's landscapes being equally unmarketable—a temporary withdrawal to the country (subsequently utilized as "Peeps into Château Life") became necessary to the courageous couple.

Five years of Mrs. Murrett's world, while increasing Sophy's tenderness for the Farlows, had left her with few illusions as to their power of advancing her fortunes; and she did not conceal from Darrow that her theatrical projects were of the vaguest. They hung mainly on the problematical goodwill of an ancient comédienne, with whom Mrs. Farlow had a slight acquaintance (extensively utilized in "Stars of the French Footlights" and "Behind the Scenes at the Français"), and who had once, with signs of approval, heard Miss Viner recite the Nuit de Mai.

"But of course I know how much that's worth," the girl broke off, with one of her flashes of shrewdness. "And besides, it isn't likely that a poor old fossil like Mme. Dolle could get anybody to listen to her now, even if she really thought I had talent. But she might introduce me to people; or at least give me a few tips. If I could manage to earn enough to pay for lessons I'd go straight to some of the big people and work with them. I'm rather hoping the Farlows may find me a chance of that kind—an engagement with some American family in Paris who would want to be 'gone round' with like the Hokes, and who'd leave me time enough to study."

In the rue de la Chaise they learned little except the exact address of the Farlows, and the fact that they had sub-let their flat before leaving. This information obtained, Darrow proposed to Miss Viner that they should stroll along the quays to a little restaurant looking out on the Seine, and there, over the *plat du jour*, consider the next step to be taken. The long walk had given her cheeks a glow indicative of wholesome hunger, and she made no difficulty about satisfying it in Darrow's company. Regaining the river they walked on in the direction of Notre Dame, delayed now and again by the young man's irresistible tendency to linger over the bookstalls, and by his ever-fresh response to the shifting beauties of the scene. For two years his eyes had been subdued to the atmospheric effects of London, to the mysterious fusion of darkly-piled city and low-lying bituminous sky; and the transparency of the French air, which left the green gardens and silvery stones so classically clear yet so softly harmonized, struck him as having a kind of conscious intelligence. Every line of the architecture, every arch of the bridges, the very sweep of the strong bright river between them, while contributing to this effect, sent forth each a separate appeal to some sensitive memory; so that, for Darrow, a walk through the Paris streets was always like the unrolling of a vast tapestry from which countless stored fragrances were shaken out.

It was a proof of the richness and multiplicity of the spectacle that it served, without incongruity, for so different a purpose as the background of Miss Viner's enjoyment. As a mere drop-scene for her personal adventure it was just as much in its place as in the evocation of great perspectives of feeling. For her, as he again perceived when they were seated at their table in a low window above the Seine, Paris was "Paris" by virtue of all its entertaining details, its endless ingenuities of pleasantness. Where else, for instance, could one find the dear little dishes of *hors d'oeuvre*, the symmetrically-laid anchovies and radishes, the thin golden shells of butter, or the wood strawberries and brown jars of cream that gave to their repast the last refinement of rusticity? Hadn't he noticed, she asked, that cooking always expressed the national character, and that French food was clever and amusing just because the people were? And in private houses, everywhere, how the dishes always resembled the talk—how the very same platitudes seemed to go into people's mouths and come out of them? Couldn't he see just what kind of menu it would make, if a fairy waved a wand and suddenly turned the conversation at a London dinner into joints and puddings? She always thought it a good sign when people liked Irish stew; it meant that they enjoyed changes and surprises, and taking life as it came; and such a beautiful Parisian version of the dish as the *navarin* that was just being set before them was like the very best kind of talk—the kind when one could never tell before-hand just what was going to be said!

Darrow, as he watched her enjoyment of their innocent feast, wondered if her vividness and vivacity were signs of her calling. She was the kind of girl in whom certain people would instantly have recognized the histrionic gift. But experience had led him to think that, except at the creative moment, the divine flame burns low in its possessors. The one or two really intelligent actresses he had known had struck him, in conversation, as either bovine or primitively "jolly". He had a notion that, save in the mind of genius, the creative process absorbs too much of the whole stuff of being to leave much surplus for personal expression; and the girl before him, with her changing face and flexible fancies, seemed destined to work in life itself rather than in any of its counterfeits.

The coffee and liqueurs were already on the table when her mind suddenly sprang back to the Farlows. She jumped up with one of her subversive movements and declared that she must telegraph at once. Darrow called for writing materials, and room was made at her elbow for the parched ink-bottle and saturated blotter of the Parisian restaurant; but the mere sight of these jaded implements seemed to paralyze Miss Viner's faculties. She hung over the telegraph-form with anxiously-drawn brow, the tip of the pen-handle pressed against her lip; and at length she raised her troubled eyes to Darrow's.

"I simply can't think how to say it."

"What—that you're staying over to see Cerdine?"

"But *am* I—am I, really?" The joy of it flamed over her face.

Darrow looked at his watch. "You could hardly get an answer to your telegram in time to take a train to Joigny this afternoon, even if you found your friends could have you."

She mused for a moment, tapping her lip with the pen. "But I must let them know I'm here. I must find out as soon as possible if they *can* have me." She laid the pen down despairingly. "I never *could* write a telegram!" she sighed.

"Try a letter, then, and tell them you'll arrive tomorrow."

This suggestion produced immediate relief, and she gave an energetic dab at the ink-bottle; but after another interval of uncertain scratching she paused again.

"Oh, it's fearful! I don't know what on earth to say. I wouldn't for the world have them know how beastly Mrs. Murrett's been."

Darrow did not think it necessary to answer. It was no business of his, after all. He lit a cigar and leaned back in his seat, letting his eyes take their fill of indolent pleasure. In the throes of invention she had pushed back her hat, loosening the stray lock which had invited his touch the night before. After looking at it for a while he stood up and wandered to the window.

Behind him he heard her pen scrape on.

"I don't want to worry them—I'm so certain they've got bothers of their own." The faltering scratches ceased again. "I wish I weren't such an idiot about writing: all the words get frightened and scurry away when I try to catch them."

He glanced back at her with a smile as she bent above her task like a school-girl struggling with a "composition." Her flushed cheek and frowning brow showed that her difficulty was genuine and not an artless device to draw him to her side. She was really powerless to put her thoughts in writing, and the inability seemed characteristic of her quick impressionable mind, and of the incessant come-and-go of her sensations. He thought of Anna Leath's letters, or rather of the few he had received, years ago, from the girl who had been Anna Summers. He saw the slender firm strokes of the pen, recalled the clear structure of the phrases, and, by an abrupt association of ideas, remembered that, at that very hour, just such a document might be awaiting him at the hotel.

What if it were there, indeed, and had brought him a complete explanation of her telegram? The revulsion of feeling produced by this thought made him look at the girl with sudden impatience. She struck him as positively stupid, and he wondered how he could have wasted half his day with her, when all the while Mrs. Leath's letter might be lying on his table. At that moment, if he could have chosen, he would have left his companion on the spot; but he had her on his hands, and must accept the consequences.

Some odd intuition seemed to make her conscious of his change of mood, for she sprang from her seat, crumpling the letter in her hand.

"I'm too stupid; but I won't keep you any longer. I'll go back to the hotel and write there."

Her colour deepened, and for the first time, as their eyes met, he noticed a faint embarrassment in hers. Could it be that his nearness was, after all, the cause of her confusion? The thought turned his vague impatience with her into a definite resentment toward himself. There was really no excuse for his having blundered into such an adventure. Why had he not shipped the girl off to Joigny by the evening train, instead of urging her to delay, and using Cerdine as a pretext? Paris was full of people he knew, and his annoyance was increased by the thought that some friend of Mrs. Leath's might see him at the play, and report his presence there with a suspiciously good-looking companion. The idea was distinctly disagreeable: he did not want the woman he adored to think he could forget her for a moment. And by this time he had fully persuaded himself that a letter from her was awaiting him, and had even gone so far as to imagine that its contents might annul the writer's telegraphed injunction, and call him to her side at once . . .

V.

AT the porter's desk a brief *"Pas de lettres"* fell destructively on the fabric of these hopes.

Mrs. Leath had not written—she had not taken the trouble to explain her telegram. Darrow turned away with a sharp pang of humiliation. Her frugal silence mocked his prodigality of hopes and fears. He had put his question to the porter once before, on returning to the hotel after luncheon; and now, coming back again in the late afternoon, he was met by the same denial. The second post was in, and had brought him nothing.

A glance at his watch showed that he had barely time to dress before taking Miss Viner out to dine; but as he turned to the lift a new thought struck him, and hurrying back into the hall he dashed off another telegram to his servant: "Have you forwarded any letter with French postmark today? Telegraph answer Terminus."

Some kind of reply would be certain to reach him on his return from the theatre, and he would then know definitely whether Mrs. Leath meant to write or not. He hastened up to his room and dressed with a lighter heart.

Miss Viner's vagrant trunk had finally found its way to its owner; and, clad in such modest splendour as it furnished, she shone at Darrow across their restaurant table. In the reaction of his wounded vanity he found her prettier and more interesting than before. Her dress, sloping away from the throat, showed the graceful set of her head on its slender neck, and the wide brim of her hat arched above her hair like a dusky halo. Pleasure danced in her eyes and on her lips, and as she shone on him between the candle-shades Darrow felt that he should not be at all sorry to be seen with her in public. He even sent a careless glance about him in the vague hope that it might fall on an acquaintance.

At the theatre her vivacity sank into a breathless hush, and she sat intent in her corner of their *baignoire*, with the gaze of a neophyte about to be initiated into the sacred mysteries. Darrow placed himself behind her, that he might catch her profile between himself and the stage. He was touched by the youthful seriousness of her expression. In spite of the experiences she must have had, and of the twenty-four years to which she owned, she struck him as intrinsically young; and he wondered how so evanescent a quality could have been preserved in the desiccating Murrett air. As the play progressed he noticed that her immobility was traversed by swift flashes of perception. She was not missing anything, and her intensity of attention when Cerdine was on the stage drew an anxious line between her brows.

After the first act she remained for a few minutes rapt and motionless; then she turned to her companion with a quick patter of questions. He gathered from them that she had been less interested in following the general drift of the play than in observing the details of its interpretation. Every gesture and inflection of the great actress's had been marked and analyzed; and Darrow felt a secret gratification in being appealed to as an authority on the histrionic art. His interest in it had hitherto been merely that of the cultivated young man curious of all forms of artistic expression; but in reply to her questions he found things to say about it which evidently struck his listener as impressive and original, and with which he himself was not, on the whole, dissatisfied. Miss Viner was much more concerned to hear his views than to express her own, and the deference with which she received his comments called from him more ideas about the theatre than he had ever supposed himself to possess.

With the second act she began to give more attention to the development of the play, though her interest was excited rather by what she called "the story" than by the conflict of character producing it. Oddly combined with her sharp apprehension of things theatrical, her knowledge of technical "dodges" and green-room precedents, her glibness about "lines" and "curtains", was the primitive simplicity of her attitude toward the tale itself, as toward something that was "really happening" and at which one assisted as at a street-accident or a quarrel overheard in the next room. She wanted to know if Darrow thought the lovers "really would" be involved in the catastrophe that threatened them, and when he reminded her that his predictions were disqualified by his having already seen the play, she exclaimed: "Oh, then, please don't tell me what's going to happen!" and the next moment was questioning him about Cerdine's theatrical situation and her private history. On the latter point some of her enquiries were of a kind that it is not in the habit of young girls to make, or even to know how to make; but her apparent unconsciousness of the fact seemed rather to reflect on her past associates than on herself.

When the second act was over, Darrow suggested their taking a turn in the *foyer*; and seated on one of its cramped red velvet sofas they watched the crowd surge up and down in a glare of lights and gilding. Then, as she complained of the heat, he led her through the press to the congested *café* at the foot of the stairs, where orangeades were thrust at them between the shoulders of packed *consommateurs*, and Darrow, lighting a cigarette while she sucked her straw, knew the primitive complacency of the man at whose companion other men stare.

On a corner of their table lay a smeared copy of a theatrical journal. It caught Sophy's eye and after poring over the page she looked up with an excited exclamation.

"They're giving *Oedipe* tomorrow afternoon at the Français! I suppose you've seen it heaps and heaps of times?"

He smiled back at her. "You must see it too. We'll go tomorrow."

She sighed at his suggestion, but without discarding it. "How can I? The last train for Joigny leaves at four."

"But you don't know yet that your friends will want you."

"I shall know tomorrow early. I asked Mrs. Farlow to telegraph as soon as she got my letter."

A twinge of compunction shot through Darrow. Her words recalled to him that on their return to the hotel after luncheon she had given him her letter to post, and that he had never thought of it again. No doubt it was still in the pocket of the coat he had taken off when he dressed for dinner. In his perturbation he pushed back his chair, and the movement made her look up at him.

"What's the matter?"

"Nothing. Only—you know I don't fancy that letter can have caught this afternoon's post."

"Not caught it? Why not?"

"Why, I'm afraid it will have been too late." He bent his head to light another cigarette.

She struck her hands together with a gesture which, to his amusement, he noticed she had caught from Cerdine.

"Oh, dear, I hadn't thought of that! But surely it will reach them in the morning?"

"Some time in the morning, I suppose. You know the French provincial post is never in a hurry. I don't believe your letter would have been delivered this evening in any case." As this idea occurred to him he felt himself almost absolved.

"Perhaps, then, I ought to have telegraphed?"

"I'll telegraph for you in the morning if you say so."

The bell announcing the close of the entr'-acte shrilled through the *café*, and she sprang to her feet.

"Oh, come, come! We mustn't miss it!"

Instantly forgetful of the Farlows, she slipped her arm through his and turned to push her way back to the theatre.

As soon as the curtain went up she as promptly forgot her companion. Watching her from the corner to which he had returned, Darrow saw that great waves of sensation were beating deliciously against her brain. It was as though every starved sensibility were throwing out feelers to the mounting tide; as though everything she was seeing, hearing, imagining, rushed in to fill the void of all she had always been denied.

Darrow, as he observed her, again felt a detached enjoyment in her pleasure. She was an extraordinary conductor of sensation: she seemed to transmit it physically, in emanations that set the blood dancing in his veins. He had not often had the opportunity of studying the effects of a perfectly fresh impression on so responsive a temperament, and he felt a fleeting desire to make its chords vibrate for his own amusement.

At the end of the next act she discovered with dismay that in their transit to the *café* she had lost the beautiful pictured programme he had bought for her. She wanted to go back and hunt for it, but Darrow assured her that he would have no trouble in getting her another. When he went out in quest of it she followed him protestingly to the door of the box, and he saw that she was distressed at the thought of his having to spend an additional franc for her. This frugality smote Darrow by its contrast to her natural bright profusion; and again he felt the desire to right so clumsy an injustice.

When he returned to the box she was still standing in the doorway, and he noticed that his were not the only eyes attracted to her. Then another impression sharply diverted his attention. Above the fagged faces of the Parisian crowd he had caught the fresh fair countenance of Owen Leath signalling a joyful recognition.

The young man, slim and eager, had detached himself from two companions of his own type, and was seeking to push through the press to his step-mother's friend. The encounter, to Darrow, could hardly have been more inopportune; it woke in him a confusion of feelings of which only the uppermost was allayed by seeing Sophy Viner, as if instinctively warned, melt back into the shadow of their box.

A minute later Owen Leath was at his side. "I was

sure it was you! Such luck to run across you! Won't you come off with us to supper after it's over? Montmartre, or wherever else you please. Those two chaps over there are friends of mine, at the Beaux Arts; both of them rather good fellows—and we'd be so glad——"

For half a second Darrow read in his hospitable eye the termination "if you'd bring the lady too"; then it deflected into: "We'd all be so glad if you'd come."

Darrow, excusing himself with thanks, lingered on for a few minutes' chat, in which every word, and every tone of his companion's voice, was like a sharp light flashed into aching eyes. He was glad when the bell called the audience to their seats, and young Leath left him with the friendly question: "We'll see you at Givré later on?"

When he rejoined Miss Viner, Darrow's first care was to find out, by a rapid inspection of the house, whether Owen Leath's seat had given him a view of their box. But the young man was not visible from it, and Darrow concluded that he had been recognized in the corridor and not at his companion's side. He scarcely knew why it seemed to him so important that this point should be settled; certainly his sense of reassurance was less due to regard for Miss Viner than to the persistent vision of grave offended eyes . . .

During the drive back to the hotel this vision was persistently kept before him by the thought that the evening post might have brought a letter from Mrs. Leath. Even if no letter had yet come, his servant might have telegraphed to say that one was on its way; and at the thought his interest in the girl at his side again cooled to the fraternal, the almost fatherly. She was no more to him, after all, than an appealing young creature to whom it was mildly agreeable to have offered an evening's diversion; and when, as they rolled into the illuminated court of the hotel, she turned with a quick movement which brought her happy face close to his, he leaned away, affecting to be absorbed in opening the door of the cab.

At the desk the night porter, after a vain search through the pigeon-holes, was disposed to think that a letter or telegram had in fact been sent up for the gentleman; and Darrow, at the announcement, could hardly wait to ascend to his room. Upstairs, he and his companion had the long dimly-lit corridor to themselves, and Sophy paused on her threshold, gathering up in one hand the pale folds of her cloak, while she held the other out to Darrow.

"If the telegram comes early I shall be off by the first train; so I suppose this is good-bye," she said, her eyes dimmed by a little shadow of regret.

Darrow, with a renewed start of contrition, perceived that he had again forgotten her letter; and as their hands met he vowed to himself that the moment she had left him he would dash down stairs to post it.

"Oh, I'll see you in the morning, of course!"

A tremor of pleasure crossed her face as he stood before her, smiling a little uncertainly.

"At any rate," she said, "I want to thank you now for my good day."

He felt in her hand the same tremor he had seen in her face. "But it's *you*, on the contrary—" he began, lifting the hand to his lips.

As he dropped it, and their eyes met, something passed through hers that was like a light carried rapidly behind a curtained window.

"Good night; you must be awfully tired," he said with a friendly abruptness, turning away without even waiting to see her pass into her room. He unlocked his door, and stumbling over the threshold groped in the darkness for the electric button. The light showed him a telegram on the table, and he forgot everything else as he caught it up.

"No letter from France," the message read.

It fell from Darrow's hand to the floor, and he dropped into a chair by the table and sat gazing at the dingy drab and olive pattern of the carpet. She had not written, then; she had not written, and it was manifest now that she did not mean to write. If she had had any intention of explaining her telegram she would certainly, within twenty-four hours, have followed it up by a letter. But she evidently did not intend to explain it, and her silence could mean only that she had no explanation to give, or else that she was too indifferent to be aware that one was needed.

Darrow, face to face with these alternatives, felt a recrudescence of boyish misery. It was no longer his hurt vanity that cried out. He told himself that he could have borne an equal amount of pain, if only it had left Mrs. Leath's image untouched; but he could not bear to think of her as trivial or insincere. The thought was so intolerable that he felt a blind desire to punish some one else for the pain it caused him.

As he sat moodily staring at the carpet its silly intricacies melted into a blur from which the eyes of Mrs. Leath again looked out at him. He saw the fine sweep of her brows, and the deep look beneath them as she had turned from him on their last evening in London. "This will be good-bye, then," she had said; and it occurred to him that her parting phrase had been the same as Sophy Viner's.

At the thought he jumped to his feet and took down from its hook the coat in which he had left Miss Viner's letter. The clock marked the third quarter after midnight, and he knew it would make no difference if he went down to the post-box now or early the next morning; but he wanted to clear his conscience, and having found the letter he went to the door.

A sound in the next room made him pause. He had become conscious again that, a few feet off, on the other side of a thin partition, a small keen flame of life was quivering and agitating the air. Sophy's face came back to him insistently. It was as vivid now as Mrs. Leath's had been a moment earlier. He recalled with a faint smile of retrospective pleasure the girl's enjoyment of her evening, and the innumerable fine feelers of sensation she had thrown out to its impressions.

It gave him a curiously close sense of her presence to think that at that moment she was living over her enjoyment as intensely as he was living over his unhappiness. His own case was irremediable, but it was easy enough to give her a few more hours of pleasure. And did she not perhaps secretly expect it of him? After all, if she had been very anxious to join her friends she would have telegraphed them on reaching Paris, instead of writing. He wondered now that he had not been struck at the moment by so artless a device to gain more time. The fact of her having practised it did not make him think less well of her; it merely strengthened the impulse to use his opportunity. She was starving, poor child, for a little amusement, a little personal life—why not give her the chance of another day in

Paris? If he did so, should he not be merely falling in with her own hopes?

At the thought his sympathy for her revived. She became of absorbing interest to him as an escape from himself and an object about which his thwarted activities could cluster. He felt less drearily alone because of her being there, on the other side of the door, and in his gratitude to her for giving him this relief he began, with indolent amusement, to plan new ways of detaining her. He dropped back into his chair, lit a cigar, and smiled a little at the image of her smiling face. He tried to imagine what incident of the day she was likely to be recalling at that particular moment, and what part he probably played in it. That it was not a small part he was certain, and the knowledge was undeniably pleasant.

Now and then a sound from her room brought before him more vividly the reality of the situation and the strangeness of the vast swarming solitude in which he and she were momentarily isolated, amid long lines of rooms each holding its separate secret. The nearness of all these other mysteries enclosing theirs gave Darrow a more intimate sense of the girl's presence, and through the fumes of his cigar his imagination continued to follow her to and fro, traced the curve of her slim young arms as she raised them to undo her hair, pictured the sliding down of her dress to the waist and then to the knees, and the whiteness of her feet as she slipped across the floor to bed . . .

He stood up and shook himself with a yawn, throwing away the end of his cigar. His glance, in following it, lit on the telegram which had dropped to the floor. The sounds in the next room had ceased, and once more he felt alone and unhappy.

Opening the window, he folded his arms on the sill and looked out on the vast light-spangled mass of the city, and then up at the dark sky, in which the morning planet stood.

VI.

At the Théâtre Français, the next afternoon, Darrow yawned and fidgeted in his seat.

The day was warm, the theatre crowded and airless, and the performance, it seemed to him, intolerably bad. He stole a glance at his companion, wondering if she shared his feelings. Her rapt profile betrayed no unrest, but politeness might have caused her to feign an interest that she did not feel. He leaned back impatiently, stifling another yawn, and trying to fix his attention on the stage. Great things were going forward there, and he was not insensible to the stern beauties of the ancient drama. But the interpretation of the play seemed to him as airless and lifeless as the atmosphere of the theatre. The players were the same whom he had often applauded in those very parts, and perhaps that fact added to the impression of staleness and conventionality produced by their performance. Surely it was time to infuse new blood into the veins of the moribund art. He had the impression that the ghosts of actors were giving a spectral performance on the shores of Styx.

Certainly it was not the most profitable way for a young man with a pretty companion to pass the golden hours of a spring afternoon. The freshness of the face at his side, reflecting the freshness of the season, suggested dapplings of sunlight through new leaves, the sound of a brook in the grass, the ripple of tree-shadows over breezy meadows . . .

When at length the fateful march of the cothurns was stayed by the single pause in the play, and Darrow had led Miss Viner out on the balcony overhanging the square before the theatre, he turned to see if she shared his feelings. But the rapturous look she gave him checked the depreciation on his lips.

"Oh, why did you bring me out here? One ought to creep away and sit in the dark till it begins again!"

"Is *that* the way they made you feel?"

"Didn't they *you*? . . . As if the gods were there all the while, just behind them, pulling the strings?" Her hands were pressed against the railing, her face shining and darkening under the wing-beats of successive impressions.

Darrow smiled in enjoyment of her pleasure. After all, he *had* felt all that, long ago; perhaps it was his own fault, rather than that of the actors, that the poetry of the play seemed to have evaporated . . . But no, he had been right in judging the performance to be dull and stale: it was simply his companion's inexperience, her lack of occasions to compare and estimate, that made her think it brilliant.

"I was afraid you were bored and wanted to come away."

"Bored?" She made a little aggrieved grimace. "You mean you thought me too ignorant and stupid to appreciate it?"

"No; not that." The hand nearest him still lay on the

railing of the balcony, and he covered it for a moment with his. As he did so he saw the colour rise and tremble in her cheek.

"Tell me just what you think," he said, bending his head a little, and only half-aware of his words.

She did not turn her face to his, but began to talk rapidly, trying to convey something of what she felt. But she was evidently unused to analyzing her aesthetic emotions, and the tumultuous rush of the drama seemed to have left her in a state of panting wonder, as though it had been a storm or some other natural cataclysm. She had no literary or historic associations to which to attach her impressions: her education had evidently not comprised a course in Greek literature. But she felt what would probably have been unperceived by many a young lady who had taken a first in classics: the ineluctable fatality of the tale, the dread sway in it of the same mysterious "luck" which pulled the threads of her own small destiny. It was not literature to her, it was fact: as actual, as near by, as what was happening to her at the moment and what the next hour held in store. Seen in this light, the play regained for Darrow its supreme and poignant reality. He pierced to the heart of its significance through all the artificial accretions with which his theories of art and the conventions of the stage had clothed it, and saw it as he had never seen it: as life.

After this there could be no question of flight, and he took her back to the theatre, content to receive his own sensations through the medium of hers. But with the continuation of the play, and the oppression of the heavy air, his attention again began to wander, straying back over the incidents of the morning.

He had been with Sophy Viner all day, and he was surprised to find how quickly the time had gone. She had hardly attempted, as the hours passed, to conceal her satisfaction on finding that no telegram came from the Farlows. "They'll have written," she had simply said; and her mind had at once flown on to the golden prospect of an afternoon at the theatre. The intervening hours had been disposed of in a stroll through the lively streets, and a repast, luxuriously lingered over, under the chestnut-boughs of a restaurant in the Champs Elysées. Everything entertained and interested her, and Darrow remarked, with an amused detachment, that she was not insensible to the impression her charms produced. Yet there was no hard edge of vanity in her sense of her prettiness: she seemed simply to be aware of it as a note in the general harmony, and to enjoy sounding the note as a singer enjoys singing.

After luncheon, as they sat over their coffee, she had again asked an immense number of questions and delivered herself of a remarkable variety of opinions. Her questions testified to a wholesome and comprehensive human curiosity, and her comments showed, like her face and her whole attitude, an odd mingling of precocious wisdom and disarming ignorance. When she talked to him about "life"—the word was often on her lips—she seemed to him like a child playing with a tiger's cub; and he said to himself that some day the child would grow up—and so would the tiger. Meanwhile, such expertness qualified by such candour made it impossible to guess the extent of her personal experience, or to estimate its effect on her character. She might be any one of a dozen definable types, or she might—more disconcertingly to her companion and more perilously to herself—be a shifting and uncrystallized mixture of them all.

Her talk, as usual, had promptly reverted to the stage. She was eager to learn about every form of dramatic expression which the metropolis of things theatrical had to offer, and her curiosity ranged from the official temples of the art to its less hallowed haunts. Her searching enquiries about a play whose production, on one of the latter scenes, had provoked a considerable amount of scandal, led Darrow to throw out laughingly: "To see *that* you'll have to wait till you're married!" and his answer had sent her off at a tangent.

"Oh, I never mean to marry," she had rejoined in a tone of youthful finality.

"I seem to have heard that before!"

"Yes; from girls who've only got to choose!" Her eyes had grown suddenly almost old. "I'd like you to see the only men who've ever wanted to marry me! One was the doctor on the steamer, when I came abroad with the Hokes: he'd been cashiered from the navy for drunkenness. The other was a deaf widower with three grown-up daughters, who kept a clockshop in Bayswater!—Besides," she rambled on, "I'm not so sure that I believe in marriage. You see I'm all for self-development and the chance to live one's life. I'm awfully modern, you know."

It was just when she proclaimed herself most awfully modern that she struck him as most helplessly backward; yet the moment after, without any bravado, or apparent desire to assume an attitude, she would propound some social axiom which could have been gathered only in the bitter soil of experience.

All these things came back to him as he sat beside

her in the theatre and watched her ingenuous absorption. It was on "the story" that her mind was fixed, and in life also, he suspected, it would always be "the story", rather than its remoter imaginative issues, that would hold her. He did not believe there were ever any echoes in her soul . . .

There was no question, however, that what she felt was felt with intensity: to the actual, the immediate, she spread vibrating strings. When the play was over, and they came out once more into the sunlight, Darrow looked down at her with a smile.

"Well?" he asked.

She made no answer. Her dark gaze seemed to rest on him without seeing him. Her cheeks and lips were pale, and the loose hair under her hat-brim clung to her forehead in damp rings. She looked like a young priestess still dazed by the fumes of the cavern.

"You poor child—it's been almost too much for you!"

She shook her head with a vague smile.

"Come," he went on, putting his hand on her arm, "let's jump into a taxi and get some air and sunshine. Look, there are hours of daylight left; and see what a night it's going to be!"

He pointed over their heads, to where a white moon hung in the misty blue above the roofs of the rue de Rivoli.

She made no answer, and he signed to a motor-cab, calling out to the driver: "To the Bois!"

As the carriage turned toward the Tuileries she roused herself. "I must go first to the hotel. There may be a message—at any rate I must decide on something."

Darrow saw that the reality of the situation had

suddenly forced itself upon her. "I *must* decide on something," she repeated.

He would have liked to postpone the return, to persuade her to drive directly to the Bois for dinner. It would have been easy enough to remind her that she could not start for Joigny that evening, and that therefore it was of no moment whether she received the Farlows' answer then or a few hours later; but for some reason he hesitated to use this argument, which had come so naturally to him the day before. After all, he knew she would find nothing at the hotel—so what did it matter if they went there?

The porter, interrogated, was not sure. He himself had received nothing for the lady, but in his absence his subordinate might have sent a letter upstairs.

Darrow and Sophy mounted together in the lift, and the young man, while she went into her room, unlocked his own door and glanced at the empty table. For him at least no message had come; and on her threshold, a moment later, she met him with the expected: "No—there's nothing!"

He feigned an unregretful surprise. "So much the better! And now, shall we drive out somewhere? Or would you rather take a boat to Bellevue? Have you ever dined there, on the terrace, by moonlight? It's not at all bad. And there's no earthly use in sitting here waiting."

She stood before him in perplexity.

"But when I wrote yesterday I asked them to telegraph. I suppose they're horribly hard up, the poor dears, and they thought a letter would do as well as a telegram." The colour had risen to her face. "That's why *I* wrote instead of telegraphing; I haven't a penny to spare myself!"

Nothing she could have said could have filled her listener with a deeper contrition. He felt the red in his own face as he recalled the motive with which he had credited her in his midnight musings. But that motive, after all, had simply been trumped up to justify his own disloyalty: he had never really believed in it. The reflection deepened his confusion, and he would have liked to take her hand in his and confess the injustice he had done her.

She may have interpreted his change of colour as an involuntary protest at being initiated into such shabby details, for she went on with a laugh: "I suppose you can hardly understand what it means to have to stop and think whether one can afford a telegram? But I've always had to consider such things. And I mustn't stay here any longer now—I must try to get a night train for Joigny. Even if the Farlows can't take me in, I can go to the hotel: it will cost less than staying here." She paused again and then exclaimed: "I ought to have thought of that sooner; I ought to have telegraphed yesterday! But I was sure I should hear from them today; and I wanted—oh, I *did* so awfully want to stay!" She threw a troubled look at Darrow. "Do you happen to remember," she asked, "what time it was when you posted my letter?"

VII.

DARROW was still standing on her threshold. As she put the question he entered the room and closed the door behind him.

His heart was beating a little faster than usual and he had no clear idea of what he was about to do or say, beyond the definite conviction that, whatever passing impulse of expiation moved him, he would not be fool enough to tell her that he had not sent her letter. He knew that most wrongdoing works, on the whole, less mischief than its useless confession; and this was clearly a case where a passing folly might be turned, by avowal, into a serious offense.

"I'm so sorry—so sorry; but you must let me help you . . . You will let me help you?" he said.

He took her hands and pressed them together between his, counting on a friendly touch to help out the insufficiency of words. He felt her yield slightly to his clasp, and hurried on without giving her time to answer.

"Isn't it a pity to spoil our good time together by regretting anything you might have done to prevent our having it?"

She drew back, freeing her hands. Her face, losing its look of appealing confidence, was suddenly sharpened by distrust.

"You didn't forget to post my letter?"

Darrow stood before her, constrained and ashamed, and ever more keenly aware that the betrayal of his distress must be a greater offense than its concealment.

"What an insinuation!" he cried, throwing out his hands with a laugh.

Her face instantly melted to laughter. "Well, then—I *won't* be sorry; I won't regret anything except that our good time is over!"

The words were so unexpected that they routed all his resolves. If she had gone on doubting him he could probably have gone on deceiving her; but her unhesitating acceptance of his word made him hate the part he was playing. At the same moment a doubt shot up its serpent head in his own bosom. Was it not he rather than she who was childishly trustful? Was she not almost too ready to take his word, and dismiss once for all the tiresome question of the letter? Considering what her experiences must have been, such trustfulness seemed open to suspicion. But the moment his eyes fell on her he was ashamed of the thought, and knew it for what it really was: another pretext to lessen his own delinquency.

"Why should our good time be over?" he asked. "Why shouldn't it last a little longer?"

She looked up, her lips parted in surprise; but before she could speak he went on: "I want you to stay with me—I want you, just for a few days, to have all the things you've never had. It's not always May and Paris—why not make the most of them now? You know me—we're not strangers—why shouldn't you treat me like a friend?"

While he spoke she had drawn away a little, but her hand still lay in his. She was pale, and her eyes were fixed on him in a gaze in which there was neither distrust or resentment, but only an ingenuous wonder. He was extraordinarily touched by her expression.

"Oh, do! You must. Listen: to prove that I'm sincere I'll tell you . . . I'll tell you I didn't post your letter . . .

I didn't post it because I wanted so much to give you a few good hours . . . and because I couldn't bear to have you go."

He had the feeling that the words were being uttered in spite of him by some malicious witness of the scene, and yet that he was not sorry to have them spoken.

The girl had listened to him in silence. She remained motionless for a moment after he had ceased to speak; then she snatched away her hand.

"You didn't post my letter? You kept it back on purpose? And you tell me so *now*, to prove to me that I'd better put myself under your protection?" She burst into a laugh that had in it all the piercing echoes of her Murrett past, and her face, at the same moment, underwent the same change, shrinking into a small malevolent white mask in which the eyes burned black. "Thank you—thank you most awfully for telling me! And for all your other kind intentions! The plan's delightful—really quite delightful, and I'm extremely flattered and obliged."

She dropped into a seat beside her dressing-table, resting her chin on her lifted hands, and laughing out at him under the elf-lock which had shaken itself down over her eyes.

Her outburst did not offend the young man; its immediate effect was that of allaying his agitation. The theatrical touch in her manner made his offense seem more venial than he had thought it a moment before.

He drew up a chair and sat down beside her. "After all," he said, in a tone of good-humoured protest, "I needn't have told you I'd kept back your letter; and my telling you seems rather strong proof that I hadn't any very nefarious designs on you."

She met this with a shrug, but he did not give her time to answer. "My designs," he continued with a smile, "were not nefarious. I saw you'd been through a bad time with Mrs. Murrett, and that there didn't seem to be much fun ahead for you; and I didn't see—and I don't yet see—the harm of trying to give you a few hours of amusement between a depressing past and a not particularly cheerful future." He paused again, and then went on, in the same tone of friendly reasonableness: "The mistake I made was not to tell you this at once—not to ask you straight out to give me a day or two, and let me try to make you forget all the things that are troubling you. I was a fool not to see that if I'd put it to you in that way you'd have accepted or refused, as you chose; but that at least you wouldn't have mistaken my intentions.—Intentions!" He stood up, walked the length of the room, and turned back to where she still sat motionless, her elbows propped on the dressing-table, her chin on her hands. "What rubbish we talk about intentions! The truth is I hadn't any: I just liked being with you. Perhaps you don't know how extraordinarily one can like being with you . . . I was depressed and adrift myself; and you made me forget my bothers; and when I found you were going—and going back to dreariness, as I was—I didn't see why we shouldn't have a few hours together first; so I left your letter in my pocket."

He saw her face melt as she listened, and suddenly she unclasped her hands and leaned to him.

"But are *you* unhappy too? Oh, I never understood—I never dreamed it! I thought you'd always had everything in the world you wanted!"

Darrow broke into a laugh at this ingenuous picture

of his state. He was ashamed of trying to better his case by an appeal to her pity, and annoyed with himself for alluding to a subject he would rather have kept out of his thoughts. But her look of sympathy had disarmed him; his heart was bitter and distracted; she was near him, her eyes were shining with compassion—he bent over her and kissed her hand.

"Forgive me—do forgive me," he said.

She stood up with a smiling head-shake. "Oh, it's not so often that people try to give me any pleasure—much less two whole days of it! I sha'n't forget how kind you've been. I shall have plenty of time to remember. But this *is* good-bye, you know. I must telegraph at once to say I'm coming."

"To say you're coming? Then I'm not forgiven?"

"Oh, you're forgiven—if that's any comfort."

"It's not, the very least, if your way of proving it is to go away!"

She hung her head in meditation. "But I can't stay. —How *can* I stay?" she broke out, as if arguing with some unseen monitor.

"Why can't you? No one knows you're here . . . No one need ever know."

She looked up, and their eyes exchanged meanings for a rapid minute. Her gaze was as clear as a boy's. "Oh, it's not *that*," she exclaimed, almost impatiently; "it's not people I'm afraid of! They've never put themselves out for me—why on earth should I care about them?"

He liked her directness as he had never liked it before. "Well, then, what is it? Not *me*, I hope?"

"No, not you: I like you. It's the money! With me that's always the root of the matter. I could never yet afford a treat in my life!"

"Is *that* all?" He laughed, relieved by her naturalness. "Look here; since we're talking as man to man—can't you trust me about that too?"

"Trust you? How do you mean? You'd better not trust *me*!" she laughed back sharply. "I might never be able to pay up!"

His gesture brushed aside the allusion. "Money may be the root of the matter; it can't be the whole of it, between friends. Don't you think one friend may accept a small service from another without looking too far ahead or weighing too many chances? The question turns entirely on what you think of me. If you like me well enough to be willing to take a few days' holiday with me, just for the pleasure of the thing, and the pleasure you'll be giving me, let's shake hands on it. If you don't like me well enough we'll shake hands too; only I shall be sorry," he ended.

"Oh, but I shall be sorry too!" Her face, as she lifted it to his, looked so small and young that Darrow felt a fugitive twinge of compunction, instantly effaced by the excitement of pursuit.

"Well, then?" He stood looking down on her, his eyes persuading her. He was now intensely aware that his nearness was having an effect which made it less and less necessary for him to choose his words, and he went on, more mindful of the inflections of his voice than of what he was actually saying: "Why on earth should we say good-bye if we're both sorry to? Won't you tell me your reason? It's not a bit like you to let anything stand in the way of your saying just what you feel. You mustn't mind offending me, you know!"

She hung before him like a leaf on the meeting of cross-currents, that the next ripple may sweep forward or whirl back. Then she flung up her head with the odd boyish movement habitual to her in moments of excitement. "What I feel? Do you want to know what I feel? That you're giving me the only chance I've ever had!"

She turned about on her heel and, dropping into the nearest chair, sank forward, her face hidden against the dressing-table.

Under the folds of her thin summer dress the modelling of her back and of her lifted arms, and the slight hollow between her shoulder-blades, recalled the faint curves of a terra-cotta statuette, some young image of grace hardly more than sketched in the clay. Darrow, as he stood looking at her, reflected that her character, for all its seeming firmness, its flashing edges of "opinion", was probably no less immature. He had not expected her to yield so suddenly to his suggestion, or to confess her yielding in that way. At first he was slightly disconcerted; then he saw how her attitude simplified his own. Her behaviour had all the indecision and awkwardness of inexperience. It showed that she was a child after all; and all he could do—all he had ever meant to do—was to give her a child's holiday to look back to.

For a moment he fancied she was crying; but the next she was on her feet and had swept round on him a face she must have turned away only to hide the first rush of her pleasure.

For a while they shone on each other without speaking; then she sprang to him and held out both hands.

"Is it true? Is it really true? Is it really going to happen to *me*?"

He felt like answering: "You're the very creature to whom it was bound to happen"; but the words had a double sense that made him wince, and instead he caught her proffered hands and stood looking at her across the length of her arms, without attempting to bend them or to draw her closer. He wanted her to know how her words had moved him; but his thoughts were blurred by the rush of the same emotion that possessed her, and his own words came with an effort.

He ended by giving her back a laugh as frank as her own, and declaring, as he dropped her hands: "All that and more too—you'll see!"

VIII.

ALL day, since the late reluctant dawn, the rain had come down in torrents. It streamed against Darrow's high-perched windows, reduced their vast prospect of roofs and chimneys to a black oily huddle, and filled the room with the drab twilight of an underground aquarium.

The streams descended with the regularity of a third day's rain, when trimming and shuffling are over, and the weather has settled down to do its worst. There were no variations of rhythm, no lyrical ups and downs: the grey lines streaking the panes were as dense and uniform as a page of unparagraphed narrative.

George Darrow had drawn his armchair to the fire. The time-table he had been studying lay on the floor, and he sat staring with dull acquiescence into the boundless blur of rain, which affected him like a vast projection of his own state of mind. Then his eyes travelled slowly about the room.

It was exactly ten days since his hurried unpacking had strewn it with the contents of his portmanteaux. His brushes and razors were spread out on the blotched marble of the chest of drawers. A stack of newspapers had accumulated on the centre table under the "electrolier", and half a dozen paper novels lay on the mantelpiece among cigar-cases and toilet bottles; but these traces of his passage had made no mark on the featureless dullness of the room, its look of being the makeshift setting of innumerable transient collocations. There was something sardonic, almost sinister, in its appearance of having deliberately "made up" for its anonymous part, all in noncommittal drabs and browns, with a carpet and paper that nobody would remember, and chairs and tables as impersonal as railway porters.

Darrow picked up the time-table and tossed it on to the table. Then he rose to his feet, lit a cigar and went to the window. Through the rain he could just discover the face of a clock in a tall building beyond the railway roofs. He pulled out his watch, compared the two time-pieces, and started the hands of his with such a rush that they flew past the hour and he had to make them repeat the circuit more deliberately. He felt a quite disproportionate irritation at the trifling blunder. When he had corrected it he went back to his chair and threw himself down, leaning back his head against his hands. Presently his cigar went out, and he got up, hunted for the matches, lit it again and returned to his seat.

The room was getting on his nerves. During the first few days, while the skies were clear, he had not noticed it, or had felt for it only the contemptuous indifference of the traveller toward a provisional shelter. But now that he was leaving it, was looking at it for the last time, it seemed to have taken complete possession of his mind, to be soaking itself into him like an ugly indelible blot. Every detail pressed itself on his notice with the familiarity of an accidental confidant: whichever way he turned, he felt the nudge of a transient intimacy . . .

The one fixed point in his immediate future was that his leave was over and that he must be back at his post in London the next morning. Within twenty-four hours he would again be in a daylight world of recognized activities, himself a busy, responsible, relatively necessary factor in the big whirring social and official machine. That fixed obligation was the fact he could think of with the least discomfort, yet for some unaccountable reason it was the one on which he found it most difficult to fix his thoughts. Whenever he did so, the room jerked him back into the circle of its insistent associations. It was extraordinary with what a microscopic minuteness of loathing he hated it all: the grimy carpet and wallpaper, the black marble mantel-piece, the clock with a gilt allegory under a dusty bell, the high-bolstered brown-counterpaned bed, the framed card of printed rules under the electric light switch, and the door of communication with the next room. He hated the door most of all . . .

At the outset, he had felt no special sense of responsibility. He was satisfied that he had struck the right note, and convinced of his power of sustaining it. The whole incident had somehow seemed, in spite of its vulgar setting and its inevitable prosaic propinquities, to be enacting itself in some unmapped region outside the pale of the usual. It was not like anything that had ever happened to him before, or in which he had ever pictured himself as likely to be involved; but that, at first, had seemed no argument against his fitness to deal with it.

Perhaps but for the three days' rain he might have got away without a doubt as to his adequacy. The rain had made all the difference. It had thrown the whole picture out of perspective, blotted out the mystery of the remoter planes and the enchantment of the middle distance, and thrust into prominence every commonplace fact of the foreground. It was the kind of situation that was not helped by being thought over; and by the perversity of circumstance he had been forced into the unwilling contemplation of its every aspect . . .

His cigar had gone out again, and he threw it into the fire and vaguely meditated getting up to find another. But the mere act of leaving his chair seemed to call for a greater exertion of the will than he was capable of, and he leaned his head back with closed eyes and listened to the drumming of the rain.

A different noise aroused him. It was the opening and closing of the door leading from the corridor into the adjoining room. He sat motionless, without opening his eyes; but now another sight forced itself under his lowered lids. It was the precise photographic picture of that other room. Everything in it rose before him and pressed itself upon his vision with the same acuity of distinctness as the objects surrounding him. A step sounded on the floor, and he knew which way the step was directed, what pieces of furniture it had to skirt, where it would probably pause, and what was likely to arrest it. He heard another sound, and recognized it as that of a wet umbrella placed in the black marble jamb of the chimneypiece, against the hearth. He caught the creak of a hinge, and instantly differentiated it as that of the wardrobe against the opposite wall. Then he heard the mouse-like squeal of a reluctant drawer, and knew it was the upper one in the chest of drawers beside the bed: the clatter which followed was caused by the mahogany toilet-glass jumping on its loosened pivots . . .

The step crossed the floor again. It was strange how much better he knew it than the person to whom it belonged! Now it was drawing near the door of communication between the two rooms. He opened his eyes and looked. The step had ceased and for a moment there was silence. Then he heard a low knock. He made no response, and after an interval he saw that the door-handle was being tentatively turned. He closed his eyes once more . . .

The door opened, and the step was in the room, coming cautiously toward him. He kept his eyes shut, relaxing his body to feign sleep. There was another pause, then a wavering soft advance, the rustle of a dress behind his chair, the warmth of two hands pressed for a moment on his lids. The palms of the hands had the lingering scent of some stuff that he had bought on the Boulevard . . . He looked up and saw a letter falling over his shoulder to his knee . . .

"Did I disturb you? I'm so sorry! They gave me this just now when I came in."

The letter, before he could catch it, had slipped between his knees to the floor. It lay there, address upward, at his feet, and while he sat staring down at the strong slender characters on the blue-gray envelope an arm reached out from behind to pick it up.

"Oh, don't—*don't!*" broke from him, and he bent over and caught the arm. The face above it was close to his.

"Don't what?"

——"take the trouble," he stammered.

He dropped the arm and stooped down. His grasp closed over the letter, he fingered its thickness and weight and calculated the number of sheets it must contain.

Suddenly he felt the pressure of the hand on his shoulder, and became aware that the face was still leaning over him, and that in a moment he would have to look up and kiss it . . .

He bent forward first and threw the unopened letter into the middle of the fire.

Book Two

IX.

THE light of the October afternoon lay on an old high-roofed house which enclosed in its long expanse of brick and yellowish stone the breadth of a grassy court filled with the shadow and sound of limes.

From the escutcheoned piers at the entrance of the court a level drive, also shaded by limes, extended to a white-barred gate beyond which an equally level avenue of grass, cut through a wood, dwindled to a blue-green blur against a sky banked with still white slopes of cloud.

In the court, half-way between house and drive, a lady stood. She held a parasol above her head, and looked now at the house-front, with its double flight of steps meeting before a glazed door under sculptured trophies, now down the drive toward the grassy cutting through the wood. Her air was less of expectancy than of contemplation: she seemed not so much to be watching for any one, or listening for an approaching sound, as letting the whole aspect of the place sink into her while she held herself open to its influence. Yet it was no less apparent that the scene was not new to her. There was no eagerness of investigation in her survey: she seemed rather to be looking about her with eyes to which, for some intimate inward reason, details long since familiar had suddenly acquired an unwonted freshness.

This was in fact the exact sensation of which Mrs. Leath was conscious as she came forth from the house and descended into the sunlit court. She had come to meet her step-son, who was likely to be returning at that hour from an afternoon's shooting in one of the more distant plantations, and she carried in her hand the letter which had sent her in search of him; but with her first step out of the house all thought of him had been effaced by another series of impressions.

The scene about her was known to satiety. She had seen Givré at all seasons of the year, and for the greater part of every year, since the far-off day of her marriage; the day when, ostensibly driving through its gates at her husband's side, she had actually been carried there on a cloud of iris-winged visions.

The possibilities which the place had then represented were still vividly present to her. The mere phrase "a French château" had called up to her youthful fancy a throng of romantic associations, poetic, pictorial and emotional; and the serene face of the old house seated in its park among the poplar-bordered meadows of middle France, had seemed, on her first sight of it, to hold out to her a fate as noble and dignified as its own mien.

Though she could still call up that phase of feeling it had long since passed, and the house had for a time become to her the very symbol of narrowness and monotony. Then, with the passing of years, it had gradually acquired a less inimical character, had become, not again a castle of dreams, evoker of fair images and romantic legend, but the shell of a life slowly adjusted to its dwelling: the place one came back to, the place where one had one's duties, one's habits and one's books, the place one would naturally live in till one died: a dull house, an inconvenient house, of which one knew all the defects, the shabbinesses, the discomforts, but to which one was so used that one could hardly, after so long a time, think one's self away from it without suffering a certain loss of identity.

Now, as it lay before her in the autumn mildness, its mistress was surprised at her own insensibility. She had been trying to see the house through the eyes of an old friend who, the next morning, would be driving up to it for the first time; and in so doing she seemed to be opening her own eyes upon it after a long interval of blindness.

The court was very still, yet full of a latent life: the wheeling and rustling of pigeons about the rectangular yews and across the sunny gravel; the sweep of rooks above the lustrous greyish-purple slates of the roof, and the stir of the tree-tops as they met the breeze which every day, at that hour, came punctually up from the river.

Just such a latent animation glowed in Anna Leath. In every nerve and vein she was conscious of that equipoise of bliss which the fearful human heart scarce dares acknowledge. She was not used to strong or full emotions; but she had always known that she should not be afraid of them. She was not afraid now; but she felt a deep inward stillness.

The immediate effect of the feeling had been to send her forth in quest of her step-son. She wanted to stroll back with him and have a quiet talk before they re-entered the house. It was always easy to talk to him, and at this moment he was the one person to whom she could have spoken without fear of disturbing her inner stillness. She was glad, for all sorts of reasons, that Madame de Chantelle and Effie were still at Ouchy with the governess, and that she and Owen had the house to themselves. And she was glad that even he was not yet in sight. She wanted to be alone a little longer; not to think, but to let the long slow waves of joy break over her one by one.

She walked out of the court and sat down on one of the benches that bordered the drive. From her seat she had a diagonal view of the long house-front and of the domed chapel terminating one of the wings. Beyond a gate in the court-yard wall the flower-garden drew its dark-green squares and raised its statues against the yellowing background of the park. In the borders only a few late pinks and crimsons smouldered, but a peacock strutting in the sun seemed to have gathered into his outspread fan all the summer glories of the place.

In Mrs. Leath's hand was the letter which had opened her eyes to these things, and a smile rose to her lips at the mere feeling of the paper between her fingers. The thrill it sent through her gave a keener edge to every sense. She felt, saw, breathed the shining world as though a thin impenetrable veil had suddenly been removed from it.

Just such a veil, she now perceived, had always hung between herself and life. It had been like the stage gauze which gives an illusive air of reality to the painted scene behind it, yet proves it, after all, to be no more than a painted scene.

She had been hardly aware, in her girlhood, of differing from others in this respect. In the well-regulated well-fed Summers world the unusual was regarded as either immoral or ill-bred, and people with emotions were not visited. Sometimes, with a sense of groping in a topsy-turvy universe, Anna had wondered why everybody about her seemed to ignore all the passions and sensations which formed the stuff of great poetry and memorable action. In a community composed entirely of people like her parents and her parents' friends she did not see how the magnificent things one read about could ever have happened. She was sure that if anything of the kind had occurred in her immediate circle her mother would have consulted the family clergyman, and her father perhaps even have rung up the police; and her sense of humour compelled her to own that, in the given conditions, these precautions might not have been unjustified.

Little by little the conditions conquered her, and she learned to regard the substance of life as a mere canvas for the embroideries of poet and painter, and its little swept and fenced and tended surface as its actual substance. It was in the visioned region of action and emotion that her fullest hours were spent; but it hardly occurred to her that they might be translated into experience, or connected with anything likely to happen to a young lady living in West Fifty-fifth Street.

She perceived, indeed, that other girls, leading outwardly the same life as herself, and seemingly unaware of her world of hidden beauty, were yet possessed of some vital secret which escaped her. There seemed to be a kind of freemasonry between them; they were wider awake than she, more alert, and surer of their wants if not of their opinions. She supposed they were "cleverer", and accepted her inferiority good-humouredly, half aware, within herself, of a reserve of unused power which the others gave no sign of possessing.

This partly consoled her for missing so much of what made their "good time"; but the resulting sense of exclusion, of being somehow laughingly but firmly debarred from a share of their privileges, threw her back on herself and deepened the reserve which made envious mothers cite her as a model of ladylike repression.

Love, she told herself, would one day release her from this spell of unreality. She was persuaded that the sublime passion was the key to the enigma; but it was difficult to relate her conception of love to the forms it wore in her experience. Two or three of the girls she had envied for their superior acquaintance with the arts of life had contracted, in the course of time, what were variously described as "romantic" or "foolish" marriages; one even made a runaway match, and languished for a while under a cloud of social reprobation. Here, then, was passion in action, romance converted to reality; yet the heroines of these exploits returned from them untransfigured, and their husbands were as dull as ever when one had to sit next to them at dinner.

Her own case, of course, would be different. Some day she would find the magic bridge between West Fifty-fifth Street and life; once or twice she had even fancied that the clue was in her hand. The first time was when she had met young Darrow. She recalled even now the stir of the encounter. But his passion swept over her like a wind that shakes the roof of the forest without reaching its still glades or rippling its hidden pools. He was extraordinarily intelligent and agreeable, and her heart beat faster when he was with her. He had a tall fair easy presence and a mind in which the lights of irony played pleasantly through the shades of feeling. She liked to hear his voice almost as much as to listen to what he was saying, and to listen to what he was saying almost as much as to feel that he was looking at her; but he wanted to kiss her, and she wanted to talk to him about books and pictures, and have him insinuate the eternal theme of their love into every subject they discussed.

Whenever they were apart a reaction set in. She wondered how she could have been so cold, called herself a prude and an idiot, questioned if any man could really care for her, and got up in the dead of night to try new ways of doing her hair. But as soon as he reappeared her head straightened itself on her slim neck and she sped her little shafts of irony, or flew her little kites of erudition, while hot and cold waves swept over her, and the things she really wanted to say choked in her throat and burned the palms of her hands.

Often she told herself that any silly girl who had waltzed through a season would know better than she how to attract a man and hold him; but when she said "a man" she did not really mean George Darrow.

Then one day, at a dinner, she saw him sitting next to one of the silly girls in question: the heroine of the elopement which had shaken West Fifty-fifth Street to its base. The young lady had come back from her adventure no less silly than when she went; and across the table the partner of her flight, a fat young man with eye-glasses, sat stolidly eating terrapin and talking about polo and investments.

The young woman was undoubtedly as silly as ever; yet after watching her for a few minutes Miss Summers perceived that she had somehow grown luminous, perilous, obscurely menacing to nice girls and the young men they intended eventually to accept. Suddenly, at the sight, a rage of possessorship awoke in her. She must save Darrow, assert her right to him at any price. Pride and reticence went down in a hurricane of jealousy. She heard him laugh, and there was something new in his laugh . . . She watched him talking, talking . . . He sat slightly sideways, a faint smile beneath his lids, lowering his voice as he lowered it when he talked to her. She caught the same inflections, but his eyes were different. It would have offended her once if he had looked at her like that. Now her one thought was that none but she had a right to be so looked at. And that girl of all others! What illusions could he have about a girl who, hardly a year ago, had made a fool of herself over the fat young man stolidly eating terrapin across the table? If that was where romance and passion ended, it was better to take to district visiting or algebra!

All night she lay awake and wondered: "What was she saying to him? How shall I learn to say such things?" and she decided that her heart would tell her—that the next time they were alone together the irresistible word would spring to her lips. He came the next day, and they were alone, and all she found was: "I didn't know that you and Kitty Mayne were such friends."

He answered with indifference that he didn't know it either, and in the reaction of relief she declared: "She's certainly ever so much prettier than she was . . ."

"She's rather good fun," he admitted, as though he had not noticed her other advantages; and suddenly Anna saw in his eyes the look she had seen there the previous evening.

She felt as if he were leagues and leagues away from her. All her hopes dissolved, and she was conscious of sitting rigidly, with high head and straight lips, while the irresistible word fled with a last wing-beat into the golden mist of her illusions . . .

She was still quivering with the pain and bewilderment of this adventure when Fraser Leath appeared. She met him first in Italy, where she was travelling with her parents; and the following winter he came to New York. In Italy he had seemed interesting: in New York he became remarkable. He seldom spoke of his life in Europe, and let drop but the most incidental allusions to the friends, the tastes, the pursuits which filled his cosmopolitan days; but in the atmosphere of West Fifty-fifth Street he seemed the embodiment of a storied past. He presented Miss Summers with a prettily-bound anthology of the old French poets and, when she showed a discriminating pleasure in the gift, observed with his grave smile: "I didn't suppose I should find any one here who would feel about these things as I do." On another occasion he asked her acceptance of a half-effaced eighteenth century pastel which he had surprisingly picked up in a New York auction-room. "I know no one but you who would really appreciate it," he explained.

He permitted himself no other comments, but these conveyed with sufficient directness that he thought her worthy of a different setting. That she should be so regarded by a man living in an atmosphere of art and beauty, and esteeming them the vital elements of life, made her feel for the first time that she was understood. Here was some one whose scale of values was the same as hers, and who thought her opinion worth hearing on the very matters which they both considered of supreme importance. The discovery restored her self-confidence, and she revealed herself to Mr. Leath as she had never known how to reveal herself to Darrow.

As the courtship progressed, and they grew more confidential, her suitor surprised and delighted her by little explosions of revolutionary sentiment. He said: "Shall you mind, I wonder, if I tell you that you live in a dreadfully conventional atmosphere?" and, seeing that she manifestly did not mind: "Of course I shall say things now and then that will horrify your dear delightful parents—I shall shock them awfully, I warn you."

In confirmation of this warning he permitted himself an occasional playful fling at the regular church-going of Mr. and Mrs. Summers, at the innocuous character of the literature in their library, and at their guileless appreciations in art. He even ventured to banter Mrs. Summers on her refusal to receive the irrepressible Kitty Mayne, who, after a rapid passage with George Darrow, was now involved in another and more flagrant adventure.

"In Europe, you know, the husband is regarded as the only judge in such matters. As long as he accepts the situation—" Mr. Leath explained to Anna, who took his view the more emphatically in order to convince herself that, personally, she had none but the most tolerant sentiments toward the lady.

The subversiveness of Mr. Leath's opinions was enhanced by the distinction of his appearance and the reserve of his manners. He was like the anarchist with a gardenia in his buttonhole who figures in the higher melodrama. Every word, every allusion, every note of his agreeably-modulated voice, gave Anna a glimpse of a society at once freer and finer, which observed the traditional forms but had discarded the underlying prejudices; whereas the world she knew had discarded many of the forms and kept almost all the prejudices.

In such an atmosphere as his an eager young woman, curious as to all the manifestations of life, yet instinctively desiring that they should come to her in terms of beauty and fine feeling, must surely find the largest scope for self-expression. Study, travel, the contact of the world, the comradeship of a polished and enlightened mind, would combine to enrich her days and form her character; and it was only in the rare moments when Mr. Leath's symmetrical blond mask bent over hers, and his kiss dropped on her like a cold smooth pebble, that she questioned the completeness of the joys he offered.

There had been a time when the walls on which her gaze now rested had shed a glare of irony on these early dreams. In the first years of her marriage the sober symmetry of Givré had suggested only her husband's neatly-balanced mind. It was a mind, she soon learned, contentedly absorbed in formulating the conventions of the unconventional. West Fifty-fifth Street was no more conscientiously concerned than Givré with the momentous question of "what people did"; it was only the type of deed investigated that was different. Mr. Leath collected his social instances with the same seriousness and patience as his snuff-boxes. He exacted a rigid conformity to his rules of non-conformity and his scepticism had the absolute accent of a dogma. He even cherished certain exceptions to his rules as the book-collector prizes a "defective" first edition. The

Protestant church-going of Anna's parents had provoked his gentle sarcasm; but he prided himself on his mother's devoutness, because Madame de Chantelle, in embracing her second husband's creed, had become part of a society which still observes the outward rites of piety.

Anna, in fact, had discovered in her amiable and elegant mother-in-law an unexpected embodiment of the West Fifty-fifth Street ideal. Mrs. Summers and Madame de Chantelle, however strongly they would have disagreed as to the authorized source of Christian dogma, would have found themselves completely in accord on all the momentous minutiae of drawing-room conduct; yet Mr. Leath treated his mother's foibles with a respect which Anna's experience of him forbade her to attribute wholly to filial affection.

In the early days, when she was still questioning the Sphinx instead of trying to find an answer to it, she ventured to tax her husband with his inconsistency.

"You say your mother won't like it if I call on that amusing little woman who came here the other day, and was let in by mistake; but Madame de Chantelle tells me she lives with her husband, and when mother refused to visit Kitty Mayne you said——"

Mr. Leath's smile arrested her. "My dear child, I don't pretend to apply the principles of logic to my poor mother's prejudices."

"But if you admit that they *are* prejudices——?"

"There are prejudices and prejudices. My mother, of course, got hers from Monsieur de Chantelle, and they seem to me as much in their place in this house as the pot-pourri in your hawthorn jar. They preserve a social tradition of which I should be sorry to lose the least perfume. Of course I don't expect you, just at first, to feel the difference, to see the *nuance*. In the case of little Madame de Vireville, for instance: you point out that she's still under her husband's roof. Very true; and if she were merely a Paris acquaintance—especially if you had met her, as one still might, in the *right kind* of house in Paris—I should be the last to object to your visiting her. But in the country it's different. Even the best provincial society is what you would call narrow: I don't deny it; and if some of our friends met Madame de Vireville at Givré—well, it would produce a bad impression. You're inclined to ridicule such considerations, but gradually you'll come to see their importance; and meanwhile, do trust me when I ask you to be guided by my mother. It is always well for a stranger in an old society to err a little on the side of what you call its prejudices but I should rather describe as its traditions."

After that she no longer tried to laugh or argue her husband out of his convictions. They *were* convictions, and therefore unassailable. Nor was any insincerity implied in the fact that they sometimes seemed to coincide with hers. There were occasions when he really did look at things as she did; but for reasons so different as to make the distance between them all the greater. Life, to Mr. Leath, was like a walk through a carefully classified museum, where, in moments of doubt, one had only to look at the number and refer to one's catalogue; to his wife it was like groping about in a huge dark lumberroom where the exploring ray of curiosity lit up now some shape of breathing beauty and now a mummy's grin.

In the first bewilderment of her new state these discoveries had had the effect of dropping another layer of gauze between herself and reality. She seemed farther than ever removed from the strong joys and pangs for which she felt herself made. She did not adopt her husband's views, but insensibly she began to live his life. She tried to throw a compensating ardour into the secret excursions of her spirit, and thus the old vicious distinction between romance and reality was re-established for her, and she resigned herself again to the belief that "real life" was neither real nor alive.

The birth of her little girl swept away this delusion. At last she felt herself in contact with the actual business of living: but even this impression was not enduring. Everything but the irreducible crude fact of child-bearing assumed, in the Leath household, the same ghostly tinge of unreality. Her husband, at the time, was all that his own ideal of a husband required. He was attentive, and even suitably moved; but as he sat by her bedside, and thoughtfully proffered to her the list of people who had "called to enquire", she looked first at him, and then at the child between them, and wondered at the blundering alchemy of Nature . . .

With the exception of the little girl herself, everything connected with that time had grown curiously remote and unimportant. The days that had moved so slowly as they passed seemed now to have plunged down headlong steeps of time; and as she sat in the autumn sun, with Darrow's letter in her hand, the history of Anna Leath appeared to its heroine like some grey shadowy tale that she might have read in an old book, one night as she was falling asleep . . .

X.

Two brown blurs emerging from the farther end of the wood-vista gradually defined themselves as her step-son and an attendant game-keeper. They grew slowly upon the bluish background, with occasional delays and re-effacements, and she sat still, waiting till they should reach the gate at the end of the drive, where the keeper would turn off to his cottage and Owen continue on to the house.

She watched his approach with a smile. From the first days of her marriage she had been drawn to the boy, but it was not until after Effie's birth that she had really begun to know him. The eager observation of her own child had shown her how much she had still to learn about the slight fair boy whom the holidays periodically restored to Givré. Owen, even then, both physically and morally, furnished her with the oddest of commentaries on his father's mien and mind. He would never, the family sighingly recognized, be nearly as handsome as Mr. Leath; but his rather charmingly unbalanced face, with its brooding forehead and petulant boyish smile, suggested to Anna what his father's countenance might have been could one have pictured its neat features disordered by a rattling breeze. She even pushed the analogy farther, and descried in her step-son's mind a quaintly-twisted reflection of her husband's. With his bursts of door-slamming activity, his fits of bookish indolence, his crude revolutionary dogmatizing and his flashes of precocious irony, the boy was not unlike a boisterous embodiment of his father's theories. It was as though Fraser Leath's ideas, accustomed to hang like marionettes on their pegs, should suddenly come down and walk. There were moments, indeed, when Owen's humours must have suggested to his progenitor the gambols of an infant Frankenstein; but to Anna they were the voice of her secret rebellions, and her tenderness to her step-son was partly based on her severity toward herself. As he had the courage she had lacked, so she meant him to have the chances she had missed; and every effort she made for him helped to keep her own hopes alive.

Her interest in Owen led her to think more often of his mother, and sometimes she would slip away and stand alone before her predecessor's portrait. Since her arrival at Givré the picture—a "full-length" by a once fashionable artist—had undergone the successive displacements of an exiled consort removed farther and farther from the throne; and Anna could not help noting that these stages coincided with the gradual decline of the artist's fame. She had a fancy that if his credit had been in the ascendant the first Mrs. Leath might have continued to throne over the drawing-room mantel-piece, even to the exclusion of her successor's effigy. Instead of this, her peregrinations had finally landed her in the shrouded solitude of the billiard-room, an apartment which no one ever entered, but where it was understood that "the light was better," or might have been if the shutters had not been always closed.

Here the poor lady, elegantly dressed, and seated in the middle of a large lonely canvas, in the blank contemplation of a gilt console, had always seemed to Anna to be waiting for visitors who never came.

"Of course they never came, you poor thing! I wonder how long it took you to find out that they never would?" Anna had more than once apostrophized her, with a derision addressed rather to herself than to the dead; but it was only after Effie's birth that it occurred to her to study more closely the face in the picture, and speculate on the kind of visitors that Owen's mother might have hoped for.

"She certainly doesn't look as if they would have been the same kind as mine: but there's no telling, from a portrait that was so obviously done 'to please the family', and that leaves Owen so unaccounted for. Well, they never came, the visitors; they never came; and she died of it. She died of it long before they buried her: I'm certain of that. Those are stone-dead eyes in the picture . . . The loneliness must have been awful, if even Owen couldn't keep her from dying of it. And to feel it so she must have *had* feelings—real live ones, the kind that twitch and tug. And all she had to look at all her life was a gilt console—yes, that's it, a gilt console screwed to the wall! That's exactly and absolutely what he is!"

She did not mean, if she could help it, that either Effie or Owen should know that loneliness, or let her know it again. They were three, now, to keep each other warm, and she embraced both children in the same passion of motherhood, as though one were not enough to shield her from her predecessor's fate.

Sometimes she fancied that Owen Leath's response was warmer than that of her own child. But then Effie was still hardly more than a baby, and Owen, from the first, had been almost "old enough to understand": certainly *did* understand now, in a tacit way that yet perpetually spoke to her. This sense of his understanding was the deepest element in their feeling for each other. There were so many things between them that were never spoken of, or even indirectly alluded to, yet that, even in their occasional discussions and differences, formed the unadduced arguments making for final agreement . . .

Musing on this, she continued to watch his approach; and her heart began to beat a little faster at the thought of what she had to say to him. But when he reached the gate she saw him pause, and after a moment he turned aside as if to gain a cross-road through the park.

She started up and waved her sunshade, but he did not see her. No doubt he meant to go back with the game-keeper, perhaps to the kennels, to see a retriever who had hurt his leg. Suddenly she was seized by the whim to overtake him. She threw down the parasol, thrust her letter into her bodice, and catching up her skirts began to run.

She was slight and light, with a natural ease and quickness of gait, but she could not recall having run a yard since she had romped with Owen in his school-days; nor did she know what impulse moved her now. She only knew that run she must, that no other motion, short of flight, would have been buoyant enough for her humour. She seemed to be keeping pace with some inward rhythm, seeking to give bodily expression to the lyric rush of her thoughts. The earth always felt elastic under her, and she had a conscious joy in treading it; but never had it been as soft and springy as today. It seemed actually to rise and meet her as she went, so that she had the feeling, which sometimes came to her in dreams, of skimming miraculously over short bright waves. The air, too, seemed to break in waves against her, sweeping by on its current all the slanted lights and moist sharp perfumes of the failing day. She panted to herself: "This is nonsense!" her blood hummed back: "But it's glorious!" and she sped on till she saw that Owen had caught sight of her and was striding back in her direction. Then she stopped and waited, flushed and laughing, her hands clasped against the letter in her breast.

"No, I'm not mad," she called out; "but there's something in the air today—don't you feel it?—And I wanted to have a little talk with you," she added as he came up to her, smiling at him and linking her arm in his.

He smiled back, but above the smile she saw the shade of anxiety which, for the last two months, had kept its fixed line between his handsome eyes.

"Owen, don't look like that! I don't want you to!" she said imperiously.

He laughed. "You said that exactly like Effie. What do you want me to do? To race with you as I do Effie? But I shouldn't have a show!" he protested, still with the little frown between his eyes.

"Where are you going?" she asked.

"To the kennels. But there's not the least need. The vet has seen Garry and he's all right. If there's anything you wanted to tell me——"

"Did I say there was? I just came out to meet you—I wanted to know if you'd had good sport."

The shadow dropped on him again. "None at all. The fact is I didn't try. Jean and I have just been knocking about in the woods. I wasn't in a sanguinary mood."

They walked on with the same light gait, so nearly of a height that keeping step came as naturally to them as breathing. Anna stole another look at the young face on a level with her own.

"You *did* say there was something you wanted to tell me," her step-son began after a pause.

"Well, there is." She slackened her pace involuntarily, and they came to a pause and stood facing each other under the limes.

"Is Darrow coming?" he asked.

She seldom blushed, but at the question a sudden heat suffused her. She held her head high.

"Yes: he's coming. I've just heard. He arrives tomorrow. But that's not——" She saw her blunder and tried to rectify it. "Or rather, yes, in a way it *is* my reason for wanting to speak to you——"

"Because he's coming?"

"Because he's not yet here."

"It's about him, then?"

He looked at her kindly, half-humourously, an almost fraternal wisdom in his smile.

"About——? No, no: I meant that I wanted to speak today because it's our last day alone together."

"Oh, I see." He had slipped his hands into the pockets of his tweed shooting jacket and lounged along at her side, his eyes bent on the moist ruts of the drive, as though the matter had lost all interest for him.

"Owen——"

He stopped again and faced her. "Look here, my dear, it's no sort of use."

"What's no use?"

"Anything on earth you can any of you say."

She challenged him: "Am *I* one of 'any of you'?"

He did not yield. "Well, then—anything on earth that even *you* can say."

"You don't in the least know what I can say—or what I mean to."

"Don't I, generally?"

She gave him this point, but only to make another. "Yes; but this is particularly. I want to say . . . Owen, you've been admirable all through."

He broke into a laugh in which the odd elder-brotherly note was once more perceptible.

"Admirable," she emphasized. "And so has *she*."

"Oh, and so have you to *her*!" His voice broke down to boyishness. "I've never lost sight of that for a minute. It's been altogether easier for her, though," he threw off presently.

"On the whole, I suppose it has. Well——" she summed up with a laugh, "aren't you all the better pleased to be told you've behaved as well as she?"

"Oh, you know, I've not done it for *you*," he tossed back at her, without the least note of hostility in the affected lightness of his tone.

"Haven't you, though, perhaps—the least bit? Because, after all, you knew I understood?"

"You've been awfully kind about pretending to."

She laughed. "You don't believe me? You must remember I had your grandmother to consider."

"Yes: and my father—and Effie, I suppose—and the outraged shades of Givré!" He paused, as if to lay more stress on the boyish sneer: "Do you likewise include the late Monsieur de Chantelle?"

His step-mother did not appear to resent the thrust. She went on, in the same tone of affectionate persuasion: "Yes: I must have seemed to you too subject to

Givré. Perhaps I have been. But you know that was not my real object in asking you to wait, to say nothing to your grandmother before her return."

He considered. "Your real object, of course, was to gain time."

"Yes—but for whom? Why not for *you*?"

"For me?" He flushed up quickly. "You don't mean——?"

She laid her hand on his arm and looked gravely into his handsome eyes.

"I mean that when your grandmother gets back from Ouchy I shall speak to her——"

"You'll speak to her . . . ?"

"Yes; if only you'll promise to give me time——"

"Time for her to send for Adelaide Painter?"

"Oh, she'll undoubtedly send for Adelaide Painter!"

The allusion touched a spring of mirth in both their minds, and they exchanged a laughing look.

"Only you must promise not to rush things. You must give me time to prepare Adelaide too," Mrs. Leath went on.

"Prepare her too?" He drew away for a better look at her. "Prepare her for what?"

"Why, to prepare your grandmother! For your marriage. Yes, that's what I mean. I'm going to see you through, you know——"

His feint of indifference broke down and he caught her hand. "Oh, you dear divine thing! I didn't dream——"

"I know you didn't." She dropped her gaze and began to walk on slowly. "I can't say you've convinced me of the wisdom of the step. Only I seem to see that other things matter more—and that not missing things matters most. Perhaps I've changed—or *your* not changing has convinced me. I'm certain now that you won't budge. And that was really all I ever cared about."

"Oh, as to not budging—I told you so months ago: you might have been sure of that! And how can you be any surer today than yesterday?"

"I don't know. I suppose one learns something every day——"

"Not at Givré!" he laughed, and shot a half-ironic look at her. "But you haven't really *been* at Givré lately—not for months! Don't you suppose I've noticed that, my dear?"

She echoed his laugh to merge it in an undenying sigh. "Poor Givré . . ."

"Poor empty Givré! With so many rooms full and yet not a soul in it—except of course my grandmother, who *is* its soul!"

They had reached the gateway of the court and stood looking with a common accord at the long soft-hued façade on which the autumn light was dying. "It looks so made to be happy in——" she murmured.

"Yes—today, today!" He pressed her arm a little. "Oh, you darling—to have given it that look for me!" He paused, and then went on in a lower voice: "Don't you feel we owe it to the poor old place to do what we can to give it that look? You, too, I mean? Come, let's make it grin from wing to wing! I've such a mad desire to say outrageous things to it—haven't you? After all, in old times there must have been living people here!"

Loosening her arm from his she continued to gaze up at the house-front, which seemed, in the plaintive decline of light, to send her back the mute appeal of something doomed.

"It *is* beautiful," she said.

"A beautiful memory! Quite perfect to take out and turn over when I'm grinding at the law in New York, and you're——" He broke off and looked at her with a questioning smile. "Come! Tell me. You and I don't have to say things to talk to each other. When you turn suddenly absent-minded and mysterious I always feel like saying: 'Come back. All is discovered'."

She returned his smile. "You know as much as I know. I promise you that."

He wavered, as if for the first time uncertain how far he might go. "I don't know Darrow as much as you know him," he presently risked.

She frowned a little. "You said just now we didn't need to say things——"

"Was *I* speaking? I thought it was your eyes——" He caught her by both elbows and spun her halfway round, so that the late sun shed a betraying gleam on her face. "They're such awfully conversational eyes! Don't you suppose they told me long ago why it's just today you've made up your mind that people have got to live their own lives—even at Givré?"

XI.

"This is the south terrace," Anna said. "Should you like to walk down to the river?"

She seemed to listen to herself speaking from a far-off airy height, and yet to be wholly gathered into the circle of consciousness which drew its glowing ring about herself and Darrow. To the aerial listener her words sounded flat and colourless, but to the self within the ring each one beat with a separate heart.

It was the day after Darrow's arrival, and he had come down early, drawn by the sweetness of the light on the lawns and gardens below his window. Anna had heard the echo of his step on the stairs, his pause in the stone-flagged hall, his voice as he asked a servant where to find her. She was at the end of the house, in the brown-panelled sitting-room which she frequented at that season because it caught the sunlight first and kept it longest. She stood near the window, in the pale band of brightness, arranging some salmon-pink geraniums in a shallow porcelain bowl. Every sensation of touch and sight was thrice-alive in her. The grey-green fur of the geranium leaves caressed her fingers and the sunlight wavering across the irregular surface of the old parquet floor made it seem as bright and shifting as the brown bed of a stream.

Darrow stood framed in the door-way of the farthest drawing-room, a light-grey figure against the black and white flagging of the hall; then he began to move toward her down the empty pale-panelled vista, crossing one after another the long reflections which a projecting cabinet or screen cast here and there upon the shining floors.

As he drew nearer, his figure was suddenly displaced by that of her husband, whom, from the same point, she had so often seen advancing down the same perspective. Straight, spare, erect, looking to right and left with quick precise turns of the head, and stopping now and then to straighten a chair or alter the position of a vase, Fraser Leath used to march toward her through the double file of furniture like a general reviewing a regiment drawn up for his inspection. At a certain point, midway across the second room, he always stopped before the mantel-piece of pinkish-yellow marble and looked at himself in the tall garlanded glass that surmounted it. She could not remember that he had ever found anything to straighten or alter in his own studied attire, but she had never known him to omit the inspection when he passed that particular mirror.

When it was over he continued more briskly on his way, and the resulting expression of satisfaction was still on his face when he entered the oak sitting-room to greet his wife . . .

The spectral projection of this little daily scene hung but for a moment before Anna, but in that moment she had time to fling a wondering glance across the distance between her past and present. Then the footsteps of the present came close, and she had to drop the geraniums to give her hand to Darrow . . .

"Yes, let us walk down to the river."

They had neither of them, as yet, found much to say to each other. Darrow had arrived late on the previous afternoon, and during the evening they had had between them Owen Leath and their own thoughts. Now they were alone for the first time and the fact was enough in itself. Yet Anna was intensely aware that as soon as they began to talk more intimately they would feel that they knew each other less well.

They passed out onto the terrace and down the steps to the gravel walk below. The delicate frosting of dew gave the grass a bluish shimmer, and the sunlight, sliding in emerald streaks along the tree-boles, gathered itself into great luminous blurs at the end of the wood-walks, and hung above the fields a watery glory like the ring about an autumn moon.

"It's good to be here," Darrow said.

They took a turn to the left and stopped for a moment to look back at the long pink house-front, plainer, friendlier, less adorned than on the side toward the court. So prolonged yet delicate had been the friction of time upon its bricks that certain expanses had the bloom and texture of old red velvet, and the patches of gold lichen spreading over them looked like the last traces of a dim embroidery. The dome of the chapel, with its gilded cross, rose above one wing, and the other ended in a conical pigeon-house, above which the birds were flying, lustrous and slatey, their breasts merged in the blue of the roof when they dropped down on it.

"And this is where you've been all these years."

They turned away and began to walk down a long tunnel of yellowing trees. Benches with mossy feet stood against the mossy edges of the path, and at its farther end it widened into a circle about a basin rimmed with stone, in which the opaque water strewn with leaves looked like a slab of gold-flecked agate. The path, growing narrower, wound on circuitously through the woods, between slender serried trunks twined with ivy. Patches of blue appeared above them through the dwindling leaves, and presently the trees drew back and showed the open fields along the river.

They walked on across the fields to the tow-path. In a curve of the wall some steps led up to a crumbling pavilion with openings choked with ivy. Anna and Darrow seated themselves on the bench projecting from the inner wall of the pavilion and looked across the river at the slopes divided into blocks of green and fawn-colour, and at the chalk-tinted village lifting its squat church-tower and grey roofs against the precisely drawn lines of the landscape. Anna sat silent, so intensely aware of Darrow's nearness that there was no surprise in the touch he laid on her hand. They looked at each other, and he smiled and said: "There are to be no more obstacles now."

"Obstacles?" The word startled her. "What obstacles?"

"Don't you remember the wording of the telegram that turned me back last May? 'Unforeseen obstacle': that was it. What *was* the earth-shaking problem, by the way? Finding a governess for Effie, wasn't it?"

"But I gave you my reason: the reason why it *was* an obstacle. I wrote you fully about it."

"Yes, I know you did." He lifted her hand and kissed it. "How far off it all seems, and how little it all matters today!"

She looked at him quickly. "Do you feel that? I suppose I'm different. I want to draw all those wasted months into today—to make them a part of it."

"But they *are*, to me. You reach back and take everything—back to the first days of all."

She frowned a little, as if struggling with an inarticulate perplexity. "It's curious how, in those first days, too, something that I didn't understand came between us."

"Oh, in those days we neither of us understood, did we? It's part of what's called the bliss of being young."

"Yes, I thought that, too: thought it, I mean, in looking back. But it couldn't, even then, have been as true of you as of me; and now——"

"Now," he said, "the only thing that matters is that we're sitting here together."

He dismissed the rest with a lightness that might have seemed conclusive evidence of her power over him. But she took no pride in such triumphs. It seemed to her that she wanted his allegiance and his adoration not so much for herself as for their mutual love, and that in treating lightly any past phase of their relation he took something from its present beauty. The colour rose to her face.

"Between you and me everything matters."

"Of course!" She felt the unperceiving sweetness of his smile. "That's why," he went on, " 'everything,' for me, is here and now: on this bench, between you and me."

She caught at the phrase. "That's what I meant: it's here and now; we can't get away from it."

"Get away from it? Do you want to? *Again?*"

Her heart was beating unsteadily. Something in her, fitfully and with reluctance, struggled to free itself, but the warmth of his nearness penetrated every sense as the sunlight steeped the landscape. Then, suddenly, she felt that she wanted no less than the whole of her happiness.

" 'Again'? But wasn't it *you*, the last time——?"

She paused, the tremor in her of Psyche holding up the lamp. But in the interrogative light of her pause her companion's features underwent no change.

"The last time? Last spring? But it was you who—for the best of reasons, as you've told me—turned me back from your very door last spring!"

She saw that he was good-humouredly ready to "thresh out," for her sentimental satisfaction, a question which, for his own, Time had so conclusively dealt with; and the sense of his readiness reassured her.

"I wrote as soon as I could," she rejoined. "I explained the delay and asked you to come. And you never even answered my letter."

"It was impossible to come then. I had to go back to my post."

"And impossible to write and tell me so?"

"Your letter was a long time coming. I had waited a week—ten days. I had some excuse for thinking, when it came, that you were in no great hurry for an answer."

"You thought that—really—after reading it?"

"I thought it."

Her heart leaped up to her throat. "Then why are you here today?"

He turned on her with a quick look of wonder. "God knows—if you can ask me that!"

"You see I was right to say I didn't understand."

He stood up abruptly and stood facing her, blocking the view over the river and the checkered slopes. "Perhaps I might say so too."

"No, no: we must neither of us have any reason for saying it again." She looked at him gravely. "Surely you and I needn't arrange the lights before we show ourselves to each other. I want you to see me just as I am, with all my irrational doubts and scruples; the old ones and the new ones too."

He came back to his seat beside her. "Never mind the old ones. They were justified—I'm willing to admit it. With the governess having suddenly to be packed off, and Effie on your hands, and your mother-in-law ill, I see the impossibility of your letting me come. I even see that, at the moment, it was difficult to write and explain. But what does all that matter now? The new scruples are the ones I want to tackle."

Again her heart trembled. She felt her happiness so near, so sure, that to strain it closer might be like a child's crushing a pet bird in its caress. But her very security urged her on. For so long her doubts had been knife-edged: now they had turned into bright harmless toys that she could toss and catch without peril!

"You didn't come, and you didn't answer my letter; and after waiting four months I wrote another."

"And I answered that one; and I'm here."

"Yes." She held his eyes. "But in my last letter I repeated exactly what I'd said in the first—the one I wrote you last June. I told you then that I was ready to give you the answer to what you'd asked me in London; and in telling you that, I told you what the answer was."

"My dearest! My dearest!" Darrow murmured.

"You ignored that letter. All summer you made no sign. And all I ask now is that you should frankly tell me why."

"I can only repeat what I've just said. I was hurt and unhappy and I doubted you. I suppose if I'd cared less I should have been more confident. I cared so much that I couldn't risk another failure. For you'd made me feel that I'd miserably failed. So I shut my eyes and set my teeth and turned my back. There's the whole pusillanimous truth of it!"

"Oh, if it's the *whole* truth——!" She let him clasp her. "There's my torment, you see. I thought that was what your silence meant till I made you break it. Now I want to be sure that I was right."

"What can I tell you to make you sure?"

"You can let me tell *you* everything first." She drew away, but without taking her hands from him. "Owen saw you in Paris," she began.

She looked at him and he faced her steadily. The light was full on his pleasantly-browned face, his grey eyes, his frank white forehead. She noticed for the first time a seal-ring in a setting of twisted silver on the hand he had kept on hers.

"In Paris? Oh, yes . . . So he did."

"He came back and told me. I think you talked to him a moment in a theatre. I asked if you'd spoken of my having put you off—or if you'd sent me any message. He didn't remember that you had."

"In a crush—in a Paris *foyer*? My dear!"

"It was absurd of me! But Owen and I have always been on odd kind of brother-and-sister terms. I think he guessed about us when he saw you with me in London. So he teased me a little and tried to make me curious about you; and when he saw he'd succeeded he told me he hadn't had time to say much to you because you were in such a hurry to get back to the lady you were with."

He still held her hands, but she felt no tremor in his,

and the blood did not stir in his brown cheek. He seemed to be honestly turning over his memories.

"Yes: and what else did he tell you?"

"Oh, not much, except that she was awfully pretty. When I asked him to describe her he said you had her tucked away in a *baignoire* and he hadn't actually seen her; but he saw the tail of her cloak, and somehow knew from that that she was pretty. One *does*, you know . . . I think he said the cloak was pink."

Darrow broke into a laugh. "Of course it was—they always are! So that was at the bottom of your doubts?"

"Not at first. I only laughed. But afterward, when I wrote you and you didn't answer—— Oh, you *do* see?" she appealed to him.

He was looking at her gently. "Yes: I see."

"It's not as if this were a light thing between us. I want you to know me as I am. If I thought that at that moment . . . when you were on your way here, almost——"

He dropped her hand and stood up. "Yes, yes—I understand."

"But do you?" Her look followed him. "I'm not a goose of a girl. I know . . . of course I *know* . . . but there are things a woman feels . . . when what she knows doesn't make any difference. It's not that I want you to explain—I mean about that particular evening. It's only that I want you to have the whole of my feeling. I didn't know what it was till I saw you again. I never dreamed I should say such things to you!"

"I never dreamed I should be here to hear you say them!" He turned back and lifting a floating end of her scarf put his lips to it. "But now that you have, *I* know—*I* know," he smiled down at her.

"You know——?"

"That this is no light thing between us. Now you may ask me anything you please! That was all I wanted to ask *you*."

For a long moment they looked at each other without speaking. She saw the dancing spirit in his eyes turn grave and darken to a passionate sternness. He stooped and kissed her, and she sat as if folded in wings.

XII.

IT was in the natural order of things that, on the way back to the house, their talk should have turned to the future.

Anna was not eager to define it. She had an extraordinary sensitiveness to the impalpable elements of happiness, and as she walked at Darrow's side her imagination flew back and forth, spinning luminous webs of feeling between herself and the scene about her. Every heightening of emotion produced for her a new effusion of beauty in visible things, and with it the sense that such moments should be lingered over and absorbed like some unrenewable miracle. She understood Darrow's impatience to see their plans take shape. She knew it must be so, she would not have had it otherwise; but to reach a point where she could fix her mind on his appeal for dates and decisions was like trying to break her way through the silver tangle of an April wood.

Darrow wished to use his diplomatic opportunities as a means of studying certain economic and social problems with which he presently hoped to deal in print; and with this in view he had asked for, and obtained, a South American appointment. Anna was ready to follow where he led, and not reluctant to put new sights as well as new thoughts between herself and her past. She had, in a direct way, only Effie and Effie's education to consider; and there seemed, after due reflection, no reason why the most anxious regard for these should not be conciliated with the demands of Darrow's career. Effie, it was evident, could be left to Madame de Chantelle's care till the couple should have organized their life; and she might even, as long as her future step-father's work retained him in distant posts, continue to divide her year between Givré and the antipodes.

As for Owen, who had reached his legal majority two years before, and was soon to attain the age fixed for the taking over of his paternal inheritance, the arrival of this date would reduce his step-mother's responsibility to a friendly concern for his welfare. This made for the prompt realization of Darrow's wishes, and there seemed no reason why the marriage should not take place within the six weeks that remained of his leave.

They passed out of the wood-walk into the open brightness of the garden. The noon sunlight sheeted with gold the bronze flanks of the polygonal yews. Chrysanthemums, russet, saffron and orange, glowed like the efflorescence of an enchanted forest; belts of red begonia purpling to wine-colour ran like smouldering flame among the borders; and above this outspread tapestry the house extended its harmonious length, the soberness of its lines softened to grace in the luminous misty air.

Darrow stood still, and Anna felt that his glance was travelling from her to the scene about them and then back to her face.

"You're sure you're prepared to give up Givré? You look so made for each other!"

"Oh, Givré——" She broke off suddenly, feeling as if her too careless tone had delivered all her past into his hands; and with one of her instinctive movements of recoil she added: "When Owen marries I shall have to give it up."

"When Owen marries? That's looking some distance ahead! I want to be told that meanwhile you'll have no regrets."

She hesitated. Why did he press her to uncover to him her poor starved past? A vague feeling of loyalty, a desire to spare what could no longer harm her, made her answer evasively: "There will probably be no 'meanwhile.' Owen may marry before long."

She had not meant to touch on the subject, for her stepson had sworn her to provisional secrecy; but since the shortness of Darrow's leave necessitated a prompt adjustment of their own plans, it was, after all, inevitable that she should give him at least a hint of Owen's.

"Owen marry? Why, he always seems like a faun in flannels! I hope he's found a dryad. There might easily be one left in these blue-and-gold woods."

"I can't tell you yet where he found his dryad, but she *is* one, I believe: at any rate she'll become the Givré woods better than I do. Only there may be difficulties——"

"Well! At that age they're not always to be wished away."

She hesitated. "Owen, at any rate, has made up his mind to overcome them; and I've promised to see him through."

She went on, after a moment's consideration, to explain that her step-son's choice was, for various reasons, not likely to commend itself to his grandmother. "She must be prepared for it, and I've promised to do the preparing. You know I always *have* seen him through things, and he rather counts on me now."

She fancied that Darrow's exclamation had in it a faint note of annoyance, and wondered if he again suspected her of seeking a pretext for postponement.

"But once Owen's future is settled, you won't, surely, for the sake of what you call seeing him through, ask that I should go away again without you?" He drew her closer as they walked. "Owen will understand, if you don't. Since he's in the same case himself I'll throw myself on his mercy. He'll see that I have the first claim on you; he won't even want you not to see it."

"Owen sees everything: I'm not afraid of that. But his future isn't settled. He's very young to marry—too young, his grandmother is sure to think—and the marriage he wants to make is not likely to convince her to the contrary."

"You don't mean that it's like his first choice?"

"Oh, no! But it's not what Madame de Chantelle would call a good match; it's not even what I call a wise one."

"Yet you're backing him up?"

"Yet I'm backing him up." She paused. "I wonder if you'll understand? What I've most wanted for him, and shall want for Effie, is that they shall always feel free to make their own mistakes, and never, if possible, be persuaded to make other people's. Even if Owen's marriage is a mistake, and has to be paid for, I believe he'll learn and grow in the paying. Of course I can't make Madame de Chantelle see this; but I can remind her that, with his character—his big rushes of impulse, his odd intervals of ebb and apathy—she may drive him into some worse blunder if she thwarts him now."

"And you mean to break the news to her as soon as she comes back from Ouchy?"

"As soon as I see my way to it. She knows the girl and likes her: that's our hope. And yet it may, in the end, prove our danger, make it harder for us all, when she learns the truth, than if Owen had chosen a stranger. I can't tell you more till I've told her: I've promised Owen not to tell any one. All I ask you is to give me time, to give me a few days at any rate. She's been wonderfully 'nice,' as she would call it, about you, and about the fact of my having soon to leave Givré; but that, again, may make it harder for Owen. At any rate, you can see, can't you, how it makes me want to stand by him? You see, I couldn't bear it if the least fraction of my happiness seemed to be stolen from his—as if it were a little scrap of happiness that had to be pieced out with other people's!" She clasped her hands on Darrow's arm. "I want our life to be like a house with all the windows lit: I'd like to string lanterns from the roof and chimneys!"

She ended with an inward tremor. All through her exposition and her appeal she had told herself that the moment could hardly have been less well chosen. In Darrow's place she would have felt, as he doubtless did, that her carefully developed argument was only the disguise of an habitual indecision. It was the hour of all others when she would have liked to affirm herself by brushing aside every obstacle to his wishes; yet it was only by opposing them that she could show the strength of character she wanted him to feel in her.

But as she talked she began to see that Darrow's face gave back no reflection of her words, that he continued to wear the abstracted look of a man who is not listening to what is said to him. It caused her a slight pang to discover that his thoughts could wander at such a moment; then, with a flush of joy she perceived the reason.

In some undefinable way she had become aware, without turning her head, that he was steeped in the sense of her nearness, absorbed in contemplating the details of her face and dress; and the discovery made the words throng to her lips. She felt herself speak with ease, authority, conviction. She said to herself: "He doesn't care what I say—it's enough that I say it—even if it's stupid he'll like me better for it . . ." She knew that every inflexion of her voice, every gesture, every characteristic of her person—its very defects, the fact that her forehead was too high, that her eyes were not large enough, that her hands, though slender, were not small, and that the fingers did not taper—she knew that these deficiencies were so many channels through which her influence streamed to him; that she pleased him in spite of them, perhaps because of them; that he wanted her as she was, and not as she would have liked to be; and for the first time she felt in her veins the security and lightness of happy love.

They reached the court and walked under the limes

toward the house. The hall door stood wide, and through the windows opening on the terrace the sun slanted across the black and white floor, the faded tapestry chairs, and Darrow's travelling coat and cap, which lay among the cloaks and rugs piled on a bench against the wall.

The sight of these garments, lying among her own wraps, gave her a sense of homely intimacy. It was as if her happiness came down from the skies and took on the plain dress of daily things. At last she seemed to hold it in her hand.

As they entered the hall her eye lit on an unstamped note conspicuously placed on the table.

"From Owen! He must have rushed off somewhere in the motor."

She felt a secret stir of pleasure at the immediate inference that she and Darrow would probably lunch alone. Then she opened the note and stared at it in wonder.

"Dear," Owen wrote, "after what you said yesterday I can't wait another hour, and I'm off to Francheuil, to catch the Dijon express and travel back with them. Don't be frightened; I won't speak unless it's safe to. Trust me for that—but I had to go."

She looked up slowly.

"He's gone to Dijon to meet his grandmother. Oh, I hope I haven't made a mistake!"

"You? Why, what have you to do with his going to Dijon?"

She hesitated. "The day before yesterday I told him, for the first time, that I meant to see him through, no matter what happened. And I'm afraid he's lost his head, and will be imprudent and spoil things. You see,

I hadn't meant to say a word to him till I'd had time to prepare Madame de Chantelle."

She felt that Darrow was looking at her and reading her thoughts, and the colour flew to her face. "Yes: it was when I heard you were coming that I told him. I wanted him to feel as I felt . . . it seemed too unkind to make him wait!"

Her hand was in his, and his arm rested for a moment on her shoulder.

"It *would* have been too unkind to make him wait."

They moved side by side toward the stairs. Through the haze of bliss enveloping her, Owen's affairs seemed curiously unimportant and remote. Nothing really mattered but this torrent of light in her veins. She put her foot on the lowest step, saying: "It's nearly luncheon time—I must take off my hat . . ." and as she started up the stairs Darrow stood below in the hall and watched her. But the distance between them did not make him seem less near: it was as if his thoughts moved with her and touched her like endearing hands.

In her bedroom she shut the door and stood still, looking about her in a fit of dreamy wonder. Her feelings were unlike any she had ever known: richer, deeper, more complete. For the first time everything in her, from head to foot, seemed to be feeding the same full current of sensation.

She took off her hat and went to the dressing-table to smooth her hair. The pressure of the hat had flattened the dark strands on her forehead; her face was paler than usual, with shadows about the eyes. She felt a pang of regret for the wasted years. "If I look like this today," she said to herself, "what will he think of me when I'm ill or worried?" She began to run her fingers through her hair, rejoicing in its thickness; then she desisted and sat still, resting her chin on her hands.

"I want him to see me as I am," she thought.

Deeper than the deepest fibre of her vanity was the triumphant sense that *as she was*, with her flattened hair, her tired pallor, her thin sleeves a little tumbled by the weight of her jacket, he would like her even better, feel her nearer, dearer, more desirable, than in all the splendours she might put on for him. In the light of this discovery she studied her face with a new intentness, seeing its defects as she had never seen them, yet seeing them through a kind of radiance, as though love were a luminous medium into which she had been bodily plunged.

She was glad now that she had confessed her doubts and her jealousy. She divined that a man in love may be flattered by such involuntary betrayals, that there are moments when respect for his liberty appeals to him less than the inability to respect it: moments so propitious that a woman's very mistakes and indiscretions may help to establish her dominion. The sense of power she had been aware of in talking to Darrow came back with ten-fold force. She felt like testing him by the most fantastic exactions, and at the same moment she longed to humble herself before him, to make herself the shadow and echo of his mood. She wanted to linger with him in a world of fancy and yet to walk at his side in the world of fact. She wanted him to feel her power and yet to love her for her ignorance and humility. She felt like a slave, and a goddess, and a girl in her teens . . .

XIII.

DARROW, late that evening, threw himself into an arm-chair before his fire and mused.

The room was propitious to meditation. The red-veiled lamp, the corners of shadow, the splashes of firelight on the curves of old full-bodied wardrobes and cabinets, gave it an air of intimacy increased by its faded hangings, its slightly frayed and threadbare rugs. Everything in it was harmoniously shabby, with a subtle sought-for shabbiness in which Darrow fancied he discerned the touch of Fraser Leath. But Fraser Leath had grown so unimportant a factor in the scheme of things that these marks of his presence caused the young man no emotion beyond that of a faint retrospective amusement.

The afternoon and evening had been perfect.

After a moment of concern over her step-son's departure, Anna had surrendered herself to her happiness with an impetuosity that Darrow had never suspected in her. Early in the afternoon they had gone out in the motor, traversing miles of sober-tinted landscape in which, here and there, a scarlet vineyard flamed, clattering through the streets of stony villages, coming out on low slopes above the river, or winding through the pale gold of narrow wood-roads with the blue of clear-cut hills at their end. Over everything lay a faint sunshine that seemed dissolved in the still air, and the smell of wet roots and decaying leaves was merged in the pungent scent of burning underbrush. Once, at the turn of a wall, they stopped the motor before a ruined gateway and, stumbling along a road full of ruts, stood before a little old deserted house, fantastically carved and chimneyed, which lay in a moat under the shade of ancient trees. They paced the paths between the trees, found a mouldy Temple of Love on an islet among reeds and plantains, and, sitting on a bench in the stable-yard, watched the pigeons circling against the sunset over their cot of patterned brick. Then the motor flew on into the dusk . . .

When they came in they sat beside the fire in the oak drawing-room, and Darrow noticed how delicately her head stood out against the sombre panelling, and mused on the enjoyment there would always be in the mere fact of watching her hands as they moved about among the tea-things . . .

They dined late, and facing her across the table, with its low lights and flowers, he felt an extraordinary pleasure in seeing her again in evening dress, and in letting his eyes dwell on the proud shy set of her head, the way her dark hair clasped it, and the girlish thinness of her neck above the slight swell of the breast. His imagination was struck by the quality of reticence in her beauty. She suggested a fine portrait kept down to a few tones, or a Greek vase on which the play of light is the only pattern.

After dinner they went out on the terrace for a look at the moon-misted park. Through the crepuscular whiteness the trees hung in blotted masses. Below the terrace, the garden drew its dark diagrams between statues that stood like muffled conspirators on the edge of the shadow. Farther off, the meadows unrolled a silver-shot tissue to the mantling of mist above the river; and the autumn stars trembled overhead like their own reflections seen in dim water.

He lit his cigar, and they walked slowly up and down the flags in the languid air, till he put an arm about her, saying: "You mustn't stay till you're chilled"; then they went back into the room and drew up their chairs to the fire.

It seemed only a moment later that she said: "It must be after eleven," and stood up and looked down on him, smiling faintly. He sat still, absorbing the look, and thinking: "There'll be evenings and evenings"—till she came nearer, bent over him, and with a hand on his shoulder said: "Good night."

He got to his feet and put his arms about her.

"Good night," he answered, and held her fast; and they gave each other a long kiss of promise and communion.

The memory of it glowed in him still as he sat over his crumbling fire; but beneath his physical exultation he felt a certain gravity of mood. His happiness was in some sort the rallying-point of many scattered purposes. He summed it up vaguely by saying to himself that to be loved by a woman like that made "all the difference" . . . He was a little tired of experimenting on life; he wanted to "take a line", to follow things up, to centralize and concentrate, and produce results. Two or three more years of diplomacy—with her beside him!—and then their real life would begin: study, travel and book-making for him, and for her—well, the joy, at any rate, of getting out of an atmosphere of bric-à-brac and card-leaving into the open air of competing activities.

The desire for change had for some time been latent in him, and his meeting with Mrs. Leath the previous spring had given it a definite direction. With such a comrade to focus and stimulate his energies he felt modestly but agreeably sure of "doing something". And under this assurance was the lurking sense that he was somehow worthy of his opportunity. His life, on the whole, had been a creditable affair. Out of modest chances and middling talents he had built himself a fairly marked personality, known some exceptional people, done a number of interesting and a few rather difficult things, and found himself, at thirty-seven, possessed of an intellectual ambition sufficient to occupy the passage to a robust and energetic old age. As for the private and personal side of his life, it had come up to the current standards, and if it had dropped, now and then, below a more ideal measure, even these declines had been brief, parenthetic, incidental. In the recognized essentials he had always remained strictly within the limit of his scruples.

From this reassuring survey of his case he came back to the contemplation of its crowning felicity. His mind turned again to his first meeting with Anna Summers and took up one by one the threads of their faintly sketched romance. He dwelt with pardonable pride on the fact that fate had so early marked him for the high privilege of possessing her: it seemed to mean that they had really, in the truest sense of the ill-used phrase, been made for each other.

Deeper still than all these satisfactions was the mere elemental sense of well-being in her presence. That, after all, was what proved her to be the woman for him: the pleasure he took in the set of her head, the way her hair grew on her forehead and at the nape, her steady gaze when he spoke, the grave freedom of her gait and gestures. He recalled every detail of her face, the fine veinings of the temples, the bluish-brown shadows in her upper lids, and the way the reflections of two stars seemed to form and break up in her eyes when he held her close to him . . .

If he had had any doubt as to the nature of her feeling for him those dissolving stars would have allayed it. She was reserved, she was shy even, was what the shallow and effusive would call "cold". She was like a picture so hung that it can be seen only at a certain angle: an angle known to no one but its possessor. The thought flattered his sense of possessorship . . . He felt that the smile on his lips would have been fatuous had it had a witness. He was thinking of her look when she had questioned him about his meeting with Owen at the theatre: less of her words than of her look, and of the effort the question cost her: the reddening of her cheek, the deepening of the strained line between her brows, the way her eyes sought shelter and then turned and drew on him. Pride and passion were in the conflict—magnificent qualities in a wife! The sight almost made up for his momentary embarrassment at the rousing of a memory which had no place in his present picture of himself. Yes! It was worth a good deal to watch that fight between her instinct and her intelligence, and know one's self the object of the struggle . . .

Mingled with these sensations were considerations of another order. He reflected with satisfaction that she was the kind of woman with whom one would like to be seen in public. It would be distinctly agreeable to follow her into drawing-rooms, to walk after her down the aisle of a theatre, to get in and out of trains with her, to say "my wife" of her to all sorts of people. He draped these details in the handsome phrase "She's a woman to be proud of", and felt that this fact somehow justified and ennobled his instinctive boyish satisfaction in loving her.

He stood up, rambled across the room and leaned out for a while into the starry night. Then he dropped again into his armchair with a sigh of deep content.

"Oh, hang it," he suddenly exclaimed, "it's the best thing that's ever happened to me, anyhow!"

The next day was even better. He felt, and knew she felt, that they had reached a clearer understanding of each other. It was as if, after a swim through bright opposing waves, with a dazzle of sun in their eyes, they had gained an inlet in the shades of a cliff, where they could float on the still surface and gaze far down into the depths.

Now and then, as they walked and talked, he felt a thrill of youthful wonder at the coincidence of their views and their experiences, at the way their minds leapt to the same point in the same instant.

"The old delusion, I suppose," he smiled to himself. "Will Nature never tire of the trick?"

But he knew it was more than that. There were moments in their talk when he felt, distinctly and unmistakably, the solid ground of friendship underneath the whirling dance of his sensations. "How I should like her if I didn't love her!" he summed it up, wondering at the miracle of such a union.

In the course of the morning a telegram had come from Owen Leath, announcing that he, his grandmother and Effie would arrive from Dijon that afternoon at four. The station of the main line was eight or ten miles from Givré, and Anna, soon after three, left in the motor to meet the travellers.

When she had gone Darrow started for a walk, planning to get back late, in order that the reunited family might have the end of the afternoon to themselves. He roamed the countryside till long after dark, and the stable-clock of Givré was striking seven as he walked up the avenue to the court.

In the hall, coming down the stairs, he encountered Anna. Her face was serene, and his first glance showed him that Owen had kept his word and that none of her forebodings had been fulfilled.

She had just come down from the school-room, where Effie and the governess were having supper; the little girl, she told him, looked immensely better for her Swiss holiday, but was dropping with sleep after the journey, and too tired to make her habitual appearance in the drawing-room before being put to bed. Madame de Chantelle was resting, but would be down for dinner; and as for Owen, Anna supposed he was off somewhere in the park—he had a passion for prowling about the park at nightfall . . .

Darrow followed her into the brown room, where the tea-table had been left for him. He declined her offer of tea, but she lingered a moment to tell him that Owen had in fact kept his word, and that Madame de

Chantelle had come back in the best of humours, and unsuspicious of the blow about to fall.

"She has enjoyed her month at Ouchy, and it has given her a lot to talk about—her symptoms, and the rival doctors, and the people at the hotel. It seems she met your Ambassadress there, and Lady Wantley, and some other London friends of yours, and she's heard what she calls 'delightful things' about you: she told me to tell you so. She attaches great importance to the fact that your grandmother was an Everard of Albany. She's prepared to open her arms to you. I don't know whether it won't make it harder for poor Owen . . . the contrast, I mean . . . There are no Ambassadresses or Everards to vouch for *his* choice! But you'll help me, won't you? You'll help me to help him? To-morrow I'll tell you the rest. Now I must rush up and tuck in Effie . . ."

"Oh, you'll see, we'll pull it off for him!" he assured her; "together, we can't fail to pull it off."

He stood and watched her with a smile as she fled down the half-lit vista to the hall.

XIV.

If Darrow, on entering the drawing-room before dinner, examined its new occupant with unusual interest, it was more on Owen Leath's account than his own.

Anna's hints had roused his interest in the lad's love

affair, and he wondered what manner of girl the heroine of the coming conflict might be. He had guessed that Owen's rebellion symbolized for his step-mother her own long struggle against the Leath conventions, and he understood that if Anna so passionately abetted him it was partly because, as she owned, she wanted his liberation to coincide with hers.

The lady who was to represent, in the impending struggle, the forces of order and tradition was seated by the fire when Darrow entered. Among the flowers and old furniture of the large pale-panelled room, Madame de Chantelle had the inanimate elegance of a figure introduced into a "still-life" to give the scale. And this, Darrow reflected, was exactly what she doubtless regarded as her chief obligation: he was sure she thought a great deal of "measure", and approved of most things only up to a certain point.

She was a woman of sixty, with a figure at once young and old-fashioned. Her fair faded tints, her quaint corseting, the *passementerie* on her tight-waisted dress, the velvet band on her tapering arm, made her resemble a "carte de visite" photograph of the middle sixties. One saw her, younger but no less invincibly lady-like, leaning on a chair with a fringed back, a curl in her neck, a locket on her tuckered bosom, toward the end of an embossed morocco album beginning with The Beauties of the Second Empire.

She received her daughter-in-law's suitor with an affability which implied her knowledge and approval of his suit. Darrow had already guessed her to be a person who would instinctively oppose any suggested changes, and then, after one had exhausted one's main arguments, unexpectedly yield to some small incidental reason, and adhere doggedly to her new position. She boasted of her old-fashioned prejudices, talked a good deal of being a grandmother, and made a show of reaching up to tap Owen's shoulder, though his height was little more than hers.

She was full of a small pale prattle about the people she had seen at Ouchy, as to whom she had the minute statistical information of a gazetteer, without any apparent sense of personal differences. She said to Darrow: "They tell me things are very much changed in America . . . Of course in my youth there *was* a Society" . . . She had no desire to return there: she was sure the standards must be so different. "There are charming people everywhere . . . and one must always look on the best side . . . but when one has lived among Traditions it's difficult to adapt one's self to the new ideas . . . These dreadful views of marriage . . . it's so hard to explain them to my French relations . . . I'm thankful to say I don't pretend to understand them myself! But *you're* an Everard—I told Anna last spring in London that one sees that instantly . . ."

She wandered off to the cooking and the service of the hotel at Ouchy. She attached great importance to gastronomic details and to the manners of hotel servants. There, too, there was a falling off, she said. "I don't know, of course; but people say it's owing to the Americans. Certainly my waiter had a way of slapping down the dishes . . . they tell me that many of them are Anarchists . . . belong to Unions, you know." She appealed to Darrow's reported knowledge of economic conditions to confirm this ominous rumour.

After dinner Owen Leath wandered into the next room, where the piano stood, and began to play among the shadows. His step-mother presently joined him, and Darrow sat alone with Madame de Chantelle.

She took up the thread of her mild chat and carried it on at the same pace as her knitting. Her conversation resembled the large loose-stranded web between her fingers: now and then she dropped a stitch, and went on regardless of the gap in the pattern.

Darrow listened with a lazy sense of well-being. In the mental lull of the after-dinner hour, with harmonious memories murmuring through his mind, and the soft tints and shadowy spaces of the fine old room charming his eyes to indolence, Madame de Chantelle's discourse seemed not out of place. He could understand that, in the long run, the atmosphere of Givré might be suffocating; but in his present mood its very limitations had a grace.

Presently he found the chance to say a word in his own behalf; and thereupon measured the advantage, never before particularly apparent to him, of being related to the Everards of Albany. Madame de Chantelle's conception of her native country—to which she had not returned since her twentieth year—reminded him of an ancient geographer's map of the Hyperborean regions. It was all a foggy blank, from which only one or two fixed outlines emerged; and one of these belonged to the Everards of Albany.

The fact that they offered such firm footing—formed, so to speak, a friendly territory on which the opposing powers could meet and treat—helped him through the task of explaining and justifying himself as the successor of Fraser Leath. Madame de Chantelle could not resist such incontestable claims. She seemed to feel her son's hovering and discriminating presence, and she gave Darrow the sense that he was being tested and approved as a last addition to the Leath Collection.

She also made him aware of the immense advantage he possessed in belonging to the diplomatic profession. She spoke of this humdrum calling as a Career, and gave Darrow to understand that she supposed him to have been seducing Duchesses when he was not negotiating Treaties. He heard again quaint phrases which romantic old ladies had used in his youth: "Brilliant diplomatic society . . . social advantages . . . the *entrée everywhere* . . . *nothing else forms* a young man in the same way . . ." and she sighingly added that she could have wished her grandson had chosen the same path to glory.

Darrow prudently suppressed his own view of the profession, as well as the fact that he had adopted it provisionally, and for reasons less social than sociological; and the talk presently passed on to the subject of his future plans.

Here again, Madame de Chantelle's awe of the Career made her admit the necessity of Anna's consenting to an early marriage. The fact that Darrow was "ordered" to South America seemed to put him in the romantic light of a young soldier charged to lead a forlorn hope: she sighed and said: "At such moments a wife's duty is at her husband's side."

The problem of Effie's future might have disturbed her, she added; but since Anna, for a time, consented to leave the little girl with her, that problem was at any rate deferred. She spoke plaintively of the responsibility of looking after her granddaughter, but Darrow divined that she enjoyed the flavour of the word more than she felt the weight of the fact.

"Effie's a perfect child. She's more like my son, perhaps, than dear Owen. She'll never intentionally give me the least trouble. But of course the responsibility will be great . . . I'm not sure I should dare to undertake it if it were not for her having such a treasure of a governess. Has Anna told you about our little governess? After all the worry we had last year, with one impossible creature after another, it seems providential, just now, to have found her. At first we were afraid she was too young; but now we've the greatest confidence in her. So clever and amusing— and *such* a lady! I don't say her education's all it might be . . . no drawing or singing . . . but one can't have everything; and she speaks Italian . . ."

Madame de Chantelle's fond insistence on the likeness between Effie Leath and her father, if not particularly gratifying to Darrow, had at least increased his desire to see the little girl. It gave him an odd feeling of discomfort to think that she should have any of the characteristics of the late Fraser Leath: he had, somehow, fantastically pictured her as the mystical offspring of the early tenderness between himself and Anna Summers.

His encounter with Effie took place the next morning, on the lawn below the terrace, where he found her, in the early sunshine, knocking about golf balls with her brother. Almost at once, and with infinite relief, he saw that the resemblance of which Madame de Chantelle boasted was mainly external. Even that discovery was slightly distasteful, though Darrow was forced to own that Fraser Leath's straight-featured fairness had lent itself to the production of a peculiarly finished image of childish purity. But it was evident that other elements had also gone to the making of Effie, and that another spirit sat in her eyes. Her serious handshake, her "pretty" greeting, were worthy of the Leath tradition, and he guessed her to be more malleable than Owen, more subject to the influences of Givré; but the shout with which she returned to her romp had in it the note of her mother's emancipation.

He had begged a holiday for her, and when Mrs. Leath appeared he and she and the little girl went off for a ramble. Anna wished her daughter to have time to make friends with Darrow before learning in what relation he was to stand to her; and the three roamed the woods and fields till the distant chime of the stable-clock made them turn back for luncheon.

Effie, who was attended by a shaggy terrier, had picked up two or three subordinate dogs at the stable; and as she trotted on ahead with her yapping escort, Anna hung back to throw a look at Darrow.

"Yes," he answered it, "she's exquisite . . . Oh, I see what I'm asking of you! But she'll be quite happy here, won't she? And you must remember it won't be for long . . ."

Anna sighed her acquiescence. "Oh, she'll be happy here. It's her nature to be happy. She'll apply herself to it, conscientiously, as she does to her lessons, and to what she calls 'being good' . . . In a way, you see, that's just what worries me. Her idea of 'being good' is to please the person she's with—she puts her whole dear little mind on it! And so, if ever she's with the wrong person——"

"But surely there's no danger of that just now? Madame de Chantelle tells me that you've at last put your hand on a perfect governess——"

Anna, without answering, glanced away from him toward her daughter.

"It's lucky, at any rate," Darrow continued, "that Madame de Chantelle thinks her so."

"Oh, I think very highly of her too."

"Highly enough to feel quite satisfied to leave her with Effie?"

"Yes. She's just the person for Effie. Only, of course, one never knows . . . She's young, and she might take it into her head to leave us . . ." After a pause she added: "I'm naturally anxious to know what you think of her."

When they entered the house the hands of the hall clock stood within a few minutes of the luncheon hour. Anna led Effie off to have her hair smoothed and Darrow wandered into the oak sitting-room, which he found untenanted. The sun lay pleasantly on its brown walls, on the scattered books and the flowers in old porcelain vases. In his eyes lingered the vision of the dark-haired mother mounting the stairs with her little fair daughter. The contrast between them seemed a last touch of grace in the complex harmony of things. He stood in the window, looking out at the park, and brooding inwardly upon his happiness . . .

He was roused by Effie's voice and the scamper of her feet down the long floors behind him.

"Here he is! Here he is!" she cried, flying over the threshold.

He turned and stooped to her with a smile, and as she caught his hand he perceived that she was trying to draw him toward some one who had paused behind her in the doorway, and whom he supposed to be her mother.

"*Here* he is!" Effie repeated, with her sweet impatience.

The figure in the doorway came forward and Darrow, looking up, found himself face to face with Sophy Viner. They stood still, a yard or two apart, and looked at each other without speaking.

As they paused there, a shadow fell across one of the terrace windows, and Owen Leath stepped whistling into the room. In his rough shooting clothes, with the glow of exercise under his fair skin, he looked extraordinarily light-hearted and happy. Darrow, with a quick side-glance, noticed this, and perceived also that the glow on the youth's cheek had deepened suddenly to red. He too stopped short, and the three stood there motionless for a barely perceptible beat of time. During its lapse, Darrow's eyes had turned back from Owen's face to that of the girl between them. He had the sense that, whatever was done, it was he who must do it, and that it must be done immediately. He went forward and held out his hand.

"How do you do, Miss Viner?"

She answered: "How do you do?" in a voice that sounded clear and natural; and the next moment he again became aware of steps behind him, and knew that Mrs. Leath was in the room.

To his strained senses there seemed to be another just measurable pause before Anna said, looking gaily about the little group: "Has Owen introduced you? This is Effie's friend, Miss Viner."

Effie, still hanging on her governess's arm, pressed herself closer with a little gesture of appropriation; and Miss Viner laid her hand on her pupil's hair.

Darrow felt that Anna's eyes had turned to him.

"I think Miss Viner and I have met already—several years ago in London."

"I remember," said Sophy Viner, in the same clear voice.

"How charming! Then we're all friends. But luncheon must be ready," said Mrs. Leath.

She turned back to the door, and the little procession moved down the two long drawing-rooms, with Effie waltzing on ahead.

XV.

MADAME de Chantelle and Anna had planned, for the afternoon, a visit to a remotely situated acquaintance whom the introduction of the motor had transformed into a neighbour. Effie was to pay for her morning's holiday by an hour or two in the school-room, and Owen suggested that he and Darrow should betake themselves to a distant covert in the desultory quest for pheasants.

Darrow was not an ardent sportsman, but any pretext for physical activity would have been acceptable at the moment; and he was glad both to get away from the house and not to be left to himself.

When he came downstairs the motor was at the door, and Anna stood before the hall mirror, swathing her hat in veils. She turned at the sound of his step and smiled at him for a long full moment.

"I'd no idea you knew Miss Viner," she said, as he helped her into her long coat.

"It came back to me, luckily, that I'd seen her two or three times in London, several years ago. She was secretary, or something of the sort, in the background of a house where I used to dine."

He loathed the slighting indifference of the phrase, but he had uttered it deliberately, had been secretly practising it all through the interminable hour at the luncheon-table. Now that it was spoken, he shivered at its note of condescension. In such cases one was almost sure to overdo . . . But Anna seemed to notice nothing unusual.

"Was she really? You must tell me all about it—tell me exactly how she struck you. I'm so glad it turns out that you know her."

" 'Know' is rather exaggerated: we used to pass each other on the stairs."

Madame de Chantelle and Owen appeared together as he spoke, and Anna, gathering up her wraps, said: "You'll tell me about that, then. Try and remember everything you can."

As he tramped through the woods at his young host's side, Darrow felt the partial relief from thought produced by exercise and the obligation to talk. Little as he cared for shooting, he had the habit of concentration which makes it natural for a man to throw himself wholly into whatever business he has in hand, and there were moments of the afternoon when a sudden whirr in the undergrowth, a vivider gleam against the hazy browns and greys of the woods, was enough to fill the foreground of his attention. But all the while, behind these voluntarily emphasized sensations, his secret consciousness continued to revolve on a loud wheel of thought. For a time it seemed to be sweeping him through deep gulfs of darkness. His sensations were too swift and swarming to be disentangled. He had an almost physical sense of struggling for air, of battling helplessly with material obstructions, as though the russet covert through which he trudged were the heart of a maleficent jungle . . .

Snatches of his companion's talk drifted to him intermittently through the confusion of his thoughts. He caught eager self-revealing phrases, and understood that Owen was saying things about himself, perhaps hinting indirectly at the hopes for which Darrow had been prepared by Anna's confidences. He had already become aware that the lad liked him, and had meant to take the first opportunity of showing that he reciprocated the feeling. But the effort of fixing his attention on Owen's words was so great that it left no power for more than the briefest and most inexpressive replies.

Young Leath, it appeared, felt that he had reached a turning-point in his career, a height from which he could impartially survey his past progress and projected endeavour. At one time he had had musical and literary yearnings, visions of desultory artistic indulgence; but these had of late been superseded by the resolute determination to plunge into practical life.

"I don't want, you see," Darrow heard him explaining, "to drift into what my grandmother, poor dear, is trying to make of me: an adjunct of Givré. I don't want—hang it all!—to slip into collecting sensations as my father collected snuffboxes. I want Effie to have Givré—it's my grandmother's, you know, to do as she likes with; and I've understood lately that if it belonged to me it would gradually gobble me up. I want to get out of it, into a life that's big and ugly and struggling. If I can extract beauty out of *that*, so much the better: that'll prove my vocation. But I want to *make* beauty, not be drowned in the ready-made, like a bee in a pot of honey."

Darrow knew that he was being appealed to for corroboration of these views and for encouragement in the course to which they pointed. To his own ears his answers sounded now curt, now irrelevant: at one moment he seemed chillingly indifferent, at another he heard himself launching out on a flood of hazy discursiveness. He dared not look at Owen, for fear of detecting the lad's surprise at these senseless transitions. And through the confusion of his inward struggles and outward loquacity he heard the ceaseless trip-hammer beat of the question: "What in God's name shall I do?" . . .

To get back to the house before Anna's return seemed his most pressing necessity. He did not clearly know why: he simply felt that he ought to be there. At one moment it occurred to him that Miss Viner might want to speak to him alone—and again, in the same flash, that it would probably be the last thing she would want . . . At any rate, he felt he ought to try to speak to *her*; or at least be prepared to do so, if the chance should occur . . .

Finally, toward four, he told his companion that he had some letters on his mind and must get back to the house and despatch them before the ladies returned. He left Owen with the beater and walked on to the edge of the covert. At the park gates he struck obliquely through the trees, following a grass avenue at the end of which he had caught a glimpse of the roof of the chapel. A grey haze had blotted out the sun and the still air clung about him tepidly. At length the house-front raised before him its expanse of damp-silvered brick, and he was struck afresh by the high decorum of its calm lines and soberly massed surfaces. It made him feel, in the turbid coil of his fears and passions, like a muddy tramp forcing his way into some pure sequestered shrine . . .

By and bye, he knew, he should have to think the complex horror out, slowly, systematically, bit by bit; but for the moment it was whirling him about so fast that he could just clutch at its sharp spikes and be tossed off again. Only one definite immediate fact stuck in his quivering grasp. He must give the girl every chance—must hold himself passive till she had taken them . . .

In the court Effie ran up to him with her leaping terrier.

"I was coming out to meet you—you and Owen. Miss Viner was coming, too, and then she couldn't because she's got such a headache. I'm afraid I gave it to her because I did my division so disgracefully. It's too bad, isn't it? But won't you walk back with me? Nurse won't mind the least bit; she'd so much rather go in to tea."

Darrow excused himself laughingly, on the plea that he had letters to write, which was much worse than having a headache, and not infrequently resulted in one.

"Oh, then you can go and write them in Owen's study. That's where gentlemen always write their letters."

She flew on with her dog and Darrow pursued his way to the house. Effie's suggestion struck him as useful. He had pictured himself as vaguely drifting about the drawing-rooms, and had perceived the difficulty of Miss Viner's having to seek him there; but the study, a small room on the right of the hall, was in easy sight from the staircase, and so situated that there would be nothing marked in his being found there in talk with her.

He went in, leaving the door open, and sat down at the writing-table. The room was a friendly heterogeneous place, the one repository, in the well-ordered and amply-servanted house, of all its unclassified odds and ends: Effie's croquet-box and fishing rods, Owen's guns and golf-sticks and racquets, his step-mother's flower-baskets and gardening implements, even Madame de Chantelle's embroidery frame, and the back numbers of the Catholic Weekly. The early twilight had begun to fall, and presently a slanting ray across the desk showed Darrow that a servant was coming across the hall with a lamp. He pulled out a sheet of note-paper and began to write at random, while the man, entering, put the lamp at his elbow and vaguely "straightened" the heap of newspapers tossed on the divan. Then his steps died away and Darrow sat leaning his head on his locked hands.

Presently another step sounded on the stairs, wavered a moment and then moved past the threshold of the study. Darrow got up and walked into the hall, which was still unlighted. In the dimness he saw Sophy Viner standing by the hall door in her hat and jacket. She stopped at sight of him, her hand on the door-bolt, and they stood for a second without speaking.

"Have you seen Effie?" she suddenly asked. "She went out to meet you."

"She *did* meet me, just now, in the court. She's gone on to join her brother."

Darrow spoke as naturally as he could, but his voice sounded to his own ears like an amateur actor's in a "light" part.

Miss Viner, without answering, drew back the bolt. He watched her in silence as the door swung open; then he said: "She has her nurse with her. She won't be long."

She stood irresolute, and he added: "I was writing in there—won't you come and have a little talk? Every one's out."

The last words struck him as not well-chosen, but there was no time to choose. She paused a second longer and then crossed the threshold of the study. At luncheon she had sat with her back to the window, and beyond noting that she had grown a little thinner, and had less colour and vivacity, he had seen no change in her; but now, as the lamplight fell on her face, its whiteness startled him.

"Poor thing . . . poor thing . . . what in heaven's name can she suppose?" he wondered.

"Do sit down—I want to talk to you," he said and pushed a chair toward her.

She did not seem to see it, or, if she did, she deliberately chose another seat. He came back to his own chair and leaned his elbows on the blotter. She faced him from the farther side of the table.

"You promised to let me hear from you now and then," he began awkwardly, and with a sharp sense of his awkwardness.

A faint smile made her face more tragic. "Did I? There was nothing to tell. I've had no history—like the happy countries . . ."

He waited a moment before asking: "You *are* happy here?"—I *was*," she said with a faint emphasis.

"Why do you say 'was'? You're surely not thinking of going? There can't be kinder people anywhere." Darrow hardly knew what he was saying; but her answer came to him with deadly definiteness.

"I suppose it depends on you whether I go or stay."

"On me?" He stared at her across Owen's scattered papers. "Good God! What can you think of me, to say that?"

The mockery of the question flashed back at him from her wretched face. She stood up, wandered away, and leaned an instant in the darkening window-frame. From there she turned to fling back at him: "Don't imagine I'm the least bit sorry for anything!"

He steadied his elbows on the table and hid his face in his hands. It was harder, oh, damnably harder, than he had expected! Arguments, expedients, palliations, evasions, all seemed to be slipping away from him: he was left face to face with the mere graceless fact of his inferiority. He lifted his head to ask at random: "You've been here, then, ever since——?"

"Since June; yes. It turned out that the Farlows were hunting for me—all the while—for *this*."

She stood facing him, her back to the window, evidently impatient to be gone, yet with something still to say, or that she expected to hear him say. The sense of her expectancy benumbed him. What in heaven's name could he say to her that was not an offense or a mockery?

"Your idea of the theatre—you gave that up at once, then?"

"Oh, the theatre!" She gave a little laugh. "I couldn't wait for the theatre. I had to take the first thing that offered; I took this."

He pushed on haltingly: "I'm glad—extremely glad—you're happy here . . . I'd counted on your letting me know if there was anything I could do . . . The theatre, now—if you still regret it—if you're not contented here . . . I know people in that line in London—I'm certain I can manage it for you when I get back——"

She moved up to the table and leaned over it to ask, in a voice that was hardly above a whisper: "Then you *do* want me to leave? Is that it?"

He dropped his arms with a groan. "Good heavens! How can you think such things? At the time, you know, I begged you to let me do what I could, but you wouldn't hear of it . . . and ever since I've been wanting to be of use—to do something, anything, to help you . . ."

She heard him through, motionless, without a quiver of the clasped hands she rested on the edge of the table.

"If you want to help me, then—you can help me to stay here," she brought out with low-toned intensity.

Through the stillness of the pause which followed, the bray of a motor-horn sounded far down the drive. Instantly she turned, with a last white look at him, and fled from the room and up the stairs. He stood motionless, benumbed by the shock of her last words. She was *afraid*, then—afraid of him—sick with fear of him! The discovery beat him down to a lower depth . . .

The motor-horn sounded again, close at hand, and he turned and went up to his room. His letter-writing was a sufficient pretext for not immediately joining the party about the tea-table, and he wanted to be alone and try to put a little order into his tumultuous thinking.

Upstairs, the room held out the intimate welcome of its lamp and fire. Everything in it exhaled the same sense of peace and stability which, two evenings before, had lulled him to complacent meditation. His armchair again invited him from the hearth, but he was too agitated to sit still, and with sunk head and hands clasped behind his back he began to wander up and down the room.

His five minutes with Sophy Viner had flashed strange lights into the shadowy corners of his consciousness. The girl's absolute candour, her hard ardent honesty, was for the moment the vividest point in his thoughts. He wondered anew, as he had wondered before, at the way in which the harsh discipline of life had stripped her of false sentiment without laying the least touch on her pride. When they had parted, five months before, she had quietly but decidedly rejected all his offers of help, even to the suggestion of his trying to further her theatrical aims: she had made it clear that she wished their brief alliance to leave no trace on their lives save that of its own smiling memory. But now that they were unexpectedly confronted in a situation which seemed, to her terrified fancy, to put her at his mercy, her first impulse was to defend her right to the place she had won, and to learn as quickly as possible if he meant to dispute it. While he had pictured her as shrinking away from him in a tremor of self-effacement she had watched his movements, made sure of her opportunity, and come straight down to "have it out" with him. He was so struck by the frankness and energy of the proceeding that for a moment he lost sight of the view of his own character implied in it.

"Poor thing . . . poor thing!" he could only go on saying; and with the repetition of the words the picture of himself as she must see him pitiably took shape again.

He understood then, for the first time, how vague, in comparison with hers, had been his own vision of the part he had played in the brief episode of their relation. The incident had left in him a sense of exasperation and self-contempt, but that, as he now perceived, was chiefly, if not altogether, as it bore on his preconceived ideal of his attitude toward another woman. He had fallen below his own standard of sentimental loyalty, and if he thought of Sophy Viner it was mainly as the chance instrument of his lapse. These considerations were not agreeable to his pride, but they were forced on him by the example of her valiant common-sense. If he had cut a sorry figure in the business, he owed it to her not to close his eyes to the fact any longer . . .

But when he opened them, what did he see? The situation, detestable at best, would yet have been relatively simple if protecting Sophy Viner had been the only duty involved in it. The fact that that duty was paramount did not do away with the contingent obligations. It was Darrow's instinct, in difficult moments, to go straight to the bottom of the difficulty; but he had never before had to take so dark a dive as this, and for the minute he shivered on the brink . . . Well, his first duty, at any rate, was to the girl: he must let her see that he meant to fulfill it to the last jot, and then try to find out how to square the fulfillment with the other problems already in his path . . .

XVI.

IN the oak room he found Mrs. Leath, her mother-in-law and Effie. The group, as he came toward it down the long drawing-rooms, composed itself prettily about the tea-table. The lamps and the fire crossed their gleams on silver and porcelain, on the bright haze of Effie's hair and on the whiteness of Anna's forehead, as she leaned back in her chair behind the tea-urn.

She did not move at Darrow's approach, but lifted to him a deep gaze of peace and confidence. The look seemed to throw about him the spell of a divine security: he felt the joy of a convalescent suddenly waking to find the sunlight on his face.

Madame de Chantelle, across her knitting, discoursed of their afternoon's excursion, with occasional pauses induced by the hypnotic effect of the fresh air; and Effie, kneeling on the hearth, softly but insistently sought to implant in her terrier's mind some notion of the relation between a vertical attitude and sugar.

Darrow took a chair behind the little girl, so that he might look across at her mother. It was almost a necessity for him, at the moment, to let his eyes rest on Anna's face, and to meet, now and then, the proud shyness of her gaze.

Madame de Chantelle presently enquired what had become of Owen, and a moment later the window behind her opened, and her grandson, gun in hand, came in from the terrace. As he stood there in the lamp-light, with dead leaves and bits of bramble clinging to his mud-spattered clothes, the scent of the night about him and its chill on his pale bright face, he really had the look of a young faun strayed in from the forest.

Effie abandoned the terrier to fly to him. "Oh, Owen, where in the world have you been? I walked miles and miles with Nurse and couldn't find you, and we met Jean and he said he didn't know where you'd gone."

"Nobody knows where I go, or what I see when I get there—that's the beauty of it!" he laughed back at her. "But if you're good," he added, "I'll tell you about it one of these days."

"Oh, now, Owen, now! I don't really believe I'll ever be much better than I am now."

"Let Owen have his tea first," her mother suggested; but the young man, declining the offer, propped his gun against the wall, and, lighting a cigarette, began to pace up and down the room in a way that reminded Darrow of his own caged wanderings. Effie pursued him with her blandishments, and for a while he poured out to her a low-voiced stream of nonsense; then he sat down beside his step-mother and leaned over to help himself to tea.

"Where's Miss Viner?" he asked, as Effie climbed up on him. "Why isn't she here to chain up this ungovernable infant?"

"Poor Miss Viner has a headache. Effie says she went to her room as soon as lessons were over, and sent word that she wouldn't be down for tea."

"Ah," said Owen, abruptly setting down his cup. He stood up, lit another cigarette, and wandered away to the piano in the room beyond.

From the twilight where he sat a lonely music, borne on fantastic chords, floated to the group about the tea-table. Under its influence Madame de Chantelle's meditative pauses increased in length and frequency, and Effie stretched herself on the hearth, her drowsy head against the dog. Presently her nurse appeared, and Anna rose at the same time. "Stop a minute in my sitting-room on your way up," she paused to say to Darrow as she went.

A few hours earlier, her request would have brought him instantly to his feet. She had given him, on the day of his arrival, an inviting glimpse of the spacious book-lined room above stairs in which she had gathered together all the tokens of her personal tastes: the retreat in which, as one might fancy, Anna Leath had hidden the restless ghost of Anna Summers; and the thought of a talk with her there had been in his mind ever since. But now he sat motionless, as if spellbound by the play of Madame de Chantelle's needles and the pulsations of Owen's fitful music.

"She will want to ask me about the girl," he repeated to himself, with a fresh sense of the insidious taint that embittered all his thoughts; the hand of the slender-columned clock on the mantel-piece had spanned a half-hour before shame at his own indecision finally drew him to his feet.

From her writing-table, where she sat over a pile of letters, Anna lifted her happy smile. The impulse to press his lips to it made him come close and draw her upward. She threw her head back, as if surprised at the abruptness of the gesture; then her face leaned to his with the slow droop of a flower. He felt again the sweep of the secret tides, and all his fears went down in them.

She sat down in the sofa-corner by the fire and he

drew an armchair close to her. His gaze roamed peacefully about the quiet room.

"It's just like you—it *is* you," he said, as his eyes came back to her.

"It's a good place to be alone in—I don't think I've ever before cared to talk with any one here."

"Let's be quiet, then: it's the best way of talking."

"Yes; but we must save it up till later. There are things I want to say to you now."

He leaned back in his chair. "Say them, then, and I'll listen."

"Oh, no. I want you to tell me about Miss Viner."

"About Miss Viner?" He summoned up a look of faint interrogation.

He thought she seemed surprised at his surprise. "It's important, naturally," she explained, "that I should find out all I can about her before I leave."

"Important on Effie's account?"

"On Effie's account—of course."

"Of course . . . But you've every reason to be satisfied, haven't you?"

"Every apparent reason. We all like her. Effie's very fond of her, and she seems to have a delightful influence on the child. But we know so little, after all—about her antecedents, I mean, and her past history. That's why I want you to try and recall everything you heard about her when you used to see her in London."

"Oh, on that score I'm afraid I sha'n't be of much use. As I told you, she was a mere shadow in the background of the house I saw her in—and that was four or five years ago . . ."

"When she was with a Mrs. Murrett?"

"Yes; an appalling woman who runs a roaring dinner-factory that used now and then to catch me in its wheels. I escaped from them long ago; but in my time there used to be half a dozen fagged 'hands' to tend the machine, and Miss Viner was one of them. I'm glad she's out of it, poor girl!"

"Then you never really saw anything of her there?"

"I never had the chance. Mrs. Murrett discouraged any competition on the part of her subordinates."

"Especially such pretty ones, I suppose?" Darrow made no comment, and she continued: "And Mrs. Murrett's own opinion—if she'd offered you one—probably wouldn't have been of much value?"

"Only in so far as her disapproval would, on general principles, have been a good mark for Miss Viner. But surely," he went on after a pause, "you could have found out about her from the people through whom you first heard of her?"

Anna smiled. "Oh, we heard of her through Adelaide Painter—;" and in reply to his glance of interrogation she explained that the lady in question was a spinster of South Braintree, Massachusetts, who, having come to Paris some thirty years earlier, to nurse a brother through an illness, had ever since protestingly and provisionally camped there in a state of contemptuous protestation oddly manifested by her never taking the slip-covers off her drawing-room chairs. Her long residence on Gallic soil had not mitigated her hostility toward the creed and customs of the race, but though she always referred to the Catholic Church as the Scarlet Woman and took the darkest views of French private life, Madame de Chantelle placed great reliance on her judgment and experience, and in every domestic crisis the irreducible Adelaide was immediately summoned to Givré.

"It's all the odder because my mother-in-law, since her second marriage, has lived so much in the country that she's practically lost sight of all her other American friends. Besides which, you can see how completely she has identified herself with Monsieur de Chantelle's nationality and adopted French habits and prejudices. Yet when anything goes wrong she always sends for Adelaide Painter, who's more American than the Stars and Stripes, and might have left South Braintree yesterday, if she hadn't, rather, brought it over with her in her trunk."

Darrow laughed. "Well, then, if South Braintree vouches for Miss Viner——"

"Oh, but only indirectly. When we had that odious adventure with Mademoiselle Grumeau, who'd been so highly recommended by Monsieur de Chantelle's aunt, the Chanoinesse, Adelaide was of course sent for, and she said at once: 'I'm not the least bit surprised. I've always told you that what you wanted for Effie was a sweet American girl, and not one of these nasty foreigners.' Unluckily she couldn't, at the moment, put her hand on a sweet American; but she presently heard of Miss Viner through the Farlows, an excellent couple who live in the Quartier Latin and write about French life for the American papers. I was only too thankful to find anyone who was vouched for by decent people; and so far I've had no cause to regret my choice. But I know, after all, very little about Miss Viner; and there are all kinds of reasons why I want, as soon as possible, to find out more—to find out all I can."

"Since you've got to leave Effie I understand your

feeling in that way. But is there, in such a case, any recommendation worth half as much as your own direct experience?"

"No; and it's been so favourable that I was ready to accept it as conclusive. Only, naturally, when I found you'd known her in London I was in hopes you'd give me some more specific reasons for liking her as much as I do."

"I'm afraid I can give you nothing more specific than my general vague impression that she seems very plucky and extremely nice."

"You don't, at any rate, know anything specific to the contrary?"

"To the contrary? How should I? I'm not conscious of ever having heard any one say two words about her. I only infer that she must have pluck and character to have stuck it out so long at Mrs. Murrett's."

"Yes, poor thing! She has pluck, certainly; and pride, too; which must have made it all the harder." Anna rose to her feet. "You don't know how glad I am that your impression's on the whole so good. I particularly wanted you to like her."

He drew her to him with a smile. "On that condition I'm prepared to love even Adelaide Painter."

"I almost hope you won't have the chance to—poor Adelaide! Her appearance here always coincides with a catastrophe."

"Oh, then I must manage to meet her elsewhere." He held Anna closer, saying to himself, as he smoothed back the hair from her forehead: "What does anything matter but just *this*?—Must I go now?" he added aloud.

She answered absently: "It must be time to dress";

then she drew back a little and laid her hands on his shoulders. "My love—oh, my dear love!" she said.

It came to him that they were the first words of endearment he had heard her speak, and their rareness gave them a magic quality of reassurance, as though no danger could strike through such a shield.

A knock on the door made them draw apart. Anna lifted her hand to her hair and Darrow stooped to examine a photograph of Effie on the writing-table.

"Come in!" Anna said.

The door opened and Sophy Viner entered. Seeing Darrow, she drew back.

"Do come in, Miss Viner," Anna repeated, looking at her kindly.

The girl, a quick red in her cheeks, still hesitated on the threshold.

"I'm so sorry; but Effie has mislaid her Latin grammar, and I thought she might have left it here. I need it to prepare for tomorrow's lesson."

"Is this it?" Darrow asked, picking up a book from the table.

"Oh, thank you!"

He held it out to her and she took it and moved to the door.

"Wait a minute, please, Miss Viner," Anna said; and as the girl turned back, she went on with her quiet smile: "Effie told us you'd gone to your room with a headache. You mustn't sit up over tomorrow's lessons if you don't feel well."

Sophy's blush deepened. "But you see I have to. Latin's one of my weak points, and there's generally only one page of this book between me and Effie." She threw the words off with a half-ironic smile. "Do excuse my disturbing you," she added.

"You didn't disturb me," Anna answered. Darrow perceived that she was looking intently at the girl, as though struck by something tense and tremulous in her face, her voice, her whole mien and attitude. "You *do* look tired. You'd much better go straight to bed. Effie won't be sorry to skip her Latin."

"Thank you—but I'm really all right," murmured Sophy Viner. Her glance, making a swift circuit of the room, dwelt for an appreciable instant on the intimate propinquity of armchair and sofa-corner; then she turned back to the door.

Book Three

XVII.

At dinner that evening Madame de Chantelle's slender monologue was thrown out over gulfs of silence. Owen was still in the same state of moody abstraction as when Darrow had left him at the piano; and even Anna's face, to her friend's vigilant eye, revealed not, perhaps, a personal preoccupation, but a vague sense of impending disturbance.

She smiled, she bore a part in the talk, her eyes dwelt on Darrow's with their usual deep reliance; but beneath the surface of her serenity his tense perceptions detected a hidden stir.

He was sufficiently self-possessed to tell himself that it was doubtless due to causes with which he was not directly concerned. He knew the question of Owen's marriage was soon to be raised, and the abrupt alteration in the young man's mood made it seem probable that he was himself the centre of the atmospheric disturbance. For a moment it occurred to Darrow that Anna might have employed her afternoon in preparing Madame de Chantelle for her grandson's impending announcement; but a glance at the elder lady's unclouded brow showed that he must seek elsewhere the clue to Owen's taciturnity and his step-mother's concern. Possibly Anna had found reason to change her own attitude in the matter, and had made the change known to Owen. But this, again, was negatived by the fact that, during the afternoon's shooting, young Leath had been in a mood of almost extravagant expansiveness, and that, from the moment of his late return to the house till just before dinner, there had been, to Darrow's certain knowledge, no possibility of a private talk between himself and his step-mother.

This obscured, if it narrowed, the field of conjecture; and Darrow's gropings threw him back on the conclusion that he was probably reading too much significance into the moods of a lad he hardly knew, and who had been described to him as subject to sudden changes of humour. As to Anna's fancied perturbation, it might simply be due to the fact that she had decided to plead Owen's cause the next day, and had perhaps already had a glimpse of the difficulties awaiting her. But Darrow knew that he was too deep in his own perplexities to judge the mental state of those about him. It might be, after all, that the variations he felt in the currents of communication were caused by his own inward tremor.

Such, at any rate, was the conclusion he had reached when, shortly after the two ladies left the drawing-room, he bade Owen good-night and went up to his room. Ever since the rapid self-colloquy which had followed on his first sight of Sophy Viner, he had known there were other questions to be faced behind the one immediately confronting him. On the score of that one, at least, his mind, if not easy, was relieved. He had done what was possible to reassure the girl, and she had apparently recognized the sincerity of his intention. He had patched up as decent a conclusion as he could to an incident that should obviously have had no sequel; but he had known all along that with the securing of Miss Viner's peace of mind only a part of his obligation was discharged, and that with that part his remaining duty was in conflict. It had been his first business to convince the girl that their secret was safe with him; but it was far from easy to square this with the equally urgent obligation of safe-guarding Anna's responsibility toward her child. Darrow was not much afraid of accidental disclosures. Both he and Sophy Viner had too much at stake not to be on their guard. The fear that beset him was of another kind, and had a profounder source. He wanted to do all he could for the girl, but the fact of having had to urge Anna to confide Effie to her was peculiarly repugnant to him. His own ideas about Sophy Viner were too mixed and indeterminate for him not to feel the risk of such an experiment; yet he found himself in the intolerable position of appearing to press it on the woman he desired above all others to protect . . .

Till late in the night his thoughts revolved in a turmoil of indecision. His pride was humbled by the discrepancy between what Sophy Viner had been to him and what he had thought of her. This discrepancy, which at the time had seemed to simplify the incident, now turned out to be its most galling complication. The bare truth, indeed, was that he had hardly thought of her at all, either at the time or since, and that he was ashamed to base his judgment of her on his meagre memory of their adventure.

The essential cheapness of the whole affair—as far as his share in it was concerned—came home to him with humiliating distinctness. He would have liked to be able to feel that, at the time at least, he had staked something more on it, and had somehow, in the sequel, had a more palpable loss to show. But the plain fact was that he hadn't spent a penny on it; which was no doubt the reason of the prodigious score it had since been rolling up. At any rate, beat about the case as he would, it was clear that he owed it to Anna—and incidentally to his own peace of mind—to find some way of securing Sophy Viner's future without leaving her installed at Givré when he and his wife should depart for their new post.

The night brought no aid to the solving of this problem; but it gave him, at any rate, the clear conviction that no time was to be lost. His first step must be to obtain from Miss Viner the chance of another and calmer talk; and he resolved to seek it at the earliest hour.

He had gathered that Effie's lessons were preceded by an early scamper in the park, and conjecturing that her governess might be with her he betook himself the next morning to the terrace, whence he wandered on to the gardens and the walks beyond.

The atmosphere was still and pale. The muffled sunlight gleamed like gold tissue through grey gauze, and the beech alleys tapered away to a blue haze blent of sky and forest. It was one of those elusive days when the familiar forms of things seem about to dissolve in a prismatic shimmer.

The stillness was presently broken by joyful barks, and Darrow, tracking the sound, overtook Effie flying down one of the long alleys at the head of her pack. Beyond her he saw Miss Viner seated near the stone-rimmed basin beside which he and Anna had paused on their first walk to the river.

The girl, coming forward at his approach, returned his greeting almost gaily. His first glance showed him that she had regained her composure, and the change in her appearance gave him the measure of her fears. For the first time he saw in her again the sidelong grace that had charmed his eyes in Paris; but he saw it now as in a painted picture.

"Shall we sit down a minute?" he asked, as Effie trotted off.

The girl looked away from him. "I'm afraid there's not much time; we must be back at lessons at half-past nine."

"But it's barely ten minutes past. Let's at least walk a little way toward the river."

She glanced down the long walk ahead of them and then back in the direction of the house. "If you like," she said in a low voice, with one of her quick fluctuations of colour; but instead of taking the way he proposed she turned toward a narrow path which branched off obliquely through the trees.

Darrow was struck, and vaguely troubled, by the change in her look and tone. There was in them an undefinable appeal, whether for help or forbearance he could not tell. Then it occurred to him that there might have been something misleading in his so pointedly seeking her, and he felt a momentary constraint. To ease it he made an abrupt dash at the truth.

"I came out to look for you because our talk of yesterday was so unsatisfactory. I want to hear more about you—about your plans and prospects. I've been wondering ever since why you've so completely given up the theatre."

Her face instantly sharpened to distrust. "I had to live," she said in an off-hand tone.

"I understand perfectly that you should like it here—for a time." His glance strayed down the gold-roofed windings ahead of them. "It's delightful: you couldn't be better placed. Only I wonder a little at your having so completely given up any idea of a different future."

She waited for a moment before answering: "I suppose I'm less restless than I used to be."

"It's certainly natural that you should be less restless here than at Mrs. Murrett's; yet somehow I don't seem to see you permanently given up to forming the young."

"What—exactly—*do* you seem to see me permanently given up to? You know you warned me rather emphatically against the theatre." She threw off the statement without impatience, as though they were discussing together the fate of a third person in whom both were benevolently interested.

Darrow considered his reply. "If I did, it was because you so emphatically refused to let me help you to a start."

She stopped short and faced him. "And you think I may let you now?"

Darrow felt the blood in his cheek. He could not understand her attitude—if indeed she had consciously taken one, and her changes of tone did not merely reflect the involuntary alternations of her mood. It humbled him to perceive once more how little he had to guide him in his judgment of her. He said to himself: "If I'd ever cared a straw for her I should know how to avoid hurting her now"—and his insensibility struck him as no better than a vulgar obtuseness. But he had a fixed purpose ahead and could only push on to it.

"I hope, at any rate, you'll listen to my reasons. There's been time, on both sides, to think them over since——" He caught himself back and hung helpless on the "since": whatever words he chose, he seemed to stumble among reminders of their past.

She walked on beside him, her eyes on the ground. "Then I'm to understand—definitely—that you *do* renew your offer?" she asked.

"With all my heart! If you'll only let me——"

She raised a hand, as though to check him. "It's extremely friendly of you—I *do* believe you mean it as a friend—but I don't quite understand why, finding me, as you say, so well placed here, you should show more anxiety about my future than at a time when I was actually, and rather desperately, adrift."

"Oh, no, not more!"

"If you show any at all, it must, at any rate, be for different reasons.—In fact, it can only be," she went on, with one of her disconcerting flashes of astuteness, "for one of two reasons; either because you feel you ought to help me, or because, for some reason, you think you owe it to Mrs. Leath to let her know what you know of me."

Darrow stood still in the path. Behind him he heard Effie's call, and at the child's voice he saw Sophy turn her head with the alertness of one who is obscurely on the watch. The look was so fugitive that he could not have said wherein it differed from her normal professional air of having her pupil on her mind.

Effie sprang past them, and Darrow took up the girl's challenge.

"What you suggest about Mrs. Leath is hardly worth answering. As to my reasons for wanting to help you, a good deal depends on the words one uses to define rather indefinite things. It's true enough that I want to help you; but the wish isn't due to . . . to any past kindness on your part, but simply to my own interest in you. Why not put it that our friendship gives me the right to intervene for what I believe to be your benefit?"

She took a few hesitating steps and then paused again. Darrow noticed that she had grown pale and that there were rings of shade about her eyes.

"You've known Mrs. Leath a long time?" she asked him suddenly.

He paused with a sense of approaching peril. "A long time—yes."

"She told me you were friends—great friends."

"Yes," he admitted, "we're great friends."

"Then you might naturally feel yourself justified in telling her that you don't think I'm the right person for Effie." He uttered a sound of protest, but she disregarded it. "I don't say you'd *like* to do it. You wouldn't: you'd hate it. And the natural alternative would be to try to persuade me that I'd be better off somewhere else than here. But supposing that failed, and you saw I was determined to stay? *Then* you might think it your duty to tell Mrs. Leath."

She laid the case before him with a cold lucidity. "I should, in your place, I believe," she ended with a little laugh.

"I shouldn't feel justified in telling her, behind your back, if I thought you unsuited for the place; but I should certainly feel justified," he rejoined after a pause, "in telling *you* if I thought the place unsuited to you."

"And that's what you're trying to tell me now?"

"Yes; but not for the reasons you imagine."

"What, then, are your reasons, if you please?"

"I've already implied them in advising you not to give up all idea of the theatre. You're too various, too gifted, too personal, to tie yourself down, at your age, to the dismal drudgery of teaching."

"And is *that* what you've told Mrs. Leath?"

She rushed the question out at him as if she expected to trip him up over it. He was moved by the simplicity of the stratagem.

"I've told her exactly nothing," he replied.

"And what—exactly—do you mean by 'nothing'? You and she were talking about me when I came into her sitting-room yesterday."

Darrow felt his blood rise at the thrust.

"I've told her, simply, that I'd seen you once or twice at Mrs. Murrett's."

"And not that you've ever seen me since?"

"And not that I've ever seen you since . . ."

"And she believes you—she completely believes you?"

He uttered a protesting exclamation, and his flush reflected itself in the girl's cheek.

"Oh, I beg your pardon! I didn't mean to ask you that." She halted, and again cast a rapid glance behind and ahead of her. Then she held out her hand. "Well, then, thank you—and let me relieve your fears. I sha'n't be Effie's governess much longer."

At the announcement, Darrow tried to merge his look of relief into the expression of friendly interest with which he grasped her hand. "You really do agree with me, then? And you'll give me a chance to talk things over with you?"

She shook her head with a faint smile. "I'm not thinking of the stage. I've had another offer: that's all."

The relief was hardly less great. After all, his personal responsibility ceased with her departure from Givré.

"You'll tell me about that, then—won't you?"

Her smile flickered up. "Oh, you'll hear about it soon . . . I must catch Effie now and drag her back to the blackboard."

She walked on for a few yards, and then paused again and confronted him. "I've been odious to you—and not quite honest," she broke out suddenly.

"Not quite honest?" he repeated, caught in a fresh wave of wonder.

"I mean, in seeming not to trust you. It's come over me again as we talked that, at heart, I've always *known* I could . . ."

Her colour rose in a bright wave, and her eyes clung to his for a swift instant of reminder and appeal. For the same space of time the past surged up in him confusedly; then a veil dropped between them.

"Here's Effie now!" she exclaimed.

He turned and saw the little girl trotting back to them, her hand in Owen Leath's.

Even through the stir of his subsiding excitement Darrow was at once aware of the change effected by the young man's approach. For a moment Sophy Viner's cheeks burned redder; then they faded to the paleness of white petals. She lost, however, nothing of the bright bravery which it was her way to turn on the unexpected. Perhaps no one less familiar with her face than Darrow would have discerned the tension of the smile she transferred from himself to Owen Leath, or have remarked that her eyes had hardened from misty grey to a shining darkness. But her observer was less struck by this than by the corresponding change in Owen Leath. The latter, when he came in sight, had been laughing and talking unconcernedly with Effie; but as his eye fell on Miss Viner his expression altered as suddenly as hers.

The change, for Darrow, was less definable; but, perhaps for that reason, it struck him as more sharply significant. Only—just what did it signify? Owen, like Sophy Viner, had the kind of face which seems less the stage on which emotions move than the very stuff they work in. In moments of excitement his odd irregular features seemed to grow fluid, to unmake and remake themselves like the shadows of clouds on a stream. Darrow, through the rapid flight of the shadows, could not seize on any specific indication of feeling: he merely perceived that the young man was unaccountably surprised at finding him with Miss Viner, and that the extent of his surprise might cover all manner of implications.

Darrow's first idea was that Owen, if he suspected that the conversation was not the result of an accidental encounter, might wonder at his step-mother's suitor being engaged, at such an hour, in private talk with her little girl's governess. The thought was so disturbing that, as the three turned back to the house, he was on the point of saying to Owen: "I came out to look for your mother." But, in the contingency he feared, even so simple a phrase might seem like an awkward attempt at explanation; and he walked on in silence at Miss Viner's side. Presently he was struck by the fact that Owen Leath and the girl were silent also; and this gave a new turn to his thoughts. Silence may be as variously shaded as speech; and that which enfolded

Darrow and his two companions seemed to his watchful perceptions to be quivering with cross-threads of communication. At first he was aware only of those that centred in his own troubled consciousness; then it occurred to him that an equal activity of intercourse was going on outside of it. Something was in fact passing mutely and rapidly between young Leath and Sophy Viner; but what it was, and whither it tended, Darrow, when they reached the house, was but just beginning to divine . . .

XVIII.

ANNA Leath, from the terrace, watched the return of the little group.

She looked down on them, as they advanced across the garden, from the serene height of her unassailable happiness. There they were, coming toward her in the mild morning light, her child, her step-son, her promised husband: the three beings who filled her life. She smiled a little at the happy picture they presented, Effie's gambols encircling it in a moving frame within which the two men came slowly forward in the silence of friendly understanding. It seemed part of the deep intimacy of the scene that they should not be talking to each other, and it did not till afterward strike her as odd that neither of them apparently felt it necessary to address a word to Sophy Viner.

Anna herself, at the moment, was floating in the

mid-current of felicity, on a tide so bright and buoyant that she seemed to be one with its warm waves. The first rush of bliss had stunned and dazzled her; but now that, each morning, she woke to the calm certainty of its recurrence, she was growing used to the sense of security it gave.

"I feel as if I could trust my happiness to carry me; as if it had grown out of me like wings." So she phrased it to Darrow, as, later in the morning, they paced the garden-paths together. His answering look gave her the same assurance of safety. The evening before he had seemed preoccupied, and the shadow of his mood had faintly encroached on the great golden orb of their blessedness; but now it was uneclipsed again, and hung above them high and bright as the sun at noon.

Upstairs in her sitting-room, that afternoon, she was thinking of these things. The morning mists had turned to rain, compelling the postponement of an excursion in which the whole party were to have joined. Effie, with her governess, had been despatched in the motor to do some shopping at Francheuil; and Anna had promised Darrow to join him, later in the afternoon, for a quick walk in the rain.

He had gone to his room after luncheon to get some belated letters off his conscience; and when he had left her she had continued to sit in the same place, her hands crossed on her knees, her head slightly bent, in an attitude of brooding retrospection. As she looked back at her past life, it seemed to her to have consisted of one ceaseless effort to pack into each hour enough to fill out its slack folds; but now each moment was like a miser's bag stretched to bursting with pure gold.

She was roused by the sound of Owen's step in the gallery outside her room. It paused at her door and in answer to his knock she called out "Come in!"

As the door closed behind him she was struck by his look of pale excitement, and an impulse of compunction made her say: "You've come to ask me why I haven't spoken to your grandmother!"

He sent about him a glance vaguely reminding her of the strange look with which Sophy Viner had swept the room the night before; then his brilliant eyes came back to her.

"I've spoken to her myself," he said.

Anna started up, incredulous.

"You've spoken to her? When?"

"Just now. I left her to come here."

Anna's first feeling was one of annoyance. There was really something comically incongruous in this boyish surrender to impulse on the part of a young man so eager to assume the responsibilities of life. She looked at him with a faintly veiled amusement.

"You asked me to help you and I promised you I would. It was hardly worth while to work out such an elaborate plan of action if you intended to take the matter out of my hands without telling me."

"Oh, don't take that tone with me!" he broke out, almost angrily.

"That tone? What tone?" She stared at his quivering face. "I might," she pursued, still half-laughing, "more properly make that request of *you*!"

Owen reddened and his vehemence suddenly subsided.

"I meant that I *had* to speak—that's all. You don't give me a chance to explain . . ."

She looked at him gently, wondering a little at her own impatience.

"Owen! Don't I always want to give you every chance? It's because I *do* that I wanted to talk to your grandmother first—that I was waiting and watching for the right moment . . ."

"The right moment? So was I. That's why I've spoken." His voice rose again and took the sharp edge it had in moments of high pressure.

His step-mother turned away and seated herself in her sofa-corner. "Oh, my dear, it's not a privilege to quarrel over! You've taken a load off my shoulders. Sit down and tell me all about it."

He stood before her, irresolute. "I can't sit down," he said.

"Walk about, then. Only tell me: I'm impatient."

His immediate response was to throw himself into the armchair at her side, where he lounged for a moment without speaking, his legs stretched out, his arms locked behind his thrown-back head. Anna, her eyes on his face, waited quietly for him to speak.

"Well—of course it was just what one expected."

"She takes it so badly, you mean?"

"All the heavy batteries were brought up: my father, Givré, Monsieur de Chantelle, the throne and the altar. Even my poor mother was dragged out of oblivion and armed with imaginary protests."

Anna sighed out her sympathy. "Well—you were prepared for all that?"

"I thought I was, till I began to hear her say it. Then it sounded so incredibly silly that I told her so."

"Oh, Owen—Owen!"

"Yes: I know. I was a fool; but I couldn't help it."

"And you've mortally offended her, I suppose? That's exactly what I wanted to prevent." She laid a hand on his shoulder. "You tiresome boy, not to wait and let me speak for you!"

He moved slightly away, so that her hand slipped from its place. "You don't understand," he said, frowning.

"I don't see how I can, till you explain. If you thought the time had come to tell your grandmother, why not have asked me to do it? I had my reasons for waiting; but if you'd told me to speak I should have done so, naturally."

He evaded her appeal by a sudden turn. "What *were* your reasons for waiting?"

Anna did not immediately answer. Her step-son's eyes were on her face, and under his gaze she felt a faint disquietude.

"I was feeling my way . . . I wanted to be absolutely sure . . ."

"Absolutely sure of what?"

She delayed again for a just perceptible instant. "Why, simply of *our* side of the case."

"But you told me you were, the other day, when we talked it over before they came back from Ouchy."

"Oh, my dear—if you think that, in such a complicated matter, every day, every hour, doesn't more or less modify one's surest sureness!"

"That's just what I'm driving at. I want to know what has modified yours."

She made a slight gesture of impatience. "What does it matter, now the thing's done? I don't know that I could give any clear reason . . ."

He got to his feet and stood looking down on her with a tormented brow. "But it's absolutely necessary that you should."

At his tone her impatience flared up. "It's not necessary that I should give you any explanation whatever, since you've taken the matter out of my hands. All I can say is that I was trying to help you: that no other thought ever entered my mind." She paused a moment and then added: "If you doubted it, you were right to do what you've done."

"Oh, I never doubted *you*!" he retorted, with a fugitive stress on the pronoun. His face had cleared to its old look of trust. "Don't be offended if I've seemed to," he went on. "I can't quite explain myself, either . . . it's all a kind of tangle, isn't it? That's why I thought I'd better speak at once; or rather why I didn't think at all, but just suddenly blurted the thing out——"

Anna gave him back his look of conciliation. "Well, the how and why don't much matter now. The point is how to deal with your grandmother. You've not told me what she means to do."

"Oh, she means to send for Adelaide Painter."

The name drew a faint note of mirth from him and relaxed both their faces to a smile.

"Perhaps," Anna added, "it's really the best thing for us all."

Owen shrugged his shoulders. "It's too preposterous and humiliating. Dragging that woman into our secrets——!"

"This could hardly be a secret much longer."

He had moved to the hearth, where he stood pushing about the small ornaments on the mantel-shelf; but at her answer he turned back to her.

"You haven't, of course, spoken of it to any one?"

"No; but I intend to now."

She paused for his reply, and as it did not come she

continued: "If Adelaide Painter's to be told there's no possible reason why I shouldn't tell Mr. Darrow."

Owen abruptly set down the little statuette between his fingers. "None whatever: I want every one to know."

She smiled a little at his over-emphasis, and was about to meet it with a word of banter when he continued, facing her: "You haven't, as yet, said a word to him?"

"I've told him nothing, except what the discussion of our own plans—his and mine—obliged me to: that you were thinking of marrying, and that I wasn't willing to leave France till I'd done what I could to see you through."

At her first words the colour had rushed to his forehead; but as she continued she saw his face compose itself and his blood subside.

"You're a brick, my dear!" he exclaimed.

"You had my word, you know."

"Yes; yes—I know." His face had clouded again. "And that's all—positively all—you've ever said to him?"

"Positively all. But why do you ask?"

He had a moment's embarrassed hesitation. "It was understood, wasn't it, that my grandmother was to be the first to know?"

"Well—and so she has been, hasn't she, since you've told her?"

He turned back to his restless shifting of the knick-knacks.

"And you're sure that nothing you've said to Darrow could possibly have given him a hint——?"

"Nothing I've said to him—certainly."

He swung about on her. "Why do you put it in that way?"

"In what way?"

"Why—as if you thought some one else might have spoken . . ."

"Some one else? Who else?" She rose to her feet. "What on earth, my dear boy, can you be driving at?"

"I'm trying to find out whether you think he knows anything definite."

"Why should I think so? Do *you*?"

"I don't know. I want to find out."

She laughed at his obstinate insistence. "To test my veracity, I suppose?" At the sound of a step in the gallery she added: "Here he is—you can ask him yourself."

She met Darrow's knock with an invitation to enter, and he came into the room and paused between herself and Owen. She was struck, as he stood there, by the contrast between his happy careless good-looks and her step-son's frowning agitation.

Darrow met her eyes with a smile. "Am I too soon? Or is our walk given up?"

"No; I was just going to get ready." She continued to linger between the two, looking slowly from one to the other. "But there's something we want to tell you first: Owen is engaged to Miss Viner."

The sense of an indefinable interrogation in Owen's mind made her, as she spoke, fix her eyes steadily on Darrow.

He had paused just opposite the window, so that, even in the rainy afternoon light, his face was clearly open to her scrutiny. For a second, immense surprise was alone visible on it: so visible that she half turned to her step-son, with a faint smile for his refuted suspicions. Why, she wondered, should Owen have thought that Darrow had already guessed his secret, and what, after all, could be so disturbing to him in this not improbable contingency? At any rate, his doubt must have been dispelled: there was nothing feigned about Darrow's astonishment. When her eyes turned back to him he was already crossing to Owen with outstretched hand, and she had, through an unaccountable faint flutter of misgiving, a mere confused sense of their exchanging the customary phrases. Her next perception was of Owen's tranquillized look, and of his smiling return of Darrow's congratulatory grasp. She had the eerie feeling of having been overswept by a shadow which there had been no cloud to cast . . .

A moment later Owen had left the room and she and Darrow were alone. He had turned away to the window and stood staring out into the down-pour.

"You're surprised at Owen's news?" she asked.

"Yes: I am surprised," he answered.

"You hadn't thought of its being Miss Viner?"

"Why should I have thought of Miss Viner?"

"You see now why I wanted so much to find out what you knew about her." He made no comment, and she pursued: "Now that you *do* know it's she, if there's anything——"

He moved back into the room and went up to her. His face was serious, with a slight shade of annoyance. "What on earth should there be? As I told you, I've never in my life heard any one say two words about Miss Viner."

Anna made no answer and they continued to face each other without moving. For the moment she had ceased to think about Sophy Viner and Owen: the only thought in her mind was that Darrow was alone with her, close to her, and that, for the first time, their hands and lips had not met.

He glanced back doubtfully at the window. "It's pouring. Perhaps you'd rather not go out?"

She hesitated, as if waiting for him to urge her. "I suppose I'd better not. I ought to go at once to my mother-in-law—Owen's just been telling her," she said.

"Ah." Darrow hazarded a smile. "That accounts for my having, on my way up, heard some one telephoning for Miss Painter!"

At the allusion they laughed together, vaguely, and Anna moved toward the door. He held it open for her and followed her out.

XIX.

He left her at the door of Madame de Chantelle's sitting-room, and plunged out alone into the rain. The wind flung about the stripped tree-tops of the avenue and dashed the stinging streams into his face. He walked to the gate and then turned into the high-road and strode along in the open, buffeted by slanting gusts. The evenly ridged fields were a blurred waste of mud, and the russet coverts which he and Owen had shot through the day before shivered desolately against a driving sky.

Darrow walked on and on, indifferent to the direction he was taking. His thoughts were tossing like the tree-tops. Anna's announcement had not come to him as a complete surprise: that morning, as he strolled back to the house with Owen Leath and Miss Viner, he had had a momentary intuition of the truth. But it had been no more than an intuition, the merest faint cloud-puff of surmise; and now it was an attested fact, darkening over the whole sky.

In respect of his own attitude, he saw at once that the discovery made no appreciable change. If he had been bound to silence before, he was no less bound to it now; the only difference lay in the fact that what he had just learned had rendered his bondage more intolerable. Hitherto he had felt for Sophy Viner's defenseless state a sympathy profoundly tinged with compunction. But now he was half-conscious of an obscure indignation against her. Superior as he had fancied himself to ready-made judgments, he was aware of cherishing the common doubt as to the disinterestedness of the woman who tries to rise above her past. No wonder she had been sick with fear on meeting him! It was in his power to do her more harm than he had dreamed . . .

Assuredly he did not want to harm her; but he did desperately want to prevent her marrying Owen Leath. He tried to get away from the feeling, to isolate and exteriorize it sufficiently to see what motives it was made of; but it remained a mere blind motion of his blood, the instinctive recoil from the thing that no amount of arguing can make "straight." His tramp, prolonged as it was, carried him no nearer to enlightenment; and after trudging through two or three sallow mudstained villages he turned about and wearily made his way back to Givré. As he walked up the black avenue, making for the lights that twinkled through its pitching branches, he had a sudden realisation of his utter helplessness. He might think and combine as he would; but there was nothing, absolutely nothing, that he could do . . .

He dropped his wet coat in the vestibule and began to mount the stairs to his room. But on the landing he was overtaken by a sober-faced maid who, in tones discreetly lowered, begged him to be so kind as to step, for a moment, into the Marquise's sitting-room. Somewhat disconcerted by the summons, he followed its bearer to the door at which, a couple of hours earlier, he had taken leave of Mrs. Leath. It opened to admit him to a large lamp-lit room which he immediately perceived to be empty; and the fact gave him time to note, even through his disturbance of mind, the interesting degree to which Madame de Chantelle's apartment "dated" and completed her. Its looped and corded curtains, its purple satin upholstery, the Sèvres jardinières, the rose-wood fire-screen, the little velvet tables edged with lace and crowded with silver knick-knacks and simpering miniatures, reconstituted an almost perfect setting for the blonde beauty of the 'sixties. Darrow wondered that Fraser Leath's filial respect should have prevailed over his æsthetic scruples to the extent of permitting such an anachronism among the eighteenth century graces of Givré; but a moment's reflection made it clear that, to its late owner, the attitude would have seemed exactly in the traditions of the place.

Madame de Chantelle's emergence from an inner room snatched Darrow from these irrelevant musings. She was already beaded and bugled for the evening, and, save for a slight pinkness of the eye-lids, her elaborate appearance revealed no mark of agitation; but Darrow noticed that, in recognition of the solemnity of the occasion, she pinched a lace handkerchief between her thumb and forefinger.

She plunged at once into the centre of the difficulty, appealing to him, in the name of all the Everards, to descend there with her to the rescue of her darling. She wasn't, she was sure, addressing herself in vain to one whose person, whose "tone," whose traditions so brilliantly declared his indebtedness to the principles she besought him to defend. Her own reception of Darrow, the confidence she had at once accorded him, must have shown him that she had instinctively felt their unanimity of sentiment on these fundamental questions. She had in fact recognized in him the one person whom, without pain to her maternal piety, she could welcome as her son's successor; and it was almost as to Owen's father that she now appealed to Darrow to aid in rescuing the wretched boy.

"Don't think, please, that I'm casting the least reflection on Anna, or showing any want of sympathy for her, when I say that I consider her partly responsible for what's happened. Anna is 'modern'—I believe that's what it's called when you read unsettling books and admire hideous pictures. Indeed," Madame de Chantelle continued, leaning confidentially forward, "I myself have always more or less lived in that atmosphere: my son, you know, was very revolutionary. Only he didn't, of course, apply his ideas: they were purely intellectual. That's what dear Anna has always failed to understand. And I'm afraid she's created the same kind of confusion in Owen's mind—led him to mix up things you read about with things you do . . . You know, of course, that she sides with him in this wretched business?"

Developing at length upon this theme, she finally narrowed down to the point of Darrow's intervention.

"My grandson, Mr. Darrow, calls me illogical and uncharitable because my feelings toward Miss Viner have changed since I've heard this news. Well! You've known her, it appears, for some years: Anna tells me you used to see her when she was a companion, or secretary or something, to a dreadfully vulgar Mrs. Murrett. And I ask you as a friend, I ask you as one of *us*, to tell me if you think a girl who has had to knock about the world in that kind of position, and at the orders of all kinds of people, is fitted to be Owen's wife . . . I'm not implying anything against her! I *liked* the girl, Mr. Darrow . . . But what's that got to do with it? I don't want her to marry my grand-son. If I'd been looking for a wife for Owen, I shouldn't have applied to the Farlows to find me one. That's what Anna won't understand; and what you must help me to make her see."

Darrow, to this appeal, could oppose only the repeated assurance of his inability to interfere. He tried to make Madame de Chantelle see that the very position he hoped to take in the household made his intervention the more hazardous. He brought up the usual arguments, and sounded the expected note of sympathy; but Madame de Chantelle's alarm had dispelled her habitual imprecision, and, though she had not many reasons to advance, her argument clung to its point like a frightened sharp-clawed animal.

"Well, then," she summed up, in response to his repeated assertions that he saw no way of helping her, "you can, at least, even if you won't say a word to the others, tell me frankly and fairly—and quite between ourselves—your personal opinion of Miss Viner, since you've known her so much longer than we have."

He protested that, if he had known her longer, he had known her much less well, and that he had already, on this point, convinced Anna of his inability to pronounce an opinion.

Madame de Chantelle drew a deep sigh of intelligence. "Your opinion of Mrs. Murrett is enough! I don't suppose you pretend to conceal *that*? And heaven knows what other unspeakable people she's been mixed up with. The only friends she can produce are called *Hoke* . . . Don't try to reason with me, Mr. Darrow. There are feelings that go deeper than facts . . . And I *know* she thought of studying for the stage . . ." Madame de Chantelle raised the corner of her lace handkerchief to her eyes. "I'm old-fashioned—like my furniture," she murmured. "And I thought I could count on you, Mr. Darrow . . ."

When Darrow, that night, regained his room, he reflected with a flash of irony that each time he entered it he brought a fresh troop of perplexities to trouble its serene seclusion. Since the day after his arrival, only forty-eight hours before, when he had set his window open to the night, and his hopes had seemed as many as its stars, each evening had brought its new problem and its renewed distress. But nothing, as yet, had approached the blank misery of mind with which he now set himself to face the fresh questions confronting him.

Sophy Viner had not shown herself at dinner, so that he had had no glimpse of her in her new character, and no means of divining the real nature of the tie between herself and Owen Leath. One thing, however, was clear: whatever her real feelings were, and however much or little she had at stake, if she had made up her mind to marry Owen she had more than enough skill and tenacity to defeat any arts that poor Madame de Chantelle could oppose to her.

Darrow himself was in fact the only person who might possibly turn her from her purpose: Madame de Chantelle, at haphazard, had hit on the surest means of saving Owen—if to prevent his marriage were to save him! Darrow, on this point, did not pretend to any fixed opinion; one feeling alone was clear and insistent in him: he did not mean, if he could help it, to let the marriage take place.

How he was to prevent it he did not know: to his tormented imagination every issue seemed closed. For a fantastic instant he was moved to follow Madame de Chantelle's suggestion and urge Anna to withdraw her approval. If his reticence, his efforts to avoid the subject, had not escaped her, she had doubtless set them down to the fact of his knowing more, and thinking less, of Sophy Viner than he had been willing to admit; and he might take advantage of this to turn her mind gradually from the project. Yet how do so without betraying his insincerity? If he had had nothing to hide he could easily have said: "It's one thing to know nothing against the girl, it's another to pretend that I think her a good match for Owen." But could he say even so much without betraying more? It was not Anna's questions, or his answers to them, that he feared, but what might cry aloud in the intervals between them. He understood now that ever since Sophy Viner's arrival at Givré he had felt in Anna the lurking sense of something unexpressed, and perhaps inexpressible, between the girl and himself . . . When at last he fell asleep he had fatalistically committed his next step to the chances of the morrow.

The first that offered itself was an encounter with Mrs. Leath as he descended the stairs the next morning. She had come down already hatted and shod for a dash to the park lodge, where one of the gatekeeper's children had had an accident. In her compact dark dress she looked more than usually straight and slim, and her face wore the pale glow it took on at any call on her energy: a kind of warrior brightness that made her small head, with its strong chin and closebound hair, like that of an amazon in a frieze.

It was their first moment alone since she had left him, the afternoon before, at her mother-in-law's door; and after a few words about the injured child their talk inevitably reverted to Owen.

Anna spoke with a smile of her "scene" with Madame de Chantelle, who belonged, poor dear, to a generation when "scenes" (in the ladylike and lachrymal sense of the term) were the tribute which sensibility was expected to pay to the unusual. Their conversation had been, in every detail, so exactly what Anna had foreseen that it had clearly not made much impression on her; but she was eager to know the result of Darrow's encounter with her mother-in-law.

"She told me she'd sent for you: she always 'sends for' people in emergencies. That again, I suppose, is *de l'époque*. And failing Adelaide Painter, who can't get here till this afternoon, there was no one but poor you to turn to."

She put it all lightly, with a lightness that seemed to his tight-strung nerves slightly, undefinably over-done. But he was so aware of his own tension that he wondered, the next moment, whether anything would ever again seem to him quite usual and insignificant and in the common order of things.

As they hastened on through the drizzle in which the

storm of the night was weeping itself out, Anna drew close under his umbrella, and at the pressure of her arm against his he recalled his walk up the Dover pier with Sophy Viner. The memory gave him a startled vision of the inevitable occasions of contact, confidence, familiarity, which his future relationship to the girl would entail, and the countless chances of betrayal that every one of them involved.

"Do tell me just what you said," he heard Anna pleading; and with sudden resolution he affirmed: "I quite understand your mother-in-law's feeling as she does."

The words, when uttered, seemed a good deal less significant than they had sounded to his inner ear; and Anna replied without surprise: "Of course. It's inevitable that she should. But we shall bring her round in time." Under the dripping dome she raised her face to his. "Don't you remember what you said the day before yesterday? 'Together we can't fail to pull it off for him!' I've told Owen that, so you're pledged and there's no going back."

The day before yesterday! Was it possible that, no longer ago, life had seemed a sufficiently simple business for a sane man to hazard such assurances?

"Anna," he questioned her abruptly, "why are you so anxious for this marriage?"

She stopped short to face him. "Why? But surely I've explained to you—or rather I've hardly had to, you seemed so in sympathy with my reasons!"

"I didn't know, then, who it was that Owen wanted to marry."

The words were out with a spring and he felt a clearer air in his brain. But her logic hemmed him in.

"You knew yesterday; and you assured me then that you hadn't a word to say——"

"Against Miss Viner?" The name, once uttered, sounded on and on in his ears. "Of course not. But that doesn't necessarily imply that I think her a good match for Owen."

Anna made no immediate answer. When she spoke it was to question: "Why don't you think her a good match for Owen?"

"Well—Madame de Chantelle's reasons seem to me not quite as negligible as you think."

"You mean the fact that she's been Mrs. Murrett's secretary, and that the people who employed her before were called Hoke? For, as far as Owen and I can make out, these are the gravest charges against her."

"Still, one can understand that the match is not what Madame de Chantelle had dreamed of."

"Oh, perfectly—if that's all you mean."

The lodge was in sight, and she hastened her step. He strode on beside her in silence, but at the gate she checked him with the question: "Is it really all you mean?"

"Of course," he heard himself declare.

"Oh, then I think I shall convince you—even if I can't, like Madame de Chantelle, summon all the Everards to my aid!" She lifted to him the look of happy laughter that sometimes brushed her with a gleam of spring.

Darrow watched her hasten along the path between the dripping chrysanthemums and enter the lodge. After she had gone in he paced up and down outside in the drizzle, waiting to learn if she had any message to send back to the house; and after the lapse of a few minutes she came out again.

The child, she said, was badly, though not dangerously, hurt, and the village doctor, who was already on hand, had asked that the surgeon, already summoned from Francheuil, should be told to bring with him certain needful appliances. Owen had started by motor to fetch the surgeon, but there was still time to communicate with the latter by telephone. The doctor furthermore begged for an immediate provision of such bandages and disinfectants as Givré itself could furnish, and Anna bade Darrow address himself to Miss Viner, who would know where to find the necessary things, and would direct one of the servants to bicycle with them to the lodge.

Darrow, as he hurried off on this errand, had at once perceived the opportunity it offered of a word with Sophy Viner. What that word was to be he did not know; but now, if ever, was the moment to make it urgent and conclusive. It was unlikely that he would again have such a chance of unobserved talk with her.

He had supposed he should find her with her pupil in the school-room; but he learned from a servant that Effie had gone to Francheuil with her step-brother, and that Miss Viner was still in her room. Darrow sent her word that he was the bearer of a message from the lodge, and a moment later he heard her coming down the stairs.

XX.

FOR a second, as she approached him, the quick tremor of her glance showed her all intent on the same thought as himself. He transmitted his instructions with mechanical precision, and she answered in the same tone, repeating his words with the intensity of attention of a child not quite sure of understanding. Then she disappeared up the stairs.

Darrow lingered on in the hall, not knowing if she meant to return, yet inwardly sure she would. At length he saw her coming down in her hat and jacket. The rain still streaked the window panes, and, in order to say something, he said: "You're not going to the lodge yourself?"

"I've sent one of the men ahead with the things; but I thought Mrs. Leath might need me."

"She didn't ask for you," he returned, wondering how he could detain her; but she answered decidedly: "I'd better go."

He held open the door, picked up his umbrella and followed her out. As they went down the steps she glanced back at him. "You've forgotten your mackintosh."

"I sha'n't need it."

She had no umbrella, and he opened his and held it out to her. She rejected it with a murmur of thanks and walked on through the thin drizzle, and he kept the umbrella over his own head, without offering to shelter her.

Rapidly and in silence they crossed the court and began to walk down the avenue. They had traversed a third of its length before Darrow said abruptly: "Wouldn't it have been fairer, when we talked together yesterday, to tell me what I've just heard from Mrs. Leath?"

"Fairer——?" She stopped short with a startled look.

"If I'd known that your future was already settled I should have spared you my gratuitous suggestions."

She walked on, more slowly, for a yard or two. "I couldn't speak yesterday. I meant to have told you today."

"Oh, I'm not reproaching you for your lack of confidence. Only, if you *had* told me, I should have been more sure of your really meaning what you said to me yesterday."

She did not ask him to what he referred, and he saw that her parting words to him lived as vividly in her memory as in his.

"Is it so important that you should be sure?" she finally questioned.

"Not to you, naturally," he returned with involuntary asperity. It was incredible, yet it was a fact, that for the moment his immediate purpose in seeking to speak to her was lost under a rush of resentment at counting for so little in her fate. Of what stuff, then, was his feeling for her made? A few hours earlier she had touched his thoughts as little as his senses; but now he felt old sleeping instincts stir in him . . .

A rush of rain dashed against his face, and, catching Sophy's hat, strained it back from her loosened hair. She put her hands to her head with a familiar gesture . . . He came closer and held his umbrella over her . . .

At the lodge he waited while she went in. The rain continued to stream down on him and he shivered in the dampness and stamped his feet on the flags. It seemed to him that a long time elapsed before the door opened and she reappeared. He glanced into the house for a glimpse of Anna, but obtained none; yet the mere sense of her nearness had completely altered his mood.

The child, Sophy told him, was doing well; but Mrs. Leath had decided to wait till the surgeon came. Darrow, as they turned away, looked through the gates, and saw the doctor's old-fashioned carriage by the road-side.

"Let me tell the doctor's boy to drive you back," he suggested; but Sophy answered: "No; I'll walk," and he moved on toward the house at her side. She expressed no surprise at his not remaining at the lodge, and again they walked on in silence through the rain. She had accepted the shelter of his umbrella, but she kept herself at such a carefully measured distance that even the slight swaying movements produced by their quick pace did not once bring her arm in touch with his; and, noticing this, he perceived that every drop of her blood must be alive to his nearness.

"What I meant just now," he began, "was that you ought to have been sure of my good wishes."

She seemed to weigh the words. "Sure enough for what?"

"To trust me a little farther than you did."

"I've told you that yesterday I wasn't free to speak."

"Well, since you are now, may I say a word to you?"

She paused perceptibly, and when she spoke it was in so low a tone that he had to bend his head to catch her answer. "I can't think what you can have to say."

"It's not easy to say here, at any rate. And indoors I sha'n't know where to say it." He glanced about him in the rain. "Let's walk over to the spring-house for a minute."

To the right of the drive, under a clump of trees, a little stucco pavilion crowned by a balustrade rose on arches of mouldering brick over a flight of steps that led down to a spring. Other steps curved up to a door above. Darrow mounted these, and opening the door entered a small circular room hung with loosened strips of painted paper whereon spectrally faded Mandarins executed elongated gestures. Some black and gold chairs with straw seats and an unsteady table of cracked lacquer stood on the floor of red-glazed tile.

Sophy had followed him without comment. He closed the door after her, and she stood motionless, as though waiting for him to speak.

"Now we can talk quietly," he said, looking at her with a smile into which he tried to put an intention of the frankest friendliness.

She merely repeated: "I can't think what you can have to say."

Her voice had lost the note of half-wistful confidence on which their talk of the previous day had closed, and she looked at him with a kind of pale hostility. Her tone made it evident that his task would be difficult, but it did not shake his resolve to go on. He sat down, and mechanically she followed his example. The table was between them and she rested her arms on its cracked edge and her chin on her interlocked hands. He looked at her and she gave him back his look.

"Have you nothing to say to *me*?" he asked at length.

A faint smile lifted, in the remembered way, the left corner of her narrowed lips.

"About my marriage?"

"About your marriage."

She continued to consider him between half-drawn

lids. "What can I say that Mrs. Leath has not already told you?"

"Mrs. Leath has told me nothing whatever but the fact— and her pleasure in it."

"Well; aren't those the two essential points?"

"The essential points to *you*? I should have thought——"

"Oh, to *you*, I meant," she put in keenly.

He flushed at the retort, but steadied himself and rejoined: "The essential point to me is, of course, that you should be doing what's really best for you."

She sat silent, with lowered lashes. At length she stretched out her arm and took up from the table a little threadbare Chinese hand-screen. She turned its ebony stem once or twice between her fingers, and as she did so Darrow was whimsically struck by the way in which their evanescent slight romance was symbolized by the fading lines on the frail silk.

"Do you think my engagement to Mr. Leath not really best for me?" she asked at length.

Darrow, before answering, waited long enough to get his words into the tersest shape—not without a sense, as he did so, of his likeness to the surgeon deliberately poising his lancet for a clean incision. "I'm not sure," he replied, "of its being the best thing for either of you."

She took the stroke steadily, but a faint red swept her face like the reflection of a blush. She continued to keep her lowered eyes on the screen.

"From whose point of view do you speak?"

"Naturally, that of the persons most concerned."

"From Owen's, then, of course? You don't think me a good match for him?"

"From yours, first of all. I don't think him a good match for you."

He brought the answer out abruptly, his eyes on her face. It had grown extremely pale, but as the meaning of his words shaped itself in her mind he saw a curious inner light dawn through her set look. She lifted her lids just far enough for a veiled glance at him, and a smile slipped through them to her trembling lips. For a moment the change merely bewildered him; then it pulled him up with a sharp jerk of apprehension.

"I don't think him a good match for you," he stammered, groping for the lost thread of his words.

She threw a vague look about the chilly rain-dimmed room. "And you've brought me here to tell me why?"

The question roused him to the sense that their minutes were numbered, and that if he did not immediately get to his point there might be no other chance of making it.

"My chief reason is that I believe he's too young and inexperienced to give you the kind of support you need."

At his words her face changed again, freezing to a tragic coldness. She stared straight ahead of her, perceptibly struggling with the tremor of her muscles; and when she had controlled it she flung out a pale-lipped pleasantry. "But you see I've always had to support myself!"

"He's a boy," Darrow pushed on, "a charming, wonderful boy; but with no more notion than a boy how to deal with the inevitable daily problems . . . the trivial stupid unimportant things that life is chiefly made up of."

"I'll deal with them for him," she rejoined.

"They'll be more than ordinarily difficult."

She shot a challenging glance at him. "You must have some special reason for saying so."

"Only my clear perception of the facts."

"What facts do you mean?"

Darrow hesitated. "You must know better than I," he returned at length, "that the way won't be made easy to you."

"Mrs. Leath, at any rate, has made it so."

"Madame de Chantelle will not."

"How do *you* know that?" she flung back.

He paused again, not sure how far it was prudent to reveal himself in the confidence of the household. Then, to avoid involving Anna, he answered: "Madame de Chantelle sent for me yesterday."

"Sent for you—to talk to you about me?" The colour rose to her forehead and her eyes burned black under lowered brows. "By what right, I should like to know? What have you to do with me, or with anything in the world that concerns me?"

Darrow instantly perceived what dread suspicion again possessed her, and the sense that it was not wholly unjustified caused him a passing pang of shame. But it did not turn him from his purpose.

"I'm an old friend of Mrs. Leath's. It's not unnatural that Madame de Chantelle should talk to me."

She dropped the screen on the table and stood up, turning on him the same small mask of wrath and scorn which had glared at him, in Paris, when he had confessed to his suppression of her letter. She walked away a step or two and then came back.

"May I ask what Madame de Chantelle said to you?"

"She made it clear that she should not encourage the marriage."

"And what was her object in making that clear to *you*?"

Darrow hesitated. "I suppose she thought——"

"That she could persuade you to turn Mrs. Leath against me?"

He was silent, and she pressed him: "Was that it?"

"That was it."

"But if you don't—if you keep your promise——"

"My promise?"

"To say nothing . . . nothing whatever . . ." Her strained look threw a haggard light along the pause.

As she spoke, the whole odiousness of the scene rushed over him. "Of course I shall say nothing . . . you know that . . ." He leaned to her and laid his hand on hers. "You know I wouldn't for the world . . ."

She drew back and hid her face with a sob. Then she sank again into her seat, stretched her arms across the table and laid her face upon them. He sat still, overwhelmed with compunction. After a long interval, in which he had painfully measured the seconds by her hard-drawn breathing, she looked up at him with a face washed clear of bitterness.

"Don't suppose I don't know what you must have thought of me!"

The cry struck him down to a lower depth of self-abasement. "My poor child," he felt like answering, "the shame of it is that I've never thought of you at all!" But he could only uselessly repeat: "I'll do anything I can to help you."

She sat silent, drumming the table with her hand. He saw that her doubt of him was allayed, and the perception made him more ashamed, as if her trust had first revealed to him how near he had come to not deserving it. Suddenly she began to speak.

"You think, then, I've no right to marry him?"

"No right? God forbid! I only meant——"

"That you'd rather I didn't marry any friend of yours." She brought it out deliberately, not as a question, but as a mere dispassionate statement of fact.

Darrow in turn stood up and wandered away helplessly to the window. He stood staring out through its small discoloured panes at the dim brown distances; then he moved back to the table.

"I'll tell you exactly what I meant. You'll be wretched if you marry a man you're not in love with."

He knew the risk of misapprehension that he ran, but he estimated his chances of success as precisely in proportion to his peril. If certain signs meant what he thought they did, he might yet—at what cost he would not stop to think—make his past pay for his future.

The girl, at his words, had lifted her head with a movement of surprise. Her eyes slowly reached his face and rested there in a gaze of deep interrogation. He held the look for a moment; then his own eyes dropped and he waited.

At length she began to speak. "You're mistaken—you're quite mistaken."

He waited a moment longer. "Mistaken——?"

"In thinking what you think. I'm as happy as if I deserved it!" she suddenly proclaimed with a laugh.

She stood up and moved toward the door. "*Now* are you satisfied?" she asked, turning her vividest face to him from the threshold.

XXI.

DOWN the avenue there came to them, with the opening of the door, the voice of Owen's motor. It was the signal which had interrupted their first talk, and again, instinctively, they drew apart at the sound. Without a word Darrow turned back into the room, while Sophy Viner went down the steps and walked back alone toward the court.

At luncheon the presence of the surgeon, and the non-appearance of Madame de Chantelle—who had excused herself on the plea of a headache—combined to shift the conversational centre of gravity; and Darrow, under shelter of the necessarily impersonal talk, had time to adjust his disguise and to perceive that the others were engaged in the same re-arrangement. It was the first time that he had seen young Leath and Sophy Viner together since he had learned of their engagement; but neither revealed more emotion than befitted the occasion. It was evident that Owen was deeply under the girl's charm, and that at the least sign from her his bliss would have broken bounds; but her reticence was justified by the tacitly recognized fact of Madame de Chantelle's disapproval. This also visibly weighed on Anna's mind, making her manner to Sophy, if no less kind, yet a trifle more constrained than if the moment of final understanding had been reached. So Darrow interpreted the tension perceptible under the fluent exchange of commonplaces in which he was diligently sharing. But he was more and more aware of his inability to test the moral atmosphere about him:

he was like a man in fever testing another's temperature by the touch.

After luncheon Anna, who was to motor the surgeon home, suggested to Darrow that he should accompany them. Effie was also of the party; and Darrow inferred that Anna wished to give her step-son a chance to be alone with his betrothed. On the way back, after the surgeon had been left at his door, the little girl sat between her mother and Darrow, and her presence kept their talk from taking a personal turn. Darrow knew that Mrs. Leath had not yet told Effie of the relation in which he was to stand to her. The premature divulging of Owen's plans had thrown their own into the background, and by common consent they continued, in the little girl's presence, on terms of an informal friendliness.

The sky had cleared after luncheon, and to prolong their excursion they returned by way of the ivy-mantled ruin which was to have been the scene of the projected picnic. This circuit brought them back to the park gates not long before sunset, and as Anna wished to stop at the lodge for news of the injured child Darrow left her there with Effie and walked on alone to the house. He had the impression that she was slightly surprised at his not waiting for her; but his inner restlessness vented itself in an intense desire for bodily movement. He would have liked to walk himself into a state of torpor; to tramp on for hours through the moist winds and the healing darkness and come back staggering with fatigue and sleep. But he had no pretext for such a flight, and he feared that, at such a moment, his prolonged absence might seem singular to Anna.

As he approached the house, the thought of her

nearness produced a swift reaction of mood. It was as if an intenser vision of her had scattered his perplexities like morning mists. At this moment, wherever she was, he knew he was safely shut away in her thoughts, and the knowledge made every other fact dwindle away to a shadow. He and she loved each other, and their love arched over them open and ample as the day: in all its sunlit spaces there was no cranny for a fear to lurk. In a few minutes he would be in her presence and would read his reassurance in her eyes. And presently, before dinner, she would contrive that they should have an hour by themselves in her sitting-room, and he would sit by the hearth and watch her quiet movements, and the way the bluish lustre on her hair purpled a little as she bent above the fire.

A carriage drove out of the court as he entered it, and in the hall his vision was dispelled by the exceedingly substantial presence of a lady in a waterproof and a tweed hat, who stood firmly planted in the centre of a pile of luggage, as to which she was giving involved but lucid directions to the footman who had just admitted her. She went on with these directions regardless of Darrow's entrance, merely fixing her small pale eyes on him while she proceeded, in a deep contralto voice, and a fluent French pronounced with the purest Boston accent, to specify the destination of her bags; and this enabled Darrow to give her back a gaze protracted enough to take in all the details of her plain thick-set person, from the square sallow face beneath bands of grey hair to the blunt boot-toes protruding under her wide walking skirt.

She submitted to this scrutiny with no more evidence of surprise than a monument examined by a tourist;

but when the fate of her luggage had been settled she turned suddenly to Darrow and, dropping her eyes from his face to his feet, asked in trenchant accents: "What sort of boots have you got on?"

Before he could summon his wits to the consideration of this question she continued in a tone of suppressed indignation: "Until Americans get used to the fact that France is under water for half the year they're perpetually risking their lives by not being properly protected. I suppose you've been tramping through all this nasty clammy mud as if you'd been taking a stroll on Boston Common."

Darrow, with a laugh, affirmed his previous experience of French dampness, and the degree to which he was on his guard against it; but the lady, with a contemptuous snort, rejoined: "You young men are all alike——"; to which she appended, after another hard look at him: "I suppose you're George Darrow? I used to know one of your mother's cousins, who married a Tunstall of Mount Vernon Street. My name is Adelaide Painter. Have you been in Boston lately? No? I'm sorry for that. I hear there have been several new houses built at the lower end of Commonwealth Avenue and I hoped you could tell me about them. I haven't been there for thirty years myself."

Miss Painter's arrival at Givré produced the same effect as the wind's hauling around to the north after days of languid weather. When Darrow joined the group about the tea-table she had already given a tingle to the air. Madame de Chantelle still remained invisible above stairs; but Darrow had the impression that even through her drawn curtains and bolted doors a stimulating whiff must have entered.

Anna was in her usual seat behind the tea-tray, and Sophy Viner presently led in her pupil. Owen was also there, seated, as usual, a little apart from the others, and following Miss Painter's massive movements and equally substantial utterances with a smile of secret intelligence which gave Darrow the idea of his having been in clandestine parley with the enemy. Darrow further took note that the girl and her suitor perceptibly avoided each other; but this might be a natural result of the tension Miss Painter had been summoned to relieve.

Sophy Viner would evidently permit no recognition of the situation save that which it lay with Madame de Chantelle to accord; but meanwhile Miss Painter had proclaimed her tacit sense of it by summoning the girl to a seat at her side.

Darrow, as he continued to observe the new-comer, who was perched on her arm-chair like a granite image on the edge of a cliff, was aware that, in a more detached frame of mind, he would have found an extreme interest in studying and classifying Miss Painter. It was not that she said anything remarkable, or betrayed any of those unspoken perceptions which give significance to the most commonplace utterances. She talked of the lateness of her train, of an impending crisis in international politics, of the difficulty of buying English tea in Paris and of the enormities of which French servants were capable; and her views on these subjects were enunciated with a uniformity of emphasis implying complete unconsciousness of any difference in their interest and importance. She always applied to the French race the distant epithet of "those people", but she betrayed an intimate acquaintance with many of its members, and an encyclopædic knowledge of the domestic habits, financial difficulties and private complications of various persons of social importance. Yet, as she evidently felt no incongruity in her attitude, so she revealed no desire to parade her familiarity with the fashionable, or indeed any sense of it as a fact to be paraded. It was evident that the titled ladies whom she spoke of as Mimi or Simone or Odette were as much "those people" to her as the *bonne* who tampered with her tea and steamed the stamps off her letters ("when, by a miracle, I don't put them in the box myself.") Her whole attitude was of a vast grim tolerance of things-as-they-came, as though she had been some wonderful automatic machine which recorded facts but had not yet been perfected to the point of sorting or labelling them.

All this, as Darrow was aware, still fell short of accounting for the influence she obviously exerted on the persons in contact with her. It brought a slight relief to his state of tension to go on wondering, while he watched and listened, just where the mystery lurked. Perhaps, after all, it was in the fact of her blank insensibility, an insensibility so devoid of egotism that it had no hardness and no grimaces, but rather the freshness of a simpler mental state. After living, as he had, as they all had, for the last few days, in an atmosphere perpetually tremulous with echoes and implications, it was restful and fortifying merely to walk into the big blank area of Miss Painter's mind, so vacuous for all its accumulated items, so echoless for all its vacuity.

His hope of a word with Anna before dinner was dispelled by her rising to take Miss Painter up to Madame de Chantelle; and he wandered away to his own room, leaving Owen and Miss Viner engaged in working out a picture-puzzle for Effie.

Madame de Chantelle—possibly as the result of her friend's ministrations—was able to appear at the dinner-table, rather pale and pink-nosed, and casting tenderly reproachful glances at her grandson, who faced them with impervious serenity; and the situation was relieved by the fact that Miss Viner, as usual, had remained in the school-room with her pupil.

Darrow conjectured that the real clash of arms would not take place till the morrow; and wishing to leave the field open to the contestants he set out early on a solitary walk. It was nearly luncheon-time when he returned from it and came upon Anna just emerging from the house. She had on her hat and jacket and was apparently coming forth to seek him, for she said at once: "Madame de Chantelle wants you to go up to her."

"To go up to her? Now?"

"That's the message she sent. She appears to rely on you to do something." She added with a smile: "Whatever it is, let's have it over!"

Darrow, through his rising sense of apprehension, wondered why, instead of merely going for a walk, he had not jumped into the first train and got out of the way till Owen's affairs were finally settled.

"But what in the name of goodness can I do?" he protested, following Anna back into the hall.

"I don't know. But Owen seems so to rely on you, too——"

"Owen! Is *he* to be there?"

"No. But you know I told him he could count on you."

"But I've said to your mother-in-law all I could."

"Well, then you can only repeat it."

This did not seem to Darrow to simplify his case as much as she appeared to think; and once more he had a movement of recoil. "There's no possible reason for my being mixed up in this affair!"

Anna gave him a reproachful glance. "Not the fact that *I* am?" she reminded him; but even this only stiffened his resistance.

"Why should you be, either—to this extent?"

The question made her pause. She glanced about the hall, as if to be sure they had it to themselves; and then, in a lowered voice: "I don't know," she suddenly confessed; "but, somehow, if *they're* not happy I feel as if we shouldn't be."

"Oh, well—" Darrow acquiesced, in the tone of the man who perforce yields to so lovely an unreasonableness. Escape was, after all, impossible, and he could only resign himself to being led to Madame de Chantelle's door.

Within, among the bric-à-brac and furbelows, he found Miss Painter seated in a redundant purple armchair with the incongruous air of a horseman bestriding a heavy mount. Madame de Chantelle sat opposite, still a little wan and disordered under her elaborate hair, and clasping the handkerchief whose visibility symbolized her distress. On the young man's entrance she sighed out a plaintive welcome, to which she immediately appended: "Mr. Darrow, I can't help feeling that at heart you're with me!"

The directness of the challenge made it easier for Darrow to protest, and he reiterated his inability to give an opinion on either side.

"But Anna declares you have—on hers!"

He could not restrain a smile at this faint flaw in an impartiality so scrupulous. Every evidence of feminine inconsequence in Anna seemed to attest her deeper subjection to the most inconsequent of passions. He had certainly promised her his help—but before he knew what he was promising.

He met Madame de Chantelle's appeal by replying: "If there were anything I could possibly say I should want it to be in Miss Viner's favour."

"You'd want it to be—yes! But could you make it so?"

"As far as facts go, I don't see how I can make it either for or against her. I've already said that I know nothing of her except that she's charming."

"As if that weren't enough—weren't all there *ought* to be!" Miss Painter put in impatiently. She seemed to address herself to Darrow, though her small eyes were fixed on her friend.

"Madame de Chantelle seems to imagine," she pursued, "that a young American girl ought to have a *dossier*—a police-record, or whatever you call it: what those awful women in the streets have here. In our country it's enough to know that a young girl's pure and lovely: people don't immediately ask her to show her bank-account and her visiting-list."

Madame de Chantelle looked plaintively at her sturdy monitress. "You don't expect me not to ask if she's got a family?"

"No; nor to think the worse of her if she hasn't. The fact that she's an orphan ought, with your ideas, to be a merit. You won't have to invite her father and mother to Givré!"

"Adelaide—Adelaide!" the mistress of Givré lamented.

"Lucretia Mary," the other returned—and Darrow spared an instant's amusement to the quaint incongruity of the name—"you know you sent for Mr. Darrow to refute me; and how can he, till he knows what I think?"

"You think it's perfectly simple to let Owen marry a girl we know nothing about?"

"No; but I don't think it's perfectly simple to prevent him."

The shrewdness of the answer increased Darrow's interest in Miss Painter. She had not hitherto struck him as being a person of much penetration, but he now felt sure that her gimlet gaze might bore to the heart of any practical problem.

Madame de Chantelle sighed out her recognition of the difficulty.

"I haven't a word to say against Miss Viner; but she's knocked about so, as it's called, that she must have been mixed up with some rather dreadful people. If only Owen could be made to see that—if one could get at a few facts, I mean. She says, for instance, that she has a sister; but it seems she doesn't even know her address!"

"If she does, she may not want to give it to you. I daresay the sister's one of the dreadful people. I've no doubt that with a little time you could rake up dozens of them: have her 'traced', as they call it in detective stories. I don't think you'd frighten Owen, but you might: it's natural enough he should have been corrupted by those foreign ideas. You might even manage to part him from the girl; but you couldn't keep him from being in love with her. I saw that when I looked them over last evening. I said to myself: 'It's a real old-fashioned American case, as sweet and sound as home-made bread.' Well, if you take his loaf away from him, what are you going to feed him with instead? Which of your nasty Paris poisons do you think he'll turn to? Supposing you succeed in keeping him out of a really bad mess—and, knowing the young man as I do, I rather think that, at this crisis, the only way to do it would be to marry him slap off to somebody else—well, then, who, may I ask, would you pick out? One of your sweet French *ingénues*, I suppose? With as much mind as a minnow and as much snap as a soft-boiled egg. You might hustle him into that kind of marriage; I daresay you could—but if I know Owen, the natural thing would happen before the first baby was weaned."

"I don't know why you insinuate such odious things against Owen!"

"Do you think it would be odious of him to return to his real love when he'd been forcibly parted from her? At any rate, it's what your French friends do, every one of them! Only they don't generally have the grace to go back to an old love; and I believe, upon my word, Owen would!"

Madame de Chantelle looked at her with a mixture of awe and exultation. "Of course you realize, Adelaide, that in suggesting this you're insinuating the most shocking things against Miss Viner?"

"When I say that if you part two young things who are dying to be happy in the lawful way it's ten to one they'll come together in an unlawful one? I'm insinuating shocking things against *you*, Lucretia Mary, in suggesting for a moment that you'll care to assume such a responsibility before your Maker. And you wouldn't, if you talked things straight out with him, instead of merely sending him messages through a miserable sinner like yourself!"

Darrow expected this assault on her adopted creed to provoke in Madame de Chantelle an explosion of pious indignation; but to his surprise she merely murmured: "I don't know what Mr. Darrow'll think of you!"

"Mr. Darrow probably knows his Bible as well as I do," Miss Painter calmly rejoined; adding a moment later, without the least perceptible change of voice or expression: "I suppose you've heard that Gisèle de Folembray's husband accuses her of being mixed up with the Duc d'Arcachon in that business of trying to sell a lot of imitation pearls to Mrs. Homer Pond, the Chicago woman the Duke's engaged to? It seems the jeweller says Gisèle brought Mrs. Pond there, and got twenty-five per cent—which of course she passed on to d'Arcachon. The poor old Duchess is in a fearful state—so afraid her son'll lose Mrs. Pond! When I think that Gisèle is old Bradford Wagstaff's granddaughter, I'm thankful he's safe in Mount Auburn!"

XXII.

It was not until late that afternoon that Darrow could claim his postponed hour with Anna. When at last he found her alone in her sitting-room it was with a sense of liberation so great that he sought no logical justification of it. He simply felt that all their destinies were in Miss Painter's grasp, and that, resistance being useless, he could only enjoy the sweets of surrender.

Anna herself seemed as happy, and for more explicable reasons. She had assisted, after luncheon, at another debate between Madame de Chantelle and her confidant, and had surmised, when she withdrew from it, that victory was permanently perched on Miss Painter's banners.

"I don't know how she does it, unless it's by the dead weight of her convictions. She detests the French so that she'd back up Owen even if she knew nothing—or knew too much—of Miss Viner. She somehow regards the match as a protest against the corruption of European morals. I told Owen that was his great chance, and he's made the most of it."

"What a tactician you are! You make me feel that I hardly know the rudiments of diplomacy," Darrow smiled at her, abandoning himself to a perilous sense of well-being.

She gave him back his smile. "I'm afraid I think nothing short of my own happiness is worth wasting any diplomacy on!"

"That's why I mean to resign from the service of my country," he rejoined with a laugh of deep content.

The feeling that both resistance and apprehension were vain was working like wine in his veins. He had done what he could to deflect the course of events: now he could only stand aside and take his chance of safety. Underneath this fatalistic feeling was the deep sense of relief that he had, after all, said and done nothing that could in the least degree affect the welfare of Sophy Viner. That fact took a millstone off his neck.

Meanwhile he gave himself up once more to the joy

of Anna's presence. They had not been alone together for two long days, and he had the lover's sense that he had forgotten, or at least underestimated, the strength of the spell she cast. Once more her eyes and her smile seemed to bound his world. He felt that their light would always move with him as the sunset moves before a ship at sea.

The next day his sense of security was increased by a decisive incident. It became known to the expectant household that Madame de Chantelle had yielded to the tremendous impact of Miss Painter's determination and that Sophy Viner had been "sent for" to the purple satin sitting-room.

At luncheon, Owen's radiant countenance proclaimed the happy sequel, and Darrow, when the party had moved back to the oak-room for coffee, deemed it discreet to wander out alone to the terrace with his cigar. The conclusion of Owen's romance brought his own plans once more to the front. Anna had promised that she would consider dates and settle details as soon as Madame de Chantelle and her grandson had been reconciled, and Darrow was eager to go into the question at once, since it was necessary that the preparations for his marriage should go forward as rapidly as possible. Anna, he knew, would not seek any farther pretext for delay; and he strolled up and down contentedly in the sunshine, certain that she would come out and reassure him as soon as the reunited family had claimed its due share of her attention.

But when she finally joined him her first word was for the younger lovers.

"I want to thank you for what you've done for Owen," she began, with her happiest smile.

"Who—I?" he laughed. "Are you confusing me with Miss Painter?"

"Perhaps I ought to say for *me*," she corrected herself. "You've been even more of a help to us than Adelaide."

"My dear child! What on earth have I done?"

"You've managed to hide from Madame de Chantelle that you don't really like poor Sophy."

Darrow felt the pallour in his cheek. "Not like her? What put such an idea into your head?"

"Oh, it's more than an idea—it's a feeling. But what difference does it make, after all? You saw her in such a different setting that it's natural you should be a little doubtful. But when you know her better I'm sure you'll feel about her as I do."

"It's going to be hard for me not to feel about everything as you do."

"Well, then—please begin with my daughter-in-law!"

He gave her back in the same tone of banter: "Agreed: if you'll agree to feel as I do about the pressing necessity of our getting married."

"I want to talk to you about that too. You don't know what a weight is off my mind! With Sophy here for good, I shall feel so differently about leaving Effie. I've seen much more accomplished governesses—to my cost!—but I've never seen a young thing more gay and kind and human. You must have noticed, though you've seen them so little together, how Effie expands when she's with her. And that, you know, is what I want. Madame de Chantelle will provide the necessary restraint." She clasped her hands on his arm. "Yes, I'm ready to go with you now. But first of all—this very moment!—you must come with me to Effie. She knows, of course, nothing of what's been happening; and I want her to be told first about *you.*"

Effie, sought throughout the house, was presently traced to the school-room, and thither Darrow mounted with Anna. He had never seen her so alight with happiness, and he had caught her buoyancy of mood. He kept repeating to himself: "It's over—it's over," as if some monstrous midnight hallucination had been routed by the return of day.

As they approached the school-room door the terrier's barks came to them through laughing remonstrances.

"She's giving him his dinner," Anna whispered, her hand in Darrow's.

"Don't forget the gold-fish!" they heard another voice call out.

Darrow halted on the threshold. "Oh—not now!"

"Not now?"

"I mean—she'd rather have you tell her first. I'll wait for you both downstairs."

He was aware that she glanced at him intently. "As you please. I'll bring her down at once."

She opened the door, and as she went in he heard her say: "No, Sophy, don't go! I want you both."

The rest of Darrow's day was a succession of empty and agitating scenes. On his way down to Givré, before he had seen Effie Leath, he had pictured somewhat sentimentally the joy of the moment when he should take her in his arms and receive her first filial kiss. Everything in him that egotistically craved for rest, stability, a comfortably organized middle-age, all the home-building instincts of the man who has sufficiently wooed and wandered, combined to throw a charm about the figure of the child who might—who should—have been his. Effie came to him trailing the cloud of glory of his first romance, giving him back the magic hour he had missed and mourned. And how different the realization of his dream had been! The child's radiant welcome, her unquestioning acceptance of this new figure in the family group, had been all that he had hoped and fancied. If Mother was so awfully happy about it, and Owen and Granny, too, how nice and cosy and comfortable it was going to be for all of them, her beaming look seemed to say; and then, suddenly, the small pink fingers he had been kissing were laid on the one flaw in the circle, on the one point which must be settled before Effie could, with complete unqualified assurance, admit the newcomer to full equality with the other gods of her Olympus.

"And is Sophy awfully happy about it too?" she had asked, loosening her hold on Darrow's neck to tilt back her head and include her mother in her questioning look.

"Why, dearest, didn't you see she was?" Anna had exclaimed, leaning to the group with radiant eyes.

"I think I should like to ask her," the child rejoined, after a minute's shy consideration; and as Darrow set her down her mother laughed: "Do, darling, do! Run off at once, and tell her we expect her to be awfully happy too."

The scene had been succeeded by others less poignant but almost as trying. Darrow cursed his luck in having, at such a moment, to run the gauntlet of a houseful of interested observers. The state of being "engaged", in itself an absurd enough predicament, even to a man only intermittently exposed, became intolerable under the continuous scrutiny of a small circle quivering with participation. Darrow was furthermore aware that, though the case of the other couple ought to have made his own less conspicuous, it was rather they who found a refuge in the shadow of his prominence. Madame de Chantelle, though she had consented to Owen's engagement and formally welcomed his betrothed, was nevertheless not sorry to show, by her reception of Darrow, of what finely-shaded degrees of cordiality she was capable. Miss Painter, having won the day for Owen, was also free to turn her attention to the newer candidate for her sympathy; and Darrow and Anna found themselves immersed in a warm bath of sentimental curiosity.

It was a relief to Darrow that he was under a positive obligation to end his visit within the next forty-eight hours. When he left London, his Ambassador had accorded him a ten days' leave. His fate being definitely settled and openly published he had no reason for asking to have the time prolonged, and when it was over he was to return to his post till the time fixed for taking up his new duties. Anna and he had therefore decided to be married, in Paris, a day or two before the departure of the steamer which was to take them to South America; and Anna, shortly after his return to England, was to go up to Paris and begin her own preparations.

In honour of the double betrothal Effie and Miss Viner were to appear that evening at dinner; and Darrow, on leaving his room, met the little girl springing down the stairs, her white ruffles and coral-coloured bows making her look like a daisy with her yellow hair for its centre. Sophy Viner was behind her pupil, and as she came into the light Darrow noticed a change in her appearance and wondered vaguely why she looked suddenly younger, more vivid, more like the little luminous ghost of his Paris memories. Then it occurred to him that it was the first time she had appeared at dinner since his arrival at Givré, and the first time, consequently, that he had seen her in evening dress. She was still at the age when the least adornment embellishes; and no doubt the mere uncovering of her young throat and neck had given her back her former brightness. But a second glance showed a more precise reason for his impression. Vaguely though he retained such details, he felt sure she was wearing the dress he had seen her in every evening in Paris. It was a simple enough dress, black, and transparent on the arms and shoulders, and he would probably not have recognized it if she had not called his attention to it in Paris by confessing that she hadn't any other. "The same dress? That proves that she's forgotten!" was his first half-ironic thought; but the next moment, with a pang of compunction, he said to himself that she had probably put it on for the same reason as before: simply because she hadn't any other.

He looked at her in silence, and for an instant, above Effie's bobbing head, she gave him back his look in a full bright gaze.

"Oh, there's Owen!" Effie cried, and whirled away down the gallery to the door from which her step-brother was emerging. As Owen bent to catch her, Sophy Viner turned abruptly back to Darrow.

"You, too?" she said with a quick laugh. "I didn't know——" And as Owen came up to them she added, in a tone that might have been meant to reach his ear: "I wish you all the luck that we can spare!"

About the dinner-table, which Effie, with Miss Viner's aid, had lavishly garlanded, the little party had an air of somewhat self-conscious festivity. In spite of flowers, champagne and a unanimous attempt at ease, there were frequent lapses in the talk, and moments of nervous groping for new subjects. Miss Painter alone seemed not only unaffected by the general perturbation but as tightly sealed up in her unconsciousness of it as a diver in his bell. To Darrow's strained attention even Owen's gusts of gaiety seemed to betray an inward sense of insecurity. After dinner, however, at the piano, he broke into a mood of extravagant hilarity and flooded the room with the splash and ripple of his music.

Darrow, sunk in a sofa corner in the lee of Miss Painter's granite bulk, smoked and listened in silence, his eyes moving from one figure to another. Madame de Chantelle, in her armchair near the fire, clasped her little granddaughter to her with the gesture of a drawing-room Niobe, and Anna, seated near them, had fallen into one of the attitudes of vivid calm which seemed to Darrow to express her inmost quality. Sophy Viner, after moving uncertainly about the room, had placed herself beyond Mrs. Leath, in a chair near the piano, where she sat with head thrown back and eyes attached to the musician, in the same rapt fixity of attention with which she had followed the players at the Français. The accident of her having fallen into the same attitude, and of her wearing the same dress, gave Darrow, as he watched her, a strange sense of double consciousness. To escape from it, his glance turned back to Anna; but from the point at which he was placed his eyes could not take in the one face without the other, and that renewed the disturbing duality of the impression. Suddenly Owen broke off with a crash of chords and jumped to his feet.

"What's the use of this, with such a moon to say it for us?"

Behind the uncurtained window a low golden orb hung like a ripe fruit against the glass.

"Yes—let's go out and listen," Anna answered. Owen threw open the window, and with his gesture a fold of the heavy star-sprinkled sky seemed to droop into the room like a drawn-in curtain. The air that entered with it had a frosty edge, and Anna bade Effie run to the hall for wraps.

Darrow said: "You must have one too," and started toward the door; but Sophy, following her pupil, cried back: "We'll bring things for everybody."

Owen had followed her, and in a moment the three reappeared, and the party went out on the terrace. The deep blue purity of the night was unveiled by mist, and the moonlight rimmed the edges of the trees with a silver blur and blanched to unnatural whiteness the statues against their walls of shade.

Darrow and Anna, with Effie between them, strolled to the farther corner of the terrace. Below them, between the fringes of the park, the lawn sloped dimly to the fields above the river. For a few minutes they stood silently side by side, touched to peace beneath the trembling beauty of the sky. When they turned back, Darrow saw that Owen and Sophy Viner, who had gone down the steps to the garden, were also walking in the direction of the house. As they advanced, Sophy paused in a patch of moonlight, between the sharp shadows of the yews, and Darrow noticed that she had thrown over her shoulders a long cloak of some light colour, which suddenly evoked her image as she had entered the restaurant at his side on the night of their first dinner in Paris. A moment later they were all together again on the terrace, and when they re-entered the drawing-room the older ladies were on their way to bed.

Effie, emboldened by the privileges of the evening, was for coaxing Owen to round it off with a game of forfeits or some such reckless climax; but Sophy, resuming her professional rôle, sounded the summons to bed. In her pupil's wake she made her round of good-nights; but when she proffered her hand to Anna, the latter ignoring the gesture held out both arms.

"Good-night, dear child," she said impulsively, and drew the girl to her kiss.

Book Four

XXIII.

THE next day was Darrow's last at Givré and, foreseeing that the afternoon and evening would have to be given to the family, he had asked Anna to devote an early hour to the final consideration of their plans. He was to meet her in the brown sitting-room at ten, and they were to walk down to the river and talk over their future in the little pavilion abutting on the wall of the park.

It was just a week since his arrival at Givré, and Anna wished, before he left, to return to the place where they had sat on their first afternoon together. Her sensitiveness to the appeal of inanimate things, to the colour and texture of whatever wove itself into the substance of her emotion, made her want to hear Darrow's voice, and to feel his eyes on her, in the spot where bliss had first flowed into her heart.

That bliss, in the interval, had wound itself into every fold of her being. Passing, in the first days, from a high shy tenderness to the rush of a secret surrender, it had gradually widened and deepened, to flow on in redoubled beauty. She thought she now knew exactly how and why she loved Darrow, and she could see her whole sky reflected in the deep and tranquil current of her love.

Early the next day, in her sitting-room, she was glancing through the letters which it was Effie's morning privilege to carry up to her. Effie meanwhile circled inquisitively about the room, where there was always something new to engage her infant fancy; and Anna, looking up, saw her suddenly arrested before a photograph of Darrow which, the day before, had taken its place on the writing-table.

Anna held out her arms with a faint blush. "You do like him, don't you, dear?"

"Oh, most awfully, dearest," Effie, against her breast, leaned back to assure her with a limpid look. "And so do Granny and Owen—and I *do* think Sophy does too," she added, after a moment's earnest pondering.

"I hope so," Anna laughed. She checked the impulse to continue: "Has she talked to you about him, that you're so sure?" She did not know what had made the question spring to her lips, but she was glad she had closed them before pronouncing it. Nothing could have been more distasteful to her than to clear up such obscurities by turning on them the tiny flame of her daughter's observation. And what, after all, now that Owen's happiness was secured, did it matter if there were certain reserves in Darrow's approval of his marriage?

A knock on the door made Anna glance at the clock. "There's Nurse to carry you off."

"It's Sophy's knock," the little girl answered, jumping down to open the door; and Miss Viner in fact stood on the threshold.

"Come in," Anna said with a smile, instantly remarking how pale she looked.

"May Effie go out for a turn with Nurse?" the girl asked. "I should like to speak to you a moment."

"Of course. This ought to be *your* holiday, as yesterday was Effie's. Run off, dear," she added, stooping to kiss the little girl.

When the door had closed she turned back to Sophy Viner with a look that sought her confidence. "I'm so glad you came, my dear. We've got so many things to talk about, just you and I together."

The confused intercourse of the last days had, in fact, left little time for any speech with Sophy but such as related to her marriage and the means of overcoming Madame de Chantelle's opposition to it. Anna had exacted of Owen that no one, not even Sophy Viner, should be given a hint of her own projects till all contingent questions had been disposed of. She had felt, from the outset, a secret reluctance to intrude her securer happiness on the doubts and fears of the young pair.

From the sofa-corner to which she had dropped back she pointed to Darrow's chair. "Come and sit by me, dear. I wanted to see you alone. There's so much to say that I hardly know where to begin."

She leaned forward, her hands clasped on the arms of the sofa, her eyes bent smilingly on Sophy's. As she did so, she noticed that the girl's unusual pallor was partly due to the slight veil of powder on her face. The discovery was distinctly disagreeable. Anna had never before noticed, on Sophy's part, any recourse to cosmetics, and, much as she wished to think herself exempt from old-fashioned prejudices, she suddenly became aware that she did not like her daughter's governess to have a powdered face. Then she reflected that the girl who sat opposite her was no longer Effie's governess, but her own future daughter-in-law; and she wondered whether Miss Viner had chosen this odd way of celebrating her independence, and whether, as Mrs. Owen Leath, she would present to the world a bedizened countenance. This idea was scarcely less distasteful than the other, and for a moment Anna continued to consider her without speaking. Then, in a flash, the truth came to her: Miss Viner had powdered her face because Miss Viner had been crying.

Anna leaned forward impulsively. "My dear child, what's the matter?" She saw the girl's blood rush up under the white mask, and hastened on: "Please don't be afraid to tell me. I do so want you to feel that you can trust me as Owen does. And you know you mustn't mind if, just at first, Madame de Chantelle occasionally relapses."

She spoke eagerly, persuasively, almost on a note of pleading. She had, in truth, so many reasons for wanting Sophy to like her: her love for Owen, her solicitude for Effie, and her own sense of the girl's fine mettle. She had always felt a romantic and almost humble admiration for those members of her sex who, from force of will, or the constraint of circumstances, had plunged into the conflict from which fate had so persistently excluded her. There were even moments when she fancied herself vaguely to blame for her immunity, and felt that she ought somehow to have affronted the perils and hardships which refused to come to her. And now, as she sat looking at Sophy Viner, so small, so slight, so visibly defenceless and undone, she still felt, through all the superiority of her worldly advantages and her seeming maturity, the same odd sense of ignorance and inexperience. She could not have said what there was in the girl's manner and expression to give her this feeling, but she was reminded, as she looked at Sophy Viner, of the other girls she had known in her youth, the girls who seemed possessed of a secret she had missed. Yes, Sophy Viner had their look—almost the obscurely menacing look of Kitty Mayne . . . Anna, with an inward smile, brushed aside the image of this forgotten rival. But she had felt, deep down, a twinge of the old pain, and she was sorry that, even for the flash of a thought, Owen's betrothed should have reminded her of so different a woman . . .

She laid her hand on the girl's. "When his grandmother sees how happy Owen is she'll be quite happy herself. If it's only that, don't be distressed. Just trust to Owen—and the future."

Sophy Viner, with an almost imperceptible recoil of her whole slight person, had drawn her hand from under the palm enclosing it.

"That's what I wanted to talk to you about—the future."

"Of course! We've all so many plans to make—and to fit into each other's. Please let's begin with yours."

The girl paused a moment, her hands clasped on the arms of her chair, her lids dropped under Anna's gaze; then she said: "I should like to make no plans at all . . . just yet . . ."

"No plans?"

"No—I should like to go away . . . my friends the Farlows would let me go to them . . ." Her voice grew firmer and she lifted her eyes to add: "I should like to leave today, if you don't mind."

Anna listened with a rising wonder.

"You want to leave Givré at once?" She gave the idea a moment's swift consideration. "You prefer to be with your friends till your marriage? I understand that—but surely you needn't rush off today? There are so many details to discuss; and before long, you know, I shall be going away too."

"Yes, I know." The girl was evidently trying to steady her voice. "But I should like to wait a few days—to have a little more time to myself."

Anna continued to consider her kindly. It was evident that she did not care to say why she wished to leave Givré so suddenly, but her disturbed face and shaken voice betrayed a more pressing motive than the natural desire to spend the weeks before her marriage under her old friends' roof. Since she had made no response to the allusion to Madame de Chantelle, Anna could but conjecture that she had had a passing disagreement with Owen; and if this were so, random interference might do more harm than good.

"My dear child, if you really want to go at once I sha'n't, of course, urge you to stay. I suppose you have spoken to Owen?"

"No. Not yet . . ."

Anna threw an astonished glance at her. "You mean to say you haven't told him?"

"I wanted to tell you first. I thought I ought to, on account of Effie." Her look cleared as she put forth this reason.

"Oh, Effie!—" Anna's smile brushed away the scruple: "Owen has a right to ask that you should consider him before you think of his sister . . . Of course you shall do just as you wish," she went on, after another thoughtful interval.

"Oh, thank you," Sophy Viner murmured and rose to her feet.

Anna rose also, vaguely seeking for some word that should break down the girl's resistance. "You'll tell Owen at once?" she finally asked.

Miss Viner, instead of replying, stood before her in manifest uncertainty, and as she did so there was a light tap on the door, and Owen Leath walked into the room.

Anna's first glance told her that his face was unclouded. He met her greeting with his happiest smile and turned to lift Sophy's hand to his lips. The perception that he was utterly unconscious of any cause for Miss Viner's agitation came to his step-mother with a sharp thrill of surprise.

"Darrow's looking for you," he said to her. "He asked me to remind you that you'd promised to go for a walk with him."

Anna glanced at the clock. "I'll go down presently." She waited and looked again at Sophy Viner, whose troubled eyes seemed to commit their message to her. "You'd better tell Owen, my dear."

Owen's look also turned on the girl. "Tell me what? Why, what's happened?"

Anna summoned a laugh to ease the vague tension of the moment. "Don't look so startled! Nothing, except that Sophy proposes to desert us for a while for the Farlows."

Owen's brow cleared. "I was afraid she'd run off before long." He glanced at Anna. "Do please keep her here as long as you can!"

Sophy intervened: "Mrs. Leath's already given me leave to go."

"Already? To go when?"

"Today," said Sophy in a low tone, her eyes on Anna's.

"Today? Why on earth should you go today?" Owen dropped back a step or two, flushing and paling under his bewildered frown. His eyes seemed to search the girl more closely. "Something's happened." He too looked at his stepmother. "I suppose she must have told you what it is?"

Anna was struck by the suddenness and vehemence of his appeal. It was as though some smouldering apprehension had lain close under the surface of his security.

"She's told me nothing except that she wishes to be with her friends. It's quite natural that she should want to go to them."

Owen visibly controlled himself. "Of course—quite natural." He spoke to Sophy. "But why didn't you tell me so? Why did you come first to my step-mother?"

Anna intervened with her calm smile. "That seems to me quite natural, too. Sophy was considerate enough to tell me first because of Effie."

He weighed it. "Very well, then: that's quite natural, as you say. And of course she must do exactly as she pleases." He still kept his eyes on the girl. "Tomorrow," he abruptly announced, "I shall go up to Paris to see you."

"Oh, no—no!" she protested.

Owen turned back to Anna. "*Now* do you say that nothing's happened?"

Under the influence of his agitation Anna felt a vague tightening of the heart. She seemed to herself like some one in a dark room about whom unseen presences are groping.

"If it's anything that Sophy wishes to tell you, no doubt she'll do so. I'm going down now, and I'll leave you here to talk it over by yourselves."

As she moved to the door the girl caught up with her. "But there's nothing to tell: why should there be? I've explained that I simply want to be quiet." Her look seemed to detain Mrs. Leath.

Owen broke in: "Is that why I mayn't go up tomorrow?"

"Not tomorrow!"

"Then when may I?"

"Later . . . in a little while . . . a few days . . ."

"In how many days?"

"Owen!" his step-mother interposed; but he seemed no longer aware of her. "If you go away today, the day that our engagement's made known, it's only fair," he persisted, "that you should tell me when I am to see you."

Sophy's eyes wavered between the two and dropped down wearily. "It's you who are not fair—when I've said I wanted to be quiet."

"But why should my coming disturb you? I'm not asking now to come tomorrow. I only ask you not to leave without telling me when I'm to see you."

"Owen, I don't understand you!" his step-mother exclaimed.

"You don't understand my asking for some explanation, some assurance, when I'm left in this way, without a word, without a sign? All I ask her to tell me is when she'll see me."

Anna turned back to Sophy Viner, who stood straight and tremulous between the two.

"After all, my dear, he's not unreasonable!"

"I'll write—I'll write," the girl repeated.

"*What* will you write?" he pressed her vehemently.

"Owen," Anna exclaimed, "you *are* unreasonable!"

He turned from Sophy to his step-mother. "I only want her to say what she means: that she's going to write to break off our engagement. Isn't that what you're going away for?"

Anna felt the contagion of his excitement. She looked at Sophy, who stood motionless, her lips set, her whole face drawn to a silent fixity of resistance.

"You ought to speak, my dear—you ought to answer him."

"I only ask him to wait——"

"Yes," Owen, broke in, "and you won't say how long!"

Both instinctively addressed themselves to Anna, who stood, nearly as shaken as themselves, between the double shock of their struggle. She looked again from Sophy's inscrutable eyes to Owen's stormy features; then she said: "What can I do, when there's clearly something between you that I don't know about?"

"Oh, if it *were* between us! Can't you see it's outside of us—outside of her, dragging at her, dragging her away from me?" Owen wheeled round again upon his step-mother.

Anna turned from him to the girl. "Is it true that you want to break your engagement? If you do, you ought to tell him now."

Owen burst into a laugh. "She doesn't dare to—she's afraid I'll guess the reason!"

A faint sound escaped from Sophy's lips, but she kept them close on whatever answer she had ready.

"If she doesn't wish to marry you, why should she be afraid to have you know the reason?"

"She's afraid to have *you* know it—not me!"

"To have *me* know it?"

He laughed again, and Anna, at his laugh, felt a sudden rush of indignation.

"Owen, you must explain what you mean!"

He looked at her hard before answering; then: "Ask Darrow!" he said.

"Owen—Owen!" Sophy Viner murmured.

XXIV.

Anna stood looking from one to the other. It had become apparent to her in a flash that Owen's retort, though it startled Sophy, did not take her by surprise; and the discovery shot its light along dark distances of fear.

The immediate inference was that Owen had guessed the reason of Darrow's disapproval of his marriage, or that, at least, he suspected Sophy Viner of knowing and dreading it. This confirmation of her own obscure doubt sent a tremor of alarm through Anna. For a moment she felt like exclaiming: "All this is really no business of mine, and I refuse to have you mix me up in it—" but her secret fear held her fast.

Sophy Viner was the first to speak.

"I should like to go now," she said in a low voice, taking a few steps toward the door.

Her tone woke Anna to the sense of her own share in the situation. "I quite agree with you, my dear, that it's useless to carry on this discussion. But since Mr. Darrow's name has been brought into it, for reasons which

I fail to guess, I want to tell you that you're both mistaken if you think he's not in sympathy with your marriage. If that's what Owen means to imply, the idea's a complete delusion."

She spoke the words deliberately and incisively, as if hoping that the sound of their utterance would stifle the whisper in her bosom.

Sophy's only answer was a vague murmur, and a movement that brought her nearer to the door; but before she could reach it Owen had placed himself in her way.

"I don't mean to imply what you think," he said, addressing his step-mother but keeping his eyes on the girl. "I don't say Darrow doesn't like our marriage; I say it's Sophy who's hated it since Darrow's been here!"

He brought out the charge in a tone of forced composure, but his lips were white and he grasped the door-knob to hide the tremor of his hand.

Anna's anger surged up with her fears. "You're absurd, Owen! I don't know why I listen to you. Why should Sophy dislike Mr. Darrow, and if she does, why should that have anything to do with her wishing to break her engagement?"

"I don't say she dislikes him! I don't say she likes him; I don't know what it is they say to each other when they're shut up together alone."

"Shut up together alone?" Anna stared. Owen seemed like a man in delirium; such an exhibition was degrading to them all. But he pushed on without seeing her look.

"Yes—the first evening she came, in the study; the next morning, early, in the park; yesterday, again, in the springhouse, when you were at the lodge with the doctor . . . I don't know what they say to each other, but they've taken every chance they could to say it . . . and to say it when they thought that no one saw them."

Anna longed to silence him, but no words came to her. It was as though all her confused apprehensions had suddenly taken definite shape. There was "something"—yes, there was "something" . . . Darrow's reticences and evasions had been more than a figment of her doubts.

The next instant brought a recoil of pride. She turned indignantly on her step-son.

"I don't half understand what you've been saying; but what you seem to hint is so preposterous, and so insulting both to Sophy and to me, that I see no reason why we should listen to you any longer."

Though her tone steadied Owen, she perceived at once that it would not deflect him from his purpose. He spoke less vehemently, but with all the more precision.

"How can it be preposterous, since it's true? Or insulting, since I don't know, any more than *you*, the meaning of what I've been seeing? If you'll be patient with me I'll try to put it quietly. What I mean is that Sophy has completely changed since she met Darrow here, and that, having noticed the change, I'm hardly to blame for having tried to find out its cause."

Anna made an effort to answer him with the same composure. "You're to blame, at any rate, for so recklessly assuming that you *have* found it out. You seem to forget that, till they met here, Sophy and Mr. Darrow hardly knew each other."

"If so, it's all the stranger that they've been so often closeted together!"

"Owen, Owen—" the girl sighed out.

He turned his haggard face to her. "Can I help it, if I've seen and known what I wasn't meant to? For God's sake give me a reason—any reason I can decently make out with! Is it my fault if, the day after you arrived, when I came back late through the garden, the curtains of the study hadn't been drawn, and I saw you there alone with Darrow?"

Anna laughed impatiently. "Really, Owen, if you make it a grievance that two people who are staying in the same house should be seen talking together——!"

"They were not talking. That's the point——"

"Not talking? How do you know? You could hardly hear them from the garden!"

"No; but I could see. *He* was sitting at my desk, with his face in his hands. *She* was standing in the window, looking away from him . . ."

He waited, as if for Sophy Viner's answer; but still she neither stirred nor spoke.

"That was the first time," he went on; "and the second was the next morning in the park. It was natural enough, their meeting there. Sophy had gone out with Effie, and Effie ran back to look for me. She told me she'd left Sophy and Darrow in the path that leads to the river, and presently we saw them ahead of us. They didn't see us at first, because they were standing looking at each other; and this time they were not speaking either. We came up close before they heard us, and all that time they never spoke, or stopped looking at each other. After that I began to wonder; and so I watched them."

"Oh, Owen!"

"Oh, I only had to wait. Yesterday, when I motored you and the doctor back from the lodge, I saw Sophy coming out of the spring-house. I supposed she'd taken shelter from the rain, and when you got out of the motor I strolled back down the avenue to meet her. But she'd disappeared—she must have taken a short cut and come into the house by the side door. I don't know why I went on to the spring-house; I suppose it was what you'd call spying. I went up the steps and found the room empty; but two chairs had been moved out from the wall and were standing near the table; and one of the Chinese screens that lie on it had dropped to the floor."

Anna sounded a faint note of irony. "Really? Sophy'd gone there for shelter, and she dropped a screen and moved a chair?"

"I said two chairs——"

"Two? What damning evidence—of I don't know what!"

"Simply of the fact that Darrow'd been there with her. As I looked out of the window I saw him close by, walking away. He must have turned the corner of the spring-house just as I got to the door."

There was another silence, during which Anna paused, not only to collect her own words but to wait for Sophy Viner's; then, as the girl made no sign, she turned to her.

"I've absolutely nothing to say to all this; but perhaps you'd like me to wait and hear your answer?"

Sophy raised her head with a quick flash of colour. "I've no answer either—except that Owen must be mad."

In the interval since she had last spoken she seemed to have regained her self-control, and her voice rang clear, with a cold edge of anger.

Anna looked at her step-son. He had grown extremely pale, and his hand fell from the door with a discouraged gesture. "That's all then? You won't give me any reason?"

"I didn't suppose it was necessary to give you or any one else a reason for talking with a friend of Mrs. Leath's under Mrs. Leath's own roof."

Owen hardly seemed to feel the retort: he kept his dogged stare on her face.

"I won't ask for one, then. I'll only ask you to give me your assurance that your talks with Darrow have had nothing to do with your suddenly deciding to leave Givré."

She hesitated, not so much with the air of weighing her answer as of questioning his right to exact any. "I give you my assurance; and now I should like to go," she said.

As she turned away, Anna intervened. "My dear, I think you ought to speak."

The girl drew herself up with a faint laugh. "To him—or to *you*?"

"To him."

She stiffened. "I've said all there is to say."

Anna drew back, her eyes on her step-son. He had left the threshold and was advancing toward Sophy Viner with a motion of desperate appeal; but as he did so there was a knock on the door. A moment's silence fell on the three; then Anna said: "Come in!"

Darrow came into the room. Seeing the three together, he looked rapidly from one to the other; then he turned to Anna with a smile.

"I came up to see if you were ready; but please send me off if I'm not wanted."

His look, his voice, the simple sense of his presence, restored Anna's shaken balance. By Owen's side he looked so strong, so urbane, so experienced, that the lad's passionate charges dwindled to mere boyish vapourings. A moment ago she had dreaded Darrow's coming; now she was glad that he was there.

She turned to him with sudden decision. "Come in, please; I want you to hear what Owen has been saying."

She caught a murmur from Sophy Viner, but disregarded it. An illuminating impulse urged her on. She, habitually so aware of her own lack of penetration, her small skill in reading hidden motives and detecting secret signals, now felt herself mysteriously inspired. She addressed herself to Sophy Viner. "It's much better for you both that this absurd question should be cleared up now." Then, turning to Darrow, she continued: "For some reason that I don't pretend to guess, Owen has taken it into his head that you've influenced Miss Viner to break her engagement."

She spoke slowly and deliberately, because she wished to give time and to gain it; time for Darrow and Sophy to receive the full impact of what she was saying, and time to observe its full effect on them. She had said to herself: "If there's nothing between them, they'll look at each other; if there *is* something, they won't;" and as she ceased to speak she felt as if all her life were in her eyes.

Sophy, after a start of protest, remained motionless, her gaze on the ground. Darrow, his face grown grave, glanced slowly from Owen Leath to Anna. With his eyes on the latter he asked: "Has Miss Viner broken her engagement?"

A moment's silence followed his question; then the girl looked up and said: "Yes!"

Owen, as she spoke, uttered a smothered exclamation and walked out of the room. She continued to stand in the same place, without appearing to notice his departure, and without vouchsafing an additional word of explanation; then, before Anna could find a cry to detain her, she too turned and went out.

"For God's sake, what's happened?" Darrow asked; but Anna, with a drop of the heart, was saying to herself that he and Sophy Viner had not looked at each other.

XXV.

ANNA stood in the middle of the room, her eyes on the door. Darrow's questioning gaze was still on her, and she said to herself with a quick-drawn breath: "If only he doesn't come near me!"

It seemed to her that she had been suddenly endowed with the fatal gift of reading the secret sense of every seemingly spontaneous look and movement, and that in his least gesture of affection she would detect a cold design.

For a moment longer he continued to look at her enquiringly; then he turned away and took up his habitual stand by the mantel-piece. She drew a deep breath of relief.

"Won't you please explain?" he said.

"I can't explain: I don't know. I didn't even know—till she told you—that she really meant to break her engagement. All I know is that she came to me just now and said she wished to leave Givré today; and that Owen, when he heard of it—for she hadn't told him—at once accused her of going away with the secret intention of throwing him over."

"And you think it's a definite break?" She perceived, as she spoke, that his brow had cleared.

"How should I know? Perhaps you can tell me."

"I?" She fancied his face clouded again, but he did not move from his tranquil attitude.

"As *I* told you," she went on, "Owen has worked himself up to imagining that for some mysterious reason you've influenced Sophy against him."

Darrow still visibly wondered. "It must indeed be a mysterious reason! He knows how slightly I know Miss Viner. Why should he imagine anything so wildly improbable?"

"I don't know that either."

"But he must have hinted at some reason."

"No: he admits he doesn't know your reason. He simply says that Sophy's manner to him has changed since she came back to Givré and that he's seen you together several times—in the park, the spring-house, I don't know where—talking alone in a way that seemed confidential—almost secret; and he draws the preposterous conclusion that you've used your influence to turn her against him."

"My influence? What kind of influence?"

"He doesn't say."

Darrow again seemed to turn over the facts she gave him. His face remained grave, but without the least trace of discomposure. "And what does Miss Viner say?"

"She says it's perfectly natural that she should occasionally talk to my friends when she's under my roof—and refuses to give him any other explanation."

"That at least is perfectly natural!"

Anna felt her cheeks flush as she answered: "Yes—but there *is* something——"

"Something——?"

"Some reason for her sudden decision to break her engagement. I can understand Owen's feeling, sorry as I am for his way of showing it. The girl owes him some sort of explanation, and as long as she refuses to give it his imagination is sure to run wild."

"She would have given it, no doubt, if he'd asked it in a different tone."

"I don't defend Owen's tone—but she knew what it was before she accepted him. She knows he's excitable and undisciplined."

"Well, she's been disciplining him a little—probably the best thing that could happen. Why not let the matter rest there?"

"Leave Owen with the idea that you *have* been the cause of the break?"

He met the question with his easy smile. "Oh, as to that—leave him with any idea of me he chooses! But leave him, at any rate, free."

"Free?" she echoed in surprise.

"Simply let things be. You've surely done all you could for him and Miss Viner. If they don't hit it off it's their own affair. What possible motive can you have for trying to interfere now?"

Her gaze widened to a deeper wonder. "Why—naturally, what he says of you!"

"I don't care a straw what he says of me! In such a situation a boy in love will snatch at the most far-fetched reason rather than face the mortifying fact that the lady may simply be tired of him."

"You don't quite understand Owen. Things go deep with him, and last long. It took him a long time to recover from his other unlucky love affair. He's romantic and extravagant: he can't live on the interest of his feelings. He worships Sophy and she seemed to be fond of him. If she's changed it's been very sudden. And if they part like this, angrily and inarticulately, it will hurt him horribly—hurt his very soul. But that, as you say, is between the two. What concerns me is his associating you with their quarrel. Owen's like my own son—if you'd seen him when I first came here you'd know why. We were like two prisoners who talk to each other by tapping on the wall. He's never forgotten it, nor I. Whether he breaks with Sophy, or whether they make it up, I can't let him think you had anything to do with it."

She raised her eyes entreatingly to Darrow's, and read in them the forbearance of the man resigned to the discussion of non-existent problems.

"I'll do whatever you want me to," he said; "but I don't yet know what it is."

His smile seemed to charge her with inconsequence, and the prick to her pride made her continue: "After all, it's not so unnatural that Owen, knowing you and Sophy to be almost strangers, should wonder what you were saying to each other when he saw you talking together."

She felt a warning tremor as she spoke, as though some instinct deeper than reason surged up in defense of its treasure. But Darrow's face was unstirred save by the flit of his half-amused smile.

"Well, my dear—and couldn't you have told him?"

"I?" she faltered out through her blush.

"You seem to forget, one and all of you, the position you put me in when I came down here: your appeal to me to see Owen through, your assurance to him that I would, Madame de Chantelle's attempt to win me over; and most of all, my own sense of the fact you've just recalled to me: the importance, for both of us, that Owen should like me. It seemed to me that the first thing to do was to get as much light as I could on the whole situation; and the obvious way of doing it was to try to know Miss Viner better. Of course I've talked with her alone—I've talked with her as often as I could. I've tried my best to find out if you were right in encouraging Owen to marry her."

She listened with a growing sense of reassurance, struggling to separate the abstract sense of his words from the persuasion in which his eyes and voice enveloped them.

"I see—I do see," she murmured.

"You must see, also, that I could hardly say this to Owen without offending him still more, and perhaps increasing the breach between Miss Viner and himself. What sort of figure should I cut if I told him I'd been trying to find out if he'd made a proper choice? In any case, it's none of my business to offer an explanation of what she justly says doesn't need one. If she declines to speak, it's obviously on the ground that Owen's insinuations are absurd; and that surely pledges me to silence."

"Yes, yes! I see," Anna repeated. "But I don't want you to explain anything to Owen."

"You haven't yet told me what you do want."

She hesitated, conscious of the difficulty of justifying her request; then: "I want you to speak to Sophy," she said.

Darrow broke into an incredulous laugh. "Considering what my previous attempts have resulted in——!"

She raised her eyes quickly. "They haven't, at least, resulted in your liking her less, in your thinking less well of her than you've told me?"

She fancied he frowned a little. "I wonder why you go back to that?"

"I want to be sure—I owe it to Owen. Won't you tell me the exact impression she's produced on you?"

"I have told you—I like Miss Viner."

"Do you still believe she's in love with Owen?"

"There was nothing in our short talks to throw any particular light on that."

"You still believe, though, that there's no reason why he shouldn't marry her?"

Again he betrayed a restrained impatience. "How can I answer that without knowing her reasons for breaking with him?"

"That's just what I want you to find out from her."

"And why in the world should she tell me?"

"Because, whatever grievance she has against Owen, she can certainly have none against me. She can't want to have Owen connect me in his mind with this wretched quarrel; and she must see that he will until he's convinced you've had no share in it."

Darrow's elbow dropped from the mantel-piece and he took a restless step or two across the room. Then he halted before her.

"Why can't you tell her this yourself?"

"Don't you see?"

He eyed her intently, and she pressed on: "You must have guessed that Owen's jealous of you."

"Jealous of me?" The blood flew up under his brown skin.

"Blind with it—what else would drive him to this folly? And I can't have her think me jealous too! I've said all I could, short of making her think so; and she's refused a word more to either of us. Our only chance now is that she should listen to you—that you should make her see the harm her silence may do."

Darrow uttered a protesting exclamation. "It's all too preposterous—what you suggest! I can't, at any rate, appeal to her on such a ground as that!"

Anna laid her hand on his arm. "Appeal to her on the ground that I'm almost Owen's mother, and that any estrangement between you and him would kill me. She knows what he is—she'll understand. Tell her to say anything, do anything, she wishes; but not to go away without speaking, not to leave *that* between us when she goes!"

She drew back a step and lifted her face to his, trying to look into his eyes more deeply than she had ever looked; but before she could discern what they expressed he had taken hold of her hands and bent his head to kiss them.

"You'll see her? You'll see her?" she entreated; and he answered: "I'll do anything in the world you want me to."

XXVI.

Darrow waited alone in the sitting-room.

No place could have been more distasteful as the scene of the talk that lay before him; but he had acceded to Anna's suggestion that it would seem more natural for her to summon Sophy Viner than for him to go in search of her. As his troubled pacings carried him back and forth a relentless hand seemed to be tearing away all the tender fibres of association that bound him to the peaceful room. Here, in this very place, he had drunk his deepest draughts of happiness, had had his lips at the fountain-head of its overflowing rivers; but now that source was poisoned and he would taste no more of an untainted cup.

For a moment he felt an actual physical anguish; then his nerves hardened for the coming struggle. He had no notion of what awaited him; but after the first instinctive recoil he had seen in a flash the urgent need of another word with Sophy Viner. He had been insincere in letting Anna think that he had consented to speak because she asked it. In reality he had been feverishly casting about for the pretext she had given him; and for some reason this trivial hypocrisy weighed on him more than all his heavy burden of deceit.

At length he heard a step behind him and Sophy Viner entered. When she saw him she paused on the threshold and half drew back.

"I was told that Mrs. Leath had sent for me."

"Mrs. Leath *did* send for you. She'll be here presently; but I asked her to let me see you first."

He spoke very gently, and there was no insincerity in his gentleness. He was profoundly moved by the change in the girl's appearance. At sight of him she had forced a smile; but it lit up her wretchedness like a candle-flame held to a dead face.

She made no reply, and Darrow went on: "You must understand my wanting to speak to you, after what I was told just now."

She interposed, with a gesture of protest: "I'm not responsible for Owen's ravings!"

"Of course——". He broke off and they stood facing each other. She lifted a hand and pushed back her loose lock with the gesture that was burnt into his memory; then she looked about her and dropped into the nearest chair.

"Well, you've got what you wanted," she said.

"What do you mean by what I wanted?"

"My engagement's broken—you heard me say so."

"Why do you say that's what I wanted? All I wished, from the beginning, was to advise you, to help you as best I could——"

"That's what you've done," she rejoined. "You've convinced me that it's best I shouldn't marry him."

Darrow broke into a despairing laugh. "At the very moment when you'd convinced me to the contrary!"

"Had I?" Her smile flickered up. "Well, I really believed it till you showed me . . . warned me . . ."

"Warned you?"

"That I'd be miserable if I married a man I didn't love."

"Don't you love him?"

She made no answer, and Darrow started up and walked away to the other end of the room. He stopped before the writing-table, where his photograph, well-dressed, handsome, self-sufficient—the portrait of a man of the world, confident of his ability to deal adequately with the most delicate situations—offered its huge fatuity to his gaze. He turned back to her. "It's rather hard on Owen, isn't it, that you should have waited until now to tell him?"

She reflected a moment before answering. "I told him as soon as I knew."

"Knew that you couldn't marry him?"

"Knew that I could never live here with him." She looked about the room, as though the very walls must speak for her.

For a moment Darrow continued to search her face perplexedly; then their eyes met in a long disastrous gaze.

"Yes——" she said, and stood up.

Below the window they heard Effie whistling for her dogs, and then, from the terrace, her mother calling her.

"There—*that* for instance," Sophy Viner said.

Darrow broke out: "It's I who ought to go!"

She kept her small pale smile. "What good would that do any of us—now?"

He covered his face with his hands. "Good God!" he groaned. "How could I tell?"

"You couldn't tell. We neither of us could." She seemed to turn the problem over critically. "After all, it might have been *you* instead of me!"

He took another distracted turn about the room and coming back to her sat down in a chair at her side. A mocking hand seemed to dash the words from his lips. There was nothing on earth that he could say to her that wasn't foolish or cruel or contemptible . . .

"My dear," he began at last, "oughtn't you, at any rate, to try?"

Her gaze grew grave. "Try to forget you?"

He flushed to the forehead. "I meant, try to give Owen more time; to give him a chance. He's madly in love with you; all the good that's in him is in your hands. His step-mother felt that from the first. And she thought—she believed——"

"She thought I could make him happy. Would she think so now?"

"Now . . . ? I don't say now. But later? Time modifies . . . rubs out . . . more quickly than you think . . . Go away, but let him hope . . . I'm going too—*we're* going—" he stumbled on the plural—"in a very few weeks: going for a long time, probably. What you're thinking of now may never happen. We may not all be here together again for years."

She heard him out in silence, her hands clasped on her knee, her eyes bent on them. "For me," she said, "you'll always be here."

"Don't say that—oh, don't! Things change . . . people change . . . You'll see!"

"You don't understand. I don't want anything to change. I don't want to forget—to rub out. At first I imagined I did; but that was a foolish mistake. As soon as I saw you again I knew it . . . It's not being here with you that I'm afraid of—in the sense you think. It's being here, or anywhere, with Owen." She stood up and bent her tragic smile on him. "I want to keep you all to myself."

The only words that came to him were futile denunciations of his folly; but the sense of their futility checked them on his lips. "Poor child—you poor child!" he heard himself vainly repeating.

Suddenly he felt the strong reaction of reality and its impetus brought him to his feet. "Whatever happens, I intend to go—to go for good," he exclaimed. "I want you to understand that. Oh, don't be afraid—I'll find a reason. But it's perfectly clear that I must go."

She uttered a protesting cry. "Go away? You? Don't you see that that would tell everything—drag everybody into the horror?"

He found no answer, and her voice dropped back to its calmer note. "What good would your going do? Do you suppose it would change anything for me?" She looked at him with a musing wistfulness. "I wonder what your feeling for me was? It seems queer that I've never really known—I suppose we *don't* know much about that kind of feeling. Is it like taking a drink when you're thirsty? . . . I used to feel as if all of me was in the palm of your hand . . ."

He bowed his humbled head, but she went on almost exultantly: "Don't for a minute think I'm sorry! It was worth every penny it cost. My mistake was in being ashamed, just at first, of its having cost such a lot. I tried to carry it off as a joke—to talk of it to myself as an 'adventure'. I'd always wanted adventures, and you'd given me one, and I tried to take your attitude about it, to 'play the game' and convince myself that I hadn't risked any more on it than you. Then, when I met you again, I suddenly saw that I *had* risked more, but that I'd won more, too—such worlds! I'd been trying all the while to put everything I could between us; now I want to sweep everything away. I'd been trying to forget how you looked; now I want to remember you always.

I'd been trying not to hear your voice; now I never want to hear any other. I've made my choice—that's all: I've had you and I mean to keep you." Her face was shining like her eyes. "To keep you hidden away here," she ended, and put her hand upon her breast.

After she had left him, Darrow continued to sit motionless, staring back into their past. Hitherto it had lingered on the edge of his mind in a vague pink blur, like one of the little rose-leaf clouds that a setting sun drops from its disk. Now it was a huge looming darkness, through which his eyes vainly strained. The whole episode was still obscure to him, save where here and there, as they talked, some phrase or gesture or intonation of the girl's had lit up a little spot in the night.

She had said: "I wonder what your feeling for me was?" and he found himself wondering too . . . He remembered distinctly enough that he had not meant the perilous passion—even in its most transient form—to play a part in their relation. In that respect his attitude had been above reproach. She was an unusually original and attractive creature, to whom he had wanted to give a few days of harmless pleasuring, and who was alert and expert enough to understand his intention and spare him the boredom of hesitations and misinterpretations. That had been his first impression, and her subsequent demeanour had justified it. She had been, from the outset, just the frank and easy comrade he had expected to find her. Was it he, then, who, in the sequel, had grown impatient of the bounds he had set himself? Was it his wounded vanity that, seeking balm for its hurt, yearned to dip deeper into the healing pool of her compassion? In his confused memory of the situation he seemed not to have been guiltless of such yearnings . . . Yet for the first few days the experiment had been perfectly successful. Her enjoyment had been unclouded and his pleasure in it undisturbed. It was very gradually—he seemed to see—that a shade of lassitude had crept over their intercourse. Perhaps it was because, when her light chatter about people failed, he found she had no other fund to draw on, or perhaps simply because of the sweetness of her laugh, or of the charm of the gesture with which, one day in the woods of Marly, she had tossed off her hat and tilted back her head at the call of a cuckoo; or because, whenever he looked at her unexpectedly, he found that she was looking at him and did not want him to know it; or perhaps, in varying degrees, because of all these things, that there had come a moment when no word seemed to fly high enough or dive deep enough to utter the sense of well-being each gave to the other, and the natural substitute for speech had been a kiss.

The kiss, at all events, had come at the precise moment to save their venture from disaster. They had reached the point when her amazing reminiscences had begun to flag, when her future had been exhaustively discussed, her theatrical prospects minutely studied, her quarrel with Mrs. Murrett retold with the last amplification of detail, and when, perhaps conscious of her exhausted resources and his dwindling interest, she had committed the fatal error of saying that she could see he was unhappy, and entreating him to tell her why . . .

From the brink of estranging confidences, and from the risk of unfavourable comparisons, his gesture had snatched her back to safety; and as soon as he had kissed her he felt that she would never bore him again. She was one of the elemental creatures whose emotion is all in their pulses, and who become inexpressive or sentimental when they try to turn sensation into speech. His caress had restored her to her natural place in the scheme of things, and Darrow felt as if he had clasped a tree and a nymph had bloomed from it . . .

The mere fact of not having to listen to her any longer added immensely to her charm. She continued, of course, to talk to him, but it didn't matter, because he no longer made any effort to follow her words, but let her voice run on as a musical undercurrent to his thoughts. She hadn't a drop of poetry in her, but she had some of the qualities that create it in others; and in moments of heat the imagination does not always feel the difference . . .

Lying beside her in the shade, Darrow felt her presence as a part of the charmed stillness of the summer woods, as the element of vague well-being that suffused his senses and lulled to sleep the ache of wounded pride. All he asked of her, as yet, was a touch on the hand or on the lips—and that she should let him go on lying there through the long warm hours, while a blackbird's song throbbed like a fountain, and the summer wind stirred in the trees, and close by, between the nearest branches and the brim of his tilted hat, a slight white figure gathered up all the floating threads of joy . . .

He recalled, too, having noticed, as he lay staring at a break in the tree-tops, a stream of mares'-tails coming up the sky. He had said to himself: "It will rain tomorrow," and the thought had made the air seem warmer and the sun more vivid on her hair . . . Perhaps if the mares'-tails had not come up the sky their adventure might have had no sequel. But the cloud brought rain, and next morning he looked out of his window into a cold grey blur. They had planned an all-day excursion down the Seine, to the two Andelys and Rouen, and now, with the long hours on their hands, they were both a little at a loss . . . There was the Louvre, of course, and the Luxembourg; but he had tried looking at pictures with her, she had first so persistently admired the worst things, and then so frankly lapsed into indifference, that he had no wish to repeat the experiment. So they went out, aimlessly, and took a cold wet walk, turning at length into the deserted arcades of the Palais Royal, and finally drifting into one of its equally deserted restaurants, where they lunched alone and somewhat dolefully, served by a wan old waiter with the look of a castaway who has given up watching for a sail . . . It was odd how the waiter's face came back to him . . .

Perhaps but for the rain it might never have happened; but what was the use of thinking of that now? He tried to turn his thoughts to more urgent issues; but, by a strange perversity of association, every detail of the day was forcing itself on his mind with an insistence from which there was no escape. Reluctantly he relived the long wet walk back to the hotel, after a tedious hour at a cinematograph show on the Boulevard. It was still raining when they withdrew from this stale spectacle, but she had obstinately refused to take a cab, had even, on the way, insisted on loitering under the dripping awnings of shop-windows and poking into draughty passages, and finally, when they had nearly reached their destination, had gone so far as to suggest that they should turn back to hunt up some show she had heard of in a theatre at the Batignolles. But at that he had somewhat irritably protested: he remembered that, for the first time, they were both rather irritable, and vaguely disposed to resist one another's suggestions. His feet were wet, and he was tired of walking, and sick of the smell of stuffy unaired theatres, and he had said he must really get back to write some letters—and so they had kept on to the hotel . . .

XXVII.

DARROW had no idea how long he had sat there when he heard Anna's hand on the door. The effort of rising, and of composing his face to meet her, gave him a factitious sense of self-control. He said to himself: "I must decide on something——" and that lifted him a hair's breadth above the whirling waters.

She came in with a lighter step, and he instantly perceived that something unforeseen and reassuring had happened.

"She's been with me. She came and found me on the terrace. We've had a long talk and she's explained everything. I feel as if I'd never known her before!"

Her voice was so moved and tender that it checked his start of apprehension.

"She's explained——?"

"It's natural, isn't it, that she should have felt a little sore at the kind of inspection she's been subjected to?

Oh, not from *you*—I don't mean that! But Madame de Chantelle's opposition—and her sending for Adelaide Painter! She told me frankly she didn't care to owe her husband to Adelaide Painter . . . She thinks now that her annoyance at feeling herself so talked over and scrutinized may have shown itself in her manner to Owen, and set him imagining the insane things he did . . . I understand all she must have felt, and I agree with her that it's best she should go away for a while. She's made me," Anna summed up, "feel as if I'd been dreadfully thick-skinned and obtuse!"

"*You?*"

"Yes. As if I'd treated her like the bric-à-brac that used to be sent down here 'on approval,' to see if it would look well with the other pieces." She added, with a sudden flush of enthusiasm: "I'm glad she's got it in her to make one feel like that!"

She seemed to wait for Darrow to agree with her, or to put some other question, and he finally found voice to ask: "Then you think it's not a final break?"

"I hope not—I've never hoped it more! I had a word with Owen, too, after I left her, and I think he understands that he must let her go without insisting on any positive promise. She's excited . . . he must let her calm down . . ."

Again she waited, and Darrow said: "Surely you can make him see that."

"She'll help me to—she's to see him, of course, before she goes. She starts immediately, by the way, with Adelaide Painter, who is motoring over to Francheuil to catch the one o'clock express—and who, of course, knows nothing of all this, and is simply to be told that Sophy has been sent for by the Farlows."

Darrow mutely signed his comprehension, and she went on: "Owen is particularly anxious that neither Adelaide nor his grandmother should have the least inkling of what's happened. The need of shielding Sophy will help him to control himself. He's coming to his senses, poor boy; he's ashamed of his wild talk already. He asked me to tell you so; no doubt he'll tell you so himself."

Darrow made a movement of protest. "Oh, as to that—the thing's not worth another word."

"Or another thought, either?" She brightened. "Promise me you won't even think of it—promise me you won't be hard on him!"

He was finding it easier to smile back at her. "Why should you think it necessary to ask my indulgence for Owen?"

She hesitated a moment, her eyes wandering from him. Then they came back with a smile. "Perhaps because I need it for myself."

"For yourself?"

"I mean, because I understand better how one can torture one's self over unrealities."

As Darrow listened, the tension of his nerves began to relax. Her gaze, so grave and yet so sweet, was like a deep pool into which he could plunge and hide himself from the hard glare of his misery. As this ecstatic sense enveloped him he found it more and more difficult to follow her words and to frame an answer; but what did anything matter, except that her voice should go on, and the syllables fall like soft touches on his tortured brain?

"Don't you know," she continued, "the bliss of waking from a bad dream in one's own quiet room, and going slowly over all the horror without being afraid of it any more? That's what I'm doing now. And that's why I understand Owen . . ." She broke off, and he felt her touch on his arm. *"Because I'd dreamed the horror too!"*

He understood her then, and stammered: "You?"

"Forgive me! And let me tell you! . . . It will help you to understand Owen . . . There *were* little things . . . little signs . . . once I had begun to watch for them: your reluctance to speak about her . . . her reserve with you . . . a sort of constraint we'd never seen in her before . . ."

She laughed up at him, and with her hands in his he contrived to say: "*Now* you understand why——?"

"Oh, I understand; of course I understand; and I want you to laugh at me—with me! Because there were other things too . . . crazier things still . . . There was even—last night on the terrace—her pink cloak . . ."

"Her pink cloak?" Now he honestly wondered, and as she saw it she blushed.

"You've forgotten about the cloak? The pink cloak that Owen saw you with at the play in Paris? Yes . . . yes . . . I was mad enough for that! . . . It does me good to laugh about it now! But you ought to know that I'm going to be a jealous woman . . . a ridiculously jealous woman . . . you ought to be warned of it in time . . ."

He had dropped her hands, and she leaned close and lifted her arms to his neck with one of her rare gestures of surrender.

"I don't know why it is; but it makes me happier now to have been so foolish!"

Her lips were parted in a noiseless laugh and the

tremor of her lashes made their shadow move on her cheek. He looked at her through a mist of pain and saw all her offered beauty held up like a cup to his lips; but as he stooped to it a darkness seemed to fall between them, her arms slipped from his shoulders and she drew away from him abruptly.

"But she *was* with you, then?" she exclaimed; and then, as he stared at her: "Oh, don't say no! Only go and look at your eyes!"

He stood speechless, and she pressed on: "Don't deny it—oh, don't deny it! What will be left for me to imagine if you do? Don't you see how every single thing cries it out? Owen sees it—he saw it again just now! When I told him she'd relented, and would see him, he said: 'Is that Darrow's doing too?' "

Darrow took the onslaught in silence. He might have spoken, have summoned up the usual phrases of banter and denial; he was not even certain that they might not, for the moment, have served their purpose if he could have uttered them without being seen. But he was as conscious of what had happened to his face as if he had obeyed Anna's bidding and looked at himself in the glass. He knew he could no more hide from her what was written there than he could efface from his soul the fiery record of what he had just lived through. There before him, staring him in the eyes, and reflecting itself in all his lineaments, was the overwhelming fact of Sophy Viner's passion and of the act by which she had attested it.

Anna was talking again, hurriedly, feverishly, and his soul was wrung by the anguish in her voice. "Do speak at last—you must speak! I don't want to ask you to harm the girl; but you must see that your silence is doing her more harm than your answering my questions could. You're leaving me only the worst things to think of her . . . she'd see that herself if she were here. What worse injury can you do her than to make me hate her—to make me feel she's plotted with you to deceive us?"

"Oh, not that!" Darrow heard his own voice before he was aware that he meant to speak. "Yes; I did see her in Paris," he went on after a pause; "but I was bound to respect her reason for not wanting it known."

Anna paled. "It *was* she at the theatre that night?"

"I was with her at the theatre one night."

"Why should she have asked you not to say so?"

"She didn't wish it known that I'd met her."

"Why shouldn't she have wished it known?"

"She had quarrelled with Mrs. Murrett and come over suddenly to Paris, and she didn't want the Farlows to hear of it. I came across her by accident, and she asked me not to speak of having seen her."

"Because of her quarrel? Because she was ashamed of her part in it?"

"Oh, no. There was nothing for her to be ashamed of. But the Farlows had found the place for her, and she didn't want them to know how suddenly she'd had to leave, and how badly Mrs. Murrett had behaved. She was in a terrible plight—the woman had even kept back her month's salary. She knew the Farlows would be awfully upset, and she wanted more time to prepare them."

Darrow heard himself speak as though the words had proceeded from other lips. His explanation sounded plausible enough, and he half-fancied Anna's look grew lighter. She waited a moment, as though to be sure he had no more to add; then she said: "But the Farlows *did* know; they told me all about it when they sent her to me."

He flushed as if she had laid a deliberate trap for him. "They may know *now*; they didn't then——"

"That's no reason for her continuing now to make a mystery of having met you."

"It's the only reason I can give you."

"Then I'll go and ask her for one myself." She turned and took a few steps toward the door.

"Anna!" He started to follow her, and then checked himself. "Don't do that!"

"Why not?"

"It's not like you . . . not generous . . ."

She stood before him straight and pale, but under her rigid face he saw the tumult of her doubt and misery.

"I don't want to be ungenerous; I don't want to pry into her secrets. But things can't be left like this. Wouldn't it be better for me to go to her? Surely she'll understand—she'll explain . . . It may be some mere trifle she's concealing: something that would horrify the Farlows, but that I shouldn't see any harm in . . ." She paused, her eyes searching his face. "A love affair, I suppose . . . that's it? You met her with some man at the theatre—and she was frightened and begged you to fib about it? Those poor young things that have to go about among us like machines—oh, if you knew how I pity them!"

"If you pity her, why not let her go?"

She stared. "Let her go—go for good, you mean? Is that the best you can say for her?"

"Let things take their course. After all, it's between herself and Owen."

"And you and me—and Effie, if Owen marries her, and I leave my child with them! Don't you see the impossibility of what you're asking? We're all bound together in this coil."

Darrow turned away with a groan. "Oh, let her go—let her go."

"Then there *is* something—something really bad? She *was* with some one when you met her? Some one with whom she was——" She broke off, and he saw her struggling with new thoughts. "If it's *that*, of course . . . Oh, don't you see," she desperately appealed to him, "that I must find out, and that it's too late now for you not to speak? Don't be afraid that I'll betray you . . . I'll never, never let a soul suspect. But I must know the truth, and surely it's best for her that I should find it out from you."

Darrow waited a moment; then he said slowly: "What you imagine's mere madness. She was at the theatre with me."

"With you?" He saw a tremor pass through her, but she controlled it instantly and faced him straight and motionless as a wounded creature in the moment before it feels its wound. "Why should you both have made a mystery of that?"

"I've told you the idea was not mine." He cast about. "She may have been afraid that Owen——"

"But that was not a reason for her asking you to tell me that you hardly knew her—that you hadn't even seen her for years." She broke off and the blood rose to her face and forehead. "Even if *she* had other reasons, there could be only one reason for your obeying her——"

Silence fell between them, a silence in which the room seemed to become suddenly resonant with voices. Darrow's gaze wandered to the window and he noticed that the gale of two days before had nearly stripped the tops of the lime-trees in the court. Anna had moved away and was resting her elbows against the mantel-piece, her head in her hands. As she stood there he took in with a new intensity of vision little details of her appearance that his eyes had often cherished: the branching blue veins in the backs of her hands, the warm shadow that her hair cast on her ear, and the colour of the hair itself, dull black with a tawny under-surface, like the wings of certain birds. He felt it to be useless to speak.

After a while she lifted her head and said: "I shall not see her again before she goes."

He made no answer, and turning to him she added: "That *is* why she's going, I suppose? Because she loves you and won't give you up?"

Darrow waited. The paltriness of conventional denial was so apparent to him that even if it could have delayed discovery he could no longer have resorted to it. Under all his other fears was the dread of dishonouring the hour.

"She *has* given me up," he said at last.

XXVIII.

WHEN he had gone out of the room Anna stood where he had left her. "I must believe him! I must believe him!" she said.

A moment before, at the moment when she had lifted her arms to his neck, she had been wrapped in a sense of complete security. All the spirits of doubt had been exorcised, and her love was once more the clear habitation in which every thought and feeling could move in blissful freedom. And then, as she raised her face to Darrow's and met his eyes, she had seemed to look into the very ruins of his soul. That was the only way she could express it. It was as though he and she had been looking at two sides of the same thing, and the side she had seen had been all light and life, and his a place of graves . . .

She didn't now recall who had spoken first, or even, very clearly, what had been said. It seemed to her only a moment later that she had found herself standing at the other end of the room—the room which had suddenly grown so small that, even with its length between them, she felt as if he touched her—crying out to him "It *is* because of you she's going!" and reading the avowal in his face.

That was his secret, then, *their* secret: he had met the girl in Paris and helped her in her straits—lent her money, Anna vaguely conjectured—and she had fallen in love with him, and on meeting him again had been suddenly overmastered by her passion. Anna, dropping back into her sofa-corner, sat staring these facts in the face.

The girl had been in a desperate plight—frightened, penniless, outraged by what had happened, and not knowing (with a woman like Mrs. Murrett) what fresh injury might impend; and Darrow, meeting her in this distracted hour, had pitied, counselled, been kind to her, with the fatal, the inevitable result. There were the facts as Anna made them out: that, at least, was their external aspect, was as much of them as she had been suffered to see; and into the secret intricacies they might cover she dared not yet project her thoughts.

"I must believe him . . . I must believe him . . ." She kept on repeating the words like a talisman. It was natural, after all, that he should have behaved as he had: defended the girl's piteous secret to the last. She too began to feel the contagion of his pity—the stir, in her breast, of feelings deeper and more native to her than the pains of jealousy. From the security of her blessedness she longed to lean over with compassionate hands . . . But Owen? What was Owen's part to be? She owed herself first to him—she was bound to protect him not only from all knowledge of the secret she had surprised, but also—and chiefly!—from its consequences. Yes: the girl must go—there could be no doubt of it—Darrow himself had seen it from the first; and at the thought she had a wild revulsion of relief, as though she had been trying to create in her heart the delusion of a generosity she could not feel . . .

The one fact on which she could stay her mind was that Sophy was leaving immediately; would be out of the house within an hour. Once she was gone, it would be easier to bring Owen to the point of understanding that the break was final; if necessary, to work upon the girl to make him see it. But that, Anna was sure, would not be necessary. It was clear that Sophy Viner was leaving Givré with no thought of ever seeing it again . . .

Suddenly, as she tried to put some order in her thoughts, she heard Owen's call at the door: "Mother!——" a name he seldom gave her. There was a new note in his voice: the note of a joyous impatience. It made her turn hastily to the glass to see what face she was about to show him; but before she had had time to compose it he was in the room and she was caught in a school-boy hug.

"It's all right! It's all right! And it's all your doing! I want to do the worst kind of penance—bell and candle and the rest. I've been through it with *her*, and now she hands me on to you, and you're to call me any names you please." He freed her with his happy laugh. "I'm to be stood in the corner till next week, and then I'm to go up to see her. And she says I owe it all to you!"

"To me?" It was the first phrase she found to clutch at as she tried to steady herself in the eddies of his joy.

"Yes: you were so patient, and so dear to her; and you saw at once what a damned ass I'd been!" She tried a smile, and it seemed to pass muster with him, for he sent it back in a broad beam. "That's not so difficult to see? No, I admit it doesn't take a microscope. But you were so wise and wonderful—you always are. I've been mad these last days, simply mad—you and she might well have washed your hands of me! And instead, it's all right—all right!"

She drew back a little, trying to keep the smile on her lips and not let him get the least glimpse of what it hid. Now if ever, indeed, it behoved her to be wise and wonderful!

"I'm so glad, dear; so glad. If only you'll always feel like that about me . . ." She stopped, hardly knowing what she said, and aghast at the idea that her own hands should have retied the knot she imagined to be broken. But she saw he had something more to say; something hard to get out, but absolutely necessary to express. He caught her hands, pulled her close, and, with his forehead drawn into its whimsical smiling wrinkles, "Look here," he cried, "if Darrow wants to call me a damned ass too you're not to stop him!"

It brought her back to a sharper sense of her central peril: of the secret to be kept from him at whatever cost to her racked nerves.

"Oh, you know, he doesn't always wait for orders!" On the whole it sounded better than she'd feared.

"You mean he's called me one already?" He accepted the fact with his gayest laugh. "Well, that saves a lot of trouble; now we can pass to the order of the day——" he broke off and glanced at the clock—"which is, you know, dear, that she's starting in about an hour; she and Adelaide must already be snatching a hasty sandwich. You'll come down to bid them good-bye?"

"Yes—of course."

There had, in fact, grown upon her while he spoke the urgency of seeing Sophy Viner again before she left. The thought was deeply distasteful: Anna shrank from encountering the girl till she had cleared a way through her own perplexities. But it was obvious that since they had separated, barely an hour earlier, the situation had taken a new shape. Sophy Viner had apparently reconsidered her decision to break amicably but definitely with Owen, and stood again in their path, a menace and a mystery; and confused impulses of resistance stirred in Anna's mind.

She felt Owen's touch on her arm. "Are you coming?"

"Yes . . . yes . . . presently."

"What's the matter? You look so strange."

"What do you mean by strange?"

"I don't know: startled—surprised——" She read what her look must be by its sudden reflection in his face.

"Do I? No wonder! You've given us all an exciting morning."

He held to his point. "You're more excited now that there's no cause for it. What on earth has happened since I saw you?"

He looked about the room, as if seeking the clue to her agitation, and in her dread of what he might guess she answered: "What has happened is simply that I'm rather tired. Will you ask Sophy to come up and see me here?"

While she waited she tried to think what she should say when the girl appeared; but she had never been more conscious of her inability to deal with the oblique and the tortuous. She had lacked the hard teachings of experience, and an instinctive disdain for whatever was less clear and open than her own conscience had kept her from learning anything of the intricacies and contradictions of other hearts. She said to herself: "I must find out——" yet everything in her recoiled from the means by which she felt it must be done . . .

Sophy Viner appeared almost immediately, dressed for departure, her little bag on her arm. She was still pale to the point of haggardness, but with a light upon her that struck Anna with surprise. Or was it, perhaps, that she was looking at the girl with new eyes: seeing her, for the first time, not as Effie's governess, not as Owen's bride, but as the embodiment of that unknown peril lurking in the background of every woman's thoughts about her lover? Anna, at any rate, with a sudden sense of estrangement, noted in her graces and snares never before perceived. It was only the flash of a primitive instinct, but it lasted long enough to make her ashamed of the darknesses it lit up in her heart . . .

She signed to Sophy to sit down on the sofa beside her. "I asked you to come up to me because I wanted to say goodbye quietly," she explained, feeling her lips tremble, but trying to speak in a tone of friendly naturalness.

The girl's only answer was a faint smile of acquiescence, and Anna, disconcerted by her silence, went on: "You've decided, then, not to break your engagement?"

Sophy Viner raised her head with a look of surprise. Evidently the question, thus abruptly put, must have sounded strangely on the lips of so ardent a partisan as Mrs. Leath! "I thought that was what you wished," she said.

"What I wished?" Anna's heart shook against her side. "I wish, of course, whatever seems best for Owen . . . It's natural, you must understand, that that consideration should come first with me . . ."

Sophy was looking at her steadily. "I supposed it was the only one that counted with you."

The curtness of retort roused Anna's latent antagonism. "It is," she said, in a hard voice that startled her as she heard it. Had she ever spoken so to any one before? She felt frightened, as though her very nature had changed without her knowing it . . . Feeling the girl's astonished gaze still on her, she continued: "The suddenness of the change has naturally surprised me. When I left you it was understood that you were to reserve your decision——"

"Yes."

"And now——?" Anna waited for a reply that did not come. She did not understand the girl's attitude, the edge of irony in her short syllables, the plainly premeditated determination to lay the burden of proof on her interlocutor. Anna felt the sudden need to lift their intercourse above this mean level of defiance and distrust. She looked appealingly at Sophy.

"Isn't it best that we should speak quite frankly? It's this change on your part that perplexes me. You can hardly be surprised at that. It's true, I asked you not to break with Owen too abruptly—and I asked it, believe me, as much for your sake as for his: I wanted you to take time to think over the difficulty that seems to have arisen between you. The fact that you felt it required thinking over seemed to show you wouldn't take the final step lightly—wouldn't, I mean, accept of Owen more than you could give him. But your change of mind obliges me to ask the question I thought you would have asked yourself. Is there any reason why you shouldn't marry Owen?"

She stopped a little breathlessly, her eyes on Sophy Viner's burning face. "Any reason——? What do you mean by a reason?"

Anna continued to look at her gravely. "Do you love some one else?" she asked.

Sophy's first look was one of wonder and a faint relief; then she gave back the other's scrutiny in a glance of indescribable reproach. "Ah, you might have waited!" she exclaimed.

"Waited——?"

"Till I'd gone: till I was out of the house. You might have known . . . you might have guessed . . ." She turned her eyes again on Anna. "I only meant to let him hope a little longer, so that he shouldn't suspect anything; of course I can't marry him," she said.

Anna stood motionless, silenced by the shock of the avowal. She too was trembling, less with anger than with a confused compassion. But the feeling was so blent with others, less generous and more obscure, that she found no words to express it, and the two women faced each other without speaking.

"I'd better go," Sophy murmured at length with lowered head.

The words roused in Anna a latent impulse of compunction. The girl looked so young, so exposed and desolate! And what thoughts must she be hiding in her heart! It was impossible that they should part in such a spirit.

"I want you to know that no one said anything . . . It was I who . . ."

Sophy looked at her. "You mean that Mr. Darrow didn't tell you? Of course not: do you suppose I thought he did? You found it out, that's all—I knew you would. In your place I should have guessed it sooner."

The words were spoken simply, without irony or emphasis; but they went through Anna like a sword. Yes, the girl would have had divinations, promptings that she had not had! She felt half envious of such a sad precocity of wisdom.

"I'm so sorry . . . so sorry . . ." she murmured.

"Things happen that way. Now I'd better go. I'd like to say good-bye to Effie."

"Oh——" it broke in a cry from Effie's mother. "Not like this—you mustn't! I feel—you make me feel too horribly: as if I were driving you away . . ." The words had rushed up from the depths of her bewildered pity.

"No one is driving me away: I had to go," she heard the girl reply.

There was another silence, during which passionate impulses of magnanimity warred in Anna with her doubts and dreads. At length, her eyes on Sophy's face: "Yes, you must go now," she began; "but later on . . . after a while, when all this is over . . . if there's no reason why you shouldn't marry Owen——" she paused a moment on the words—"I shouldn't want you to think I stood between you . . ."

"You?" Sophy flushed again, and then grew pale. She seemed to try to speak, but no words came.

"Yes! It was not true when I said just now that I was thinking only of Owen. I'm sorry—oh, so sorry!—for you too. Your life—I know how hard it's been; and mine . . . mine's so full . . . Happy women understand best!" Anna drew near and touched the girl's hand; then she began again, pouring all her soul into the broken phrases: "It's terrible now . . . you see no future; but if, by and bye . . . you know best . . . but you're so young . . . and at your age things *do* pass. If there's no reason, no real reason, why you shouldn't marry Owen, I *want* him to hope, I'll help him to hope . . . if you say so . . ."

With the urgency of her pleading her clasp tightened on Sophy's hand, but it warmed to no responsive tremor:

the girl seemed numb, and Anna was frightened by the stony silence of her look. "I suppose I'm not more than half a woman," she mused, "for I don't want my happiness to hurt her;" and aloud she repeated: "If only you'll tell me there's no reason——"

The girl did not speak; but suddenly, like a snapped branch, she bent, stooped down to the hand that clasped her, and laid her lips upon it in a stream of weeping. She cried silently, continuously, abundantly, as though Anna's touch had released the waters of some deep spring of pain; then, as Anna, moved and half afraid, leaned over her with a sound of pity, she stood up and turned away.

"You're going, then—for good—like this?" Anna moved toward her and stopped. Sophy stopped too, with eyes that shrank from her.

"Oh——" Anna cried, and hid her face.

The girl walked across the room and paused again in the doorway. From there she flung back: "I wanted it—I chose it. He was good to me—no one ever was so good!"

The door-handle turned, and Anna heard her go.

XXIX.

HER first thought was: "He's going too in a few hours— I needn't see him again before he leaves . . ." At that moment the possibility of having to look in Darrow's face and hear him speak seemed to her more unendurable than anything else she could imagine. Then, on the next wave of feeling, came the desire to confront him at once and wring from him she knew not what: avowal, denial, justification, anything that should open some channel of escape to the flood of her pent-up anguish.

She had told Owen she was tired, and this seemed a sufficient reason for remaining upstairs when the motor came to the door and Miss Painter and Sophy Viner were borne off in it; sufficient also for sending word to Madame de Chantelle that she would not come down till after luncheon. Having despatched her maid with this message, she lay down on her sofa and stared before her into darkness . . .

She had been unhappy before, and the vision of old miseries flocked like hungry ghosts about her fresh pain: she recalled her youthful disappointment, the failure of her marriage, the wasted years that followed; but those were negative sorrows, denials and postponements of life. She seemed in no way related to their shadowy victim, she who was stretched on this fiery rack of the irreparable. She had suffered before— yes, but lucidly, reflectively, elegiacally: now she was suffering as a hurt animal must, blindly, furiously, with the single fierce animal longing that the awful pain should stop . . .

She heard her maid knock, and she hid her face and made no answer. The knocking continued, and the discipline of habit at length made her lift her head, compose her face and hold out her hand to the note the woman brought her. It was a word from Darrow—"May I see you?"—and she said at once, in a voice that sounded thin and empty: "Ask Mr. Darrow to come up."

The maid enquired if she wished to have her hair smoothed first, and she answered that it didn't matter; but when the door had closed, the instinct of pride drew her to her feet and she looked at herself in the glass above the mantelpiece and passed her hands over her hair. Her eyes were burning and her face looked tired and thinner; otherwise she could see no change in her appearance, and she wondered that at such a moment her body should seem as unrelated to the self that writhed within her as if it had been a statue or a picture.

The maid reopened the door to show in Darrow, and he paused a moment on the threshold, as if waiting for Anna to speak. He was extremely pale, but he looked neither ashamed nor uncertain, and she said to herself, with a perverse thrill of appreciation: "He's as proud as I am."

Aloud she asked: "You wanted to see me?"

"Naturally," he replied in a grave voice.

"Don't! It's useless. I know everything. Nothing you can say will help."

At the direct affirmation he turned even paler, and

his eyes, which he kept resolutely fixed on her, confessed his misery.

"You allow me no voice in deciding that?"

"Deciding what?"

"That there's nothing more to be said?" He waited for her to answer, and then went on: "I don't even know what you mean by 'everything'."

"Oh, I don't know what more there is! I know enough. I implored her to deny it, and she couldn't . . . What can you and I have to say to each other?" Her voice broke into a sob. The animal anguish was upon her again—just a blind cry against her pain!

Darrow kept his head high and his eyes steady. "It must be as you wish; and yet it's not like you to be afraid."

"Afraid?"

"To talk things out—to face them."

"It's for *you* to face this—not me!"

"All I ask is to face it—but with you." Once more he paused. "Won't you tell me what Miss Viner told you?"

"Oh, she's generous—to the utmost!" The pain caught her like a physical throe. It suddenly came to her how the girl must have loved him to be so generous—what memories there must be between them!

"Oh, go, please go. It's too horrible! Why should I have to see you?" she stammered, lifting her hands to her eyes.

With her face hidden she waited to hear him move away, to hear the door open and close again, as, a few hours earlier, it had opened and closed on Sophy Viner. But Darrow made no sound or movement: he too was waiting. Anna felt a thrill of resentment: his presence was an outrage on her sorrow, a humiliation to her pride. It was strange that he should wait for her to tell him so!

"You want me to leave Givré?" he asked at length. She made no answer, and he went on: "Of course I'll do as you wish; but if I go now am I not to see you again?"

His voice was firm: his pride was answering her pride!

She faltered: "You must see it's useless——"

"I might remind you that you're dismissing me without a hearing——"

"Without a hearing? I've heard you both!"

——"but I won't," he continued, "remind you of that, or of anything or any one but Owen."

"Owen——?"

"Yes; if we could somehow spare him——"

She had dropped her hands and turned her startled eyes on him. It seemed to her an age since she had thought of Owen!

"You see, don't you," Darrow continued, "that if you send me away now——"

She interrupted: "Yes, I see——" and there was a long silence between them. At length she said, very low: "I don't want any one else to suffer as I'm suffering . . ."

"Owen knows I meant to leave tomorrow," Darrow went on. "Any sudden change of plan may make him think . . ."

Oh, she saw his inevitable logic: the horror of it was on every side of her! It had seemed possible to control her grief and face Darrow calmly while she was upheld by the belief that this was their last hour together, that after he had passed out of the room there would be no fear of seeing him again, no fear that his nearness, his look, his voice, and all the unseen influences that flowed from him, would dissolve her soul to weakness. But her courage failed at the idea of having to conspire with him to shield Owen, of keeping up with him, for Owen's sake, a feint of union and felicity. To live at Darrow's side in seeming intimacy and harmony for another twenty-four hours seemed harder than to live without him for all the rest of her days. Her strength failed her, and she threw herself down and buried her sobs in the cushions where she had so often hidden a face aglow with happiness.

"Anna——" His voice was close to her. "Let me talk to you quietly. It's not worthy of either of us to be afraid."

Words of endearment would have offended her; but her heart rose at the call to her courage.

"I've no defense to make," he went on. "The facts are miserable enough; but at least I want you to see them as they are. Above all, I want you to know the truth about Miss Viner——"

The name sent the blood to Anna's forehead. She raised her head and faced him. "Why should I know more of her than what she's told me? I never wish to hear her name again!"

"It's because you feel about her in that way that I ask you—in the name of common charity—to let me give you the facts as they are, and not as you've probably imagined them."

"I've told you I don't think uncharitably of her. I don't want to think of her at all!"

"That's why I tell you you're afraid."

"Afraid?"

"Yes. You've always said you wanted, above all, to look at life, at the human problem, as it is, without fear and without hypocrisy; and it's not always a pleasant thing to look at." He broke off, and then began again: "Don't think this a plea for myself! I don't want to say a word to lessen my offense. I don't want to talk of myself at all. Even if I did, I probably couldn't make you understand—I don't, myself, as I look back. Be just to me—it's your right; all I ask you is to be generous to Miss Viner . . ."

She stood up trembling. "You're free to be as generous to her as you please!"

"Yes: you've made it clear to me that I'm free. But there's nothing I can do for her that will help her half as much as your understanding her would."

"Nothing you can do for her? You can marry her!"

His face hardened. "You certainly couldn't wish her a worse fate!"

"It must have been what she expected . . . relied on . . ." He was silent, and she broke out: "Or what *is* she? What are you? It's too horrible! On your way here . . . to *me* . . ." She felt the tears in her throat and stopped.

"That was it," he said bluntly. She stared at him.

"I was on my way to you—after repeated delays and postponements of your own making. At the very last you turned me back with a mere word—and without explanation. I waited for a letter; and none came. I'm not saying this to justify myself. I'm simply trying to make you understand. I felt hurt and bitter and bewildered. I thought you meant to give me up. And suddenly, in my way, I found some one to be sorry for, to be of use to. That, I swear to you, was the way it began. The rest was a moment's folly . . . a flash of madness . . . as such things are. We've never seen each other since . . ."

Anna was looking at him coldly. "You sufficiently describe her in saying that!"

"Yes, if you measure her by conventional standards—which is what you always declare you never do."

"Conventional standards? A girl who——" She was checked by a sudden rush of almost physical repugnance. Suddenly she broke out: "I always thought her an adventuress!"

"Always?"

"I don't mean always . . . but after you came . . ."

"She's not an adventuress."

"You mean that she professes to act on the new theories? The stuff that awful women rave about on platforms?"

"Oh, I don't think she pretended to have a theory——"

"She hadn't even *that* excuse?"

"She had the excuse of her loneliness, her unhappiness—of miseries and humiliations that a woman like you can't even guess. She had nothing to look back to but indifference or unkindness—nothing to look forward to but anxiety. She saw I was sorry for her and it touched her. She made too much of it—she exaggerated it. I ought to have seen the danger, but I didn't. There's no possible excuse for what I did."

Anna listened to him in speechless misery. Every word he spoke threw back a disintegrating light on their own past. He had come to her with an open face and a clear conscience—come to her from this! If his security was the security of falsehood it was horrible; if it meant that he had forgotten, it was worse. She would have liked to stop her ears, to close her eyes, to shut out every sight and sound and suggestion of a world in which such things could be; and at the same time she was tormented by the desire to know more, to understand better, to feel herself less ignorant and inexpert in matters which made so much of the stuff of human experience. What did he mean by "a moment's folly, a flash of madness"? How did people enter on such adventures, how pass out of them without more visible traces of their havoc? Her imagination recoiled from the vision of a sudden debasing familiarity: it seemed to her that her thoughts would never again be pure . . .

"I swear to you," she heard Darrow saying, "it was simply that, and nothing more."

She wondered at his composure, his competence, at his knowing so exactly what to say. No doubt men often had to make such explanations: they had the formulas by heart . . . A leaden lassitude descended on her. She passed from flame and torment into a colourless cold world where everything surrounding her seemed equally indifferent and remote. For a moment she simply ceased to feel.

She became aware that Darrow was waiting for her to speak, and she made an effort to represent to herself the meaning of what he had just said; but her mind was as blank as a blurred mirror. Finally she brought out: "I don't think I understand what you've told me."

"No; you don't understand," he returned with sudden bitterness; and on his lips the charge of incomprehension seemed an offense to her.

"I don't want to—about such things!"

He answered almost harshly: "Don't be afraid . . . you never will . . ." and for an instant they faced each other like enemies. Then the tears swelled in her throat at his reproach.

"You mean I don't feel things—I'm too hard?"

"No: you're too high . . . too fine . . . such things are too far from you."

He paused, as if conscious of the futility of going on with whatever he had meant to say, and again, for a short space, they confronted each other, no longer as enemies—so it seemed to her—but as beings of different language who had forgotten the few words they had learned of each other's speech.

Darrow broke the silence. "It's best, on all accounts, that I should stay till tomorrow; but I needn't intrude on you; we needn't meet again alone. I only want to be sure I know your wishes." He spoke the short sentences in a level voice, as though he were summing up the results of a business conference.

Anna looked at him vaguely. "My wishes?"

"As to Owen——"

At that she started. "They must never meet again!"

"It's not likely they will. What I meant was, that it depends on you to spare him . . ."

She answered steadily: "He shall never know," and after another interval Darrow said: "This is good-bye, then."

At the word she seemed to understand for the first time whither the flying moments had been leading them. Resentment and indignation died down, and all her consciousness resolved itself into the mere visual sense that he was there before her, near enough for her to lift her hand and touch him, and that in another instant the place where he stood would be empty.

She felt a mortal weakness, a craven impulse to cry

out to him to stay, a longing to throw herself into his arms, and take refuge there from the unendurable anguish he had caused her. Then the vision called up another thought: "I shall never know what that girl has known . . ." and the recoil of pride flung her back on the sharp edges of her anguish.

"Good-bye," she said, in dread lest he should read her face; and she stood motionless, her head high, while he walked to the door and went out.

Book Five

XXX.

ANNA Leath, three days later, sat in Miss Painter's drawing-room in the rue de Matignon.

Coming up precipitately that morning from the country, she had reached Paris at one o'clock and Miss Painter's landing some ten minutes later. Miss Painter's mouldy little manservant, dissembling a napkin under his arm, had mildly attempted to oppose her entrance; but Anna, insisting, had gone straight to the dining-room and surprised her friend—who ate as furtively as certain animals—over a strange meal of cold mutton and lemonade. Ignoring the embarrassment she caused, she had set forth the object of her journey, and Miss Painter, always hatted and booted for action, had immediately hastened out, leaving her to the solitude of the bare fireless drawing-room with its eternal slip-covers and "bowed" shutters.

In this inhospitable obscurity Anna had sat alone for close upon two hours. Both obscurity and solitude were acceptable to her, and impatient as she was to hear the result of the errand on which she had despatched her hostess, she desired still more to be alone. During her long meditation in a white-swathed chair before the muffled hearth she had been able for the first time to clear a way through the darkness and confusion of her thoughts. The way did not go far, and her attempt to trace it was as weak and spasmodic as a convalescent's first efforts to pick up the thread of living. She seemed to herself like some one struggling to rise from a long sickness of which it would have been so much easier to die. At Givré she had fallen into a kind of torpor, a deadness of soul traversed by wild flashes of pain; but whether she suffered or whether she was numb, she seemed equally remote from her real living and doing self.

It was only the discovery—that very morning—of Owen's unannounced departure for Paris that had caught her out of her dream and forced her back to action. The dread of what this flight might imply, and of the consequences that might result from it, had roused her to the sense of her responsibility, and from the moment when she had resolved to follow her step-son, and had made her rapid preparations for pursuit, her mind had begun to work again, feverishly, fitfully, but still with something of its normal order. In the train she had been too agitated, too preoccupied with what might next await her, to give her thoughts to anything but the turning over of dread alternatives; but Miss Painter's imperviousness had steadied her, and while she waited for the sound of the latch-key she resolutely returned upon herself.

With respect to her outward course she could at least tell herself that she had held to her purpose. She had, as people said, "kept up" during the twenty-four hours preceding George Darrow's departure; had gone with a calm face about her usual business, and even contrived not too obviously to avoid him. Then, the next day before dawn, from behind the closed shutters where she had kept for half the night her dry-eyed vigil, she had heard him drive off to the train which brought its passengers to Paris in time for the Calais express.

The fact of his taking that train, of his travelling so straight and far away from her, gave to what had happened the implacable outline of reality. He was gone; he would not come back; and her life had ended just as she had dreamed it was beginning. She had no doubt, at first, as to the absolute inevitability of this conclusion. The man who had driven away from her house in the autumn dawn was not the man she had loved; he was a stranger with whom she had not a single thought in common. It was terrible, indeed, that he wore the face and spoke in the voice of her friend, and that, as long as he was under one roof with her, the mere way in which he moved and looked could bridge at a stroke the gulf between them. That, no doubt, was the fault of her exaggerated sensibility to outward things: she was frightened to see how it enslaved her. A day or two before she had supposed the sense of honour was her deepest sentiment: if she had smiled at the conventions of others it was because they were too trivial, not because they were too grave. There were certain dishonours with which she had never dreamed that any pact could be made: she had had an incorruptible passion for good faith and fairness.

She had supposed that, once Darrow was gone, once she was safe from the danger of seeing and hearing him, this high devotion would sustain her. She had believed it would be possible to separate the image of the man she had thought him from that of the man he was. She had even foreseen the hour when she might raise a mournful shrine to the memory of the Darrow she had loved, without fear that his double's shadow would desecrate it. But now she had begun to understand that the two men were really one. The Darrow she worshipped was inseparable from the Darrow she abhorred; and the inevitable conclusion was that both must go, and she be left in the desert of a sorrow without memories . . .

But if the future was thus void, the present was all too full. Never had blow more complex repercussions; and to remember Owen was to cease to think of herself. What impulse, what apprehension, had sent him suddenly to Paris? And why had he thought it needful to conceal his going from her? When Sophy Viner had left, it had been with the understanding that he was to await her summons; and it seemed improbable that he would break his pledge, and seek her without leave, unless his lover's intuition had warned him of some fresh danger. Anna recalled how quickly he had read the alarm in her face when he had rushed back to her sitting-room with the news that Miss Viner had promised to see him again in Paris. To be so promptly roused, his suspicions must have been but half-asleep; and since then, no doubt, if she and Darrow had dissembled, so had he. To her proud directness it was degrading to think that they had been living together like enemies who spy upon each other's movements: she felt a desperate longing for the days which had seemed so dull and narrow, but in which she had walked with her head high and her eyes unguarded.

She had come up to Paris hardly knowing what peril she feared, and still less how she could avert it. If Owen meant to see Miss Viner—and what other object could he have?—they must already be together, and it was too late to interfere. It had indeed occurred to

Anna that Paris might not be his objective point: that his real purpose in leaving Givré without her knowledge had been to follow Darrow to London and exact the truth of him. But even to her alarmed imagination this seemed improbable. She and Darrow, to the last, had kept up so complete a feint of harmony that, whatever Owen had surmised, he could scarcely have risked acting on his suspicions. If he still felt the need of an explanation, it was almost certainly of Sophy Viner that he would ask it; and it was in quest of Sophy Viner that Anna had despatched Miss Painter.

She had found a blessed refuge from her perplexities in the stolid Adelaide's unawareness. One could so absolutely count on Miss Painter's guessing no more than one chose, and yet acting astutely on such hints as one vouchsafed her! She was like a well-trained retriever whose interest in his prey ceases when he lays it at his mater's feet. Anna, on arriving, had explained that Owen's unannounced flight had made her fear some fresh misunderstanding between himself and Miss Viner. In the interests of peace she had thought it best to follow him; but she hastily added that she did not wish to see Sophy, but only, if possible, to learn from her where Owen was. With these brief instructions Miss Painter had started out; but she was a woman of many occupations, and had given her visitor to understand that before returning she should have to call on a friend who had just arrived from Boston, and afterward despatch to another exiled compatriot a supply of cranberries and brandied peaches from the American grocery in the Champs Elysées.

Gradually, as the moments passed, Anna began to feel the reaction which, in moments of extreme nervous tension, follows on any effort of the will. She seemed to have gone as far as her courage would carry her, and she shrank more and more from the thought of Miss Painter's return, since whatever information the latter brought would necessitate some fresh decision. What should she say to Owen if she found him? What could she say that should not betray the one thing she would give her life to hide from him? "Give her life"— how the phrase derided her! It was a gift she would not have bestowed on her worst enemy. She would not have had Sophy Viner live the hours she was living now . . .

She tried again to look steadily and calmly at the picture that the image of the girl evoked. She had an idea that she ought to accustom herself to its contemplation. If life was like that, why the sooner one got used to it the better . . . But no! Life was not like that. Her adventure was a hideous accident. She dreaded above all the temptation to generalise from her own case, to doubt the high things she had lived by and seek a cheap solace in belittling what fate had refused her. There *was* such love as she had dreamed, and she meant to go on believing in it, and cherishing the thought that she was worthy of it. What had happened to her was grotesque and mean and miserable; but she herself was none of these things, and never, never would she make of herself the mock that fate had made of her . . .

She could not, as yet, bear to think deliberately of Darrow; but she kept on repeating to herself "By and bye that will come too." Even now she was determined not to let his image be distorted by her suffering. As soon as she could, she would try to single out for remembrance the individual things she had liked in him before she had loved him altogether. No "spiritual exercise" devised by the discipline of piety could have been more torturing; but its very cruelty attracted her. She wanted to wear herself out with new pains . . .

XXXI.

THE sound of Miss Painter's latch-key made her start. She was still a bundle of quivering fears to whom each coming moment seemed a menace.

There was a slight interval, and a sound of voices in the hall; then Miss Painter's vigorous hand was on the door.

Anna stood up as she came in. "You've found him?"

"I've found Sophy."

"And Owen?—has she seen him? Is he here?"

"*She's* here: in the hall. She wants to speak to you."

"Here—*now?*" Anna found no voice for more.

"She drove back with me," Miss Painter continued in the tone of impartial narrative. "The cabman was impertinent. I've got his number." She fumbled in a stout black reticule.

"Oh, I can't—" broke from Anna; but she collected herself, remembering that to betray her unwillingness to see the girl was to risk revealing much more.

"She thought you might be too tired to see her: she wouldn't come in till I'd found out."

Anna drew a quick breath. An instant's thought had told her that Sophy Viner would hardly have taken such a step unless something more important had happened. "Ask her to come, please," she said.

Miss Painter, from the threshold, turned back to announce her intention of going immediately to the police station to report the cabman's delinquency; then she passed out, and Sophy Viner entered.

The look in the girl's face showed that she had indeed come unwillingly; yet she seemed animated by an eager resoluteness that made Anna ashamed of her tremors. For a moment they looked at each other in silence, as if the thoughts between them were packed too thick for speech; then Anna said, in a voice from which she strove to take the edge of hardness: "You know where Owen is, Miss Painter tells me."

"Yes; that was my reason for asking you to see me." Sophy spoke simply, without constraint or hesitation.

"I thought he'd promised you—" Anna interposed.

"He did; but he broke his promise. That's what I thought I ought to tell you."

"Thank you." Anna went on tentatively: "He left Givré this morning without a word. I followed him because I was afraid . . ."

She broke off again and the girl took up her phrase. "You were afraid he'd guessed? He *has* . . ."

"What do you mean—guessed what?"

"That you know something he doesn't . . . something that made you glad to have me go."

"Oh—" Anna moaned. If she had wanted more pain she had it now. "He's told you this?" she faltered.

"He hasn't told me, because I haven't seen him. I kept him off—I made Mrs. Farlow get rid of him. But he's written me what he came to say; and that was it."

"Oh, poor Owen!" broke from Anna. Through all the intricacies of her suffering she felt the separate pang of his.

"And I want to ask you," the girl continued, "to let me see him; for of course," she added in the same strange voice of energy, "I wouldn't unless you consented."

"To see him?" Anna tried to gather together her startled thoughts. "What use would it be? What could you tell him?"

"I want to tell him the truth," said Sophy Viner.

The two women looked at each other, and a burning blush rose to Anna's forehead. "I don't understand," she faltered.

Sophy waited a moment; then she lowered her voice to say: "I don't want him to think worse of me than he need . . ."

"Worse?"

"Yes—to think such things as you're thinking now . . . I want him to know exactly what happened . . . then I want to bid him good-bye."

Anna tried to clear a way through her own wonder and confusion. She felt herself obscurely moved.

"Wouldn't it be worse for him——?"

"To hear the truth? It would be better, at any rate, for you and Mr. Darrow."

At the sound of the name Anna lifted her head quickly. "I've only my step-son to consider!"

The girl threw a startled look at her. "You don't mean—you're not going to give him up?"

Anna felt her lips harden. "I don't think it's of any use to talk of that."

"Oh, I know! It's my fault for not knowing how to say what I want you to hear. Your words are different; you know how to choose them. Mine offend you . . . and the dread of it makes me blunder. That's why, the other day, I couldn't say anything . . . couldn't make things clear to you. But now I *must*, even if you hate it!" She drew a step nearer, her slender figure swayed forward in a passion of entreaty. "Do listen to me! What you've said is dreadful. How can you speak of him in that voice? Don't you see that I went away so that he shouldn't have to lose you?"

Anna looked at her coldly. "Are you speaking of Mr. Darrow? I don't know why you think your going or staying can in any way affect our relations."

"You mean that you *have* given him up—because of me? Oh, how could you? You can't really love him! —And yet," the girl suddenly added, "you must, or you'd be more sorry for me!"

"I'm very sorry for you," Anna said, feeling as if the iron band about her heart pressed on it a little less inexorably.

"Then why won't you hear me? Why won't you try to understand? It's all so different from what you imagine!"

"I've never judged you."

"I'm not thinking of myself. He loves you!"

"I thought you'd come to speak of Owen."

Sophy Viner seemed not to hear her. "He's never loved any one else. Even those few days . . . I knew it all the while . . . he never cared for me."

"Please don't say any more!" Anna said.

"I know it must seem strange to you that I should say so much. I shock you, I offend you: you think me a creature without shame. So I am—but not in the sense you think! I'm not ashamed of having loved him; no; and I'm not ashamed of telling you so. It's that that justifies me—and him too . . . Oh, let me tell you how it happened! He was sorry for me: he saw I cared. I *knew* that was all he ever felt. I could see he was thinking of some one else. I knew it was only for a week . . . He never said a word to mislead me . . . I wanted to be happy just once—and I didn't dream of the harm I might be doing him!"

Anna could not speak. She hardly knew, as yet, what the girl's words conveyed to her, save the sense of their tragic fervour; but she was conscious of being in the presence of an intenser passion than she had ever felt.

"I am sorry for you." She paused. "But why do you say this to me?" After another interval she exclaimed: "You'd no right to let Owen love you."

"No; that was wrong. At least what's happened since has made it so. If things had been different I think I could have made Owen happy. You were all so good to me—I wanted so to stay with you! I suppose you'll say that makes it worse: my daring to dream I had the right . . . But all that doesn't matter now. I won't see Owen unless you're willing. I should have liked to tell him what I've tried to tell you; but you must know better; you feel things in a finer way. Only you'll have to help him if I can't. He cares a great deal . . . it's going to hurt him . . ."

Anna trembled. "Oh, I know! What can I do?"

"You can go straight back to Givré—now, at once! So that Owen shall never know you've followed him." Sophy's clasped hands reached out urgently. "And you can send for Mr. Darrow—bring him back. Owen must be convinced that he's mistaken, and nothing else will convince him. Afterward I'll find a pretext—oh, I promise you! But first he must see for himself that nothing's changed for you."

Anna stood motionless, subdued and dominated. The girl's ardour swept her like a wind.

"Oh, can't I move you? Some day you'll know!" Sophy pleaded, her eyes full of tears.

Anna saw them, and felt a fullness in her throat. Again the band about her heart seemed loosened. She wanted to find a word, but could not: all within her was too dark and violent. She gave the girl a speechless look.

"I do believe you," she said suddenly; then she turned and walked out of the room.

XXXII.

SHE drove from Miss Painter's to her own apartment. The maid-servant who had it in charge had been apprised of her coming, and had opened one or two of the rooms, and prepared a fire in her bedroom. Anna shut herself in, refusing the woman's ministrations. She felt cold and faint, and after she had taken off her hat and cloak she knelt down by the fire and stretched her hands to it.

In one respect, at least, it was clear to her that she would do well to follow Sophy Viner's counsel. It had been an act of folly to follow Owen, and her first business was to get back to Givré before him. But the only train leaving that evening was a slow one, which did not reach Francheuil till midnight, and she knew that her taking it would excite Madame de

Chantelle's wonder and lead to interminable talk. She had come up to Paris on the pretext of finding a new governess for Effie, and the natural thing was to defer her return till the next morning. She knew Owen well enough to be sure that he would make another attempt to see Miss Viner, and failing that, would write again and await her answer; so that there was no likelihood of his reaching Givré till the following evening.

Her sense of relief at not having to start out at once showed her for the first time how tired she was. The *bonne* had suggested a cup of tea, but the dread of having any one about her had made Anna refuse, and she had eaten nothing since morning but a sandwich bought at a buffet. She was too tired to get up, but stretching out her arm she drew toward her the armchair which stood beside the hearth and rested her head against its cushions. Gradually the warmth of the fire stole into her veins and her heaviness of soul was replaced by a dreamy buoyancy. She seemed to be seated on the hearth in her sitting-room at Givré, and Darrow was beside her, in the chair against which she leaned. He put his arms about her shoulders and drawing her head back looked into her eyes. "Of all the ways you do your hair, that's the way I like best," he said . . .

A log dropped, and she sat up with a start. There was a warmth in her heart, and she was smiling. Then she looked about her, and saw where she was, and the glory fell. She hid her face and sobbed.

Presently she perceived that it was growing dark, and getting up stiffly she began to undo the things in her bag and spread them on the dressing-table. She shrank from lighting the lights, and groped her way about, trying to find what she needed. She seemed immeasurably far off from every one, and most of all from herself. It was as if her consciousness had been transmitted to some stranger whose thoughts and gestures were indifferent to her . . .

Suddenly she heard a shrill tinkle, and with a beating heart she stood still in the middle of the room. It was the telephone in her dressing-room—a call, no doubt, from Adelaide Painter. Or could Owen have learned she was in town? The thought alarmed her and she opened the door and stumbled across the unlit room to the instrument. She held it to her ear, and heard Darrow's voice pronounce her name.

"Will you let me see you? I've come back—I had to come. Miss Painter told me you were here."

She began to tremble, and feared that he would guess it from her voice. She did not know what she answered: she heard him say: "I can't hear." She called "Yes!" and laid the telephone down, and caught it up again—but he was gone. She wondered if her "Yes" had reached him.

She sat in her chair and listened. Why had she said that she would see him? What did she mean to say to him when he came? Now and then, as she sat there, the sense of his presence enveloped her as in her dream, and she shut her eyes and felt his arms about her. Then she woke to reality and shivered. A long time elapsed, and at length she said to herself: "He isn't coming."

The door-bell rang as she said it, and she stood up, cold and trembling. She thought: "Can he imagine there's any use in coming?" and moved forward to bid the servant say she could not see him.

The door opened and she saw him standing in the

drawing-room. The room was cold and fireless, and a hard glare fell from the wall-lights on the shrouded furniture and the white slips covering the curtains. He looked pale and stern, with a frown of fatigue between his eyes; and she remembered that in three days he had travelled from Givré to London and back. It seemed incredible that all that had befallen her should have been compressed within the space of three days!

"Thank you," he said as she came in.

She answered: "It's better, I suppose——"

He came toward her and took her in his arms. She struggled a little, afraid of yielding, but he pressed her to him, not bending to her but holding her fast, as though he had found her after a long search: she heard his hurried breathing. It seemed to come from her own breast, so close he held her; and it was she who, at last, lifted up her face and drew down his.

She freed herself and went and sat on a sofa at the other end of the room. A mirror between the shrouded window-curtains showed her crumpled travelling dress and the white face under her disordered hair.

She found her voice, and asked him how he had been able to leave London. He answered that he had managed—he'd arranged it; and she saw he hardly heard what she was saying.

"I had to see you," he went on, and moved nearer, sitting down at her side.

"Yes; we must think of Owen——"

"Oh, Owen—!"

Her mind had flown back to Sophy Viner's plea that she should let Darrow return to Givré in order that Owen might be persuaded of the folly of his suspicions. The suggestion was absurd, of course. She could not ask Darrow to lend himself to such a fraud, even had she had the inhuman courage to play her part in it. She was suddenly overwhelmed by the futility of every attempt to reconstruct her ruined world. No, it was useless; and since it was useless, every moment with Darrow was pure pain . . .

"I've come to talk of myself, not of Owen," she heard him saying. "When you sent me away the other day I understood that it couldn't be otherwise—then. But it's not possible that you and I should part like that. If I'm to lose you, it must be for a better reason."

"A better reason?"

"Yes: a deeper one. One that means a fundamental disaccord between us. This one doesn't—in spite of everything it doesn't. That's what I want you to see, and have the courage to acknowledge."

"If I saw it I should have the courage!"

"Yes: courage was the wrong word. You have that. That's why I'm here."

"But I don't see it," she continued sadly. "So it's useless, isn't it?—and so cruel . . ." He was about to speak, but she went on: "I shall never understand it—never!"

He looked at her. "You will some day: you were made to feel everything——"

"I should have thought this was a case of not feeling——"

"On my part, you mean?" He faced her resolutely. "Yes, it was: to my shame . . . What I meant was that when you've lived a little longer you'll see what complex blunderers we all are: how we're struck blind sometimes, and mad sometimes—and then, when our sight and our senses come back, how we have to set to work, and build up, little by little, bit by bit, the precious things we'd smashed to atoms without knowing it. Life's just a perpetual piecing together of broken bits."

She looked up quickly. "That's what I feel: that you ought to——"

He stood up, interrupting her with a gesture. "Oh, don't—don't say what you're going to! Men don't give their lives away like that. If you won't have mine, it's at least my own, to do the best I can with."

"The best you can—that's what I mean! How can there be a 'best' for you that's made of some one else's worst?"

He sat down again with a groan. "I don't know! It seemed such a slight thing—all on the surface—and I've gone aground on it because it *was* on the surface. I see the horror of it just as you do. But I see, a little more clearly, the extent, and the limits, of my wrong. It's not as black as you imagine."

She lowered her voice to say: "I suppose I shall never understand; but she seems to love you . . ."

"There's my shame! That I didn't guess it, didn't fly from it. You say you'll never understand: but why shouldn't you? Is it anything to be proud of, to know so little of the strings that pull us? If you knew a little more, I could tell you how such things happen without offending you; and perhaps you'd listen without condemning me."

"I don't condemn you." She was dizzy with struggling impulses. She longed to cry out: "I *do* understand! I've understood ever since you've been here!" For she was aware, in her own bosom, of sensations so separate from her romantic thoughts of him that she saw her body and soul divided against themselves. She recalled having read somewhere that in ancient Rome the slaves were not allowed to wear a distinctive dress lest they should recognize each other and learn their numbers and their power. So, in herself, she discerned for the first time instincts and desires, which, mute and unmarked, had gone to and fro in the dim passages of her mind, and now hailed each other with a cry of mutiny.

"Oh, I don't know what to think!" she broke out. "You say you didn't know she loved you. But you know it now. Doesn't that show you how you can put the broken bits together?"

"Can you seriously think it would be doing so to marry one woman while I care for another?"

"Oh, I don't know . . . I don't know . . ." The sense of her weakness made her try to harden herself against his arguments.

"You do know! We've often talked of such things: of the monstrousness of useless sacrifices. If I'm to expiate, it's not in that way." He added abruptly: "It's in having to say this to you now . . ."

She found no answer.

Through the silent apartment they heard the sudden peal of the door-bell, and she rose to her feet. "Owen!" she instantly exclaimed.

"Is Owen in Paris?"

She explained in a rapid undertone what she had learned from Sophy Viner.

"Shall I leave you?" Darrow asked.

"Yes . . . no . . ." She moved to the dining-room door, with the half-formed purpose of making him pass out, and then turned back. "It may be Adelaide."

They heard the outer door open, and a moment later Owen walked into the room. He was pale, with excited eyes: as they fell on Darrow, Anna saw his start of wonder. He made a slight sign of recognition, and then went up to his stepmother with an air of exaggerated gaiety.

"You furtive person! I ran across the omniscient Adelaide and heard from her that you'd rushed up suddenly and secretly——" He stood between Anna and Darrow, strained, questioning, dangerously on edge.

"I came up to meet Mr. Darrow," Anna answered. "His leave's been prolonged—he's going back with me."

The words seemed to have uttered themselves without her will, yet she felt a great sense of freedom as she spoke them.

The hard tension of Owen's face changed to incredulous surprise. He looked at Darrow.

"The merest luck . . . a colleague whose wife was ill . . . I came straight back," she heard the latter tranquilly explaining. His self-command helped to steady her, and she smiled at Owen.

"We'll all go back together tomorrow morning," she said as she slipped her arm through his.

XXXIII.

OWEN Leath did not go back with his step-mother to Givré. In reply to her suggestion he announced his intention of staying on a day or two longer in Paris.

Anna left alone by the first train the next morning. Darrow was to follow in the afternoon. When Owen had left them the evening before, Darrow waited a moment for her to speak; then, as she said nothing, he asked her if she really wished him to return to Givré. She made a mute sign of assent, and he added: "For you know that, much as I'm ready to do for Owen, I can't do that for him—I can't go back to be sent away again."

"No—no!"

He came nearer, and looked at her, and she went to him. All her fears seemed to fall from her as he held her. It was a different feeling from any she had known before: confused and turbid, as if secret shames and rancours stirred in it, yet richer, deeper, more enslaving. She leaned her head back and shut her eyes beneath his kisses. She knew now that she could never give him up.

Nevertheless she asked him, the next morning, to let her go back alone to Givré. She wanted time to think. She was convinced that what had happened was inevitable, that she and Darrow belonged to each other, and that he was right in saying no past folly could ever put them asunder. If there was a shade of difference in her feeling for him it was that of an added intensity. She felt restless, insecure out of his sight: she had a sense of incompleteness, of passionate dependence, that was somehow at variance with her own conception of her character.

It was partly the consciousness of this change in herself that made her want to be alone. The solitude of her inner life had given her the habit of these hours of self-examination, and she needed them as she needed her morning plunge into cold water.

During the journey she tried to review what had

happened in the light of her new decision and of her sudden relief from pain. She seemed to herself to have passed through some fiery initiation from which she had emerged seared and quivering, but clutching to her breast a magic talisman. Sophy Viner had cried out to her: "Some day you'll know!" and Darrow had used the same words. They meant, she supposed, that when she had explored the intricacies and darknesses of her own heart her judgment of others would be less absolute. Well, she knew now—knew weaknesses and strengths she had not dreamed of, and the deep discord and still deeper complicities between what thought in her and what blindly wanted . . .

Her mind turned anxiously to Owen. At least the blow that was to fall on him would not seem to have been inflicted by her hand. He would be left with the impression that his breach with Sophy Viner was due to one of the ordinary causes of such disruptions: though he must lose her, his memory of her would not be poisoned. Anna never for a moment permitted herself the delusion that she had renewed her promise to Darrow in order to spare her step-son this last refinement of misery. She knew she had been prompted by the irresistible impulse to hold fast to what was most precious to her, and that Owen's arrival on the scene had been the pretext for her decision, and not its cause; yet she felt herself fortified by the thought of what she had spared him. It was as though a star she had been used to follow had shed its familiar ray on ways unknown to her.

All through these meditations ran the undercurrent of an absolute trust in Sophy Viner. She thought of the girl with a mingling of antipathy and confidence. It was humiliating to her pride to recognize kindred impulses in a character which she would have liked to feel completely alien to her. But what indeed was the girl really like? She seemed to have no scruples and a thousand delicacies. She had given herself to Darrow, and concealed the episode from Owen Leath, with no more apparent sense of debasement than the vulgarest of adventuresses; yet she had instantly obeyed the voice of her heart when it bade her part from the one and serve the other.

Anna tried to picture what the girl's life must have been: what experiences, what initiations, had formed her. But her own training had been too different: there were veils she could not lift. She looked back at her married life, and its colourless uniformity took on an air of high restraint and order. Was it because she had been so incurious that it had worn that look to her? It struck her with amazement that she had never given a thought to her husband's past, or wondered what he did and where he went when he was away from her. If she had been asked what she supposed he thought about when they were apart, she would instantly have answered: his snuff-boxes. It had never occurred to her that he might have passions, interests, preoccupations of which she was absolutely ignorant. Yet he went up to Paris rather regularly: ostensibly to attend sales and exhibitions, or to confer with dealers and collectors. She tried to picture him, straight, trim, beautifully brushed and varnished, walking furtively down a quiet street, and looking about him before he slipped into a doorway. She understood now that she had been cold to him: what more likely than that he had sought compensations? All men were like that, she supposed—no doubt her simplicity had amused him.

In the act of transposing Fraser Leath into a Don Juan she was pulled up by the ironic perception that she was simply trying to justify Darrow. She wanted to think that all men were "like that" because Darrow was "like that": she wanted to justify her acceptance of the fact by persuading herself that only through such concessions could women like herself hope to keep what they could not give up. And suddenly she was filled with anger at her blindness, and then at her disastrous attempt to see. Why had she forced the truth out of Darrow? If only she had held her tongue nothing need ever have been known. Sophy Viner would have broken her engagement, Owen would have been sent around the world, and her own dream would have been unshattered. But she had probed, insisted, cross-examined, not rested till she had dragged the secret to the light. She was one of the luckless women who always have the wrong audacities, and who always know it . . .

Was it she, Anna Leath, who was picturing herself to herself in that way? She recoiled from her thoughts as if with a sense of demoniac possession, and there flashed through her the longing to return to her old state of fearless ignorance. If at that moment she could have kept Darrow from following her to Givré she would have done so . . .

But he came; and with the sight of him the turmoil fell and she felt herself reassured, rehabilitated. He arrived toward dusk, and she motored to Francheuil to meet him. She wanted to see him as soon as possible, for she had divined, through the new insight that was in her, that only his presence could restore her to a normal view of things. In the motor, as they left the town and turned into the high-road, he lifted her hand and kissed it, and she leaned against him, and felt the currents flow between them. She was grateful to him for not saying anything, and for not expecting her to speak. She said to herself: "He never makes a mistake—he always knows what to do"; and then she thought with a start that it was doubtless because he had so often been in such situations. The idea that his tact was a kind of professional expertness filled her with repugnance, and insensibly she drew away from him. He made no motion to bring her nearer, and she instantly thought that that was calculated too. She sat beside him in frozen misery, wondering whether, henceforth, she would measure in this way his every look and gesture. Neither of them spoke again till the motor turned under the dark arch of the avenue, and they saw the lights of Givré twinkling at its end. Then Darrow laid his hand on hers and said: "I know, dear—" and the hardness in her melted. "He's suffering as I am," she thought; and for a moment the baleful fact between them seemed to draw them closer instead of walling them up in their separate wretchedness.

It was wonderful to be once more re-entering the doors of Givré with him, and as the old house received them into its mellow silence she had again the sense of passing out of a dreadful dream into the reassurance of kindly and familiar things. It did not seem possible that these quiet rooms, so full of the slowly-distilled accumulations of a fastidious taste, should have been the scene of tragic dissensions. The memory of them seemed to be shut out into the night with the closing and barring of its doors.

At the tea-table in the oak-room they found Madame

de Chantelle and Effie. The little girl, catching sight of Darrow, raced down the drawing-rooms to meet him, and returned in triumph on his shoulder. Anna looked at them with a smile. Effie, for all her graces, was chary of such favours, and her mother knew that in according them to Darrow she had admitted him to the circle where Owen had hitherto ruled.

Over the tea-table Darrow gave Madame de Chantelle the explanation of his sudden return from England. On reaching London, he told her, he had found that the secretary he was to have replaced was detained there by the illness of his wife. The Ambassador, knowing Darrow's urgent reasons for wishing to be in France, had immediately proposed his going back, and awaiting at Givré the summons to relieve his colleague; and he had jumped into the first train, without even waiting to telegraph the news of his release. He spoke naturally, easily, in his usual quiet voice, taking his tea from Effie, helping himself to the toast she handed, and stooping now and then to stroke the dozing terrier. And suddenly, as Anna listened to his explanation, she asked herself if it were true.

The question, of course, was absurd. There was no possible reason why he should invent a false account of his return, and every probability that the version he gave was the real one. But he had looked and spoken in the same way when he had answered her probing questions about Sophy Viner, and she reflected with a chill of fear that she would never again know if he were speaking the truth or not. She was sure he loved her, and she did not fear his insincerity as much as her own distrust of him. For a moment it seemed to her that this must corrupt the very source of love; then she said to herself: "By and bye, when I am altogether his, we shall be so near each other that there will be no room for any doubts between us." But the doubts were there now, one moment lulled to quiescence, the next more torturingly alert. When the nurse appeared to summon Effie, the little girl, after kissing her grandmother, entrenched herself on Darrow's knee with the imperious demand to be carried up to bed; and Anna, while she laughingly protested, said to herself with a pang: "Can I give her a father about whom I think such things?"

The thought of Effie, and of what she owed to Effie, had been the fundamental reason for her delays and hesitations when she and Darrow had come together again in England. Her own feeling was so clear that but for that scruple she would have put her hand in his at once. But till she had seen him again she had never considered the possibility of remarriage, and when it suddenly confronted her it seemed, for the moment, to disorganize the life she had planned for herself and her child. She had not spoken of this to Darrow because it appeared to her a subject to be debated within her own conscience. The question, then, was not as to his fitness to become the guide and guardian of her child; nor did she fear that her love for him would deprive Effie of the least fraction of her tenderness, since she did not think of love as something measured and exhaustible but as a treasure perpetually renewed. What she questioned was her right to introduce into her life any interests and duties which might rob Effie of a part of her time, or lessen the closeness of their daily intercourse.

She had decided this question as it was inevitable that she should; but now another was before her. Assuredly, at her age, there was no possible reason why she should cloister herself to bring up her daughter; but there was every reason for not marrying a man in whom her own faith was not complete . . .

XXXIV.

WHEN she woke the next morning she felt a great lightness of heart. She recalled her last awakening at Givré, three days before, when it had seemed as though all her life had gone down in darkness. Now Darrow was once more under the same roof with her, and once more his nearness sufficed to make the looming horror drop away. She could almost have smiled at her scruples of the night before: as she looked back on them they seemed to belong to the old ignorant timorous time when she had feared to look life in the face, and had been blind to the mysteries and contradictions of the human heart because her own had not been revealed to her. Darrow had said: "You were made to feel everything"; and to feel was surely better than to judge.

When she came downstairs he was already in the oak-room with Effie and Madame de Chantelle, and the sense of reassurance which his presence gave her was merged in the relief of not being able to speak of what was between them. But there it was, inevitably, and whenever they looked at each other they saw it. In her dread of giving it a more tangible shape she tried to devise means of keeping the little girl with her, and, when the latter had been called away by the nurse, found an excuse for following Madame de Chantelle upstairs to the purple sitting-room. But a confidential talk with Madame de Chantelle implied the detailed discussion of plans of which Anna could hardly yet bear to consider the vaguest outline: the date of her marriage, the relative advantages of sailing from London or Lisbon, the possibility of hiring a habitable house at their new post; and, when these problems were exhausted, the application of the same method to the subject of Owen's future.

His grandmother, having no suspicion of the real reason of Sophy Viner's departure, had thought it "extremely suitable" of the young girl to withdraw to the shelter of her old friends' roof in the hour of bridal preparation. This maidenly retreat had in fact impressed Madame de Chantelle so favourably that she was disposed for the first time to talk over Owen's projects; and as every human event translated itself for her into terms of social and domestic detail, Anna had perforce to travel the same round again. She felt a momentary relief when Darrow presently joined them; but his coming served only to draw the conversation back to the question of their own future, and Anna felt a new pang as she heard him calmly and lucidly discussing it. Did such self-possession imply indifference or insincerity? In that problem her mind perpetually revolved; and she dreaded the one answer as much as the other.

She was resolved to keep on her course as though nothing had happened: to marry Darrow and never let the consciousness of the past intrude itself between them; but she was beginning to feel that the only way of attaining to this state of detachment from the irreparable was once for all to turn back with him to its contemplation. As soon as this desire had germinated it became so strong in her that she regretted having promised Effie to take her out for the afternoon. But she could think of no pretext for disappointing the little girl, and soon after luncheon the three set forth in the motor to show Darrow a château famous in the annals of the region. During their excursion Anna found it impossible to guess from his demeanour if Effie's presence between them was as much of a strain to his composure as to hers. He remained imperturbably good-humoured and appreciative while they went the round of the monument, and she remarked only that when he thought himself unnoticed his face grew grave and his answers came less promptly.

On the way back, two or three miles from Givré, she suddenly proposed that they should walk home through the forest which skirted that side of the park. Darrow acquiesced, and they got out and sent Effie on in the motor. Their way led through a bit of sober French woodland, flat as a faded tapestry, but with gleams of live emerald lingering here and there among its browns and ochres. The luminous grey air gave vividness to its dying colours, and veiled the distant glimpses of the landscape in soft uncertainty. In such a solitude Anna had fancied it would be easier to speak; but as she walked beside Darrow over the deep soundless flooring of brown moss the words on her lips took flight again. It seemed impossible to break the spell of quiet joy which his presence laid on her, and when he began to talk of the place they had just visited she answered his questions and then waited for what he should say next . . . No, decidedly she could not speak;

she no longer even knew what she had meant to say . . .

The same experience repeated itself several times that day and the next. When she and Darrow were apart she exhausted herself in appeal and interrogation, she formulated with a fervent lucidity every point in her imaginary argument. But as soon as she was alone with him something deeper than reason and subtler than shyness laid its benumbing touch upon her, and the desire to speak became merely a dim disquietude, through which his looks, his words, his touch, reached her as through a mist of bodily pain. Yet this inertia was torn by wild flashes of resistance, and when they were apart she began to prepare again what she meant to say to him.

She knew he could not be with her without being aware of this inner turmoil, and she hoped he would break the spell by some releasing word. But she presently understood that he recognized the futility of words, and was resolutely bent on holding her to her own purpose of behaving as if nothing had happened. Once more she inwardly accused him of insensibility, and her imagination was beset by tormenting visions of his past . . . Had such things happened to him before? If the episode had been an isolated accident—"a moment of folly and madness", as he had called it—she could understand, or at least begin to understand (for at a certain point her imagination always turned back); but if it were a mere link in a chain of similar experiments, the thought of it dishonoured her whole past . . .

Effie, in the interregnum between governesses, had been given leave to dine downstairs; and Anna, on the evening of Darrow's return, kept the little girl with her till long after the nurse had signalled from the drawing-room door. When at length she had been carried off, Anna proposed a game of cards, and after this diversion had drawn to its languid close she said good-night to Darrow and followed Madame de Chantelle upstairs. But Madame de Chantelle never sat up late, and the second evening, with the amiably implied intention of leaving Anna and Darrow to themselves, she took an earlier leave of them than usual.

Anna sat silent, listening to her small stiff steps as they minced down the hall and died out in the distance. Madame de Chantelle had broken her wooden embroidery frame, and Darrow, having offered to repair it, had drawn his chair up to a table that held a lamp. Anna watched him as he sat with bent head and knitted brows, trying to fit together the disjoined pieces. The sight of him, so tranquilly absorbed in this trifling business, seemed to give to the quiet room a perfume of intimacy, to fill it with a sense of sweet familiar habit; and it came over her again that she knew nothing of the inner thoughts of this man who was sitting by her as a husband might. The lamplight fell on his white forehead, on the healthy brown of his cheek, the backs of his thin sun-burnt hands. As she watched the hands her sense of them became as vivid as a touch, and she said to herself: "That other woman has sat and watched him as I am doing. She has known him as I have never known him . . . Perhaps he is thinking of that now. Or perhaps he has forgotten it all as completely as I have forgotten everything that happened to me before he came . . ."

He looked young, active, stored with strength and energy; not the man for vain repinings or long memories. She wondered what she had to hold or satisfy him.

He loved her now; she had no doubt of that; but how could she hope to keep him? They were so nearly of an age that already she felt herself his senior. As yet the difference was not visible; outwardly at least they were matched; but ill-health or unhappiness would soon do away with this equality. She thought with a pang of bitterness: "He won't grow any older because he doesn't feel things; and because he doesn't, I *shall* . . ."

And when she ceased to please him, what then? Had he the tradition of faith to the spoken vow, or the deeper piety of the unspoken dedication? What was his theory, what his inner conviction in such matters? But what did she care for his convictions or his theories? No doubt he loved her now, and believed he would always go on loving her, and was persuaded that, if he ceased to, his loyalty would be proof against the change. What she wanted to know was not what he thought about it in advance, but what would impel or restrain him at the crucial hour. She put no faith in her own arts: she was too sure of having none! And if some beneficent enchanter had bestowed them on her, she knew now that she would have rejected the gift. She could hardly conceive of wanting the kind of love that was a state one could be cozened into . . .

Darrow, putting away the frame, walked across the room and sat down beside her; and she felt he had something special to say.

"They're sure to send for me in a day or two now," he began.

She made no answer, and he continued: "You'll tell me before I go what day I'm to come back and get you?"

It was the first time since his return to Givré that

he had made any direct allusion to the date of their marriage; and instead of answering him she broke out: "There's something I've been wanting you to know. The other day in Paris I saw Miss Viner."

She saw him flush with the intensity of his surprise.

"You sent for her?"

"No; she heard from Adelaide that I was in Paris and she came. She came because she wanted to urge me to marry you. I thought you ought to know what she had done."

Darrow stood up. "I'm glad you've told me." He spoke with a visible effort at composure. Her eyes followed him as he moved away.

"Is that all?" he asked after an interval.

"It seems to me a great deal."

"It's what she'd already asked me." His voice showed her how deeply he was moved, and a throb of jealousy shot through her.

"Oh, it was for your sake, I know!" He made no answer, and she added: "She's been exceedingly generous . . . Why shouldn't we speak of it?"

She had lowered her head, but through her dropped lids she seemed to be watching the crowded scene of his face.

"I've not shrunk from speaking of it."

"Speaking of *her*, then, I mean. It seems to me that if I could talk to you about her I should know better——"

She broke off, confused, and he questioned: "What is it you want to know better?"

The colour rose to her forehead. How could she tell him what she scarcely dared own to herself? There was nothing she did not want to know, no fold or cranny of his secret that her awakened imagination did not strain to penetrate; but she could not expose Sophy Viner to the base fingerings of a retrospective jealousy, nor Darrow to the temptation of belittling her in the effort to better his own case. The girl had been magnificent, and the only worthy return that Anna could make was to take Darrow from her without a question if she took him at all . . .

She lifted her eyes to his face. "I think I only wanted to speak her name. It's not right that we should seem so afraid of it. If I were really afraid of it I should have to give you up," she said.

He bent over her and caught her to him. "Ah, you can't give me up now!" he exclaimed.

She suffered him to hold her fast without speaking; but the old dread was between them again, and it was on her lips to cry out: "How can I help it, when I *am* so afraid?"

XXXV.

THE next morning the dread was still there, and she understood that she must snatch herself out of the torpor of the will into which she had been gradually sinking, and tell Darrow that she could not be his wife.

The knowledge came to her in the watches of a sleepless night, when, through the tears of disenchanted passion, she stared back upon her past. There it lay before her, her sole romance, in all its paltry poverty, the cheapest of cheap adventures, the most pitiful of sentimental blunders. She looked about her room, the room where, for so many years, if her heart had been quiescent her thoughts had been alive, and pictured herself henceforth cowering before a throng of mean suspicions, of unavowed compromises and concessions. In that moment of self-searching she saw that Sophy Viner had chosen the better part, and that certain renunciations might enrich where possession would have left a desert.

Passionate reactions of instinct fought against these efforts of her will. Why should past or future coerce her, when the present was so securely hers? Why insanely surrender what the other would after all never have? Her sense of irony whispered that if she sent away Darrow it would not be to Sophy Viner, but to the first woman who crossed his path—as, in a similar hour, Sophy Viner herself had crossed it . . . But the mere fact that she could think such things of him sent her shuddering back to the opposite pole. She pictured herself gradually subdued to such a conception of life and love, she pictured Effie growing up under the influence of the woman she saw herself becoming—and she hid her eyes from the humiliation of the picture . . .

They were at luncheon when the summons that Darrow expected was brought to him. He handed the telegram to Anna, and she learned that his Ambassador, on the way to a German cure, was to be in Paris the next evening and wished to confer with him there before he went back to London. The idea that the decisive moment was at hand was so agitating to her that when luncheon was over she slipped away to the terrace and thence went down alone to the garden. The day was grey but mild, with the heaviness of decay in the air. She rambled on aimlessly, following under the denuded boughs the path she and Darrow had taken on their first walk to the river. She was sure he would not try to overtake her: sure he would guess why she wished to be alone. There were moments when it seemed to double her loneliness to be so certain of his reading her heart while she was so desperately ignorant of his . . .

She wandered on for more than an hour, and when she returned to the house she saw, as she entered the hall, that Darrow was seated at the desk in Owen's study. He heard her step, and looking up turned in his chair without rising. Their eyes met, and she saw that his were clear and smiling. He had a heap of papers at his elbow and was evidently engaged in some official correspondence. She wondered that he could address himself so composedly to his task, and then ironically reflected that such detachment was a sign of his superiority. She crossed the threshold and went toward him; but as she advanced she had a sudden vision of Owen, standing outside in the cold autumn dusk and watching Darrow and Sophy Viner as they faced each other across the lamplit desk . . . The evocation was so vivid that it caught her breath like a blow, and she sank down helplessly on the divan among the piled-up books. Distinctly, at the moment, she understood that the end had come. "When he speaks to me I will tell him!" she thought . . .

Darrow, laying aside his pen, looked at her for a moment in silence; then he stood up and shut the door.

"I must go to-morrow early," he said, sitting down beside her. His voice was grave, with a slight tinge of sadness. She said to herself: "He knows what I am feeling . . ." and now the thought made her feel less alone. The expression of his face was stern and yet tender: for the first time she understood what he had suffered.

She had no doubt as to the necessity of giving him up, but it was impossible to tell him so then. She stood up and said: "I'll leave you to your letters." He made no protest, but merely answered: "You'll come down presently for a walk?" and it occurred to her at once that she would walk down to the river with him, and give herself for the last time the tragic luxury of sitting at his side in the little pavilion. "Perhaps," she thought, "it will be easier to tell him there."

It did not, on the way home from their walk, become any easier to tell him; but her secret decision to do so before he left gave her a kind of factitious calm and laid a melancholy ecstasy upon the hour. Still skirting the subject that fanned their very faces with its flame, they clung persistently to other topics, and it seemed to Anna that their minds had never been nearer together than in this hour when their hearts were so separate. In the glow of interchanged love she had grown less conscious of that other glow of interchanged thought which had once illumined her mind. She had forgotten how Darrow had widened her world and lengthened out all her perspectives, and with a pang of double destitution she saw herself alone among her shrunken thoughts.

For the first time, then, she had a clear vision of what her life would be without him. She imagined herself trying to take up the daily round, and all that had lightened and animated it seemed equally lifeless and vain. She tried to think of herself as wholly absorbed in her daughter's development, like other mothers she had seen; but she supposed those mothers must have had stored memories of happiness to nourish them. She had had nothing, and all her starved youth still claimed its due.

When she went up to dress for dinner she said to herself: "I'll have my last evening with him, and then, before we say good night, I'll tell him."

This postponement did not seem unjustified. Darrow had shown her how he dreaded vain words, how resolved he was to avoid all fruitless discussion. He must have been intensely aware of what had been going on in her mind since his return, yet when she had attempted to reveal it to him he had turned from the revelation. She was therefore merely following the line he had traced in behaving, till the final moment came, as though there were nothing more to say . . .

That moment seemed at last to be at hand when, at her usual hour after dinner, Madame de Chantelle rose to go upstairs. She lingered a little to bid good-bye to Darrow, whom she was not likely to see in the morning; and her affable allusions to his prompt return sounded in Anna's ear like the note of destiny.

A cold rain had fallen all day, and for greater warmth and intimacy they had gone after dinner to the oak-room, shutting out the chilly vista of the farther drawing-rooms. The autumn wind, coming up from the river, cried about the house with a voice of loss and separation; and Anna and Darrow sat silent, as if they feared to break the hush that shut them in. The solitude, the fire-light, the harmony of soft hangings and old dim pictures, wove about them a spell of security through which Anna felt, far down in her heart, the muffled beat of an inextinguishable bliss. How could she have thought that this last moment would be the moment to speak to him, when it seemed to have gathered up into its flight all the scattered splendours of her dream?

XXXVI.

DARROW continued to stand by the door after it had closed. Anna felt that he was looking at her, and sat still, disdaining to seek refuge in any evasive word or movement. For the last time she wanted to let him take from her the fulness of what the sight of her could give.

He crossed over and sat down on the sofa. For a moment neither of them spoke; then he said: "To-night, dearest, I must have my answer."

She straightened herself under the shock of his seeming to take the very words from her lips.

"To-night?" was all that she could falter.

"I must be off by the early train. There won't be more than a moment in the morning."

He had taken her hand, and she said to herself that she must free it before she could go on with what she had to say. Then she rejected this concession to a weakness she was resolved to defy. To the end she would leave her hand in his hand, her eyes in his eyes: she would not, in their final hour together, be afraid of any part of her love for him.

"You'll tell me to-night, dear," he insisted gently; and his insistence gave her the strength to speak.

"There's something I must ask you," she broke out, perceiving, as she heard her words, that they were not in the least what she had meant to say.

He sat still, waiting, and she pressed on: "Do such things happen to men often?"

The quiet room seemed to resound with the long reverberations of her question. She looked away from him, and he released her and stood up.

"I don't know what happens to other men. Such a thing never happened to me . . ."

She turned her eyes back to his face. She felt like a traveller on a giddy path between a cliff and a precipice: there was nothing for it now but to go on.

"Had it . . . had it begun . . . before you met her in Paris?"

"No; a thousand times no! I've told you the facts as they were."

"All the facts?"

He turned abruptly. "What do you mean?"

Her throat was dry and the loud pulses drummed in her temples.

"I mean—about her . . . Perhaps you knew . . . knew things about her . . . beforehand."

She stopped. The room had grown profoundly still. A log dropped to the hearth and broke there in a hissing shower.

Darrow spoke in a clear voice. "I knew nothing, absolutely nothing," he said.

She had the answer to her inmost doubt—to her last shameful unavowed hope. She sat powerless under her woe.

He walked to the fireplace and pushed back the broken log with his foot. A flame shot out of it, and in the upward glare she saw his pale face, stern with misery

"Is that all?" he asked.

She made a slight sign with her head and he came slowly back to her. "Then is this to be good-bye?"

Again she signed a faint assent, and he made no effort to touch her or draw nearer. "You understand that I sha'n't come back?"

He was looking at her, and she tried to return his look, but her eyes were blind with tears, and in dread of his seeing them she got up and walked away. He did not follow her, and she stood with her back to him, staring at a bowl of carnations on a little table strewn with books. Her tears magnified everything she looked at, and the streaked petals of the carnations, their fringed edges and frail curled stamens, pressed upon her, huge and vivid. She noticed among the books a volume of verse he had sent her from England, and tried to remember whether it was before or after . . .

She felt that he was waiting for her to speak, and at last she turned to him. "I shall see you to-morrow before you go . . ."

He made no answer.

She moved toward the door and he held it open for her. She saw his hand on the door, and his seal ring in its setting of twisted silver; and the sense of the end of all things came to her.

They walked down the drawing-rooms, between the shadowy reflections of screens and cabinets, and mounted the stairs side by side. At the end of the gallery, a lamp brought out turbid gleams in the smoky battle-piece above it.

On the landing Darrow stopped; his room was the

nearest to the stairs. "Good night," he said, holding out his hand.

As Anna gave him hers the springs of grief broke loose in her. She struggled with her sobs, and subdued them; but her breath came unevenly, and to hide her agitation she leaned on him and pressed her face against his arm.

"Don't—don't," he whispered, soothing her.

Her troubled breathing sounded loudly in the silence of the sleeping house. She pressed her lips tight, but could not stop the nervous pulsations in her throat, and he put an arm about her and, opening his door, drew her across the threshold of his room. The door shut behind her and she sat down on the lounge at the foot of the bed. The pulsations in her throat had ceased, but she knew they would begin again if she tried to speak.

Darrow walked away and leaned against the mantel-piece. The red-veiled lamp shone on his books and papers, on the arm-chair by the fire, and the scattered objects on his dressing-table. A log glimmered on the hearth, and the room was warm and faintly smoke-scented. It was the first time she had ever been in a room he lived in, among his personal possessions and the traces of his daily usage. Every object about her seemed to contain a particle of himself: the whole air breathed of him, steeping her in the sense of his intimate presence.

Suddenly she thought: "This is what Sophy Viner knew" . . . and with a torturing precision she pictured them alone in such a scene . . . Had he taken the girl to an hotel . . . where did people go in such cases? Wherever they were, the silence of night had been around them, and the things he used had been strewn about the room . . . Anna, ashamed of dwelling on the detested vision, stood up with a confused impulse of flight; then a wave of contrary feeling arrested her and she paused with lowered head.

Darrow had come forward as she rose, and she perceived that he was waiting for her to bid him good night. It was clear that no other possibility had even brushed his mind; and the fact, for some dim reason, humiliated her. "Why not . . . why not?" something whispered in her, as though his forbearance, his tacit recognition of her pride, were a slight on other qualities she wanted him to feel in her.

"In the morning, then?" she heard him say.

"Yes, in the morning," she repeated.

She continued to stand in the same place, looking vaguely about the room. For once before they parted—since part they must—she longed to be to him all that Sophy Viner had been; but she remained rooted to the floor, unable to find a word or imagine a gesture that should express her meaning. Exasperated by her helplessness, she thought: "Don't I feel things as other women do?"

Her eye fell on a note-case she had given him. It was worn at the corners with the friction of his pocket and distended with thickly packed papers. She wondered if he carried her letters in it, and she put her hand out and touched it.

All that he and she had ever felt or seen, their close encounters of word and look, and the closer contact of their silences, trembled through her at the touch. She remembered things he had said that had been like new skies above her head: ways he had that seemed a part of the air she breathed. The faint warmth of her girlish love came back to her, gathering heat as it passed through her thoughts; and her heart rocked like a boat on the surge of its long long memories. "It's because I love him in too many ways," she thought; and slowly she turned to the door.

She was aware that Darrow was still silently watching her, but he neither stirred nor spoke till she had reached the threshold. Then he met her there and caught her in his arms.

"Not to-night—don't tell me to-night!" he whispered; and she leaned away from him, closing her eyes for an instant, and then slowly opening them to the flood of light in his.

XXXVII.

ANNA and Darrow, the next day, sat alone in a compartment of the Paris train.

Anna, when they entered it, had put herself in the farthest corner and placed her bag on the adjoining seat. She had decided suddenly to accompany Darrow to Paris, had even persuaded him to wait for a later train in order that they might travel together. She had an intense longing to be with him, an almost morbid terror of losing sight of him for a moment: when he jumped out of the train and ran back along the platform to buy a newspaper for her she felt as though she should never see him again, and shivered with the cold misery of her last journey to Paris, when she had thought herself parted from him forever. Yet she wanted to keep him at a distance, on the other side of the compartment, and as the train moved out of the station she drew from her bag the letters she had thrust in it as she left the house, and began to glance over them so that her lowered lids should hide her eyes from him.

She was his now, his for life: there could never again be any question of sacrificing herself to Effie's welfare, or to any other abstract conception of duty. Effie of course would not suffer; Anna would pay for her bliss as a wife by redoubled devotion as a mother. Her scruples were not overcome; but for the time their voices were drowned in the tumultuous rumour of her happiness.

As she opened her letters she was conscious that Darrow's gaze was fixed on her, and gradually it drew her eyes upward, and she drank deep of the passionate tenderness in his. Then the blood rose to her face and she felt again the desire to shield herself. She turned back to her letters and her glance lit on an envelope inscribed in Owen's hand.

Her heart began to beat oppressively: she was in a mood when the simplest things seemed ominous. What could Owen have to say to her? Only the first page was covered, and it contained simply the announcement that, in the company of a young compatriot who was studying at the Beaux Arts, he had planned to leave for Spain the following evening.

"He hasn't seen her, then!" was Anna's instant thought; and her feeling was a strange compound of humiliation and relief. The girl had kept her word, lived up to the line of conduct she had set herself; and

Anna had failed in the same attempt. She did not reproach herself with her failure; but she would have been happier if there had been less discrepancy between her words to Sophy Viner and the act which had followed them. It irritated her obscurely that the girl should have been so much surer of her power to carry out her purpose . . .

Anna looked up and saw that Darrow's eyes were on the newspaper. He seemed calm and secure, almost indifferent to her presence. "Will it become a matter of course to him so soon?" she wondered with a twinge of jealousy. She sat motionless, her eyes fixed on him, trying to make him feel the attraction of her gaze as she felt his. It surprised and shamed her to detect a new element in her love for him: a sort of suspicious tyrannical tenderness that seemed to deprive it of all serenity. Finally he looked up, his smile enveloped her, and she felt herself his in every fibre, his so completely and inseparably that she saw the vanity of imagining any other fate for herself.

To give herself a countenance she held out Owen's letter. He took it and glanced down the page, his face grown grave. She waited nervously till he looked up.

"That's a good plan; the best thing that could happen," he said, a just perceptible shade of constraint in his tone.

"Oh, yes," she hastily assented. She was aware of a faint current of relief silently circulating between them. They were both glad that Owen was going, that for a while he would be out of their way; and it seemed to her horrible that so much of the stuff of their happiness should be made of such unavowed feelings . . .

"I shall see him this evening," she said, wishing

Darrow to feel that she was not afraid of meeting her step-son.

"Yes, of course; perhaps he might dine with you."

The words struck her as strangely obtuse. Darrow was to meet his Ambassador at the station on the latter's arrival, and would in all probability have to spend the evening with him, and Anna knew he had been concerned at the thought of having to leave her alone. But how could he speak in that careless tone of her dining with Owen? She lowered her voice to say: "I'm afraid he's desperately unhappy."

He answered, with a tinge of impatience: "It's much the best thing that he should travel."

"Yes—but don't you feel . . ." She broke off. She knew how he disliked these idle returns on the irrevocable, and her fear of doing or saying what he disliked was tinged by a new instinct of subserviency against which her pride revolted. She thought to herself: "He will see the change, and grow indifferent to me as he did to *her* . . ." and for a moment it seemed to her that she was reliving the experience of Sophy Viner.

Darrow made no attempt to learn the end of her unfinished sentence. He handed back Owen's letter and returned to his newspaper; and when he looked up from it a few minutes later it was with a clear brow and a smile that irresistibly drew her back to happier thoughts.

The train was just entering a station, and a moment later their compartment was invaded by a commonplace couple preoccupied with the bestowal of bulging packages. Anna, at their approach, felt the possessive pride of the woman in love when strangers are between herself and the man she loves. She asked Darrow to open the window, to place her bag in the net, to roll her rug into a cushion for her feet; and while he was thus busied with her she was conscious of a new devotion in his tone, in his way of bending over her and meeting her eyes. He went back to his seat, and they looked at each other like lovers smiling at a happy secret.

Anna, before going back to Givré, had suggested Owen's moving into her apartment, but he had preferred to remain at the hotel to which he had sent his luggage, and on arriving in Paris she decided to drive there at once. She was impatient to have the meeting over, and glad that Darrow was obliged to leave her at the station in order to look up a colleague at the Embassy. She dreaded his seeing Owen again, and yet dared not tell him so; and to ensure his remaining away she mentioned an urgent engagement with her dress-maker and a long list of commissions to be executed for Madame de Chantelle.

"I shall see you to-morrow morning," she said; but he replied with a smile that he would certainly find time to come to her for a moment on his way back from meeting the Ambassador; and when he had put her in a cab he leaned through the window to press his lips to hers.

She blushed like a girl, thinking, half vexed, half happy: "Yesterday he would not have done it . . ." and a dozen scarcely definable differences in his look and manner seemed all at once to be summed up in the boyish act. "After all, I'm engaged to him," she reflected, and then smiled at the absurdity of the word. The next instant, with a pang of self-reproach, she remembered Sophy Viner's cry: "I knew all the while he didn't care . . ." "Poor thing, oh poor thing!" Anna murmured . . .

At Owen's hotel she waited in a tremor while the porter went in search of him. Word was presently brought back that he was in his room and begged her to come up, and as she crossed the hall she caught sight of his portmanteaux lying on the floor, already labelled for departure.

Owen sat at a table writing, his back to the door; and when he stood up the window was behind him, so that, in the rainy afternoon light, his features were barely discernible.

"Dearest—so you're really off?" she said, hesitating a moment on the threshold.

He pushed a chair forward, and they sat down, each waiting for the other to speak. Finally she put some random question about his travelling-companion, a slow shy meditative youth whom he had once or twice brought down to Givré. She reflected that it was natural he should have given this uncommunicative comrade the preference over his livelier acquaintances, and aloud she said: "I'm so glad Fred Rempson can go with you."

Owen answered in the same tone, and for a few minutes their talk dragged itself on over a dry waste of commonplaces. Anna noticed that, though ready enough to impart his own plans, Owen studiously abstained from putting any questions about hers. It was evident from his allusions that he meant to be away for some time, and he presently asked her if she would give instructions about packing and sending after him some winter clothes he had left at Givré. This gave her the opportunity to say that she expected to go back within a day or two and would attend to the matter as soon as she returned. She added: "I came up this morning with George, who is going on to London to-morrow," intending, by the use of Darrow's Christian name, to give Owen the chance to speak of her marriage. But he made no comment, and she continued to hear the name sounding on unfamiliarly between them.

The room was almost dark, and she finally stood up and glanced about for the light-switch, saying: "I can't see you, dear."

"Oh, don't—I hate the light!" Owen exclaimed, catching her by the wrist and pushing her back into her seat. He gave a nervous laugh and added: "I'm half-blind with neuralgia. I suppose it's this beastly rain."

"Yes; it will do you good to get down to Spain."

She asked if he had the remedies the doctor had given him for a previous attack, and on his replying that he didn't know what he'd done with the stuff, she sprang up, offering to go to the chemist's. It was a relief to have something to do for him, and she knew from his "Oh, thanks—would you?" that it was a relief to him to have a pretext for not detaining her. His natural impulse would have been to declare that he didn't want any drugs, and would be all right in no time; and his acquiescence showed her how profoundly he felt the uselessness of their trying to prolong their talk. His face was now no more than a white blur in the dusk, but she felt its indistinctness as a veil drawn over aching intensities of expression. "He knows . . . he knows . . ." she said to herself, and wondered whether the truth had been revealed to him by some corroborative fact or by the sheer force of divination.

He had risen also, and was clearly waiting for her to go, and she turned to the door, saying: "I'll be back in a moment."

"Oh, don't come up again, please!" He paused, embarrassed. "I mean—I may not be here. I've got to go and pick up Rempson, and see about some final things with him."

She stopped on the threshold with a sinking heart. He meant this to be their leave-taking, then—and he had not even asked her when she was to be married, or spoken of seeing her again before she set out for the other side of the world.

"Owen!" she cried, and turned back.

He stood mutely before her in the dimness.

"You haven't told me how long you're to be gone."

"How long? Oh, you see . . . that's rather vague . . . I hate definite dates, you know . . ."

He paused and she saw he did not mean to help her out. She tried to say: "You'll be here for my wedding?" but could not bring the words to her lips. Instead she murmured: "In six weeks I shall be going too . . ." and he rejoined, as if he had expected the announcement and prepared his answer: "Oh, by that time, very likely . . ."

"At any rate, I won't say good-bye," she stammered, feeling the tears beneath her veil.

"No, no; rather not!" he declared; but he made no movement, and she went up and threw her arms about him. "You'll write me, won't you?"

"Of course, of course——"

Her hands slipped down into his, and for a minute they held each other dumbly in the darkness; then he gave a vague laugh and said: "It's really time to light up." He pressed the electric button with one hand while with the other he opened the door; and she passed out without daring to turn back, lest the light on his face should show her what she feared to see.

XXXVIII.

ANNA drove to the chemist's for Owen's remedy. On the way she stopped her cab at a book-shop, and emerged from it laden with literature. She knew what would interest Owen, and what he was likely to have read, and she had made her choice among the newest publications with the promptness of a discriminating reader. But on the way back to the hotel she was overcome by the irony of adding this mental panacea to the other. There was something grotesque and almost mocking in the idea of offering a judicious selection of literature to a man setting out on such a journey. "He knows . . . he knows . . ." she kept on repeating; and giving the porter the parcel from the chemist's she drove away without leaving the books.

She went to her apartment, whither her maid had preceded her. There was a fire in the drawing-room and the tea-table stood ready by the hearth. The stormy rain beat against the uncurtained windows, and she thought of Owen, who would soon be driving through it to the station, alone with his bitter thoughts. She had been proud of the fact that he had always sought her help in difficult hours; and now, in the most difficult of all, she was the one being to whom he could not turn. Between them, henceforth, there would always be the wall of an insurmountable silence . . . She strained her aching thoughts to guess how the truth had come to him. Had he seen the girl, and had she told him? Instinctively, Anna rejected this conjecture. But what need was there of assuming an explicit statement, when every breath they had drawn for the last weeks had been charged with the immanent secret? As she looked back over the days since Darrow's first arrival at Givré she perceived that at no time had any one deliberately spoken, or anything been accidentally disclosed. The truth had come to light by the force of its irresistible pressure; and the perception gave her a startled sense of hidden powers, of a chaos of attractions and repulsions far beneath the ordered surfaces of intercourse. She looked back with melancholy derision on her old conception of life, as a kind of welllit and well-policed suburb to dark places one need never know about. Here they were, these dark places, in her own bosom, and henceforth she would always have to traverse them to reach the beings she loved best!

She was still sitting beside the untouched tea-table when she heard Darrow's voice in the hall. She started up, saying to herself: "I must tell him that Owen knows . . ." but when the door opened and she saw his face, still lit by the same smile of boyish triumph, she felt anew the uselessness of speaking . . . Had he ever supposed that Owen would not know? Probably, from the height of his greater experience, he had seen long since that all that happened was inevitable; and the thought of it, at any rate, was clearly not weighing on him now.

He was already dressed for the evening, and as he came toward her he said: "The Ambassador's booked for an official dinner and I'm free after all. Where shall we dine?"

Anna had pictured herself sitting alone all the evening with her wretched thoughts, and the fact of having to put them out of her mind for the next few hours gave her an immediate sensation of relief. Already her pulses were dancing to the tune of Darrow's, and as they smiled at each other she thought: "Nothing can ever change the fact that I belong to him."

"Where shall we dine?" he repeated gaily, and she named a well-known restaurant for which she had once heard him express a preference. But as she did so she fancied she saw a shadow on his face, and instantly she said to herself: "It was there he went with her!"

"Oh, no, not there, after all!" she interrupted herself; and now she was sure his colour deepened.

"Where shall it be, then?"

She noticed that he did not ask the reason of her change, and this convinced her that she had guessed the truth, and that he knew she had guessed it. "He will always know what I am thinking, and he will never dare to ask me," she thought; and she saw between them the same insurmountable wall of silence as between herself and Owen, a wall of glass through which they could watch each other's faintest motions but which no sound could ever traverse . . .

They drove to a restaurant on the Boulevard, and there, in their intimate corner of the serried scene, the sense of what was unspoken between them gradually ceased to oppress her. He looked so light-hearted and handsome, so ingenuously proud of her, so openly happy at being with her, that no other fact could seem real in his presence. He had learned that the Ambassador was to spend two days in Paris, and he had reason to hope that in consequence his own departure for London would be deferred. He was exhilarated by the prospect of being with Anna for a few hours longer, and she did not ask herself if his exhilaration were a sign of insensibility, for she was too conscious of his power of swaying her moods not to be secretly proud of affecting his.

They lingered for some time over the fruit and coffee, and when they rose to go Darrow suggested that, if she felt disposed for the play, they were not too late for the second part of the programme at one of the smaller theatres.

His mention of the hour recalled Owen to her thoughts. She saw his train rushing southward through the storm, and, in a corner of the swaying compartment, his face, white and indistinct as it had loomed on her in the rainy twilight. It was horrible to be thus perpetually paying for her happiness!

Darrow had called for a theatrical journal, and he presently looked up from it to say: "I hear the second play at the Athéné is amusing."

It was on Anna's lips to acquiesce; but as she was about to speak she wondered if it were not at the Athéné that Owen had seen Darrow with Sophy Viner. She was not sure he had even mentioned the theatre, but the mere possibility was enough to darken her sky. It was hateful to her to think of accompanying Darrow to places where the girl had been with him. She tried to reason away this scruple, she even reminded herself with a bitter irony that whenever she was in Darrow's arms she was where the girl had been before her—but she could not shake off her superstitious dread of being with him in any of the scenes of the Parisian episode.

She replied that she was too tired for the play, and they drove back to her apartment. At the foot of the stairs she half-turned to wish him good night, but he appeared not to notice her gesture and followed her up to her door.

"This is ever so much better than the theatre," he said as they entered the drawing-room.

She had crossed the room and was bending over the hearth to light the fire. She knew he was approaching her, and that in a moment he would have drawn the cloak from her shoulders and laid his lips on her neck, just below the gathered-up hair. These privileges were his and, however deferently and tenderly he claimed them, the joyous ease of his manner marked a difference and proclaimed a right.

"After the theatre they came home like this," she thought; and at the same instant she felt his hands on her shoulders and shrank back.

"Don't—oh, don't!" she cried, drawing her cloak about her. She saw from his astonished stare that her face must be quivering with pain.

"Anna! What on earth is the matter?"

"Owen knows!" she broke out, with a confused desire to justify herself.

Darrow's countenance changed. "Did he tell you so? What did he say?"

"Nothing! I knew it from the things he didn't say."

"You had a talk with him this afternoon?"

"Yes: for a few minutes. I could see he didn't want me to stay."

She had dropped into a chair, and sat there huddled, still holding her cloak about her shoulders.

Darrow did not dispute her assumption, and she noticed that he expressed no surprise. He sat down at a little distance from her, turning about in his fingers the cigar-case he had drawn out as they came in. At length he said: "Had he seen Miss Viner?"

She shrank from the sound of the name. "No . . . I don't think so . . . I'm sure he hadn't . . ."

They remained silent, looking away from one another. Finally Darrow stood up and took a few steps across the room. He came back and paused before her, his eyes on her face.

"I think you ought to tell me what you mean to do."

She raised her head and gave him back his look. "Nothing I do can help Owen!"

"No; but things can't go on like this." He paused, as if to measure his words. "I fill you with aversion," he exclaimed.

She started up, half-sobbing. "No—oh, no!"

"Poor child—you can't see your face!"

She lifted her hands as if to hide it, and turning away from him bowed her head upon the mantel-shelf. She felt that he was standing a little way behind her, but he made no attempt to touch her or come nearer.

"I know you've felt as I've felt," he said in a low voice—"that we belong to each other and that nothing can alter that. But other thoughts come, and you can't banish them. Whenever you see me you remember . . . you associate me with things you abhor . . . You've been generous—immeasurably. You've given me all the chances a woman could; but if it's only made you suffer, what's the use?"

She turned to him with a tear-stained face. "It hasn't only done that."

"Oh, no! I know . . . There've been moments . . ." He took her hand and raised it to his lips. "They'll be with me as long as I live. But I can't see you paying such a price for them. I'm not worth what I'm costing you."

She continued to gaze at him through tear-dilated eyes; and suddenly she flung out the question: "Wasn't it the Athéné you took her to that evening?"

"Anna—Anna!"

"Yes; I want to know now: to know everything. Perhaps that will make me forget. I ought to have made you tell me before. Wherever we go, I imagine you've been there with her . . . I see you together. I want to know how it began, where you went, why you left her . . . I can't go on in this darkness any longer!"

She did not know what had prompted her passionate outburst, but already she felt lighter, freer, as if at last the evil spell were broken. "I want to know everything," she repeated. "It's the only way to make me forget."

After she had ceased speaking Darrow remained where he was, his arms folded, his eyes lowered, immovable. She waited, her gaze on his face.

"Aren't you going to tell me?"

"No."

The blood rushed to her temples. "You won't? Why not?"

"If I did, do you suppose you'd forget that?"

"Oh—" she moaned, and turned away from him.

"You see it's impossible," he went on. "I've done a thing I loathe, and to atone for it you ask me to do another. What sort of satisfaction would that give you? It would put something irremediable between us."

She leaned her elbow against the mantel-shelf and hid her face in her hands. She had the sense that she was vainly throwing away her last hope of happiness, yet she could do nothing, think of nothing, to save it. The conjecture flashed through her: "Should I be at peace if I gave him up?" and she remembered the desolation of the days after she had sent him away, and understood that that hope was vain. The tears welled through her lids and ran slowly down between her fingers.

"Good-bye," she heard him say, and his footsteps turned to the door.

She tried to raise her head, but the weight of her despair bowed it down. She said to herself: "This is the end . . . he won't try to appeal to me again . . ." and she remained in a sort of tranced rigidity, perceiving without feeling the fateful lapse of the seconds. Then the cords that bound her seemed to snap, and she lifted her head and saw him going.

"Why, he's mine—he's mine! He's no one else's!" His face was turned to her and the look in his eyes swept away all her terrors. She no longer understood what had prompted her senseless outcry; and the mortal sweetness of loving him became again the one real fact in the world.

XXXIX.

ANNA, the next day, woke to a humiliated memory of the previous evening.

Darrow had been right in saying that their sacrifice would benefit no one; yet she seemed dimly to discern that there were obligations not to be tested by that standard. She owed it, at any rate, as much to his pride as to hers to abstain from the repetition of such scenes; and she had learned that it was beyond her power to do so while they were together. Yet when he had given her the chance to free herself, everything had vanished from her mind but the blind fear of losing him; and she saw that he and she were as profoundly and inextricably bound together as two trees with interwoven roots.

For a long time she brooded on her plight, vaguely conscious that the only escape from it must come from some external chance. And slowly the occasion shaped itself in her mind. It was Sophy Viner only who could save her—Sophy Viner only who could give her back her lost serenity. She would seek the girl out and tell her that she had given Darrow up; and that step once taken there would be no retracing it, and she would perforce have to go forward alone.

Any pretext for action was a kind of anodyne, and she despatched her maid to the Farlows' with a note asking if Miss Viner would receive her. There was a long delay before the maid returned, and when at last she appeared it was with a slip of paper on which an address was written, and a verbal message to the effect that Miss Viner had left some days previously, and was staying with her sister in a hotel near the Place de l'Etoile. The maid added that Mrs. Farlow, on the plea that Miss Viner's plans were uncertain, had at first made some difficulty about giving this information; and Anna guessed that the girl had left her friends' roof, and instructed them to withhold her address, with the object of avoiding Owen. "She's kept faith with herself and I haven't," Anna mused; and the thought was a fresh incentive to action.

Darrow had announced his intention of coming soon after luncheon, and the morning was already so far advanced that Anna, still mistrustful of her strength, decided to drive immediately to the address Mrs. Farlow had given. On the way there she tried to recall what she had heard of Sophy Viner's sister, but beyond the girl's enthusiastic report of the absent Laura's loveliness she could remember only certain vague allusions of Mrs. Farlow's to her artistic endowments and matrimonial vicissitudes. Darrow had mentioned her but once, and in the briefest terms, as having apparently very little concern for Sophy's welfare, and being, at any rate, too geographically remote to give her any practical support; and Anna wondered what chance had brought her to her sister's side at this conjunction. Mrs. Farlow had spoken of her as a celebrity (in what line Anna failed to recall); but Mrs. Farlow's celebrities were legion, and the name on the slip of paper—Mrs. McTarvie-Birch—did not seem to have any definite association with fame.

While Anna waited in the dingy vestibule of the *Hôtel Chicago* she had so distinct a vision of what she meant to say to Sophy Viner that the girl seemed already to be before her; and her heart dropped from all the height of its courage when the porter, after a long delay, returned with the announcement that Miss Viner was no longer in the hotel. Anna, doubtful if she understood, asked if he merely meant that the young lady was out at the moment; but he replied that she had gone away the day before. Beyond this he had no information to impart, and after a moment's hesitation Anna sent him back to enquire if Mrs. McTarvie-Birch would receive her. She reflected that Sophy had probably pledged her sister to the same secrecy as Mrs. Farlow, and that a personal appeal to Mrs. Birch might lead to less negative results.

There was another long interval of suspense before the porter reappeared with an affirmative answer; and a third while an exiguous and hesitating lift bore her up past a succession of shabby landings.

When the last was reached, and her guide had directed her down a winding passage that smelt of seagoing luggage, she found herself before a door through which a strong odour of tobacco reached her simultaneously with the sounds of a suppressed altercation. Her knock was followed by a silence, and after a minute or two the door was opened by a handsome young man whose ruffled hair and general air of creased disorder led her to conclude that he had just risen from a long-limbed sprawl on a sofa strewn with tumbled cushions. This sofa, and a grand piano bearing a basket of faded roses, a biscuit-tin and a devastated breakfast tray, almost filled the narrow sitting-room, in the remaining corner of which another man, short, swarthy and humble, sat examining the lining of his hat.

Anna paused in doubt; but on her naming Mrs.

Birch the young man politely invited her to enter, at the same time casting an impatient glance at the mute spectator in the background.

The latter, raising his eyes, which were round and bulging, fixed them, not on the young man but on Anna, whom, for a moment, he scrutinized as searchingly as the interior of his hat. Under his gaze she had the sense of being minutely catalogued and valued; and the impression, when he finally rose and moved toward the door, of having been accepted as a better guarantee than he had had any reason to hope for. On the threshold his glance crossed that of the young man in an exchange of intelligence as full as it was rapid; and this brief scene left Anna so oddly enlightened that she felt no surprise when her companion, pushing an arm-chair forward, sociably asked her if she wouldn't have a cigarette. Her polite refusal provoked the remark that *he* would, if she'd no objection; and while he groped for matches in his loose pockets, and behind the photographs and letters crowding the narrow mantel-shelf, she ventured another enquiry for Mrs. Birch.

"Just a minute," he smiled; "I think the *masseur's* with her." He spoke in a smooth denationalized English, which, like the look in his long-lashed eyes and the promptness of his charming smile, suggested a long training in all the arts of expediency. Having finally discovered a match-box on the floor beside the sofa, he lit his cigarette and dropped back among the cushions; and on Anna's remarking that she was sorry to disturb Mrs. Birch he replied that that was all right, and that she always kept everybody waiting.

After this, through the haze of his perpetually renewed cigarettes, they continued to chat for some time of indifferent topics; but when at last Anna again suggested the possibility of her seeing Mrs. Birch he rose from his corner with a slight shrug, and murmuring: "She's perfectly hopeless," lounged off through an inner door.

Anna was still wondering when and in what conjunction of circumstances the much-married Laura had acquired a partner so conspicuous for his personal charms, when the young man returned to announce: "She says it's all right, if you don't mind seeing her in bed."

He drew aside to let Anna pass, and she found herself in a dim untidy scented room, with a pink curtain pinned across its single window, and a lady with a great deal of fair hair and uncovered neck smiling at her from a pink bed on which an immense powder-puff trailed.

"You don't mind, do you? He costs such a frightful lot that I can't afford to send him off," Mrs. Birch explained, extending a thickly-ringed hand to Anna, and leaving her in doubt as to whether the person alluded to were her *masseur* or her husband. Before a reply was possible there was a convulsive stir beneath the pink expanse, and something that resembled another powder-puff hurled itself at Anna with a volley of sounds like the popping of Lilliputian champagne corks. Mrs. Birch, flinging herself forward, gasped out: "If you'd just give him a caramel . . . there, in that box on the dressing-table . . . it's the only earthly thing to stop him . . ." and when Anna had proffered this sop to her assailant, and he had withdrawn with it beneath the bedspread, his mistress sank back with a laugh.

"Isn't he a beauty? The Prince gave him to me down

at Nice the other day—but he's perfectly awful," she confessed, beaming intimately on her visitor. In the roseate penumbra of the bed-curtains she presented to Anna's startled gaze an odd chromo-like resemblance to Sophy Viner, or a suggestion, rather, of what Sophy Viner might, with the years and in spite of the powder-puff, become. Larger, blonder, heavier-featured, she yet had glances and movements that disturbingly suggested what was freshest and most engaging in the girl; and as she stretched her bare plump arm across the bed she seemed to be pulling back the veil from dingy distances of family history.

"Do sit down, if there's a place to sit on," she cordially advised; adding, as Anna took the edge of a chair hung with miscellaneous raiment: "My singing takes so much time that I don't get a chance to walk the fat off—that's the worst of being an artist."

Anna murmured an assent. "I hope it hasn't inconvenienced you to see me; I told Mr. Birch——"

"Mr. *who?*" the recumbent beauty asked; and then: "Oh, *Jimmy!*" she faintly laughed, as if more for her own enlightenment than Anna's.

The latter continued eagerly: "I understand from Mrs. Farlow that your sister was with you, and I ventured to come up because I wanted to ask you when I should have a chance of finding her."

Mrs. McTarvie-Birch threw back her head with a long stare. "Do you mean to say the idiot at the door didn't tell you? Sophy went away last night."

"Last night?" Anna echoed. A sudden terror had possessed her. Could it be that the girl had tricked them all and gone with Owen? The idea was incredible, yet it took such hold of her that she could hardly steady her lips to say: "The porter did tell me, but I thought perhaps he was mistaken. Mrs. Farlow seemed to think that I should find her here."

"It was all so sudden that I don't suppose she had time to let the Farlows know. She didn't get Mrs. Murrett's wire till yesterday, and she just pitched her things into a trunk and rushed——"

"Mrs. Murrett?"

"Why, yes. Sophy's gone to India with Mrs. Murrett; they're to meet at Brindisi," Sophy's sister said with a calm smile.

Anna sat motionless, gazing at the disordered room, the pink bed, the trivial face among the pillows.

Mrs. McTarvie-Birch pursued: "They had a fearful kick-up last spring—I daresay you knew about it—but I told Sophy she'd better lump it, as long as the old woman was willing to . . . As an artist, of course, it's perfectly impossible for me to have her with me . . ."

"Of course," Anna mechanically assented.

Through the confused pain of her thoughts she was hardly aware that Mrs. Birch's explanations were still continuing. "Naturally I didn't altogether approve of her going back to that beast of a woman. I said all I could . . . I told her she was a fool to chuck up such a place as yours. But Sophy's restless—always was—and she's taken it into her head she'd rather travel . . ."

Anna rose from her seat, groping for some formula of leave-taking. The pushing back of her chair roused the white dog's smouldering animosity, and he drowned his mistress's further confidences in another outburst of hysterics. Through the tumult Anna signed an inaudible farewell, and Mrs. Birch, having momentarily succeeded in suppressing her pet under a pillow, called out: "Do come again! I'd love to sing to you."

Anna murmured a word of thanks and turned to the door. As she opened it she heard her hostess crying after her: "Jimmy! Do you hear me? Jimmy *Brance!*" and then, there being no response from the person summoned: "*Do* tell him he must go and call the lift for you!"

THE END.

About the Author

AMERICA'S most famous woman of letters, and the first woman to win the Pulitzer Prize, **Edith Wharton** was born into one of the last "leisured class" families in New York City, as she put it, in 1862. Educated privately, she was married to Edward Wharton in 1885, and for the next few years, they spent their time in the high society of Newport (Rhode Island), then Lenox (Massachusetts) and Europe. It was in Europe that Wharton first met Henry James, who was to have a profound and lasting influence on her life and work. Wharton's first published book was a work of nonfiction, in collaboration with Ogden Codman, *The Decoration of Houses* (1897), but from early on, her marriage had been a source of distress, and she was advised by her doctor to write fiction to relieve her nervous tension. Wharton's first short stories appeared in *Scribner's Magazine,* and though she published several volumes of fiction around the turn of the century, including *The Greater Inclination* (1899), *The Touchstone* (1900), *Crucial Instances* (1901), *The Valley of Decision* (1902), *Sanctuary* (1903), and *The Descent of Man and Other Stories* (1904), it wasn't until 1905, with the publication of the bestselling *The House of Mirth,* that she was recognized as one of the most important novelists of her time for her keen social insight and subtle sense of satire. In 1906, Wharton visited Paris, which inspired *Madame de Treymes* (1907), and made her home there in 1907, finally divorcing her husband in 1912. The years before the outbreak of World War I represent the core of her artistic achievement, when *Ethan Frome* (1911), *The Reef* (1912), and *The Custom of the Country* (1913) were published. During the war, she remained in France organizing relief for Belgian refugees, for which she was later awarded the Legion of Honor. She also wrote two novels about the war, *The Marne* (1918) and *A Son at the Front* (1923), and continued, in France, to write about New England and the Newport society she had known so well in *Summer* (1917), the companion to *Ethan Frome,* and *The Age of Innocence* (1920), for which she won the Pulitzer Prize. Wharton died in France in 1937. Her other works include *Old New York* (1924), *The Mother's Recompense* (1925), *The Writing of Fiction* (1925), *The Children* (1928), *Hudson River Bracketed* (1929), and her autobiography, *A Backward Glance* (1934).